# NOWHERE

**CAMRYN VAN LINGEN**

The butterfly is a fragile testament to resilience.
Its delicate wings, now a symphony of colors, remind us that
every struggle is a brushstroke in the masterpiece of our
becoming. Only through trial and transformation can true
beauty be attained.

# CHAPTER 1
# NAYA

The evening air is warm with the promise of summer, stars twinkling in the sky overhead. Naya heads down the sidewalk with purpose, knowing her destination is right around the corner. She pauses momentarily, appreciating the clear skies one last time before the streetlights dim the stars' beauty.

Behind her, footsteps sound, reminding her to keep moving. She sees the familiar torn window awnings ahead, quickening her pace to the grocery store. One foot illuminates with the lights of her nearby safe haven before she's suddenly yanked backwards by her long hair. A hand clamps over her mouth, silencing her screams for help as she's dragged into a dark alleyway nearby.

"Why's a pretty thing like you walking all alone out here?" a raspy voice whispers, his breath hot against her ear. "Don't you know it's not safe at night?"

Naya feels his hold on the hair at the base of her neck tighten as he leans in to smell it. She feels sick, panic overtaking her. As the man drags her deeper into the dark alley, she reaches for her purse, remembering the small pepper spray buried within.

Her hands graze the worn fabric, fingers seconds from unclasping the latch before he notices her movement. A pocketknife clicks into place and the man places it against her throat.

"I wouldn't do that if I were you."

Still unable to respond, his hand firmly placed over her mouth, Naya whimpers softly. A tear involuntarily snakes its way down her cheek. The man slides a dirty finger along her face, wiping it away.

"Now, don't cry. I won't hurt you if you just cooperate," he says, still stroking the side of her face.

Naya is repulsed by his touch but does her best to nod, hoping he'll release her enough to get away.

"I'm going to reach into your purse, and you won't scream when I release my hand. When I get what I want, you can walk away." He frees her mouth, feeling his way down her side.

The man gropes more than he needs to before digging through her purse. Worried his excessive touch is foreshadowing for what's to come, Naya ignores his warning and screams, hoping someone will hear her.

His hand clamps back over her mouth, much tighter than before, the knife digging into her neck. She winces as it draws blood.

"What did I say? You're going to pay for that."

In a flash, he pins her against the brick wall, shoving her cheek into the rough stone. Although he's no longer covering her mouth, the only sound that comes out are sobs that rack her body. She's going to die here.

"Please don't do this," she begs. "Just let me go."

The man moves his knife to her face, tracing its edge lightly along her chin. His other hand tugs her hair harder, wrenching her head back.

"I'll have my way with you first."

His words send desperation flooding through her, and she makes an effort to scream through her sobs.

He yells in frustration when footsteps sound on the street, moving toward them. Someone heard her!

Hope swells in her chest but is quickly replaced by a sudden, sharp pain in her temple. She feels the warmth of blood trickle down her face and realizes he's cutting along her hairline.

Naya screams in pain.

"Now you'll have something to remember me by. Not so pretty anymore."

The knife continues its searing path toward her cheekbone, the intense pain making her dizzy. And then, it stops, and she crumples to the ground, watching through blurry eyes as the man rips her purse off her body and takes off down the alley.

Blood drips into her eyes and she turns to see two people rushing toward her. She reaches up to touch the wound, her hand coming away drenched in blood. Their voices feel faraway, a fresh wave of panic and nausea taking hold at the sight of that much blood.

The two strangers, now kneeling beside her, exchange hurried words as they assess the extent of her injuries. Time seems to blur as Naya struggles to stay conscious, her vision swimming in and out of focus. She can hear the distant wail of sirens growing closer and latches onto the knowledge that she's going to be okay.

The scar along her hairline is pink, still healing. She runs her fingers over the length of it, shivering at the memories of that night. Her long black hair easily covers the scar, but she hates it. It holds memories of what he did to her.

Naya picks up the brush on the bathroom counter, detangling her wet hair. She brushes through it with force, as if she can erase the feeling of him touching it, using it to restrain her. She changed her shampoo, unable to bear the scent of the old one. Every time she smelled it she thought of him doing the same thing.

Her brush gets caught on a knot of hair, evoking a visceral reaction from her as she remembers the feel of his hands knotted in her hair. She lets the brush clatter to the floor, bracing herself against the counter. Staring into the mirror, she sees the fear in her eyes and hates herself for it. They used to be so full of life.

In a moment of clarity, she realizes what has to happen. Digging through the drawers of the bathroom vanity, she searches for the shine of silver metal. Naya finds the scissors in the third drawer, closing her hands around them. Before she second-guesses it, she grabs a strand of hair and cuts.

It drops to the floor, followed by another and another as she wildly chops at her hair. She understands, now, the saying about hair holding memories. With each snip of the scissors, she feels like she's shedding not just hair, but the remnants of her experience. By the time she finishes, the wavy strands barely touch her shoulder.

Naya stares at her new look in the mirror. She feels lighter, as if a weight has been lifted off her. It was cathartic to cut them away.

Running her fingers along the ends, she marvels at the softness of the freshly severed strands between her fingertips. As she holds them lightly, she looks at the young woman staring back at her in the mirror. She's not the same as she was before, but she's stronger now. And she's ready to make new memories.

# CHAPTER 2
# ATLAS

"Notify the anesthesiologist! Get them back in here!" someone shouts, their voice muffled as if speaking underwater.

Atlas feels pressure on the back of his neck, accompanied by an intense flash of pain. He can tell he's lying face down, his body unable to move. Breathing is difficult and he feels a sense of helplessness.

More shouts echo around him but he's unable to make out all of what they're saying. The beeping of monitors grows louder.

"His blood pressure is dropping!" another person yells.

Atlas hears doors swing open and urgent footsteps approaching his bedside. An ache flows through his arm as more medication is pushed into his veins.

The pain in his neck dulls. His awareness grows foggy.

"Don't mess this up! This thing costs a fortune, and we can't afford to find another patient," a deep voice booms.

It's the last thing Atlas remembers before being plunged back into darkness.

Shapes and shadows dance at the edge of his perception, elusive and fleeting. Voices echo through his mind, distorted and fragmented. Fluorescent lights blind him as he's wheeled through sterile white halls. He comes to a halt, grateful for the dim lights in whatever room they ended up in.

"Atlas, can you hear me?" a voice asks, tone laced with concern.

He struggles to focus, his mind still muddled by the remnants of anesthesia. He tries to speak, but his words come out slurred and unintelligible.

"Don't strain yourself. Take your time."

A cool hand is placed against his feverish forehead. It feels good to close his eyes and he slips once more into oblivion.

Atlas has no idea how long he lays there, drifting in and out of consciousness. He grapples with fragments of memory flickering through his mind. With a groan, he attempts to stay awake and clear the haze of anesthesia. It's like his head is full of cotton, affecting his ability to focus. He flexes his fingers and toes, feeling for all his extremities. Then he rubs a hand over his abdomen, assessing for bandages, tubes, or anything unordinary. Nothing seems amiss.

"Hello again!" a voice says. "Think you'll be able to stick around this time?"

They must've sensed his movements and noticed he was waking up. Curious who is talking to him, Atlas pushes past the clouds in his head through sheer force of will. Clarity slowly returns, sharpening his senses. An ache at the base of his skull is suddenly very noticeable.

"How are you feeling?" they ask, drawing his attention.

Across from him, Atlas sees a well-dressed man sitting in the armchair. There's an air of authority to him that puts Atlas on edge.

"Confused," Atlas replies. "What happened?"

"You underwent a surgical procedure. We've implanted some advanced technology in your brain."

Bile rises in his throat, the man's comment hard to process. "I'm sorry, what? Advanced technology in my brain?"

"Let's just say it's cutting-edge, designed to enhance certain capabilities. I'm afraid I can't go into specifics at the moment."

"Enhance capabilities? What does that mean? Did I agree to this? Why can't I remember?"

"All in due time, Atlas," the man says, rising from the armchair as if to leave.

"Wait, I want to know what you did to me!" Atlas shouts, panicked at the thought of him leaving without answers.

"Trust that it's for the greater good."

"Trust? I don't even know who you are!"

"And soon, you won't even remember this conversation," he replies grimly, briskly walking out the door without looking back.

"Hey! Where are you going?" Atlas shouts after the man. "Why wouldn't I remember? Answer my questions!"

His heart leaps at the sound of footsteps drawing closer. *It will all make sense when he comes back to answer my questions,* Atlas thinks to himself, trying to calm the panic now taking over.

It's not the man who returns, though. Instead, several nurses sweep into his room wheeling unknown devices along with them. They begin unwinding various tubes and IV lines, clearly prepping to hook him up to them.

"What are those? Who are you?" Atlas says, wildly looking from one nurse to the next.

They avoid eye contact, continuing to work.

"Answer me! What are you going to do to me?"

In his panic, he doesn't notice one of the nurses pulling restraints from the side of the bed. With deft hands, she buckles him tight against the bed.

"This is for your own safety," she whispers. "Try to relax."

"Relax?" he says incredulously. "Do you restrain all your patients? What kind of hospital is this? I've done nothing wrong!"

His yelling is interrupted by a prick in his arm as another nurse starts an IV. Atlas's attempts to escape are weak, the other nurse holding him down. His movements only serve to make the IV more painful. When the nurse finishes, she repeats the process on the other arm.

"What is this for?" Atlas implores, hoping the nurses will share more information with him. "Please, at least tell me what you're hooking me up to. I deserve to know."

He stares at the nurses, hoping to make eye contact with them. Maybe if they would actually look at him, they'd recognize he's human too and take pity on him. They don't. He feels like he's being treated like a test subject.

Hoping to reduce the pain of the second IV, he cooperates with them and sits still. As he waits, he realizes it's no use fighting with them. They won't help. He decides after they leave, he'll unbuckle himself and rip them out. Getting out of this place is now top priority.

What he didn't consider, however, was the steady trickle of medication that now flows into his first IV. The sensation of cold travels up his arm, followed by dread at what it will do. He feels a haze creep back into his brain, dulling his senses. The medication's effect is rapid and all-encompassing, dragging him into darkness.

The forest flies past in a blur, a chaotic symphony of green and brown as leaves and branches are crushed underfoot. Each step propels him forward, closer to the beckoning expanse of blue sky ahead. The urgency of his flight is palpable, a wild desperation driving him onward.

Leaves rustle and branches groan, as if pleading for him to halt, to reconsider his reckless dash into the unknown. He ignores them, his focus fixed solely on the promise of freedom that lies just beyond the forest's edge.

As he sprints into a small clearing, the chaos of the forest fades into the background, replaced by the steady pounding of his heart. The landscape stretches out before him, hills and far away trees forming a distant tapestry against the horizon.

Racing forward, an open door looms ahead like the mouth of an ancient creature. An exit sign glows above it, urging him closer. His thoughts are consumed by the need to escape, to outrun the specter of pursuit that hangs heavy in the air. The voices draw nearer, a chorus of urgency and dread that spurs him onward.

With a final burst of speed, he reaches the door, his momentum carrying him over the threshold and into the darkness beyond. For a fleeting moment, he is weightless, suspended in the shadows.

And then, he is falling, hurtling downwards with the inevitability of fate. Solid ground rushes up to meet him, a cruel reminder of his mortality, and for a heartbeat, he is consumed by sheer terror. But even as the world spins around him, a flicker of defiance ignites within his chest.

In that moment of chaos and uncertainty, he finds a strange sense of clarity, a realization that he is not alone. The wind whispers words of encouragement in his ear, a gentle reminder that he is not defined by the fall, but by the strength of his spirit.

And so, as he hurtles toward the ground below, he spreads his arms wide and embraces the unknown. For in the depths of his descent, he discovers a truth that transcends fear and uncertainty—that sometimes, it is only in the act of falling that we truly learn how to fly.

# CHAPTER 3
# NAYA

Naya gasps awake, clutching her chest and trying to catch her breath. It's been two months since the incident, and she's only had a few dreams that have felt that real. They've all been about that night, though. She's never had a dream like this one before. Who was that boy and why was there a random door in the middle of a forest?

Still jarred from her dream, she rolls out of bed and pads down the carpeted stairs. The hum of the refrigerator greets her as she enters the kitchen to grab a glass of water. A glance at the clock shows it's four in the morning. Her parents and sister are asleep upstairs.

Rather than go back to bed, she sits on the faded living room couch, staring out the window. Her mind replays the image of the boy enveloped in darkness as he went through the door. What made him take such a daring leap into the unknown?

Lost in thought, Naya absently sips her water, the cool liquid doing little to calm her mind. She wonders if the dream had any significance or if it was merely a product of her overactive imagination.

She recalls the freedom of escape, relief evident on the boy's face. Then a shudder rolls through her, her mind unable to push away the sensation of sheer terror as he plummeted toward the ground moments later. It all felt so real.

As the minutes tick by, the world outside begins to stir, the first rays of dawn creeping over the horizon. Faint sunlight casts long shadows across the living room, illuminating the familiar objects scattered haphazardly around the room—her mom's Bible on the coffee table, a vase of wilting flowers on the windowsill, and a stack of old magazines in the corner.

The warmth of dawn lulls Naya closer to sleep, the dream still haunting her thoughts. As she tries to grasp hold of it again, it eludes her like the fleeting shadows of the night. Setting her glass on the coffee table, Naya welcomes the peace of sleep.

"Naya!" her sister says, shaking her awake a few short hours later. "Wake up!"

Groggily, she rubs her eyes and yawns, stretching like a cat to shake off the remnants of sleep.

"I'm up, I'm up," she replies.

"Are you sure? You still look pretty asleep to me. Why are you on the couch?"

"Couldn't sleep. That's also why I probably still look like a zombie," Naya says, pausing before saying any more.

Should she tell her sister about the strange dream? They tell each other everything but Naya feels strangely apprehensive about sharing. Eager to forget the unsettling dream, she heads into the kitchen to prepare breakfast, but Harper beats her to it.

"You sit down and relax. I got this," she says, pushing Naya into one of the dining chairs.

"I thought I was the big sister?" Naya asks.

Harper sticks her tongue out at her before unwrapping the stale loaf of bread on the counter. She shoves a few slices into the rusty toaster and grabs two jars of jam from the fridge.

"Strawberry or grape?"

"Is that even a question?" Naya asks.

With a smile, Harper grabs the grape jam and spreads it across the freshly toasted bread. When she's finished, she sets it down in front of Naya before returning to the kitchen to smear strawberry on her slice. Jam preference is one of the few differences between them, Naya favoring the subtle tanginess of grape over the cloying sweetness of strawberry.

Naya crunches into the toast, missing the savor of peanut butter. They ran out just a few days ago and she's not too eager to go to the grocery store. Her mom will go when she finds the time. As they eat in comfortable silence, Naya hears footsteps upstairs. Her parents must be getting ready for the day.

Harper shoves the last of her toast in her mouth and preps breakfast for her parents just as they come into the kitchen.

"Grape for you," she says, setting a plate in front of their mother, "and strawberry for you," handing a plate to their father.

They smile at her, eating quickly before putting the dishes in the sink, kissing her and Harper on the cheek, and bustling out the door. Glancing at the clock, Naya realizes she needs to do the same. It will be her first day back since returning from the hospital and she doesn't want to be late. Mr. Jenkins has been gracious enough already.

"Will you be okay today?" Harper asks with concern.

"Of course! It's time I go back. I've been sitting around the house long enough," she replies. "How else do you think we keep up with that hungry belly of yours?" Naya teases, hoping to joke away her nerves.

She ruffles Harper's hair as she walks by, dropping her dish in the sink and staring out the kitchen window. The day outside is beautiful, but she still feels nervous. The past two months she's only gone further than the driveway when she absolutely needed to.

"You know I'm almost a teenager, I know why you really have to go back!"

Naya stops, nervousness prickling her palms. Must they have this conversation today?

"And why's that?" she replies.

"Everything is so expensive we can't afford it anymore. It's not like I haven't noticed how little Mom brings home from the grocery store lately. You don't have to pretend everything is fine with me."

Naya sighs, a mixture of relief and concern flitting across her face. It's good Harper doesn't know exactly how bad things have become, but she shouldn't have to bear the weight of even this.

"You're right, I'm sorry. I just don't want you to have to grow up so fast. Live a little, let us adults take care of things" she says, wrapping her sister in a hug.

She's at the perfect height now where Naya can rest her chin on the crown of Harper's head. The scent of strawberry shampoo drifts off her hair.

"You'll still make time to hang out, right?" Harper asks, staring up at Naya.

"I promise, once things settle down, we'll find time to hang out."

"Okay," she concedes, her reply muffled against Naya's chest.

"Be good today. Stay out of trouble now that I won't be around during the day," Naya reminds, grabbing her worn leather backpack and rushing out the door before she lets fear take hold.

Her bike is waiting for her in the garage, dusty from months of disuse. She gingerly wheels it out onto the driveway and climbs on. The warm summer breeze tousles her short black hair as she pedals through the crowded sidewalks and bustling traffic.

There are less cars on the road these days, people opting for cheaper modes of transportation like bikes and mopeds. Just as many choose to walk, hurrying through the crowds to get where they need to be. Naya passes a corner store where people are lined up down the road, waiting for their turn. They must be having one of their rare flash sales on expired food.

Rounding the next corner, she slows to a stop in front of Bargain Bytes, the run-down computer shop she's worked at since graduating high school. The shop is a relic of a bygone era, its faded sign barely visible through grime-streaked windows. Carefully maneuvering her bike through the front doors, she parks it unceremoniously in the back of the shop. Even locked, she doesn't trust it outside.

"Ah, Naya! Right on time as always," Mr. Jenkins exclaims, looking up from his work with a warm smile. "You're sure you're up to being back?"

"Absolutely, Mr. Jenkins! I'm determined to get that computer working today!" she says, mustering up all her enthusiasm.

"And I have absolute faith you will," he replies, pushing up the glasses on the bridge of his nose.

Naya's gaze flits momentarily to his hand where a delicate birthmark in the shape of a butterfly graces his weathered skin. It's a small detail, but one that never fails to bring a smile to her face, a gentle contrast to his gruff exterior. Mr. Jenkins notices her glance and offers her a brief, knowing smile.

Naya is grateful for Mr. Jenkins, who has become like family to her over the years. Initially reserved and distant when he first hired her, she worked hard to break through his shell and build a genuine connection.

Settling in behind the counter, Naya takes in the familiar scent of old electronics and dust. The air is thick with the hum of outdated machinery and the faint crackle of static electricity. She feels a little nervous but knows it will be good to occupy her mind with work and get back into a normal routine.

Despite the shop's dilapidated appearance, Naya feels a sense of fondness for the place. It was here, amidst the clutter and chaos of the shop floor, that she first discovered her passion for technology. Though the world outside changes constantly, this small corner of the city has been a constant in her life the last several years.

Returning her attention to the laptop in front of her, a mixture of resignation and determination settles over her. With each passing day, the demand for outdated technology wanes. Newer, more efficient tech dominates the market but very few can afford it. Restoring the beat-up laptop in front of her is her typical task, the shop's clients wanting to get as much out of their old tech as possible. As the shop's survival becomes more uncertain, Naya ensures some of her time is devoted to new gadgets as well. Mr. Jenkins has helped her hone her skills, teaching her everything he knows.

Time flies by, Naya finding herself lost in a sea of wires and circuit boards, tinkering with the old laptop. Despite her best efforts, the machine remains stubbornly unresponsive, its screen flashing with error messages and glitches. While she may have gotten it running, it's been utterly uncooperative after that.

Frustrated but undeterred, she decides to give her brain a break. She tidies up her workspace, sorting the various parts she's left scattered across her small desk.

"How's your project going?" Naya asks, wandering over to Mr. Jenkins where he stares through a magnifying glass at a tiny gadget.

He grunts in frustration, putting the gadget down momentarily to look at Naya.

"You know, back in my day, you could actually see what you were working with. Now it's like trying to fix a puzzle with tweezers!"

Naya laughs. "And don't even get me started on the connectors. Soon I'll even need a magnifying glass to plug them in!"

Mr. Jenkins sighs, patting the large computer sitting under his desk. "Makes you appreciate the simplicity of old technology, doesn't it?"

"Definitely. At least we can say it keeps us on our toes, right? Always learning something new in this field."

"That's the spirit, Naya! Adaptability is key in the world of technology. Just keep those steady hands and sharp eyes and you'll pass me up in no time," he says with a wink, returning to the tiny gadget in his hands.

Naya wanders through the store a while longer, organizing as she goes. Soon, she's back to work, determined to solve the problem and prove herself capable. Although several more hours pass, she emerges victorious, the laptop purring contentedly beneath her skilled touch. With a sense of pride and satisfaction, she powers down the machine and prepares to close up shop for the night.

Mr. Jenkins still tinkers at his desk, a lamp now on to aid him in his work. She doesn't know how he does it all day and night, hunched over in his chair squinting in concentration.

"Alright, I'll see you tomorrow Mr. Jenkins. Take a break for me, will you?"

Mr. Jenkins looks up from his work with a rueful grin. "I'll try. The client wants this fixed as soon as possible. You know how the rich folk are."

Naya turns to leave, stopping just before the doors. The sun is dipping below the horizon and night is fast approaching. She feels her heart rate spike at the thought of being out in the dark again.

"Naya, get home safe, will ya?" Mr. Jenkins says, noticing her trepidation.

She nods over at him and wheels her bicycle outside, locking the door before shutting it behind her. The neon lights of the city come alive around her, casting a vibrant glow over the sidewalks and storefronts. With her backpack slung over her shoulder, she sets off toward home, weaving through the crowded streets faster than she used to. She wants to get home as fast as possible.

As she rides through the familiar paths of her neighborhood, the rhythmic sound of her pedals fills the air and she's able to relax slightly. Her house appears up ahead and Naya sighs in relief. *One day at a time*, she thinks to herself, *just one day at a time.*

# CHAPTER 4
# ATLAS

Slowly regaining consciousness, Atlas finds himself in a disoriented state, his mind struggling to make sense of his surroundings. Blinking away the drowsiness, he tries to sit up, only to realize his body feels heavy and restrained. Panicking, he glances around the room, taking in the sterile white walls and the maze of wires and tubes snaking their way across the floor. His heart pounds in his chest as he realizes the array of medical equipment he's hooked up to. The slight movement of his arm tugs on the intricate web of IV lines tethering him to the various machines and monitors.

Fear and confusion grip him as he struggles to piece together what happened, his memory fragmented and hazy. The last thing he remembers is the sensation of falling, the rush of wind against his face as he plummeted into the abyss below. But now, as he lies in this unfamiliar hospital space, he can't shake the feeling that something is terribly wrong.

Pushing past the pounding in his head, Atlas summons his strength and manages to sit up awkwardly in the bed. The restraints around his arms are surprisingly easy to remove, as if they weren't expecting opposition. Were they there for his own safety? Why can't he remember how he got here?

With a grimace of pain, he tears the IV lines from his skin. The monitors immediately start beeping, sounds of warning for nurses inevitably nearby. He staggers to his feet, his muscles worryingly fatigued. His body feels heavy and weak, moving as if it forgot how to respond to his brain. How long has he been here?

Surveying the room for an exit, he spots one in the corner. The determination to escape this nightmarish prison fuels his steps, drawing him closer to the door. Pressing his ear against the wood, he listens for footsteps. Nothing so far. He pushes it open and steps out into the hall, navigating the labyrinth in search of the outdoors.

As he nears a corner, footsteps sound in front of him. With a surge of panic, he presses himself against the wall and they mercifully head in the opposite direction. The fear coursing through his veins urges him onwards, despite the ever-growing pounding in his head. He catches his reflection in a glass frame on the wall, noticing his hair is slightly longer and cheekbones more pronounced. A faded red reflection in the corner also catches his eye and he whips around to see an exit sign further down the hall.

He lunges toward it, grasping the handle with trembling fingers and pushing it open. The outside world greets him with blinding sunlight, the warmth a welcome feeling on his now pale skin. For a moment, Atlas hesitates, his eyes wide with disbelief as he takes in the sight before him. He's jolted back to reality when the sound of shouts and alarms erupt behind him.

Looking around, he tries to determine his location. It seems he's at the third floor's emergency exit. The rusty metal stairs groan beneath him as he races toward the bottom, eager to outrun whatever follows behind. As he moves, his muscles slowly regain mobility as if finally waking from a deep slumber. He makes it to the last flight when it shakes beneath him, signaling others have joined his descent.

Forgoing caution, he launches himself over the side, landing precariously on the cracked asphalt below. The hospital gown tugs open behind him, but he has no time to worry about modesty, rushing forward and away from the building.

"Stop!" someone shouts behind him.

He doesn't dare look back, urging his muscles to carry him further. A forest looms ahead, strange to be so close to a hospital but perfect for hiding an escapee. Branches crunch under his bare feet, his run through the forest eerily resembling what he thought he'd been doing moments before waking up.

Atlas is unsure how long he's been running, the woods too similar to feel very different. His muscles scream from disuse, begging for a break. He gives in, the shouts of his pursuers having quieted long ago. Collapsing onto the forest floor, he rests against a tree. The adrenaline that fueled his escape is beginning to fade.

Birds chirp in the distance. A squirrel scuttles up a tree somewhere nearby. The forest around him thrums with life, distant calls of wildlife reminding him he's not alone out here.

Running his hands through his hair now damp with sweat, his fingers catch on a small scar at the base of his skull.

That's new.

He grimaces as he feels the dried blood crusting down his arms from where he ripped out the IVs, but he's relieved the bleeding has stopped. Atlas sighs as he glances down at himself, realizing how disheveled he must look. The hospital gown barely covers him, and his bare feet are caked with dirt and dried blood. He'll need to find proper clothes soon if he wants to avoid drawing attention to himself.

For now, hunger gnaws at his stomach, demanding his full attention. When was the last time he ate? He tries to recall his last meal, but his memories are hazy and fragmented, like pieces of a puzzle that refuse to fit together.

With a frustrated growl, Atlas pushes himself to his feet determined to put more distance between himself and the hospital before nightfall. He re-ties the gown behind him as best as he can and sets off into the woods once more.

The canopy of trees overhead casts long shadows across the forest floor, obscuring his path and adding to the sense of isolation surrounding him. Every rustle of leaves or snap of twigs sends a shiver down his spine, his senses heightened as he listens for any signs of danger.

Despite the urgency of his situation, Atlas can't help but feel a sense of wonder at the beauty of the wilderness around him. The scent of earth and pine is strong. Shafts of golden sunlight filter through the dense foliage, casting a warm glow over everything they touch.

As he walks, Atlas keeps his eyes peeled for any signs of civilization, hoping to find shelter before the sun goes down. His stomach rumbles loudly, a constant reminder of his hunger, and he curses himself for not thinking to grab something to eat before fleeing the hospital. He trudges along, despair creeping in.

Pushing through the underbrush, he emerges into a small clearing bathed in dappled sunlight. His eyes widen in surprise, hope swelling in his chest as he spots a rustic cabin nestled among the trees. Relief floods through him, his footsteps quickening with anticipation.

He steps gingerly onto the small wooden porch and approaches the door. Turning the handle reveals it's locked. Summoning his remaining strength, he rams his shoulder against the door, breaking the rusted lock out of the rotted wooden frame.

Inside, simple wooden furniture surrounds a fireplace, everything covered in a fine layer of dust. A threadbare rug covers the floor, its muted colors doing little to liven the space.

On one side of the room is a small kitchenette tucked into the corner. Pots and pans hang from hooks over a cast-iron stove. Opposite the kitchenette, a narrow staircase leads to a loft area where a simple bed is nestled beneath a patchwork quilt. Sunlight filters through a small window above, casting a golden glow over the room and illuminating the cozy alcove.

Atlas settles into the armchair beside the fireplace, feeling overwhelmed with gratitude for the unexpected sanctuary he's found amidst the wilderness.

# CHAPTER 5
# NAYA

As Naya steps through the creaky door of the computer shop the next morning, she's greeted by the familiar sights and sounds of her workplace. The faint hum of computers fills the air, mingling with the soft click of a keyboard and the occasional beep of a printer in the corner. Mr. Jenkins looks up from his workbench as she enters, a twinkle of excitement in his eyes despite the bags under them. He must've been up all night working again.

"Good morning, Naya," he says, beckoning her over. "I've got something interesting to show you."

Curious, Naya approaches. "What is it, Mr. Jenkins?" She scans the cluttered workbench for clues.

Mr. Jenkins leans in conspiratorially, his voice dropping to a whisper. "I've been hearing some rumors lately," he says, his tone grave. "Whispers of a new virtual reality technology being developed by the government."

Naya's eyes widen in surprise. "Virtual reality?" she repeats, her mind racing with possibilities. "But what would the government want with VR technology?"

Mr. Jenkins shrugs, his expression troubled. "That's the million-dollar question," he says. "Some say they're using it for military training, others think it's for surveillance purposes. Whatever the case, it's got people talking."

As Naya absorbs this new information, a sense of unease settles over her. The thought of the government developing advanced VR technology raises more questions than answers, and she can't shake the feeling that there's more to this story than meets the eye.

"What else have you heard?"

"Not much. I've been doing some digging, but it seems like they're keeping it under wraps for now. But mark my words, Naya, this could be big."

Pushing her concerns aside, she heads to her desk to focus on work. No sense fretting about something so unknown. She has enough worries on her plate as it is.

Throughout the day, snippets of conversation drift through the shop, each one adding a piece to the puzzle of the government's mysterious VR project. Some customers speak in hushed tones about the potential applications of the technology, while others express concerns about the implications of such advanced surveillance capabilities. Although wary of the reason, both Naya and Mr. Jenkins are elated at the increased traffic in the shop. Several new clients come in asking for repairs on their old devices and soon, they are buried in work.

The bell above the door chimes again, announcing the arrival of a new client. Naya looks up to see an elderly gentleman shuffling through the entrance. Seeing as Mr. Jenkins has his nose buried in a computer tower, she knows this client will be hers.

"Good afternoon, how can I help you today?" Naya asks with a warm smile, setting aside the tablet she'd been working on.

The man approaches the counter, clutching an old device in his hands. "I'm hoping you can help me with this," he says, his voice tinged with a hint of uncertainty.

Naya examines the device, noting the worn casing and outdated design. "What seems to be the problem?" she inquires.

The man hesitates for a moment before speaking. "Well, you see, this old radio has been in my family for generations," he explains. "It's a cherished heirloom, but lately, it's been acting up. I was hoping you could take a look and see if you can fix it."

Naya smiles understandingly, sensing the sentimental value attached to the device. "Of course, I'll do my best to help," she assures him, taking the radio from his hands and placing it on the counter.

As she begins to inspect it, the man fidgets nervously, his eyes darting around the shop. "I'm not very good with all these new gadgets and gizmos," he admits, his voice barely above a whisper. "I prefer things simple, like they used to be. Nowadays, there's no telling who could be listening in."

Unsure how to respond, Naya nods sympathetically. With gentle reassurance, she sets to work on repairing the old radio, her skilled hands deftly navigating the intricate circuitry. As she works, she shares stories with the man, exchanging anecdotes about the joys of simpler times, although he has much more experience than her. She enjoys hearing about the days before the economic crash and wishes Harper would have grown up in a world like that. Naya, at least, had a few good years she can remember.

By the time Naya finishes the repairs, the man's face lights up with gratitude, his eyes shining with appreciation. "Thank you, my dear," he says, his voice filled with emotion. "You've done more than just fix a radio. You've not only restored a piece of my family's history, but my peace of mind."

The man pays, setting the money on the counter before briefly embracing Naya's hand in his. With a parting smile, he grabs the radio and leaves the shop. The bell above the door chimes softly in his wake and Naya smiles contentedly.

In a world of ever-changing technology, moments like these remind her of the timeless value of human connection. So often she forgets the countless memories tied to these old devices and how many people she can help, one repair at a time.

"Way to go, kiddo," Mr. Jenkins praises, pausing from his work to pat her on the shoulder as she walks past. "It's like you never even took a break."

Naya chuckles, her face flushed with pride at his compliment. Mr. Jenkins has taught her so much; it means a lot to receive his praise.

Uplifted from her conversations, she says a prayer of gratitude before focusing back on the battered tablet. Before long, closing time approaches. As she sets the tablet aside for the day, a familiar anxiety creeps up, something the elderly gentleman said resurfacing in her mind. *There's no telling who could be listening in.*

The thought of someone surveilling her home, listening in to her family's conversations makes her feel sick. She makes a mental note to check all their devices when she gets home tonight.

Wandering over to Mr. Jenkins' desk, she shuts off his desk lamp and moves his magnifying glass to the side. He glances up at her in surprise, clearly perturbed she disrupted his workflow.

"You promised you'd take a break, remember? It doesn't look like you've stopped working since I left you last night," Naya says with concern.

Removing his glasses, Mr. Jenkins scrubs a weathered hand over his face.

"You got me there," he replies with a sigh. "You can't expect me to take a break today after all the new clients we got, though, can you?" He looks around the room at all the newly inventoried devices.

"Yes, I do. Even with all the new clients. How are you supposed to take care of their devices if you aren't taking care of yourself, first?"

"What would I do without you, Naya?" he says with a tired smile.

"Pass out on top of a computer and drool all over the keyboard," she says with a grin, recalling the first day she came into the shop after he hired her.

Thankfully, he's only done it a few times since having her around. He probably went right back to that habit while she was gone, though.

Mr. Jenkins rubs the back of his neck, a bit embarrassed. "Not the greatest first impression of your boss, huh? Best not ask how I survived two months without you, then."

"Actually, it just proves to me how hard you work and how much you care about this place."

He grunts at the compliment. "Get home safe, I'll see you tomorrow."

"Yes, sir!" she says, gathering her confidence before wheeling her bike out the doors.

Her ride home gives her plenty of time to stew in her thoughts, replaying the snippets of conversation from the day. What could've happened in one day to suddenly spread such rumors around the city? Whatever it was, she's thankful for the distraction from her usual nighttime thoughts. Tomorrow, she'll try to find out more details. For now, though, she can't shake the feeling that their world is on the brink of a major upheaval, and she's determined to be ready for whatever comes next.

# CHAPTER 6
# ATLAS

Sunlight streams through the window above the bed, casting a warm glow over the patterned quilt covering Atlas like a cocoon. Despite his best efforts to block out the relentless rays, they filter through the fabric, illuminating the room with their golden hue.

"Five more minutes," Atlas mutters, his voice muffled by the quilt as he burrows deeper into its folds. He clings to the hope that the sun will take pity on his tired body and grant him a few more moments of rest.

But the sun is unforgiving, its rays dancing across the room with unwavering determination. With a resigned sigh, Atlas relents, pushing the quilt aside and sitting up in bed with a groan.

"Fine, I'm up," he grumbles, rubbing the sleep from his eyes.

As Atlas swings his legs over the edge of the bed, he can't shake the unsettling feeling that washes over him. *Maybe I really am going crazy*, he thinks, *if I'm already talking to myself this early in the morning.*

With a shake of his head, Atlas pushes aside his doubts and forces his tired mind to focus. He can't afford to dwell on his situation, not when there are still so many unanswered questions and people out looking for him.

Rising to his feet, he stretches his weary muscles. Atlas descends the narrow staircase and heads to the kitchenette. Empty cans of soup and fruit litter the small countertop, remnants of his dinner the night before. He reaches back into the cabinets, fishing out a can of fruit cocktail for breakfast. There are only a few cans of various foods left, so he must eat more sparingly.

After drinking the last bit of juice in the can, he sets it down and goes to work rummaging through the meager belongings scattered around the small cabin. His eyes light up as he spots a weathered backpack tucked away in the alcove, its faded fabric showing signs of age but still sturdy enough for his needs.

He begins to fill the backpack with essentials: a few cans of food scavenged from the sparse pantry, a water bottle half-filled from the stream outside, and a handful of survival supplies salvaged from the makeshift storage shelves. He's grateful for the modest provisions the previous owners left behind.

Once the backpack is packed to his satisfaction, he turns his attention to his attire. He grabs a faded blue jacket hanging from a hook on the wall, pulling it on over the black T-shirt and worn denim pants he found in the closet last night. The clothes are a bit too small for his tall frame, but he's grateful there were clothes at all. Atlas was eager to shed the uncomfortable hospital gown, a reminder of the sterile prison he left behind.

With one last glance around the cabin, he takes a deep breath and steps outside into the humid morning air. Atlas shuts the cabin door behind him as much as the broken frame allows and hops off the porch. The journey ahead feels much more doable with proper clothes and the pair of sturdy boots he found tucked by the fireplace.

Passing through the clearing and back into the thick of the woods, the ground beneath his feet grows increasingly uneven. The tangled underbrush tugs at his clothes with each step. Despite the physical strain, he presses on, his senses alert for any signs of danger. The only sound is the soft rustle of leaves overhead and the occasional chirp of a bird in the distance.

After what feels like hours of trudging through the dense forest, Atlas stumbles upon another small clearing. His breath catches in his throat as he takes in the narrow dirt road stretching before him, its surface rutted and uneven from years of neglect.

He hesitates, not sure which way to go. The road stretches in both directions, disappearing into the forest on either side. With no clear indication of which way to go, he decides to trust his instincts and follows the road to the left, his heart pounding as he sets off into the unknown.

As he walks, Atlas keeps a wary eye out for any signs of civilization. The trees loom overhead like silent sentinels, their branches casting eerie shadows across the dusty ground. He lets his thoughts drift back to the hospital where his journey began. He remembers the sterile white walls, the faint smell of antiseptic that lingered in the air, and the sense of confusion that clouded his mind. The memories are hazy, like fragments of a dream.

Lost in his thoughts, Atlas scarcely notices as the road begins to curve and wind its way through the forest, leading him deeper into the heart of the wilderness. His mind races with questions and uncertainties, each one more perplexing than the last.

Suddenly, a flash of movement catches his eye. He blinks, his gaze sharpening as he scans the horizon. Ahead, lies a sprawling city, its skyline rising against the backdrop of the forest. Tall buildings tower overhead, their windows glinting in the sunlight.

Fear keeps him rooted to the spot, memories of being chased still clouding his judgment. What if he runs into someone who recognizes him and takes him back? How will he know who to trust? Knowing there's no way to tell, he decides to be extra cautious.

Atlas pushes on toward the city, the smells of the forest growing fainter. The trees give way to fields and farmhouses as he walks, the sound of people echoing through the air. A sidewalk approaches up ahead, connected to rows of cookie-cutter houses. Atlas walks through the neighborhood, watching children play and people stroll by.

Slowly, the houses become businesses and restaurants, the heart of the city growing closer. He presses forward, a busy street coming into view. Pedestrians bustle along the sidewalks, some with faces obscured by masks. Mopeds and bikes whiz by, people rushing to get to their destination. His senses are overwhelmed by the sights and sounds of the urban landscape.

Atlas navigates the maze of streets, stunned by the stark contrast of the city to the quiet solitude of the forest. He scans the crowds for any sign of familiarity, noting the way people stare at him as he walks by. There's a sense of energy and life in the city that he finds both exhilarating and overbearing. But amidst the chaos and clamor, Atlas remains focused. He's here for a reason. There are answers waiting to be found amidst the dilapidated buildings and busy streets.

Focused on scanning far ahead in search of where to go, Atlas fails to notice the person hurrying toward him until it's too late. With a sudden collision, he finds himself stumbling backward, nearly losing his balance as he collides with a stranger.

"Hey, watch where you're going!" the person snaps, shooting him a scowl before hurrying off down the sidewalk.

Shaken by the encounter, Atlas reaches up to rub his forehead, a pounding in his head drowning out his surroundings. His brain feels like it's about to explode when a memory hits him, vivid and unbidden, crashing over him with overwhelming force.

Atlas gathers items from around his dorm room, stuffing them into a backpack. It looks like the one he carries now, its fabric worn and weathered from years of use.

Glancing back, he sees another man in the room, his face blurred. The man points to a laptop on the desk and Atlas grabs it, adding it to his backpack before zipping it closed.

Slinging the bag over his shoulder, Atlas hurries out the door and makes his way across a manicured lawn. Right as he recognizes it as a college campus, the memory fades as quickly as it began.

He's left standing on the crowded sidewalk, heart pounding in his chest. Atlas reaches behind him to touch the backpack for reassurance only to realize it's not there. Frantically, he looks around, scanning for the person who bumped into him, but they are nowhere to be found. Panic sets in as he realizes the gravity of the situation—he's lost his only means of survival in this unfamiliar city.

Desperate, Atlas begins to push his way through the crowds, scanning the sidewalks and alleys for any sign of the missing backpack. But it's no use—the busy streets offer no clues, and the backpack remains stubbornly out of reach.

With a sinking feeling in the pit of his stomach, Atlas stops in the middle of the sidewalk. He's lost and alone in a city he doesn't understand, with no idea where to turn or who to trust.

He swipes a hand across his forehead, wiping away the faint sheen of sweat now coating his skin as he tries to make sense of what just happened. But there's no time to dwell on the memory, a steely determination taking hold. He's faced so much and has come too far to give up now. Fixing his eyes on the horizon, he sets off once more. He really can't trust anyone in this city.

# CHAPTER 7
# NAYA

Every day starts the same, Naya's routine serving as a steady anchor amidst the sea of fears that flood her mind. She finds comfort in the predictability, a shield against the uncertainties beyond her doorstep.

Except today is different.

Whispers run rampant through the streets, people scuttling around more nervously than before. Are people really that worried about this new government VR? Naya checked all the devices in her house last night after her family was fast asleep and found nothing. It put her mind at ease but now, the nerves are back. As she rounds the last corner on her route, distracted by conversations flitting through the city, she narrowly avoids colliding with a stranger.

Her bike swerves to the side at the last moment, heart skipping a beat. She catches a glimpse of the startled stranger, his features obscured by the morning light. There's something undeniably captivating about him, a flash of dark hair, a hint of stubble, and eyes that seem to hold secrets.

For a fleeting moment, time seems to stand still as they make eye contact, Naya's pulse quickening in response. But just as quickly as he appeared, the stranger is gone, disappearing into the flow of morning commuters.

Shaking her head to clear her thoughts, Naya spares a glance behind her hoping to spot the young man again. But he's gone. She hops back on her bike, the wheels spinning beneath her with a rhythmic hum. Her mind replays the near miss collision, wondering who she almost ran into. While she lives in a city, it's not the sprawling metropolis one might envision. The more intimate community means she can recognize many of the faces that grace its streets. Someone as distinctive as him would undoubtedly have caught her eye before. A face like that is hard to forget. Still, something about him was also strangely familiar.

As she wheels her way into the computer shop, she's still distracted, searching through her memories for snippets of the man. She sees a flash of dark hair tousled by the wind and tries to grab hold of the memory, but it eludes her. Naya is still in a daze when she realizes Mr. Jenkins is waving his hand in front of her face, trying to tell her something.

"Earth to Naya!" he says, hunching down to stare directly in her eyes. "Are you okay? Did something happen on your way here?"

Startled, she steps back, stumbling into her bike which she must've let crash to the floor behind her. "Sorry, Mr. Jenkins. I guess I was just lost in my thoughts."

"Yeah, you drifted in here like you'd just seen a ghost! You're not hurt, are you?"

Naya appreciates his concern and reassures him she's fine. Absentmindedly, she hauls her bike against the back wall and gets to work. She sits behind the desk, her fingers tapping on the keyboard as she attempts to troubleshoot the stubborn tablet from yesterday. Her mind, however, refuses to cooperate.

Naya works through the morning, doing her best to focus. Though the time passes quickly, she gets very little done. Restarting the tablet for the millionth time, she notices the clock on the home screen says it's almost noon. Naya sighs and rests her chin on one hand. She stares down at the flickering screen, frustrated with her lack of progress.

Mr. Jenkins notices Naya's faraway look and furrowed brow. With a concerned expression, he approaches her, his voice breaking through the fog of her thoughts.

"Naya, are you sure you're alright? You seem very distracted today."

Naya blinks and looks up, realizing she's been staring blankly at the tablet screen for several minutes. She forces a smile, attempting to mask her inner turmoil. "I'm fine, Mr. Jenkins. Just a little tired, I guess."

He studies her for a moment, his forehead creased with worry. "You know what? I think you could use a break. I don't want you to push yourself too hard. Why don't you go home early today? I'll manage the shop for the rest of the day."

"Are you sure?"

"Of course. And what was it you said to me yesterday? You can't help others if you don't help yourself first?"

"Something like that," Naya agrees with a small smile. "Thanks Mr. Jenkins."

Naya cleans up her desk and gathers her things, heading out the shop with a parting wave. Harper will be thrilled she's coming home early. The anticipation of her younger sister's excitement energizes her ride home.

As she bikes into the driveway, Harper runs out the front door with a wide grin. "You're home early! Does that mean we get to hang out?"

Naya returns her sister's infectious smile. "Absolutely! Now the question is, what should we do?"

With the afternoon stretching ahead of them, Naya and Harper brainstorm ideas for how to spend their unexpected time together. Harper's eyes light up with excitement as she suggests a variety of activities, ranging from organizing a scavenger hunt around the house to exploring the nearby park.

After some deliberation, they settle on a make-do picnic in the backyard, Naya preferring to stay home. She retrieves a worn blanket from the closet while Harper excitedly rummages through the sparse pantry, pulling out the few remaining snacks they have on hand.

Naya picks a spot under the maple tree, laying the blanket on the dry grass. Harper arranges the meager picnic spread with meticulous care, making the most of what little they have. With the finishing touches in place, they both settle down on the blanket, surrounded by their modest feast.

They chat animatedly as they eat, enjoying the warmth of the summer air. Despite their limited means, they've managed to create a cozy moment of joy amid their difficult circumstances. Harper spreads grape jam onto a piece of bread and Naya gives her a puzzled look.

"Since when do you like grape jam?" she asks.

Harper stops mid-chew, a blank expression on her face. "Oh, I don't?" Tilting her head in thought, she shrugs and adopts a sudden British accent. "Perhaps I've acquired a more sophisticated palette."

"And grape is more sophisticated than strawberry?" Naya retorts in her own British accent, trying to keep the mood light after Harper's suddenly strange behavior.

"So how come you came home early today?" Harper inquires, changing the subject. Her question is a bit hard to decipher around her mouthful of grape covered toast. "You didn't have another panic attack, did you?"

"No, nothing like that. Mr. Jenkins just caught me zoning out, so he sent me home. I felt bad at first, but honestly, I'm glad he did. My brain refuses to focus today."

"Busy day at the shop then?"

"Sometimes. Yesterday was a zoo." Naya takes a bite of her sandwich, comfortable in the silence as they eat.

"Something interesting did happen on my way to work this morning, though" Naya reveals, suddenly excited to fill Harper in about her encounter this morning.

"Oh, spill it! Hardly anything interesting happens anymore!" She props her chin in one hand, fully focused on Naya's answer. Her eyes are full of hopefulness and Naya notices her other hand fiddling with the butterfly necklace around her neck.

Naya startles at the sight of the jewelry, certain her sister had lost it a while back. Questioning whether that was just another weird dream she had, Naya gets lost in her thoughts.

"Hey, don't leave me hanging here," Harper interjects.

Jolted back to the present, Naya smiles apologetically. "I nearly crashed my bike into a cute guy," she states.

For a split second, Harper looks strangely disappointed by her answer. Then, as if Naya imagined it, Harper's eyebrows shoot up in surprise.

"A CUTE GUY?!" she practically screams. "You never talk about boys with me!!!"

*Now I've done it*, Naya thinks, wincing from the shrill of Harper's exclamation. She forgets how boy crazy Harper can be.

"Well considering you just about blew my eardrums out, maybe that's why I keep the boy drama to myself," Naya teases.

Harper pouts her lips dramatically. "Sorry, sorry! Tell me more! Cute is high praise coming from you. It takes a lot to get your attention. Especially—" Harper stops mid-sentence.

"Especially what?"

"Since that night," Harper says softly, as if she's scared to mention it.

Naya grimaces, saddened by how her experience has affected the whole family. She's doing much better than two months ago, but a relationship is still the last thing on her mind.

Collecting her thoughts, Naya continues, describing what she remembers about the young man from this morning.

Harper lays on her back while she talks, staring at the sky as if she can see him take shape in the clouds.

"Considering you had like a two second encounter with him, you sure noticed every detail." Harper pokes Naya and looks over at her with a smile. "Is it because he reminded you of someone?"

Naya simply shrugs in return, unsure how to respond. He did seem strangely familiar. She blushes as she recalls the details of his face, realizing Harper's right. She really did notice a lot. Ignoring the fluttery feeling in her chest, Naya focuses on the progress she's making. It's a good sign she can notice anything about a man after being so close to him. Usually, she succumbs to her trauma-induced fears and bolts away as fast as possible.

Hoping to calm her restless mind, Naya lays down to gaze at the sky with her sister. Her short black hair blends with Harper's, the only difference being length. Harper still likes to keep her hair long no matter how many times Naya tries to convince her of the practicality of short hair. It suits her, though. Harper's long, dark waves give her an innocence Naya's attacker took from her. Even so, Naya has grown very fond of her short hair. It's much easier to maintain.

The clouds drift lazily overhead, a gentle breeze contrasting the blazing sun. It feels good to do nothing, simply enjoying the outdoors and each other's company. Before long, both girls drift off to sleep in the afternoon shade.

# CHAPTER 8

# ATLAS

Sweat drips down Atlas's forehead. He swipes it away, though he's so hot it won't do much good. He's been wandering through the city all day, the afternoon heat scorching his too-pale skin. It makes him wonder just how long he was inside that hospital.

As he continues to wind through the busy city streets, he feels anxious. Everything seems unfamiliar, yet strangely familiar at the same time. He passes by crowds of people, their faces blending together in a blur of anonymity. Since recalling a memory yesterday, he's been searching for anything that might trigger another one.

Walking closer to what appears to be a marketplace, a familiar scent catches his attention. Nearby, a lone street vendor is selling freshly baked pastries. As he approaches, memories flood his mind—a similar scent from his past, lazy Sunday mornings, and eating pastries while holding someone's hand. Fleeting seconds of a past he can't remember.

Shaking off the haze of his returning memories, Atlas gets closer in hopes more will surface. Unfortunately, staring at the array of delicious desserts does nothing to spark his recollection. He nods apologetically at the vendor now staring awkwardly at him. He was probably hoping he would buy something. Atlas's stomach rumbles, a reminder of his desperate situation since the loss of his backpack yesterday.

Hastily walking away, Atlas searches for the reprieve of shade. A narrow alleyway between two brick buildings catches his attention, the small space currently shielded from the sun. The subtle shift in temperature is immediate, and he relaxes against the coolness of the bricks. Memories continue to flicker in and out of focus, teasing him with blurry fragments that make no sense. He rubs his temple, hoping to ease the pounding headache that tends to follow the memories.

Determined to regain his bearings, Atlas formulates a plan. Memories can wait. Just because he's in a city, doesn't mean he's any better off than the forest. It's almost worse, surrounded by food and goods he can't just steal like back at the cabin.

With a sigh, he racks his brain for anything of note from his journey throughout the day. The girl on the bike from this morning comes to mind, and he recalls the way her dark eyes shone gold in the morning sun. Why had she looked at him so intently?

He shoves that thought aside, retracing his steps until he recalls passing a park on his way into the city. It shouldn't be too far from here.

Pushing himself off the wall, Atlas sets off toward the park. The rhythmic thud of his footsteps focuses him, and he ignores the stares of people as he passes. What is with people in this city? It's like he has a tattoo in the middle of his forehead screaming 'Look at me!'

Lowering his head, he continues, his long strides making quick work of the distance to the park. Upon arriving, he finds himself standing in stark contrast to the chaotic cityscape. Despite the dilapidated appearance of the city, the park has managed to retain a semblance of its former beauty. While not as meticulously maintained as in better times, the greenery still flourishes, albeit with patches of wilting grass and overgrown shrubbery.

The towering trees, though showing signs of neglect, provide a welcome respite from the concrete jungle beyond. Their leaves rustle mournfully in the breeze, whispering tales of better days gone by. The flower beds, once vibrant with color, now lie neglected, their blossoms faded and withered.

Worn wooden benches adorn the path, their green paint chipped and peeling. The playground equipment, though rusted and in need of repair, is still being used by the city's children. Their laughter is a bittersweet reminder of the childhood he can't recall.

A bright blue butterfly catches his attention as it flutters past, its path directing his gaze toward the public bathroom. Atlas strides closer, noticing the graffiti on the exterior. The shape of a crudely drawn eye catches his attention, the words "They're always watching" scrawled underneath. The paint still looks somewhat fresh. A shiver runs down his spine and he involuntarily glances over his shoulder.

Turning away from the ominous message, Atlas tests the water fountain sitting between the two restrooms. Rusty colored water trickles out the spout before stopping completely, a horrible whining sound taking its place. Great.

In search of another option, Atlas pushes open the men's door. It creaks on its hinges, revealing a dimly lit interior. The bathroom is cramped and musty, air heavy with the scent of mildew and neglect. The tiles on the floor are cracked and grimy, while the sinks are stained with rust and calcium deposits. A flickering fluorescent light casts eerie shadows across the room, adding to the overall sense of decay.

The stalls offer little privacy, their doors hanging askew on rusty hinges. Graffiti covers every available surface, a colorful mosaic of crude drawings and profane messages. Several of the toilets are stained and overflowing, their plumbing long overdue for repairs.

Despite its dismal condition, the bathroom still seems usable, a steady stream of water running from the sink when

Atlas turns it on. He's so thirsty he ignores the grime surrounding him and drinks directly from the tap, greedily gulping the water down.

He drinks his fill, settling the hunger pangs in his stomach temporarily. Exiting the bathroom, he tries not to think about what diseases he could've just given himself. Beggars can't be choosers.

Shielding his eyes from the sun, Atlas scans the park once more and notices a fountain in the center. Its waters lie stagnant, growing murky with bacteria. And yet, it still exudes a quiet dignity, calling Atlas closer.

As he approaches, he's surprised to see a familiar butterfly drinking from a puddle on the fountain's ledge. *Even butterflies get thirsty*, he thinks. Stepping closer, he notices a glimmer of sunlight reflecting off the water's surface. Atlas peers through a break in the scum.

There, along the bottom of the fountain, lie scattered coins shimmering like lost treasures in the murky depths. With a pang of desperation, he realizes that these forgotten coins could be his ticket to survival in this unforgiving city.

Ignoring the disapproving and curious glances of people walking by, Atlas rolls up his sleeves and wades into the fountain, his hands groping blindly in the tepid water. With each handful of coins he retrieves, his heart sinks a little lower. The coins are few and far between, and most are coated in algae and grime.

Undeterred, Atlas continues his search, his fingers brushing against something hard and metallic. Pulling it from the water, he reveals a tarnished silver coin. It stands in stark contrast to the other rusted copper coins he'd collected so far. A few more minutes of searching yield only a few more. He wades back to the edge of the fountain, counting his meager haul. It might barely be enough to purchase one of those pastries from the vendor and his heart swells with hope.

Racing back to the bathroom, Atlas attempts to clean up his appearance by drying off his clothes with the weak hand dryers. It takes far too long to make any progress, so he forgoes it in favor of fixing his hair in the cracked mirror. Raking his hand through the dark brown curls, he manages to tame them only slightly. He rubs a hand along his chiseled jaw, now covered in two-day old stubble. His hazel eyes have grown hollow, evident of all he's been through. Atlas hardly recognizes who he's become.

Turning away from his reflection, he heads through the park and back toward the pastry vendor. A small crowd surrounds the stall and Atlas reluctantly gets in line. He's still counting his change when he reaches the register. Embarrassment floods through him, knowing the people behind him will quickly grow impatient the longer he takes. After counting the last coin, he realizes it's still not enough for the cheapest item on the menu.

"Um, I'm so sorry. I thought I had enough," Atlas says to the man behind the register, disappointment evident in his tone.

He pockets the change, ready to flee from this awkward situation when a hand touches his shoulder. Atlas whips around in surprise to see a small family standing before him, the father now releasing his grip on his shoulder. His face is weathered and worn, lined with creases of years of hard work and struggle. Despite the fatigue in his eyes, he gives a warm smile. Next to him stands a woman, her expression gentle yet determined. Her eyes betray a depth of compassion and understanding, reflecting a lifetime of caring for her family and those in need.

Behind them are two girls, strikingly similar in appearance besides the age difference and varying length of hair. Gazing closer at the older of the two, he immediately recognizes the chopped wavy hair and glowing brown eyes. It's the girl from this morning.

Startled by the recognition, Atlas doesn't notice the handful of coins the man now holds toward him. He regains his composure and accepts the humble gesture. A lump forms in his throat, Atlas feeling overcome with emotion at the kindness and generosity of these strangers. He glances back at the girl and sees a flicker of something in her eyes—understanding, perhaps, or a shared sense of empathy.

With a grateful nod, he returns his attention to the man. "Thank you. I don't even know what to say," he manages, voice thick with emotion.

The man gives him a reassuring smile, patting him gently on the back. "No need for thanks, son. We've all got to look out for each other in times like these and trust that the Lord will provide. Take care of yourself out there."

With a smile of gratitude, Atlas purchases a pastry and disappears into the crowd. He spares a glance back at the family to find the brown-eyed girl watching him intently.

Taken off-guard, Atlas ducks into the familiar alleyway and braces himself against the wall, his heart beating rapidly. The smell of the pastry in his hands draws his attention, making his mouth water. It's an apple turnover, its simplicity reminiscent of the warmth of home. The golden crust is flaky and delicate in his hands, and he sinks his teeth into it, savoring every bite.

# NAYA

"Keep up, Naya!" her dad calls, turning to glance back at her.

His voice startles her out of her thoughts, and she notices just how far back she's fallen. She jogs to catch up, settling in beside Harper on the sidewalk.

"Are you going to eat that?" Harper points at the untouched brownie in her hands.

Naya instinctively pulls it closer. "Of course! Just because you scarfed yours down doesn't mean you get mine too," she retorts playfully, bopping Harper on the nose.

She puts her hands up in mock surrender. "Just thought I'd ask!"

Taking a bite of her brownie, Naya shoots Harper a smug look as if to say, '*See? I'm eating it.*' The rich chocolate flavor floods her senses, a rare treat that she relishes with each mouthful. When their parents suggested they go out for dessert, both Harper and Naya jumped at the chance. It's a rare treat for them, and the promise of chocolate still manages to coax Naya out of the house.

What she didn't expect to find at their favorite pastry vendor was the cute boy she'd been gossiping about earlier this afternoon. Naya's mind wanders back to the encounter, remembering his look when her dad offered him money. The mix of gratitude and humility on the boy's face had tugged at her heartstrings.

"You've been quiet since we left the vendor, sweetheart. Everything alright?" her mom inquires, falling back to walk next to her.

Naya blinks, refocusing on the present moment. "Oh, sorry, Mom. I was just thinking about something."

Her dad, still walking a few steps ahead, turns back with a concerned expression. "Everything alright, kiddo?"

They probably think she's fretting about being out in public again, recalling the events of that horrible night.

"Yeah, Dad, I'm fine," she says, hoping to reassure them. "I was thinking about the boy at the pastry vendor. The one you gave money to."

"What about him?"

"I'm not sure," she admits. "I just feel bad. I wonder what his situation is?"

Her dad's response is measured, tone imbued with wisdom that Naya admires. "Good question, kiddo. All I know is he looked like he needed some help, and we were happy to give it to him. In a world like this, one act of kindness can change someone's life. I'm grateful we have the means to help."

Naya's mom nods in agreement. "Yes, we are very blessed." She hugs Naya to her side, matching her strides as they continue walking.

"I know you've been through a lot lately, but I hope you don't lose that kind heart of yours," her mom murmurs, the words a gentle reminder of the values they hold dear. "It's desperately needed nowadays."

"Thanks, Mom. I'm trying," Naya replies, offering a small smile. Her heart swells with love and appreciation for her family. As she watches Harper skip happily ahead, a sense of profound gratitude washes over her.

Naya silently thanks God for her family, something she does frequently. They've been such an incredible support for her, giving her grace while she recovers from the trauma. It's rare to see families still together, untouched by death, disease, or divorce. Her family's faith is what holds them together, offering hope in a world so full of darkness.

Her mind drifts back to the boy, wondering what kind of support system he might have. Does he have a family to lean on, or is he all alone? His handful of coins certainly hinted at the challenges he must be facing.

"Before we head home, can we make a quick stop at the grocery store? We're running low on food," Naya's mom gently interjects, glancing over at her in search of approval.

Naya's heart skips a beat at the mention of the grocery store. Her mom knows she hasn't been back since that night. Suppressing a shiver, she nods hesitantly, trying to push aside the unease threatening to overwhelm her. She needs to face her fears eventually.

"Sure, Mom. No problem," she manages, her voice tight with apprehension.

They make their way to the store, the familiar sights and sounds doing little to ease Naya's nerves. With each step closer, her pulse quickens, memories clawing at her mind.

As they enter, Naya can't shake the feeling of being watched, the hairs on the back of her neck standing on end. She forces herself to focus on the task at hand, trailing behind her family as they gather items off the sparse shelves.

Rounding the corner, Naya's breath catches in her throat. There, standing at the end of the aisle, is a figure that sends a chill down her spine. It's the same man from that night, his eyes locking onto hers with a chilling intensity.

Panic surges through Naya's veins and she stumbles backward, struggling to maintain her composure. She grips her mother's arm, voice trembling as she whispers, "Mom, we need to go. Now."

Her mother turns to her, confusion evident in her eyes. "What's wrong, Naya?"

Naya's gaze flickers back to the man, only to realize it's not him. Relief washes over her as she realizes it was a figment of her imagination.

"Never mind. It's nothing," she dismisses, her voice rising in embarrassment. "Just my mind playing tricks on me."

Her mom envelops her in a comforting embrace, her warmth a balm against Naya's frayed nerves. Her dad glances over at their encounter, keeping Harper busy at the other end of the aisle.

"It's okay, sweetheart," her mom says soothingly. "Let's get out of here."

She keeps Naya close as they checkout and head home. Naya chastises herself for letting her trauma continue to haunt her. But even as she tries to push the memories aside, they linger in the recesses of her mind, refusing to be ignored.

By the time they reach home, Naya's nerves are stretched taut. As she heads inside, a verse comes to mind, one of her favorites as of late.

*Even though I walk through the valley of the shadow of death, I will fear no evil, for you are with me. Your rod and your staff, they comfort me.*

It's Psalm 23, a reminder that the Lord is her shepherd, comforting her in times of need. The verse playing through her mind feels as though He is speaking directly to her, a perfect reminder for the moment she's in.

She's struggled with her faith these last couple months, wondering why this happened to her. Though she doesn't have the answer, Naya knows that it's in her weakness that she is drawn closer to Him, relying on His strength and understanding rather than her own.

# CHAPTER 10

# ATLAS

Wandering the city streets makes each day blur into the next, marked only by the cold nights spent huddled against alleyway walls and the gnawing ache in Atlas's stomach. It's been about a week since the delicious apple turnover. Since then, he scours dumpsters for scraps of food, the pangs of hunger a constant companion.

He's visited the local shelter several times, but it's always full. The third time, they were kind enough not to send him away empty-handed, offering leftovers and hand-me-down clothes. It was during one of those desperate searches for shelter that he stumbled upon a junkyard at the outskirts of the city. Its towering piles of discarded objects held a variety of treasures for him to sort through.

One of them was the battered laptop he now holds. He's been working up the courage to enter Bargain Bytes, the run-down computer shop he stands in front of. After his many tours through the city, he settled on this one because it looked like the cheapest option in the city. It also looks like the type of place where he won't be judged for walking in with a junkyard laptop.

Having access to the internet would be lifesaving, helping him recover memories more quickly. Atlas has no money left, planning to flee the computer shop after they've diagnosed the laptop's problem.

With a deep breath, he steps into the dimly lit interior, the musty scent of old electronics welcoming him. An older man with glasses looks up from his desk and behind him, a young woman follows suit. A flicker of recognition crosses her features and Atlas's heart lodges in his throat.

It's the brown-eyed girl. Why does he keep running into her? This might mess up his whole plan.

"Hey there," she greets, pushing back a strand of hair that escaped from behind her ear. "What can I do for you?"

Atlas clears his throat, suddenly feeling self-conscious under her piercing gaze. "Um, I was just wondering if you could help me with something," he says, trying to keep his voice steady.

She nods. "Of course, what do you need?"

Atlas sets the laptop on the front counter, and she walks closer. "I'm not sure what's wrong with it. Would you be able to tell me?"

"Sure, let me take a look."

As she examines the device, Atlas notices the way she moves with a subtle confidence.

"So, what's your name?" she asks, breaking the silence as she continues her work.

Atlas hesitates, unsure whether to reveal his identity. "I'm… just passing through," he replies evasively.

"Well, it's nice to meet you," she says with a smile, likely sensing his reluctance to share more. "I'm Naya."

He returns her smile, feeling a sense of relief at the friendly gesture. "Nice to meet you, Naya." He's grateful for her willingness to help him even though he's a stranger.

As she works to examine the laptop, Atlas steals glances at her. He wonders if fate keeps bringing them together for a reason. He definitely didn't expect to ever see her again, let alone only a week later.

"Alright, I've got good news and bad news," she says, looking up from the laptop. "Good news is, I think I can get it working again."

"What's the bad news?"

"It needs pretty extensive repairs to be functional. The screen is cracked, keys are missing, and many of the internal components are corroded and coated in grime. What did you say happened to this thing?"

Atlas racks his brain for an answer. "Uh, it was left in the attic, and I didn't realize there was a hole in the roof." It was the best he could come up with.

"You should take better care of your devices," she says, her tone a little skeptical. "So, would you like it refurbished?"

"No, that's alright," he replies, knowing it will cost a fortune. Atlas is disappointed it's also too much to try and fix on his own.

He grabs the beat-up laptop off the counter and turns to leave, rushing toward the door.

"Hey," Naya calls after him. "You might be better off just buying a newer one. We sell nice, refurbished ones if you're interested."

He looks at her with a resigned smile. "Thanks, I'll think about it."

Letting the door close behind him, he wanders across the street into a shaded alley. He sinks down to the ground, resting his head on his hands. Frustration rises in him, and he throws the laptop at the opposite wall. It clatters against the brick, breaking the plastic case.

Tears well up in his eyes and he angrily swipes them away. He just can't catch a break! All his efforts feel in vain, with only a few small items from his scavenging to show for a week of being in the city. He pulls a rusted lighter out of his pocket, flicking it open and closed with a satisfying click. The simple movement calms his racing mind.

Reflected light momentarily blinds him as the sun continues its ascent. He shields his eyes, looking left to realize he can still see Bargain Bytes across the street. Squinting, he spots Naya helping another customer. Atlas moves closer to the end of the alley to get a better look, needing something to distract him from his pity party.

Though the windows of the shop are rather dirty, Atlas is still able to notice the determined set to her jaw. The customer must say something funny because Naya grins. It's dazzling, though it doesn't quite reach her eyes. Atlas senses a vulnerability in her gaze, a hint of pain she masks with a smile. Despite the distance between them, he feels drawn to her, a silent observer captivated by this puzzling, brown-eyed girl.

"Naya," he whispers to himself, wanting to remember her name. Suddenly, he feels embarrassed for watching her. He hopes she can't see him in the dim alleyway. Turning away, he glances over at the broken laptop on the ground and decides to take another look. *Enough of all this self-pity*, he thinks to himself, determined to make some progress.

# CHAPTER 11
# NAYA

Looking up from her newest job, an old smartwatch, Naya notices a glint of light across the street. Setting the watch down, she squints through the shop's grimy windows, barely able to make out a silhouette. Curious, she moves closer and immediately recognizes the lean frame and tousled strands of hair that now fall over his forehead.

He's inspecting the laptop he brought in, the light reflecting off its surface. Her mother's words about the importance of kindness echo in her mind, and she feels a pull toward this mysterious boy.

Quickly gathering various discarded parts from the shop, she grabs her toolkit and heads toward the front door. "Hey, Mr. Jenkins. I'll be right back."

"Where are you going?" he asks, looking up in surprise.

"There's just something I need to do quick. I'll be fine, I promise."

"Alright. You know this will count toward your lunch break, right? I'm really sorry but I can't afford to pay you if you're not in the shop."

"Of course, no biggie, Mr. J." she replies, pushing the door open and heading across the street.

Naya recalls the several encounters she's had with this handsome stranger. Maybe he's been put in her path for a reason.

"Hey," she calls out, stopping at the edge of the sidewalk. "I couldn't help but notice you out here."

He turns to face her, startled by her presence. His striking hazel eyes lock onto hers, a sense of vulnerability in them that catches her off guard. He almost looks like he's been crying.

"Sorry, I can leave," he responds, hastily scooping up the laptop and rising to his feet. His lean frame towers over her petite stature and she has to look up at him to make eye contact.

"No, you're fine. I just noticed you struggling with that laptop and thought maybe I could lend a hand." Naya holds up her toolkit.

He stares at her in silence for a few seconds before saying, "I don't have any money to pay you."

"Good thing I'm not asking for any," she says, a reassuring smile playing on her lips.

Naya walks into the alley, sitting on the ground and setting her equipment beside her. He pauses in surprise before following behind, sitting along the opposite wall to face her.

"My name is Atlas, by the way," he says, handing over the laptop.

"Atlas. That's a nice name." She notes the way his hands tremble slightly as he releases the laptop into her hands.

Naya sets to work, moving with practiced ease as she carefully dismantles the broken laptop.

"I can't promise miracles, but I can at least get it running."

"That's more than enough," Atlas replies, seeming a bit more comfortable with her presence.

She notices him watching her as she replaces parts, carefully fitting the new ones amidst the others that still work. Heat floods her cheeks at the intensity of his gaze, and she tries to focus on her task. Although they remain silent, it's not uncomfortable. Before long, Naya has pieced the laptop back together.

"Moment of truth," she says, pressing the power button.

Naya gives a shout of victory as it flickers to life. Only parts of the screen work where the cracks don't mar its surface. But it works all the same. She spins it around on her lap so it faces Atlas, looking up to see his reaction. At first, he simply gazes at the screen as if he can't quite believe what just happened. Then, a mix of awe and gratitude wash over his features, his lips parting in silent amazement.

"Wow," he breathes, his voice barely above a whisper. "I don't know how to thank you. This means a lot."

Naya senses a profound appreciation in his tone and she feels touched by his genuine gratitude. Moments like these are what continue to compel her to help others despite all she's been through.

"It was nothing, really," she says modestly, though her heart swells with pride. "Just a few tweaks here and there. It looks like it's good to go now, you'll just have to work around the cracked screen and missing keys."

Atlas nods, a soft expression on his face. "Thank you, Naya. I can't tell you how much this means to me. You've been a real lifesaver."

She blushes at his compliment and the sound of her name on his lips. Atlas places the laptop on his lap, eyes flitting across the screen as he tests it out. She feels a sense of closeness to him as she watches, a bond she can't quite describe. Despite their limited interactions, she's comfortable in his presence.

"Oh, that's not good," Atlas suddenly exclaims.

Naya crouches beside him to see what he means. A low battery warning appears in the corner of the screen.

"No big deal. I'm surprised it even had enough battery to power on. You'll just have to charge it when you get home." She glances over at him, noticing how close they are.

Atlas drops his head into his hands with a sigh.

"You do have a charger, right?" Naya questions.

"No," he says into his palms, clearly feeling defeated.

She doesn't press him any further, though she wonders why he has a laptop with no charger.

"I probably have one in the shop you can use."

"Really?" Atlas says, turning toward her.

"Yeah, I'm sure Mr. Jenkins won't mind. He loves me," she says with a wink. "Come on!"

Atlas follows her back into the shop. Mr. Jenkins raises a curious eyebrow at them. "I made a new friend. I hope you don't mind."

"As long as he doesn't distract you from your work," Mr. Jenkins says with a grunt of resignation.

Naya leans in closer to Atlas, whispering, "Told you he likes me."

She leads him to her desk, moving a large computer monitor off a wooden chair so he can sit. He stands near her desk awkwardly, only sitting down when she pats the chair and beckons him over.

"Here." Naya holds a charging cable out to him. "There's an outlet right behind you."

"Thanks."

"No problem! I'll leave you to it while it charges." She gets him set-up with the shop's Wi-Fi before returning to her work.

The rest of her shift flies by as she keeps herself busy. Atlas is as quiet as a mouse, typing away on his laptop. She's curious what's keeping him so intrigued but doesn't pry for answers. As she cleans up her desk for the night, Atlas's stomach growls loudly.

He grips his stomach in embarrassment, avoiding eye contact.

"Do you want to come over for dinner?" she blurts without thinking.

Atlas looks up, likely as shocked as she is by her offer. A range of emotions cross his face, as if he's not sure how to respond.

"You can hitch a ride on the back of my bike if you want." She's surprised by her sudden boldness.

"You've done enough for me already, I shouldn't." He stands and unplugs the charger from the wall, handing it back to her. "Thanks for letting me use this."

"Yeah," she says, distracted by the disappointment now pooling in her stomach. Naya hadn't realized how much she was enjoying his quiet company.

Atlas walks past her to exit the shop.

"Wait," she says, grabbing his arm.

He turns around in surprise and she drops her hand, once again shocked by her own actions. She has no idea why she hates the thought of him leaving.

"It's really not a big deal. Come over. My mom is a great cook."

Naya recalls the day her dad bought his pastry and wonders when he last had a good meal. The silence between them is a bit strained and she feels suddenly embarrassed by her brazen behavior.

"I'm sorry. I don't know why I'm being so pushy. You don't have—"

"Sure, that would be nice."

# CHAPTER 12
# ATLAS

Outside Bargain Bytes, Atlas patiently stands on the sidewalk as Naya converses with Mr. Jenkins inside. While he waits, he begins to second-guess his decision to join her for dinner. Her family has already been so generous and they're still practically strangers. The offer of a real meal is just too tempting to refuse. His stomach growls again at the thought.

The door hinge creaks in front of him as Naya exits the shop with her bike. She stands and surveys him, nerves fluttering in his stomach as she does.

"Um, so, I think it might be easiest if you steer. You're a little tall to ride on the back."

Atlas hesitates briefly before agreeing, realizing she's right.

"I can take your laptop too. It should fit in my backpack."

After securing it on her back, she gives him a relieved smile and climbs on behind him. Her hands settle on his shoulders, surprisingly warm. It's a strange sensation, but not an entirely unwelcome one.

With Naya's directions, they set off toward her house. As they ride, Atlas feels more comfortable with her. Despite their limited interaction, she continues to show him kindness and generosity.

Arriving at Naya's house, Atlas feels a strong sense of déjà vu. The house is a modest two-story structure, painted in an earthy taupe. The front yard is small but well-maintained.

"I can take it from here." Naya hops off the back of the bike and gestures to the handlebars.

Atlas clamors off, releasing them into her hands and watching as she guides it into the garage.

As they enter the front door, Atlas is welcomed by a cozy atmosphere. The interior decor is simple yet tasteful, the walls adorned with framed artwork, family photos, and bookshelves. A delicious aroma wafts through the air, prompting another growl from Atlas's stomach.

Voices in the kitchen set Atlas on edge.

"Let me introduce you to my parents," Naya says, guiding him around a staircase and into the kitchen.

They are greeted by the surprised expressions of her parents, Naya quickly introducing him while they exchange polite greetings.

"Welcome, Atlas. I'm Celeste. This is my husband, Silas. Please, make yourself at home," Naya's mom says warmly.

Atlas makes his way awkwardly to the table and has a seat, noticing as Celeste asks to have a word with Naya. They leave the kitchen briefly and Atlas is fairly certain it's about him. It's probably safe to assume Naya doesn't bring strangers to the house very often, let alone strangers of the opposite gender.

The noise of someone descending the stairs draws Atlas's attention, and he turns to see a girl slide into the kitchen, her socks slippery against the wood floor. She stops dead in her tracks when she spots Atlas and stares at him, mouth agape.

He waves, unsure how to respond. "Hi."

"Who are you?"

"Atlas," he responds, still deciding what else to say. Can he call himself a friend of Naya's?

Silas breaks the silence for him. "He's a friend of Naya's and he's joining us for dinner tonight. Be polite, Harper."

She gives him an embarrassed grin, moving to help her dad set the table. Naya and her mom return shortly after to help.

Sitting down to dinner, Naya's family exudes a sense of warmth and comfort. They all grasp hands and Naya reaches out to Atlas.

"We're going to say grace, if that's alright."

"Yeah," Atlas says, taking her hand.

"Dear Heavenly Father," Silas starts. "We thank you for the blessings you continue to pour out in our lives. We are grateful to welcome a new friend to join us in sharing this meal. Thank you for the hands that prepared this food and bless it to our bodies. Amen."

"Amen," Atlas echoes.

Food is dished out and conversation flows easily, Naya's parents asking polite questions about Atlas and his background. He shares what he can remember, knowing his answers are rather vague. As he eats, he has to stop himself from devouring the food. It's the best thing he's had in a long time, and he wants to savor every bite of it.

"You sure like the food," Harper notes from across the table.

Naya shoots her a look and Atlas chuckles. "It's delicious. Thank you again. I'm lucky to have met you all."

Celeste smiles gratefully at him. "It's not a problem, though I don't think it was luck that brought you here."

Atlas isn't quite sure what she's hinting at, but he returns her smile all the same.

A short while later, the table is cleared away and Atlas insists on helping with the dishes. He already feels bad for doing nothing to help set the table. Naya's parents exchange a quick glance, before agreeing.

"We're glad you could join us tonight, Atlas," Celeste says, patting his hand as he dries the last of the plates. "You're welcome here anytime."

Atlas smiles gratefully, humbled by her open invitation. "Thank you again for having me. It was a delicious meal."

Behind him, Atlas can feel Harper boring a hole through his head as she eyes him skeptically. "So, Atlas," she begins, twirling a lock of hair around her finger, "what do you do?"

Atlas chokes, taken aback by her sudden question. "Um, well, I'm… I'm kind of between things at the moment," he admits, a hint of embarrassment coloring his cheeks.

Harper nods thoughtfully. "Do you like video games?" she asks, eyes lighting up with excitement.

Before Atlas can respond, Naya intervenes. "Harper, let Atlas finish up. I'm sure he doesn't want to be pestered with all your questions." She gently pushes her sister toward the living room.

Once the dishes are done, Atlas heads to the front door with a goodbye. He starts to shut the door behind him when Naya follows, joining him on the front step. The soft glow of the porch light casts shadows across their faces as they stand in the cool night air.

"I'm glad you decided to come tonight," Naya says softly, her gaze meeting his.

"Me too. Your family is incredibly kind. Thank you."

"Yeah, they're really something. I love them to bits. Take care on your way home, Atlas. Maybe I'll see you around?"

A pang of disappointment hits him, knowing he doesn't have a home to go back to. "Yeah, maybe."

Sleep finds Atlas easily as he settles into the familiar alley, his stomach full for the first time in a while. It's almost as unexpected as the dream that follows.

Atlas swiftly makes his way down the cramped grocery aisle, eyes scanning the shelves for his favorite cereal. Spotting the last box nestled among the other breakfast goods, a smile tugs at his lips. Fate seems to be smiling upon him today.

He reaches out to claim his prize, just as another hand latches onto it. He looks over in surprise, meeting the eyes of a young woman in a tense moment of silent confrontation. He's not about to give up the last box.

As she realizes he isn't going to let her have it, her expression turns from determination to frustration. He can see the annoyance flickering in her intense brown eyes but can't suppress the smug satisfaction that wells up within him.

"First come, first served," Atlas says, his tone laced with amusement as he pulls the cereal box closer.

"You've got to be kidding me," she exclaims, brows furrowing in irritation. "I was here first!"

She doesn't release her grip on the box, pulling it back toward her. Atlas chuckles, her petite frame not very intimidating next to his tall one.

"Great minds think alike, I suppose. Though I appreciate your taste in cereal, this one is mine. Better luck next time."

"In a perfect world, maybe," she replies, her voice tinged with resignation. "I've been trying to get my hands on these for the last month."

Atlas feels a hint of guilt but pushes it aside. He's been after these for a while now too. The grocery store never keeps a reliable stock of items.

He surveys the young woman, noticing how she's resorted to nervously twirling her long hair around her finger.

"Looks like we have a standoff, then," Atlas says, an idea forming in his mind.

The woman's irritation returns. "And what do you suppose we do about it?"

His eyes sparkle with mischief as he pulls a coin out of his pocket. "Why don't we flip a coin? Winner gets the cereal, loser walks away empty-handed," he proposes casually.

Her eyes narrow and she squares her shoulders. "Fine," she shoots back, her voice laced with defiance.

Atlas loves a challenge. "Ladies first. Heads or tails?"

"Heads."

Without loosening his grip on the cereal, he tosses the coin into the air. It catches the fluorescent grocery store lights with a flicker of silver before descending into Atlas's waiting palm. Releasing his grip on the cereal box, he swiftly slaps the coin onto the back of his opposite hand.

"Tails," he declares, a victorious grin spreading across his face. "Looks like luck is on my side today."

Locking eyes with the young woman, he's shocked by her resigned smile.

She sighs. "Thanks for adding some fun to my loss. Maybe there's more than just luck on your side."

For a moment, Atlas is speechless, his mind struggling to process her graceful acceptance of defeat. It wasn't the reaction he had anticipated, and he's momentarily disarmed by her calm demeanor.

Regaining his composure, Atlas admires the woman's poise. "Well, I suppose luck favors the bold," he replies, a hint of admiration coloring his tone.

She hands him the cereal box, the brush of her fingers sending a jolt of electricity coursing through him.

"See you around, Brown Eyes," he says, turning to leave.

He glances behind him as he exits the aisle, a sense of intrigue urging him to look back. Her brown eyes are watching him as he leaves, and she smiles softly, sending butterflies through his stomach.

# CHAPTER 13
# NAYA

Naya settles into her room, the soft glow of her desk lamp casting a warm hue over the space. Walking past her bed, she sits in her creaky desk chair and powers up her computer. The moon is bright, illuminating the modest wooden desk below the window. Naya pulls the beige curtains closed. Although the moon is beautiful, she doesn't like the feeling of being watched.

With a crack of her knuckles, she opens a browser and sends her fingers flying across the keyboard. After spending all day with Atlas, Naya wants to find out everything she can about him.

Not knowing much, Naya starts with '*Atlas mid-twenties Havenwood.*'

Sifting through pages of search results, she furrows her brow in concentration. Naya knows her search was vague, but there isn't a single helpful link. She buckles down, realizing this will be harder than she thought.

After an hour of digging, Naya leans back in frustration.

"Who is this guy?" she says to no one.

It's as if Atlas is a ghost, his presence completely erased from the digital world. No social media profiles, no online records—nothing. It's like he doesn't exist beyond their chance encounters.

Feeling a twinge of unease, Naya continues scrolling through endless web pages, each time coming away empty handed. It's like chasing shadows in the dark, the more she searches, the more elusive Atlas becomes.

Ready to give up for the night, Naya scrolls through one more social media page. Then, a glimmer of something catches her eye—a small thumbnail in the corner of the screen. With trembling fingers, Naya clicks on it.

And there he is, staring back at her from the screen. The photo is cropped, and Naya notices the shoulder of another person next to him. She tries to zoom in to see who it might belong to when the image suddenly disappears. An error page now replaces it.

Clicking rapidly, Naya tries to find it again, upset she didn't think to save it to her computer.

"No! Come back!" she shouts at her computer.

Groaning in frustration, she twirls in her chair. As the initial anger of losing the image ebbs away, the realization of what just happened hits her. Whirling around, she manually powers down her computer, heart racing. Someone knows the picture was found and made an effort to erase it. And fast.

Breathing hard, Naya tears through her room, inspecting every device and hidden crevice. The feeling of being watched consumes her, intensifying her urgency to find whatever might be lurking in the shadows of her own home.

She's standing on her bed inspecting one of her framed pictures when she's startled by a knock on her door.

"Naya? What's going on?" Harper opens the door, concern shadowing her youthful features.

Naya glances around her room at the mess she made. Books from her now empty shelf lay scattered on the floor, the comforter is torn off the bed, and her lamp is dismantled on her desk. Harper's eyes widen as she takes in the disarray.

"Hey, Harper. Sorry, I was, uh, looking for something," she stammers, not wanting to worry her younger sister.

"Looking for what? Did you lose something important?" she asks, stepping inside and surveying the chaos around her.

Naya hesitates, unsure how to explain her paranoia. "Uh, just some… personal stuff. Nothing to worry about." She forces a reassuring smile as she climbs off the bed.

But Harper isn't convinced. "Are you sure? You seem really worked up." She gently touches Naya's arm in support.

With a sigh, Naya realizes her sister is much too perceptive to be kept in the dark. "Okay, fine. I've just been feeling like… like someone's watching me, you know? Like there's something in here, watching everything I do," she admits, her voice barely above a whisper.

Harper's expression softens and she sits on Naya's bed. "I'm sure it's nothing. You've just been under a lot of stress lately, going back to work and all." She pats the spot next to her, motioning for Naya to join.

Naya sits and Harper wraps her arms around her in a comforting embrace. She burrows her face into the silkiness of her hair, breathing in the familiar scent. "I don't know, Harper. It just feels so real."

"Just like your nightmares, all you need to do when it feels real is wake up. Remember where you really are."

Naya holds her sister in silence, pondering her words.

"We'll figure it out together, okay?" Harper's words are filled with determination. "You've made it through these last couple months so I know you can make it through this."

Naya nods, grateful for her sister's support. "Yeah, okay. Thanks, Harper," she murmurs, a glimmer of hope returning amidst the chaos of her fears.

"Let me help you get your room back in order." Harper picks up the frame Naya laid on her bed.

"I'd appreciate it."

It takes a while to clean up even with Harper's help. Naya never would've imagined her mere minutes of chaos would require an eternity to fix. Once Naya finishes putting the pieces of her lamp back together, the two girls collapse back onto her bed.

"Just how long were you ransacking your room?" Harper says incredulously.

Naya grins ruefully. "Not that long."

They both sigh, relaxing into the soft gray comforter.

"Sleepover?" Naya suggests hopefully, not wanting to be alone in her room tonight.

"Absolutely." In a flash, Harper runs out the door, only to return moments later with her pillow.

Naya laughs.

"What?" Harper asks. "You know I hate your extra pillow. It's uncomfortable."

Harper settles onto Naya's bed, arranging her pillow just right. "You know it's probably been a couple weeks since our last sleepover. Have your nightmares stopped?"

Naya ponders Harper's question, realizing the last dream she had was the one of the boy running through the door. She hasn't had a nightmare since.

"Yeah, you're right."

"That's great, Naya!" Harper smiles warmly. "Another sleepover won't hurt though, right?"

Naya crushes her sister into a bear hug and turns off the lights. Before long, she hears Harper's faint snores. Staring at the ceiling, she wishes she could fall asleep that fast but too many thoughts are still swirling through her mind.

She says a quick prayer, trying to let her worries go.

*Lord,*

*I have so many questions and so few answers. Please give me your strength and patience to continue walking with you one day at a time. Thank you for the many blessings in my life—my family, no nightmares, good health, and my job at Bargain Bytes. Oh, and thanks for bringing Atlas into my life. I don't know if I'll see him again, but I trust your plan for my life and whatever you have in store. I want to continue to be your hands and feet, letting your love shine through me onto others.*

*Amen.*

# CHAPTER 14

# ATLAS

Atlas jolts awake, the remnants of the memory still fluttering in his mind. He tries to grasp onto it, but it slips away like sand through his fingers, overshadowed by a growing ache in his head. Grimacing, he absentmindedly runs his fingers along the scar on his neck.

*Who was that woman?* he thinks. *When did that happen?*

He tries to picture her face, but it's blurred in his memory. Slumping back against the brick wall, he massages his temples, hoping to ease the pounding headache. Unsure what's causing them, he decides to look it up. Connecting to the nearby coffee shop's Wi-Fi, Atlas does a quick search on his new laptop.

Results suggest anything from migraines and sinus infections to traumatic head injuries and various diseases. Atlas wishes he could remember if he's always suffered from migraines or if it's a recent occurrence. He scrolls through more articles, absorbing information about sleep patterns, diet, and stress.

As he navigates through search results, an online forum catches his eye, the topic focusing on Government VR Technology. Intrigued, Atlas clicks on the forum thread, his eyes scanning through the posts with growing concern. Users speculate about rumors of a new government-funded Virtual Reality technology program.

Reading further, Atlas is unsettled by the various suggestions for its purpose, with some users adamant the tech is for surveillance and mind control.

One particularly chilling post catches Atlas's attention. It describes a supposed insider leak, claiming the government is using VR to manipulate and monitor citizens without their knowledge. The post alleges that participants in VR simulations are unknowingly subjected to psychological experiments, their thoughts and behaviors analyzed.

The similarity to his own experience sends a shiver down Atlas's spine. Is he one of the so-called participants? Overwhelmed by questions, Atlas closes the browser tab. The prospect of his thoughts and behaviors now in the hands of the government fills him with dread. He shuts the computer and stares blankly at the wall in front of him.

As the morning sun casts its faint glow over the city, Atlas decides to head to the local grocery store to clear his head. Naya's parents were generous enough to give him a bit of money before he left last night.

Before entering, he straightens his clothes and hair, wanting to look more presentable. He pastes a smile on his face, hoping to appear like a charming young man rather than one haunted by unanswered questions.

Wandering through the aisles, Atlas spots a familiar box of cereal. The vibrant packaging calls out to him, exactly the same as in his memory. With a sense of curiosity and trepidation, he picks it up and heads to the checkout counter, grabbing a bottle of water along the way.

At the cashier, he places the box and bottled water on the counter and digs into his pockets for the money. It's not much, but it's enough to cover the cost. As he pays, he musters up the courage to ask about job openings at the store. He desperately needs to start making money of his own.

"Sorry, we're not hiring right now," the cashier replies with a polite smile, already ringing up his purchase.

Atlas nods, feeling disappointed at yet another dead end. With a murmured thanks, he takes his purchase and heads back out into the humid morning air. Ripping open the cereal box, he grabs a handful and shovels it into his mouth. The cereal is good, the taste both familiar and foreign at the same time. Although he's slowly remembering bits of his past, he still feels detached from it, like he's a completely different person.

While he eats, he wanders through the city streets, not concerned with where his feet will take him. His reflection in a shop window catches his attention and he's shocked to find himself in front of Bargain Bytes. Distracted by the ridiculous sight of him standing there with his hand stuffed in a cereal box, he doesn't notice Naya staring at him through the window.

The dinging of the bell above the shop door alerts him to her presence.

"Nice breakfast you got there," she says, a grin tugging at the corner of her full lips.

Atlas feels his face heat up with embarrassment, quickly pulling his hand out of the box and closing it.

He clears his throat awkwardly, swallowing his last handful of cereal. "Yeah, Harvest Crunch is my favorite."

Naya's eyebrows raise in surprise. "Mine too. Although there aren't many cereal options to begin with these days."

She puts her hands in the pockets of her shorts, gently rocking on her heels. "So, what brings you back here?"

"Just wandering by, I guess. And maybe hoping to see a certain someone," he admits, surprising himself.

Naya smirks playfully, arching one eyebrow. "Oh, really? No need to be shy, I can go get Mr. Jenkins for you."

Atlas grins, feeling confident as he meets her gaze. "He's a nice guy, but I much prefer your company."

Now it's Naya's turn to blush, a delicate pink gracing her cheeks.

She laughs softly, a melodic sound that makes his heart beat faster. "Woah, who's this sudden smooth talker?"

Atlas shrugs, appreciating the compliment. He's glad to know some of his past charm is still there, although he's a little rusty. "So, what's on your agenda today?"

"Just the usual. Fixing up some gadgets, cleaning the shop."

"Sounds nice," Atlas remarks, a sudden thought occurring to him. "The shop wouldn't happen to be hiring, would it?

# CHAPTER 15

# NAYA

Naya's heart jumps at his unexpected question, intrigued by the idea of working with Atlas. She hides her excitement behind a composed smile. "Hmm, I'm not sure, but it wouldn't hurt to ask. Come on, let's go inside and find out." Although she's almost positive Mr. Jenkins isn't looking to hire anytime soon, she's determined to change his mind.

Entering the shop, Naya leads Atlas to Mr. Jenkins's desk. He looks up from his work, glancing between Naya and Atlas with a confused expression.

"Good morning, Mr. Jenkins. You might remember me from yesterday," Atlas starts. "I was wondering if Bargain Bytes has any job openings?"

Naya flashes Mr. Jenkins a hopeful smile, her eyes flickering with determination. "Mr. Jenkins, Atlas is a quick learner. He's got a knack for problem-solving and is incredibly resourceful." She glances over at Atlas who's staring at her in surprise.

Mr. Jenkins furrows his brow, clearly considering her words carefully. "Well, we're not exactly rolling in profits."

"Not yet but having an extra pair of hands around here could really speed up our repairs and help us serve more customers!" she exclaims, raising her brows and silently pleading with him to consider it further.

The old man pauses for a moment, the silence stretching out like an eternity. Naya can hear the nervous shuffling of Atlas's feet against the worn linoleum floors.

"I can't promise much in terms of pay."

Atlas nods eagerly. "Whatever you can offer would be greatly appreciated, sir."

Naya watches as Mr. Jenkins appraises Atlas with a sigh.

"Well, Naya, if you're confident in his abilities, I'll give him a chance."

"Thank you, Mr. Jenkins," Atlas says. "I won't let you down."

With a grunt and a nod of his head, Mr. Jenkins goes back to his work. Naya motions for Atlas to wait by her desk and he tentatively heads that way.

Moving closer to Mr. Jenkins, Naya hugs him softly. "Thanks again. You're not just doing me a favor, Mr. Jenkins. You're giving Atlas a chance, and I know he'll make the most of it."

Mr. Jenkins chuckles. "You're welcome, Naya. Something tells me Atlas will be very helpful, not just for the shop, but for you too."

With a laugh, Naya releases him and joins Atlas at her desk in the back of the shop.

"Thanks for sticking up for me," he says quietly. "You didn't have to say all that."

"Anytime, it's all true."

Throughout the day, Naya shows Atlas the ropes of his new job and finds herself enjoying his company more than she expected. They quickly fall into a rhythm, with Atlas proving to be a diligent and enthusiastic learner. Naya guides him through the basics of repairing and troubleshooting electronics, impressed by his natural curiosity and willingness to ask questions.

As they work side by side, she demonstrates how to dismantle a laptop and identify its components, patiently walking him through each step. Despite the occasional mishap, they work very well together.

By the end of the day, Naya is satisfied with his progress.

"Not bad for your first day on the job." She gives him a playful nudge.

Atlas returns her smile, his hazel eyes bright with gratitude. "Thanks to you, Naya. You're a surprisingly patient teacher."

"Hey, watch it mister!" she says in mock warning. "I got you this job and I can get it taken away, too."

"Didn't mean to upset the boss lady," he jokes.

Now that Atlas is more comfortable with her, she's learning a lot about his personality. He's remarkably funny and charming, traits he kept well hidden beneath his previously cold demeanor. But there's still an aura of mystery surrounding him she hasn't quite unraveled. She wants to know more about his past, but decides it'd be best to start with the basics.

"What's your favorite color?" she blurts.

"Navy blue," he replies promptly. "Like the sky when the moon is just a sliver among an ocean of stars."

"Wow, that's rather poetic."

Atlas shrugs. "That's just what comes to mind when I think of the color. What's your favorite?"

"Black."

"That's not even a color!" Atlas protests.

"Hold on a minute, you didn't let me finish!" Naya exclaims. "First, black is actually a combination of all the colors, so you're wrong. Second, it's elegant, sophisticated, and timeless. There's a rich, velvety quality about black I just love."

"Huh, I'd never thought about it that way before," Atlas admits.

"What's your favorite food?"

"Why all the questions?" he says warily, already shying away even though the questions aren't that deep.

"Well, I figured now that we work together, I should get to know you a little better!" Naya knows there's more to it than that but she's not ready to admit it.

"Alright. Um… I'm not sure what my favorite food is. Maybe just a burger?"

"Hm, not my first choice but okay. I really like grilled cheese sandwiches."

"And that's better than a burger? I'll have to agree to disagree." Atlas rises from his chair, stretching after sitting all day.

"You'll change your mind after trying my mom's grilled cheese! They're, uh, amazing," Naya replies, faltering over her words when the edge of Atlas's shirt rides up, revealing part of his toned abdomen underneath.

Quickly averting her eyes, Naya busies herself with tidying her desk, hoping to conceal her flushed cheeks.

"I'll take your word for it," he says, thankfully unaware of her wandering eyes.

Naya stands alongside him, putting a few things away and willing her heart rate to return to normal. As Naya and Atlas head toward the exit, Mr. Jenkins looks up from his work.

"Closing time already?" He glances over at the clock in surprise. "Well, you two get home safe and don't get into any trouble."

Naya notices the hint of amusement in his voice and nods, offering a coy smile. "We'll see you tomorrow, Mr. Jenkins."

Atlas chimes in with a polite nod. "Thanks again for the opportunity, sir."

Mr. Jenkins waves them off with a grin. "No problem, just don't forget to lock up on your way out."

With a final wave, Naya and Atlas step out into the cool evening air, the faint sound of the bell chiming behind them as they leave.

"I guess I'll see you tomorrow," she says, looking up at Atlas.

"Definitely. Thanks again for today."

Naya's heart skips a beat at the sight of his genuine smile. "Of course."

She hops on her bike and heads toward home, unable to deny the flutter of anticipation in her chest at seeing him again tomorrow.

# CHAPTER 16
# ATLAS

"Please!" Atlas gives Naya his best puppy dog eyes. "It's not like it's that expensive. I want to return the favor!"

Naya eyes the pastry vendor across the street. After work, Atlas asked her to go on a walk, wanting to surprise her by buying her favorite pastry.

"But your first paycheck should be for you," she argues gently, concern evident in her furrowed brow. "That's two weeks of hard work!"

"You've done so much for me, Naya. Let me do this for you."

With a soft sigh, Naya relents, her resistance melting away under his earnest gaze. "Okay, but just this once," she concedes.

Atlas beams at her, leading the way across the street to the vendor. As they approach, the aroma of freshly baked pastries wafts toward them. They exchange a few words with the vendor, selecting their favorite pastries from the display. As Atlas hands over the money, he feels a sense of satisfaction. It's a small gesture, but it means the world to him to be able to finally do something nice for Naya.

Walking away with pastries in hand, Atlas hears unexpected laughter. He looks over at Naya but it's not her. A memory has surfaced, playing out before his eyes like he's reliving the moment.

The woman from before walks next to him, her face still unclear. Atlas feels nervous and excited, caught up in her laughter and the scent of baked goods.

"I can't believe Mr. Cereal Thief bought me a pastry," she says playfully, giving him an incredulous side-eye.

Atlas chuckles, charmed by her nickname for him. "Running into you again can't be a coincidence. It's fate telling me I need to repay you for taking the last box of Harvest Crunch."

"Possibly. Or maybe you're some creep who's stalking me now." The hint of a smile tugs at her lips.

"How did you figure it out already?" he replies with mock surprise. "I thought I was keeping a really low profile."

She laughs again and Atlas is pleased he can elicit that reaction from her.

"Seriously, though," he starts, "sorry about the other day. I still feel bad. Although my stomach doesn't."

She whacks his arm. "Don't rub it in. You're not so good at these apology things, are you?"

"I'll work on that for next time."

"Oh, you think there's going to be a next time? How presumptuous of you, Cereal Thief."

"Well, I can hope."

Her face flushes at his boldness. She's about to say something when Atlas blinks and the memory is gone.

Naya stands beside him once more, concern clouding her face as she looks over at him.

"Where did you go in that head of yours? Are you okay?"

Perplexed by the whirlwind of emotions stirred up by his memory, Atlas simply nods. "Yeah, I'm okay."

Naya gives him a skeptical look but doesn't push for more answers. He's grateful, not knowing what to say, anyway.

They walk in silence for several blocks, Atlas wrestling with conflicting emotions. He still knows nothing about this mysterious woman but feels torn between his past self and the present.

Atlas steals a glance at Naya. He appreciates how comfortable they've gotten around each other and finds himself always eagerly anticipating seeing her.

"Hey, let's take a detour," Atlas suggests. "I know a place."

"Okay" Naya says, curiosity evident on her face.

Atlas leads them to the park, finding a bench and sitting down. He gazes over at the fountain, remembering wading through the murky water.

"You look lost in thought again. You know if you ever need someone to talk to, I'm here," she offers gently.

Her words stir a sense of gratitude and warmth within him. Although he's slowly revealed more about himself, he's still hesitant to share the whole escaping from a hospital with missing memories thing.

"Thanks, Naya," he replies sincerely. "I appreciate that."

"You're a pretty secretive guy," she says, gazing at him intently.

Atlas stares back, unsure how to respond.

Averting her eyes, Naya clears her throat. "I have a confession."

Atlas's heart leaps into his throat at her words.

"I may have done a little research on you."

Atlas can't hide the look of shock on his face. "You what?"

She stares at the sidewalk, avoiding eye contact. "You know, just a quick internet search to look for your social media accounts and stuff."

He mentally kicks himself for not thinking of that first. He's been more focused on searching for the mysterious hospital facility and government VR tech. Sweat pricks his palms at the thought of what Naya found.

"And? Did I pass your inspection?" he says, attempting to hide his apprehension with a hint of charm.

Naya turns her head to look at him. There's a hint of fear now darkening her usually warm brown eyes.

"That's what's weird. You're like a ghost, Atlas. I found almost nothing."

His heart rate quickens at her words. "Almost nothing?" He needs to know what she managed to find.

"I may have exaggerated when I said I did a little research," she admits. "I spent a lot longer looking into you when my first search came back suspiciously empty."

Naya looks around nervously, leaning in closer to Atlas when she spots a few people walking in the park.

"The only thing I found was one picture of you with someone."

"With who?"

"I couldn't tell. The photo was cropped. And only seconds after I found the image, it disappeared completely," she says, dropping her voice to a whisper.

"Disappeared? What do you mean?" Ominous thoughts pop up in his mind, thinking back to the forum post about government surveillance.

"Like someone deleted it. Atlas, are you in trouble?"

Dropping his head into his hands, he folds into himself and hunches over on the bench. The desire to tell Naya everything is very tempting, but he doesn't want to scare her away. Lost in his inner turmoil, he jumps in surprise when he feels Naya touch the scar on the back of his neck.

"Sorry. A butterfly landed on your neck." She points in the direction it went. "What is the scar from? I've never noticed it before."

A shiver runs along his spine, though he's not sure if it's from her touch or the chilling mystery of the scar. Maybe both.

"I don't know."

Naya's face scrunches in confusion. "That's a sensitive spot. You don't know how you got it?"

She moves closer, examining the raised ridge. "It seems it was repaired very professionally."

Suddenly, a sharp shock of electricity makes Atlas jerk away from her touch.

They stare at each other in surprise, Naya holding the side of her head and Atlas touching his neck.

"That was weird," he remarks.

"Must be static electricity," she says sheepishly. "Sorry."

"It's okay." He brushes the sensation away, lingering on the way her cool fingers felt on his skin.

"Naya?"

"Hm?"

"There's something I want to tell you, but this really isn't the place to do it." He glances around at the park, more people now strolling through it.

"Alright," she says tentatively, one eyebrow raised. "My house?"

# CHAPTER 17
## NAYA

"Atlas! It's so good to see you again," her mom says as Naya and Atlas walk into the house together.

"You too, ma'am."

"Always so polite. Call me Celeste." She ushers them into the foyer and shuts the front door. "Naya tells me you work at Bargain Bytes now?"

"That's right."

"How are you liking it? Naya seems to really enjoy working with you."

"Mom!" Naya chides, embarrassment heating her face.

Atlas smiles over at her, only adding to the blush now creeping onto her face.

"I enjoy working with her too. Mr. Jenkins is a very nice guy as well."

"Glad to hear it." Her mom grins at both of them.

"Well, we're going to hang out upstairs for a bit." Naya hopes her mom will take the hint and let them be, not wanting to be embarrassed any further.

"Let me know if you need anything."

"Much appreciated, Celeste," Atlas replies, following Naya up the stairs.

As they reach her bedroom, Naya hears the patter of footsteps in Harper's bedroom. Looking down the hall, she sees her sister stick her head out of her room.

"Atlas is here?" she asks excitedly.

She runs down the hall and grabs Atlas by the hand, trying to drag him to her room. "Come play video games with me! I've been stuck on this last level forever. I'm sure you'd know how to beat it though."

"Since when were you best friends with Atlas?"

"Since today!" She shoots her sister a death glare.

"Sorry, he came over to hang out with me, Harper. Maybe we can all play games later, okay?" Naya says, trying to stay patient.

"Pretty please?" Harper begs, returning her attention to Atlas, still holding onto his arm.

Atlas smiles at Naya before bending down so he's closer to Harper's level. "It sounds fun, but I'm not really in the mood for a game right now."

Harper looks dejected.

"Maybe later, after I've had a chat with Naya?" Atlas asks.

Naya appreciates how Atlas treats her sister, considering her feelings with kindness even though she's been nothing but needy and demanding.

Suddenly shy, Harper drops Atlas's hand and nods before scampering back to her room. A few seconds later she pops her head back into the hallway. "You can come too, Naya. If you want."

Naya smiles, glad her sister still wants to include her. "Of course."

Naya directs Atlas into her bedroom and shuts the door behind them, hoping for no more distractions.

"Sorry about all that. Make yourself comfortable."

She watches as Atlas pulls her desk chair out and takes a seat. Naya sits on the edge of her bed, crossing her legs in front of her. Now that they're in her room, she feels a little on edge. Atlas looks around, and she follows his gaze. Hopefully there's nothing embarrassing laying around.

"Your room is nice," he says finally.

"It's nothing too crazy. I'm sure yours is just as cozy."

Atlas sighs. "Well, I guess that's as good a place to start as any."

Unsure what he means, Naya just waits for him to continue.

"I don't have my own bedroom."

"Oh, so you share one with siblings or something?" Naya guesses. She had assumed his family wasn't the most well-off, so it makes sense.

"No. I don't live in a house at all. And I don't have a family."

Stunned into silence, Naya tries to keep her expression neutral, not wanting to interrupt him.

Atlas stares at his hands folded in his lap. "I've been living on the streets."

"Atlas, why haven't you said anything?" Naya exclaims, unable to hold back her emotions. She feels guilty, wondering how she'd been so blind to his situation.

He looks up at her now, his hazel eyes full of vulnerability. "Because it's embarrassing, and I don't want to just keep taking handouts from your family."

"Handouts? Are you so thick-headed you can't see it's so much more than that?" Naya's anger wells up, disappointed in his explanation. "I care about you!"

Atlas meets her eyes in surprise. Hope flickers through them before it's quickly replaced by fear.

"There's more I've been keeping from you, and I don't know if you'll still feel that way after I tell you."

Naya's anger is gone in a flash, the chill of worry flowing through her veins. "Tell me."

"Days before I ran into you, I woke up in some sort of hospital facility attached to strange medical equipment. I was scared and confused, with little to no memories of who I was or why I was there." He turns to look out the window, letting his words sink in.

"There was a forest nearby," he continues. "I wandered for a while and stumbled upon a cabin where I gathered my strength and then eventually made my way to the city. The first day I got here, my backpack was stolen, and I was left with nothing."

"And you've been living on the streets since," Naya finishes for him.

She stares at the wall in front of her, pondering everything he just said. Although his circumstances are a little frightening and unusual, she doesn't feel any differently about him.

"Atlas, I still care about you."

He turns in the chair to look at her, uncertainty written all over his handsome features.

Naya scoots closer on the bed, letting her leg dangle over the side. Tentatively, she reaches for his hand that's now clenched into a tight fist in his lap. He lets her take it, relaxing into her touch.

"Thank you for trusting me with all this. I'm sorry you've been going through it alone."

"I don't know what to do," he says, his voice shaky with emotion.

"We'll figure it out. Together. I want to help."

They sit like that for a while, content in the silence. Naya likes the way his hand feels in hers, strong and solid. She absentmindedly runs her thumb along the back of his hand as she thinks, wondering where to start in the search for answers. Her eyes land on a cardboard box in her closet, an idea hitting her like lightning.

"I've got it!" Naya declares, shocking Atlas out of his stupor. "You can stay in my old apartment! It's a small loft above Bargain Bytes."

"You used to live in an apartment?" Atlas inquires.

"Yeah, before, uh, something happened to me." Naya ignores the questioning look in his eyes, not wanting to talk about the incident right now. "Anyway, I moved back home after that, and it's been sitting empty since. I have a feeling Mr. Jenkins is saving it for me when I'm ready to go back, even though he says he's just having trouble finding a new tenant."

"You think he'd let me stay there? He already said he can barely afford to pay me to work there."

"Trust me, Mr. Jenkins is a softie. If he knew your situation, he'd gladly let you have the place."

"And if I don't want to tell him?"

Naya gives Atlas a disappointed look. "Even if it will get you an apartment?"

He sighs. "I suppose. I'll tell him tomorrow."

"Perfect!"

Although it won't solve all his problems, it's a great place to start.

"You can sleep here tonight," Naya suggests.

Atlas snaps his head in her direction. "Here?"

"Don't sound so disgusted!" she jokes.

Naya knows he might find her suggestion strange but having him stay over feels right somehow.

"No, it's just, will that be okay?"

His hesitation is evident, and she wonders what other thoughts are racing through his mind.

"I'm twenty-two. Even though I've been living at home, my parents respect my decisions. They'll be fine with it," she quickly reassures him, trying to sound casual.

"Alright," he relents.

"And I know another person who will be elated you're sleeping over," Naya says with a smile.

# CHAPTER 18

# ATLAS

The dim glow of the old gaming console illuminates Harper's room. Naya and Atlas sits cross-legged on the floor, their eyes glued to the screen. The sound of rapid button-mashing fills the air as they navigate the game together.

Harper leans against the headboard of her bed, her expression a mixture of amusement and concern as she watches them play. "I told you it's not easy! You're never going to make it past this level."

Naya frowns in concentration, her fingers moving deftly across the controller. "We'll see about that," she replies, her competitive spirit coming out.

Atlas remains silent, his focus unwavering as he navigates his character through the virtual maze.

"Remember, sometimes the only way out is through…" Harper comments.

Atlas momentarily turns away from the screen to look at Harper behind him. "That's… oddly profound."

She smiles and the light from the screen reflects off the gold butterfly necklace hanging around her neck. "Just a little nugget of wisdom for you. Now go kick some virtual butt!"

Atlas gives her a mock salute before returning his attention back to the game. The more they navigate through the maze, the more the walls shift and turn, as if adapting to their previous attempts. Naya and Atlas quickly realize they need to communicate more, honing in on a solid strategy to beat this level.

Harper breaks through their focus, scooting closer to where they sit on the floor at the foot of her bed. "You know, sometimes things aren't what they seem in this game."

Naya pauses, turning to look into her sister's amber eyes. "What do you mean?"

"Well, you might think it's just a video game, but what if it's more than that?"

Atlas makes eye contact with Naya before looking over at Harper. "Like what?"

"Like, a simulation of sorts. A way to escape this reality," Harper suggests, eyes wide at the idea.

"Harper, it's just a game. Don't read too much into it," Naya huffs, turning back to the screen.

Atlas follows suit, but Harper's words linger in the back of his mind as they progress through the level. His thoughts wander back to his experiences before waking up in the hospital. The machine he was hooked up to felt so real, but it was clearly some sort of simulation. Naya nudges his shoulder, jostling him back to the present.

"Focus, I see an exit!" she says as their characters finally finish the maze and encounter the final boss.

"Maybe I've needed two experts to solve this level all along," Harper notes. "You've made it farther than me. Just remember, sometimes the only way to win is to realize it's not real."

"Harper, seriously, what are you talking about?" Naya's eyes never leave the screen as they attack the final monster. "You're being really weird tonight."

"So you're saying she's not always like this?" Atlas gives Harper a lopsided grin.

"Very funny, Atlas," Harper deadpans. "Just because I'm young doesn't mean I don't have good advice. Now focus and beat this level for me."

Atlas stares at the ceiling several hours later, unable to sleep. He shifts amongst the pile of pillows and blankets Naya retrieved earlier. It's a ridiculous amount, but she felt bad for making him sleep on the floor. Atlas doesn't mind, it's certainly more comfortable than the cold ground outside.

Naya had offered the couch downstairs, but he didn't feel as comfortable down there. He likes the small, cozy feel of Naya's bedroom better. In the dark, the light of the moon reflects off the frames hanging on the walls. Some hold quotes and pieces of art, while others have family photos in them.

In one, Naya hugs Harper, both grinning ear to ear. She looks so happy, a light in her brown eyes that Atlas doesn't see very often. As he stares, he notices her hair is longer in the picture and wonders how long ago it was taken.

Turning to lay on his side, he tries to calm his fears. Today went much better than he expected. He should be thrilled Naya knows everything and didn't run for the hills. Instead, he's filled with anxiety over including her in his drama. He doesn't want her to get caught up in whatever might happen next.

Though his apprehension doesn't fade, Naya's rhythmic breathing eventually pulls him into sleep.

Atlas dreams about her bedroom of all things. He's laying comfortably on Naya's bed, watching her type away on her desktop computer. Glancing around the room, he's now in several of the photos hanging on the wall. His eyes land on one in particular, where it's now him holding Naya tight, instead of Naya holding Harper. They're both smiling at each other, an emotion in their eyes he can't quite decipher.

Atlas feels comfortable and loved, a feeling he's been missing lately. If only it were real.

# CHAPTER 19
# NAYA

"Here it is." Naya unlocks the door to the small loft nestled above Bargain Bytes.

It didn't take much to convince Mr. Jenkins to let Atlas stay here, especially after he learned about his current living situation. They agreed he would take a smaller paycheck, some of it now made up with living in the loft.

Atlas wanders through the small space, starting with the kitchen on his left and making his way toward the back where the bedroom and bathroom are. Naya has a seat on the worn, faded couch next to the kitchen, propping her feet up on the small, stained coffee table. It's almost weird being back. She'd forgotten what the space felt like and missed the scent of old books mixed with faint hints of coffee.

Atlas emerges from the bedroom and joins her on the couch. "Wow, Naya. This is nicer than anything I could've ever gotten myself. Thank you." He looks over at her. "You clean up after yourself, well, too."

She grabs the nearest pillow, hitting him over the head with it. "I wasn't going to leave it a pigsty when I moved out! What do you take me for?"

"I'm kidding! Have mercy," he says amidst his laughter, shielding his head with his hands as she continues hitting him.

This is one of the first times she's heard Atlas laugh this much. Warmth swells in her chest knowing she's the cause of it. Putting the pillow back down, she watches as he adjusts his mop of dark brown hair. His whole demeanor is more relaxed since telling her his secrets. It suits him.

Atlas notices her watching him and smirks. "Like what you see?"

Naya grabs the pillow and holds it up threateningly. "Don't make me hit you again."

"Is that a challenge? Because I love a little friendly competition." He grabs the other pillow and wiggles his eyebrows at her.

Naya rolls her eyes, tossing the pillow unceremoniously into his lap. "Let's get to work. Don't want to upset Mr. Jenkins into taking the apartment back."

Heading back down the stairs, Naya tosses the loft key up to Atlas.

"You might need this later."

Atlas catches it easily, pocketing it with a thankful smile.

"It's about time you started working. What am I paying you for?" Mr. Jenkins scolds as they walk into the shop.

Naya sees the hint of a grin on his face, but lets Atlas sweat it out a bit before saying anything.

"Sorry sir, won't happen again," Atlas replies hastily, nodding his head in acknowledgement.

Mr. Jenkins can't hold back his grin any longer and it breaks free, lighting up his whole face. "I'm just messing with you, boy! It's not like we're busy or anything."

Naya laughs, glancing over at Atlas's relieved expression. "You'll start picking up on Mr. Jenkins's sense of humor at some point. If he's actually mad, you'll know it."

"You betcha," Mr. Jenkins agrees. "It takes a lot to get me to that point, though. As long as you don't push my buttons, you'll be fine."

"Ha, that's a good one Mr. J," Atlas compliments.

Mr. Jenkins raises an eyebrow at him in confusion. "What was?"

Naya tries to stifle her laughter behind her hand, knowing Mr. Jenkins has no idea what he just said was funny. A play on words isn't his style.

"Pushing your buttons? Like a computer?" Atlas wears a wary smile as he tries to explain the joke.

"Oh, glad you thought it was funny," Mr. Jenkins responds, a hint of self-deprecation in his tone. "I'm not much of a jokester. Half the time, I feel like one of the computers I work on," he quips, giving Atlas a cryptic wink.

The bell chimes above the door, ending their side conversation. Naya pushes Atlas toward the front counter, implying it's his turn to take a client. He glances back at her in surprise, pointing at himself and mouthing, "*Me?*"

Naya nods her head with a smirk and gives him two thumbs up. "You've got this," she whispers. "I'll be listening in if you need anything."

Standing nearby, she gives Atlas space to assist the customer without hovering like a concerned parent. He handles the introduction with ease, but Naya grows worried as the customer relays their issue. It sounds like the customer's computer operating system isn't functioning properly.

Naya is about to step in, knowing Atlas doesn't have the knowledge to fix a problem like that, when he gets to work without even batting an eye. She watches, mouth agape, as he opens the terminal and starts entering commands like a pro.

"Looks like it was just a corrupted system file," he says. "It should be ready to go, now!"

The client is very pleased with his efficient service, and Naya peeks over at Mr. Jenkins. He smiles knowingly, as if he knew all along Atlas could do it.

Strange.

Looking back at Atlas, she sees him taking the client's payment and waving goodbye. He turns to look at her, a triumphant smile on his face.

"Heck yeah! That was easy!"

"How did you know how to do that?" Naya questions. "I haven't taught you how to use a terminal. Or any backend commands for that matter."

Atlas ponders for a moment before shrugging and pulling out his own laptop. "I'm not sure, I just click this, and then that—"

He walks through the process on his device before suddenly doubling over, his hand pressed to his temple. Naya rushes to his side, trying to determine what's causing his pain.

"Atlas? Are you okay?" she asks worriedly.

He doesn't respond for a while, his eyes moving rapidly behind closed lids. When he finally opens them again, there's a sense of clarity in his hazel eyes.

"Did you remember something?" Naya guesses, hoping it will help in their search for answers.

"Yeah. Apparently, I was some sort of programmer."

Stunned, Naya isn't sure how to respond. She paces between her desk and the front counter, trying to piece together what this means. Mr. Jenkins eyes them curiously from his desk but doesn't get involved.

Atlas rubs his temples, watching her pace in silence. "Naya," he says finally, stilling her movements. "It was one memory, don't stress over it."

"But this could be big!" With a huff, Naya grabs his hand and pulls him to her desk, pushing him into the wooden chair nearby. "What do you remember? Tell me everything."

She sits in her creaky desk chair, wheeling closer so their knees are practically touching.

Atlas squeezes his eyes shut as if trying to picture the memory in his mind. He grimaces in pain before blinking his eyes open with a frustrated sigh. "Every time I try to remember more, this pounding headache drowns them out."

"It's okay, Atlas. Take your time. Just start with what you did manage to see."

# CHAPTER 20
# ATLAS

Images of an industrial building flash through his mind, accompanied by the rhythmic sound of typing and mouse-clicks. Rows of computers line the room, their screens glowing in the dim fluorescent light. As he describes the scene to Naya, Atlas vividly recounts sitting at a table, fingers dancing across the keyboard as he enters a series of commands into the computer terminal. Beside him, a man leans in, inquiring about the progress of the program he is working on.

As Atlas replays the memory, the details become clearer. He remembers the feeling of satisfaction as lines of code flow effortlessly from his fingertips. The young man beside him nods in approval at Atlas's work, clearly excited by his progress.

Atlas remembers saying something, but can't remember what, the memory fading as he blinks back to the present. How could he possess such advanced skills in programming when he has no recollection of ever learning them?

Looking at Naya, he tries to make sense of his thoughts. "It's strange, isn't it? That memory felt so vivid, yet I can't place where or when it happened."

"The mind is tricky like that," she says, mulling over all that he just told her. "Do you remember anything specific about the man you saw?"

Atlas thinks back, focusing on the details. "Yeah, actually." He's surprised he hadn't noticed it sooner. "He has a butterfly tattoo on his hand with the word *Mom* underneath it."

"A butterfly, huh? We've been seeing a lot of those lately, both real and otherwise" Naya responds, glancing over in Mr. Jenkins's direction.

Atlas follows her gaze, squinting to see what she might've been looking at. A shiver ripples through him at the sight of his hand, a butterfly-shaped birthmark in almost the same spot as the mystery man's tattoo.

"Coincidence?" Atlas knows Naya will understand what he's asking.

She shrugs in reply. "Maybe. Maybe not."

Uncertain what to do with their revelation, Naya and Atlas return to working on devices for clients.

"Let's see if I can remember any other cool tricks," he says to Naya, hoping working with the tech will help jog his memory.

Unfortunately, the rest of the day is uneventful, with no new memories surfacing. Atlas can't hide his disappointment and Naya quickly notices his forlorn expression.

"You can't solve all your problems in a day. Take it easy, Atlas. Enjoy that new loft of yours."

She wheels her bike out of the store, waving before letting the door close behind her. It's strange not to be leaving with her, the cluttered shop feeling suddenly empty. The only sounds are Mr. Jenkins's mouse clicks as he works on his latest computer.

"Hey, Mr. Jenkins, mind if I ask you something?" Atlas meanders over to stand beside his desk.

The old man looks up from his work and takes off his glasses. He rubs his eyes and Atlas notices the butterfly birthmark again.

"Shoot, kid. What's on your mind?" Mr. Jenkins prompts.

"It's just… Well, have you ever had that feeling like you're supposed to remember something, but you can't quite put your finger on it?"

Mr. Jenkins chuckles, a knowing glint in his eye. "You're not the only one, Atlas. Happens to the best of us. Memories can be elusive little devils sometimes."

Atlas nods in understanding. "Yeah, I guess you're right. It's probably nothing."

Leaning in slightly, Mr. Jenkins lowers his voice. "But sometimes, those memories come back when you least expect them to. Keep your eyes open, Atlas. You never know what you might find."

Atlas raises his eyebrows at the man's sudden intensity. "Thanks, Mr. Jenkins. I'll keep that in mind."

With a sigh, Mr. Jenkins shuts his computer and stands. "Anytime. Now, let's get this place locked up for the night and I'll leave you to your shiny new place."

Locking up is easy, and Atlas is soon left standing alone in the loft upstairs. The dirty windows emit only a dim light, and the creaks and groans of the old building only add to the sense of isolation.

It's strange being alone again. Atlas hadn't realized how much time he's been spending with Naya lately. Trying to push aside his lingering doubts, Atlas focuses instead on the simple comforts of his new home. The soft hum of the refrigerator, the faint scent of dust, and the feeling of finally having a roof over his head.

His footsteps echo softly against the weathered floorboards. He runs his fingers along the faded wallpaper, tracing the intricate patterns etched into its surface. In the corner, a stack of dusty books catches his eye, their spines cracked, and pages yellowed with age. He flips through a few of them, but their contents offer no insight.

Surveying the shelves above the kitchen counters, he spots a few plates and mugs left behind. With nothing of his own to contribute, he appreciates the random assortment of items that fill the space. Atlas opens the fridge and peers inside. He's not sure what he was expecting, but still feels a twinge of disappointment at the empty shelves within.

With a sigh, Atlas sinks onto the worn couch only a few steps from the kitchen. His thoughts swirl with unanswered questions. Mr. Jenkins's comment keeps looping through his mind, a nagging sensation in his gut telling him he's forgetting something important.

As exhaustion finally begins to weigh down his eyelids, Atlas resolves to confront his concerns in the morning. For now, all he wants is to lose himself in the comforting embrace of sleep, even if it's only temporary relief from the uncertainties that haunt his mind.

# CHAPTER 21
# NAYA

Naya sits across from Atlas in a booth at the diner, the soft hum of conversation and clinking of dishes creating a warm ambiance. The diner bustles with activity, the aroma of freshly brewed coffee mingling with the tantalizing scent of fried food.

It was a busy week at work and Naya thought they deserved to treat themselves on this fine Saturday afternoon. Though the food is expensive here, it's delicious. Hence why the diner is always busy.

"So, any new revelations?" Naya sips on her soda and leans forward expectantly.

Atlas shakes his head, a hint of frustration evident in his tone. "Not much. Just bits and pieces. Nothing concrete."

"Well, don't worry. We'll get there," Naya reassures him, her hand reaching across the table to offer support.

Their conversation is momentarily interrupted as the waitress approaches, a notepad and pen in hand. "What can I get for you two today?"

Naya glances at Atlas, a playful twinkle in her eye. "I'll have the grilled cheese with fries."

Atlas chuckles at her choice, a fond smile gracing his lips. "I'll do the brunch special, please. And a side of hash browns."

As the waitress departs to place their order, Naya turns her attention back to Atlas, her gaze softening with affection. "A brunch guy, huh? I wondered if you'd get a burger."

"Not today." He leans into the table conspiratorially. "I thought you only liked your mom's grilled cheese?"

Naya leans in too. "Then you weren't listening hard enough, mister. I said you'd change your mind if you tried hers, not that it's the only kind I like. The diner makes a top tier grilled cheese as well."

Atlas wrinkles his nose at the mention of the food and Naya laughs. "Maybe I should make you try a bite."

"In your dreams," he replies quickly, leaning back into the booth.

"Speaking of dreams, tell me about these bits and pieces you've remembered."

Atlas recounts snippets of conversation about advanced technology and secretive projects, hinting at a deeper involvement in something significant. Naya's mind flashes back to her conversation with Mr. Jenkins about the government VR technology, but quickly dismisses it. That's a recent occurrence so there's no way Atlas was involved.

Atlas finishes explaining his memories, his tone laced with disappointment. He's probably beating himself up again for not remembering more. Naya gives him an encouraging smile, understanding the frustration of trying to put together a puzzle with missing pieces.

"That's important information, Atlas. We can't expect everything to come rushing back all at once. That would be too easy," she says with a rueful grin.

They fall into a comfortable silence for a moment, each lost in their own thoughts. Then, an idea strikes Naya.

"You know what we should do?" she says, feeling a spark of determination. "We should go back to that facility you escaped from. Maybe there's something there that could jog your memory. Or records of your stay or something!"

Atlas's eyes widen at the suggestion, apprehension flickering in their depths. "Break into a highly secure facility? That sounds risky, Naya."

Naya's grin widens, thrilled by the idea of getting out of the city. "Exactly. Plus, it'll be fun."

Atlas narrows his eyes. "You have a strange definition of fun."

"Hey, where's your sense of adventure?" Naya teases, trying to calm his nerves. She knows it could be dangerous bringing him back there but feels like it's the only way to get more solid leads.

The waitress returns, setting their meals on the table. Naya digs into her grilled cheese, enjoying each bite. She notices Atlas watching her and rips off a piece of her sandwich to hold out to him.

"You know you want to," she says, waving it in front of his face.

"Fine," he relents, popping the small piece into his mouth.

Naya watches intently as his face contorts with disgust. Her eyebrows raise in concern, suddenly feeling bad for making him try it.

Then, he starts laughing, pointing at her concerned expression. "I'm sorry, I'm just kidding. It's not that bad."

She scowls at him. Glancing down at his meal, she snags a piece of bacon off his plate.

"Hey! That's my food," he scolds playfully.

"Payment for eating part of my sandwich." She crunches into the bacon, making a show of enjoying the greasy goodness. His responding grin makes her stomach flip.

With each passing moment, Naya finds herself drawn to Atlas in ways she can't quite explain—a warmth spreading through her chest when their eyes meet, a flutter of excitement when their hands brush against each other.

She breaks eye contact, engrossing herself in her sandwich. Naya feels his eyes on her but avoids looking at him as if he'll be able to see her innermost thoughts. She's surprised when he reaches over to steal a fry off her plate.

"You have your own potatoes, why do you want mine?"

"They looked good," he says simply, shoving the fry into his mouth. As he chews, his forehead wrinkles and he grabs his head.

He's remembering something.

# CHAPTER 22

# ATLAS

The diner is alive with chatter in his memory, the aroma of sizzling burgers wafting through the air. Across from him sits the mystery woman. Looking at her makes him nervous.

"So, tell me something interesting about yourself." Her eyes sparkle with mischief as she steals a fry off his plate and dips it in her milkshake.

Atlas pretends to ponder her question for a moment before responding with a playful grin. "Well, did you know that I once saved a cat from a tree?"

The woman raises an eyebrow, clearly not buying his exaggerated claim. "Really? And here I was thinking you were just another boring tech guy."

Atlas laughs, feeling a sense of ease wash over him in her presence. He likes being around her. "Well, you know what they say—never judge a book by its cover."

"Touché. I still let you take me out on a date, though, didn't I?"

"After several attempts," Atlas replies, remembering the many failed times he tried to convince her.

"What can I say, Cereal Thief, you made an interesting first impression." She shrugs.

"You are never going to let me live that down, are you?"

"We'll see, Atlas."

The sound of his name on her lips brings him back to reality, leaving him with a lingering sense of longing. He looks across the table at Naya to see her saying his name.

"That was a longer one. You good?" She searches his eyes for an answer.

Shame courses through him as he realizes he just had a memory of another woman while in Naya's presence. He looks away, not sure what to say. Though he's grateful for remembering more, these memories stir up a whirlwind of emotions, leaving him feeling torn between the past and the present. His mind races, unsure how to explain this sudden recollection to Naya.

"Atlas?"

He meets her gaze, not wanting to keep her waiting. "Yeah, I'm okay. Just collecting my thoughts, sorry."

Naya nods, sensing his reluctance to share. She focuses on her plate, eating more of her fries. Atlas does the same, glad for her patience. He'll share when he's ready.

While they eat, Atlas considers his current feelings for Naya compared to the mystery woman from his memories. Both stir up a mix of nerves and excitement within him. But there's only one he truly wants, and she's sitting right in front of him.

Atlas stares at the way Naya's short, wavy hair frames her face. She radiates a unique blend of fierce kindness. It's a quality that makes you instinctively wary of crossing her yet draws you in with the promise of unwavering affection if you earn her favor.

She must sense him watching her because she looks up from her food, giving him a small smile. Instantly, he feels a pang of sadness for shutting her out so quickly after recalling his memory. She's been nothing but kind, generous, and understanding, so why is he so afraid to tell her?

"I remembered a first date I had here at the diner," he blurts, laying it all out there before he changes his mind.

Naya's eyes widen in surprise, and he thinks he sees a flicker of jealousy in her eyes. Seeing that emotion from her makes his stomach do a somersault.

"Interesting. Did you recognize who she was?"

"No," Atlas replies immediately. He plays with his food, preparing for what he's about to say next.

Naya notices his nerves and sets her sandwich down, leaning against the booth as if to brace herself.

"This isn't the first memory I've had of her, and in each one, I can never clearly see her face," Atlas admits. "I'm not sure why."

Naya purses her lips and Atlas stares at them involuntarily before averting his eyes.

"Could it be because she was very important to you?" she asks.

Atlas shakes his head. "I feel like that doesn't make sense. If she was so important to me, don't you think her face would be one I couldn't forget?"

Naya picks up a fry and chews on it, thinking over his question. "Not necessarily," she replies. "Think about it. Whoever or whatever is suppressing your memories took them from you for a reason. So, the more important the memory is, the harder it will be to recall."

"That actually makes a lot of sense," Atlas concedes, finishing the last of his hashbrowns.

He sees a mischievous smile return to Naya's face and worries what she's thinking.

"This is even more reason why we need to go back to that facility!"

"I don't see how that relates to this. Plus, I already told you it's risky!" Atlas argues, more concerned with her safety than getting answers.

"I have a hypothesis that your more important memories are triggered by extremely similar present circumstances. Do you concur?"

Atlas thinks back to what he's recalled so far. Most of the ones with the mystery woman were triggered by similar actions and environments whereas others only needed one or the other. Atlas nods at Naya, motioning for her to continue.

"So, in order to remember what happened to you, you need to go back to the place where it occurred."

"And if your hypothesis is wrong?"

"Then at least we can snoop around for other information or digital records or something," Naya asserts, clearly not wanting to let this go.

Atlas gives her a lopsided grin, shaking his head at her. "You're stubborn, you know that?"

"I prefer the word determined," she says. "Is that a yes?"

"It's a maybe. There's a lot we would need to do to be prepared for something like that," Atlas warns, still hoping to dissuade her.

"Then we better start preparing now." Naya finishes the last of her food and waves the waitress over for their checks.

Before he knows it, they're out the door and headed through the busy city streets. Atlas struggles to keep up with Naya's hurried strides.

"Where are we going?" he yells.

"Your place."

# CHAPTER 23

# NAYA

Naya and Atlas enter softly through the shop door. She stops to collect a small box of discarded tech at her desk before following him up the steps to his loft. Atlas fumbles with the key, seeming nervous. She tries to stay focused on her plans, but thoughts of the first date he remembered keep clouding her judgment. Jealousy flares up at the idea of Atlas having an important woman in his life.

The door swings open on creaky hinges, drawing Naya out of her thoughts. As they enter his loft, Atlas rushes to tidy up the space. She takes a moment to survey the main room, noticing the eclectic assortment of items scattered about. Books, papers, and various electronic gadgets lay strewn across surfaces, evidence of Atlas's relentless pursuit of answers.

Despite the clutter, there's a sense of purpose to the room. Naya admires his unwavering commitment to uncovering the truth about his past despite what it might hold.

"Sorry," he mumbles, moving books off the couch so Naya has room to sit. "I've been reading a lot and doing more research, trying to trigger more memories."

"Makes sense. What about all the random tech?" she asks curiously.

He gives her a shy smile. "Still trying to uncover the rest of my so-called programming skills."

"Still nothing, huh?"

Atlas just shakes his head, sitting on the couch beside her. "So why did you want to come here?"

Naya holds the box of parts up for him to see. "For these. And whatever else we can find that's being unused around the shop."

Atlas tilts his head, still confused.

"To build things for our trip! If we're going to do this right, we need good tech to do it. Plus, I figured we could plan better here. No little sister distractions." Naya smirks.

"Alright. What kind of tech are you thinking?"

"My first thought is communications. We probably both don't need to go into the facility since that will increase our chances of getting caught."

Atlas nods again, following her line of reasoning. "Which means we need a way to communicate."

"Exactly."

Naya starts sifting through the box, pulling out various items and setting them on the coffee table. Atlas picks a few up as she does, inspecting them.

"Ringing any bells?" She watches as he squints at an old circuit board.

"Nope. I'm afraid I might be useless in this venture."

"No way! You're the brains of this operation. You've actually been inside this place before."

Getting off the couch, Naya hunts down a piece of paper and pencil. She sets it down on the coffee table in front of Atlas. "Draw me a map."

An hour later, Naya has sorted through her whole box of parts and Atlas is onto his third page of map-making. They pour over each other's progress, Atlas recounting what he remembers of the facility and Naya explaining her plan for a rudimentary comms device.

"Alright, so if we use these old transistors and this wire, we can rig up a basic communication device," Naya explains, pointing to various components spread out on the table.

Atlas nods, his brow furrowed in concentration. "Will it have long enough range for only one of us to go into the facility?"

"I'll make sure it does," Naya reassures.

She points to a spot on his map where the edge of the forest is across from the facility. "One of us will wait right at the edge of the forest to get as close to the facility as possible while still maintaining cover."

Atlas looks satisfied with her plan and they both go back to work, diving deeper into their preparations. Naya sketches out the schematics for the communication device while Atlas scours the internet for any additional information he can find about the facility. They bounce ideas off each other, refining their plans and addressing any potential obstacles they might encounter.

The afternoon turns to evening, and they take a break for dinner. Atlas rummages through his cabinets for options. With a grin, he produces two packs of instant noodles.

"You gotta love these things," he says playfully. "Cheap but oh, so good."

Naya laughs, watching as Atlas preps both packs. She could get used to him cooking for her.

"Careful, it's hot," he says a few minutes later, setting a bowl on the coffee table in front of her.

Naya scoots off the couch to sit on the floor closer to the table and Atlas does the same. Over steaming bowls of noodles, they discuss their strategy for getting past the facility's security measures and accessing the information they need.

"We'll need to be careful." Naya takes a thoughtful bite of her noodles.

"That's what I've been trying to tell you," Atlas nags. "They probably heightened their security after I escaped."

"So how will we get in?"

Amidst the slurping of their noodles, an idea forms in Naya's mind. She looks over at Atlas with a mischievous grin.

He gives her a worried look. "Uh oh, what did you come up with?"

"We need a disguise. And what better to blend in with than a nurse uniform! I'll dress up in scrubs and try to get in with the other nurses after their break or something," Naya explains excitedly, the plan forming as she speaks.

Atlas quickly shakes his head. "Absolutely not. What am I supposed to do outside?"

"Keep watch?" she suggests. "They would recognize you if you went in!"

Naya watches as a flurry of emotions cross Atlas's face.

"I just can't let you be the one to go in there," he says softly. "I don't know what I'd do if something happened to you because of my mess."

"I appreciate your concern, but I can handle myself," Naya states confidently.

It feels good to know he cares so much but she sees no other way of getting in. Looking over at Atlas, she can practically see the gears turning in his head.

"A mask," he mumbles. "What if I wore a surgical mask?"

"You could, but I don't know how well that would disguise you."

"And a surgical cap."

Naya gives him a skeptical look. He's really trying to get her to stay outside.

"It makes the most sense, Naya. I know my way around better than you. Plus, you said it yourself! The location seems to trigger my memory, which means I need to go inside."

Naya presses her lips together, unable to argue. Atlas makes a good point. "Alright genius, then what am I doing while waiting outside?"

He grins victoriously, relief washing over his face. "Can you hack?"

# CHAPTER 24
# ATLAS

The setting sun casts a warm glow through the windows of the loft. Atlas slumps into the couch beside Naya, the exhaustion of hours spent poring over plans and strategies weighing heavily on his shoulders. His gaze drifts over the array of papers scattered across the coffee table—his crude maps, Naya's intricate schematics, and a list of essential items they'll need moving forward.

With a sigh, Atlas rubs his weary eyes, feeling the apprehension of their impending journey settling in his chest. They've finally reached a consensus on their approach—he'll be the one to infiltrate the facility, while Naya provides support from a safe distance, hacking into security cameras and keeping watch from the cover of the nearby forest. It's still risky, but they're out of options.

Glancing at Naya, Atlas can see the determination on her face, a reflection of his own resolve. She continues to sift through information, her fingers darting across the keyboard with practiced ease. Just moments ago, she proved her hacking prowess by effortlessly breaching the security of a government website.

"Find anything interesting?" Atlas asks, hoping she learned something more about the mysterious facility.

Naya looks back at him and shakes her head. "Nope. They're keeping this place under wraps. It's just as much of a ghost as you are in the digital world," she says with a wink.

Despite the gravity of their situation, Naya always manages to stay upbeat. It's infectious and Atlas wonders how she does it.

Naya shuts her laptop and sits back on the couch next to Atlas. Their shoulders touch and they relax in the warmth of each other's company. Atlas looks over at Naya now laying with her head on the back of the couch, eyes closed. Her short hair fans out around her, falling away from her face. His eyes trace her profile, following the peak of her nose down to her rosy pink lips.

Atlas feels a flicker of something at the sight of her—a nervous thrill at being so close. She shifts her head slightly, exposing a pink scar along her hairline. Without thinking, Atlas reaches out, tracing the delicate skin with his fingers.

Naya jerks away in surprise, suddenly breathing hard.

"Sorry," Atlas says, profusely blushing. Why did he do that? And why does he feel so hurt by her reaction?

She must see the hurt in his eyes because she scoots back toward him, touching his arm in reassurance. "It's not you, Atlas." Pausing, she looks toward the door of his loft. "Can I show you something?"

Atlas nods tentatively, following Naya as they enter the short hallway and head to the only other door upstairs. She pulls out her keys and finds the one for the shop, slotting it in and opening the door to reveal another set of stairs. Without a word, they ascend the steps, Atlas's curiosity growing.

Through another door at the top, Atlas and Naya step onto the roof of Bargain Bytes. The view is breathtaking, a gentle breeze ruffling their hair.

"This is where I used to come when I needed to clear my head," Naya says, her voice soft with nostalgia. "It's amazing how being up here can make everything seem so small."

Atlas follows Naya to the edge, bracing himself against the railing. He watches as her eyes trace the lights that dot the skyline. Looking up, a sea of stars greets him. The clear skies make for a perfect night of stargazing. He looks back down to Naya standing beside him.

"It's beautiful," he breathes.

Naya gives him a sad smile. "It reminds me of that night." She sighs, looking over at him. "I think it's my turn to be honest."

Atlas arches a brow, worry already forming a pit in his stomach.

Naya points at something in the distance, and Atlas squints to see it. "The grocery store?"

Naya takes a deep breath. "About three months ago now, I was attacked in the alley beside the grocery store. That's how I got my scar." She wraps her arms around herself.

"I'm so sorry, Naya." He wants to reach out and hold her, but doesn't, unsure how she'd react.

She shrugs and they stand together in silence, the bustling city below a distant murmur against the backdrop of their thoughts. While Naya looks out at the city, Atlas finds himself captivated by her presence. In the soft glow of the city lights, he sees more than just her outer beauty. Despite the challenges she faced, there's an undeniable radiance about her. In that moment, there's nothing she could say or do to diminish the brilliance that emanates from within her.

"How do you do it?" he asks suddenly, prompting Naya to turn back toward him.

"Do what?"

"Stay so positive?" Atlas thinks about all she's done for him, a stranger she knew nothing about. "And offer such kindness to strangers after what happened to you?"

"It wasn't immediate. I had a lot I needed to work through, but my family was a big support system. My faith too, that helped a lot."

"Faith? But aren't you angry at God for letting it happen to you?" Atlas asks, surprised by her answer.

"Maybe at first. I mean, I'm only human. But I realized it's not Him who makes bad things happen."

"But he's in control of everything."

"And he gave some of that control to us by giving us free will. With that, comes the choices we make, and both the good and evil consequences that go along with it. We live in a fallen world, Atlas. You can't have good without evil."

Atlas doesn't know what to say, unable to fathom faith that strong. He's been wrestling with his own for a while, wondering why all this is happening to him.

"So, I must've made a lot of bad choices to lead to all this crazy stuff that's been happening to me," he concludes.

Naya shakes her head. "Not necessarily. Sure, maybe you made some, but it's other people's choices that often affect us as well."

The tension in their conversation eases when she gives him a wry smile. "Are you saying I'm one of your bad choices?"

Atlas smiles at the absurdity of Naya ever being a bad choice. "Hell, no. You are one of the best things that has ever happened to me."

Even in the dim light, he can see the effect his words have on her. A deep blush rapidly spreads across her face.

"You too, Atlas," she replies, so quietly Atlas almost misses it.

Unable to hold back, Atlas reaches for her hand, threading his fingers through hers. She looks up at him, searing him with her gaze.

"What we've been through is a lot, but I think if it hadn't happened, we wouldn't have met," she muses softly.

Atlas tugs her closer, their foreheads gently touching. Naya's words resonate with him, and he realizes he can't fathom a reality where they hadn't met. "And I'd do it all over again to be here with you, Brown Eyes."

The nickname slips from his lips involuntarily and Naya smiles softly. But Atlas's reaction is visceral, shame and anger surging through him. The woman from his past flashes through his mind, causing him to stumble backward.

His heart thunders in his chest, a relentless rhythm. How dare those memories of *her* persist, invading his mind even as he stands here with Naya. He tries to mask his turmoil, to conceal the emotions churning inside him, but he knows he can't hide it from Naya's discerning gaze. She reaches out to steady him, concern etched on her features.

"Atlas, what's wrong?" Her voice is laced with genuine worry.

He struggles to find the words, to explain the flood of emotions that threaten to overwhelm him. But the words elude him, slipping through his fingers like grains of sand.

"It's nothing," he manages to choke out, but even to his own ears, the words sound hollow and unconvincing.

Naya studies him intently, her gaze piercing through his defenses. Atlas takes a shaky breath, trying to regain his composure, but a memory triggers, unbidden. He tries to push it away, but it refuses to loosen its grip on him, pulling him into the past.

Atlas sits under the twinkling stars, the soft glow of the moonlight illuminating the landscape around them. He turns to the woman beside him, her warm amber eyes reflecting the celestial beauty above.

"Brown Eyes," he murmurs, the endearment slipping effortlessly from his lips. "Look!" He points toward the sky where a shooting star streaks across the night.

"You know, I read somewhere that each star holds a wish," she says, her voice a soft melody in the quiet of the night. "What would you wish for, Atlas?"

He gazes up at the heavens, his mind swimming with answers. But in that moment, with her by his side, there's only one thing that truly matters.

"I don't need to wish for anything," he replies, his voice barely above a whisper. "Because right now, I have everything I could ever want."

She grins over at him. "You're so cheesy."

Atlas gives her a playful shove. "Sorry. What I meant to say is I'd wish for a million dollars. Then, I'd be set for life."

"Not in this economy," she replies with a laugh. "What would you even do with a million dollars?"

His eyes sparkle with mischief. "Buy a bunch of Harvest Crunch."

She doubles over with laughter, clutching her stomach. "I should've known you were going to say something like that!" she shouts. "And that's precisely why I will never let the name Cereal Thief die."

"Maybe I like that nickname." He leans close to her. "It reminds me of the first day we met."

# CHAPTER 25
# NAYA

Naya sits on the roof with Atlas's head in her lap, cradling him gently while the memory passes. When he opens his eyes, they're full of confusion and a hint of something she doesn't recognize.

"Naya?" He sits up and looks around. "Why are we on the ground?"

"You collapsed. What happened? A memory has never affected you like that before."

Atlas winces, his expression clouded with discomfort, likely from the headache that always follows a memory. "I tried to fight it."

"The memory?" she asks, perplexed.

Why would he resist something he's been working so hard to unlock? She watches him closely, her gaze searching his for understanding as he moves to sit directly across from her.

"It was her again," he confesses softly, his tone heavy with apology.

Naya's heart sinks at his words, a pang of hurt piercing through her. Insecurity and disappointment creep in at the thought of the moment they had together triggering something similar from his past. She pushes her own feelings aside, attempting to decipher what might've caused the memory.

"The nickname," Atlas adds, as if sensing her unspoken questions.

Her stomach twists with a fresh wave of discomfort. The affectionate term he used for her suddenly feels tainted, overshadowed by his past. She struggles to mask her disappointment, wondering how much of their connection is genuine and how much is merely a reflection of his memories. Was any of it really for her?

Naya stands, moving back to the edge of the roof to clear her mind. Suddenly, being around Atlas is the last thing she wants. Her eyes sting with the promise of tears and she wishes she were alone.

Behind her, she hears his tentative footsteps approach.

"Naya, what are you thinking?" he asks softly.

She doesn't look at him, knowing it will send her tears cascading down her face. She doesn't want that. Not in front of him.

Tonight, she felt vulnerable with him, his actions igniting a spark of hope that he reciprocates her feelings. But now, she feels her walls going back up, keeping him at a distance. Though he's done nothing wrong, his memories are hard to handle. And insecurity is a wicked thing.

Steeling herself, she takes a deep breath before speaking. "Can you tell the difference?" she questions. "Between your feelings for her and for me?"

Naya turns to look at Atlas. He pauses before answering, face scrunched in concentration as he thinks. His uncertainty sends another wave of disappointment crashing over her. She should've known better than to start falling for a guy who's stuck in the past.

Before he can respond, she heads toward the stairs. "I'm sorry Atlas, I need to go." She tries to keep her voice from wavering as tears blur her vision.

"Naya!" he calls after her, reaching out as she walks past him.

"I'll see you on Monday, Atlas." She smiles sadly, flying down the stairs and out of Bargain Bytes as fast as she can.

She clumsily locks the door behind her, a tear dripping onto the door handle. Naya angrily wipes them away, upset that her emotions are getting the better of her.

Halfway home, the ache in her throat becomes unbearable, and she finally allows her tears to spill over. Naya regrets not opting for her bike today, the fear of navigating the darkness on foot only exacerbating her already fragile emotional state.

With each step, her mind replays the evening, the words spoken and unspoken hanging heavy in the air. She wonders if she should have said more, been more honest about how she truly feels. Or should she have waited to hear what Atlas wanted to say? But her fear and insecurity whispered doubts into her ear, begging her to flee.

As she rounds the corner onto her street, the familiar sight of her house comes into view. Relief washes over her, and she walks faster, eager to escape the suffocating grip of her own thoughts. Reaching her doorstep, she lets out a shaky breath and unlocks the door with trembling hands.

"Naya, is that you?" her mom calls from the kitchen.

"Yeah," she replies, disguising the emotion in her voice. "I think I'm going to bed early tonight."

She hears her mom walking toward the foyer and beelines it up the steps, not wanting to explain why she's crying.

"Are you alright?"

"Fine, Mom," she dismisses, entering her bedroom and closing the door behind her with a soft click.

Alone in the safety of her own space, Naya allows herself to crumble. She sinks to the floor, tears flowing freely now, as she lets herself feel everything she'd been holding back. With each shuddering breath, Naya confronts the tangled mess of emotions that have been simmering beneath the surface.

Though she knows it's not fair to Atlas to be so upset, she lets herself cry through it. As the tension in her throat eases and the tears stop flowing, a strange sort of catharsis sets in, leaving her feeling lighter. Naya isn't sure how she'll face Atlas after the way she left him but resolves to worry about it later.

Picking herself up off the floor, she dries her cheeks and collapses into bed. Despite her emotional turmoil, helping Atlas regain his memories is still her top priority. Moving forward, she resolves to keep her emotions in check. She won't let how she feels about him get in the way anymore. As they continue their preparations, she'll need a clear mind, anyway.

*Friends,* she tells herself. *Being friends is still good.*

A soft knock at the door interrupts her thoughts.

"Naya? Can I come in?" Harper asks.

"Sure."

Shutting the door behind her, Harper joins Naya on the bed. She snuggles into her, the warmth of her embrace easing Naya's frayed nerves.

"I heard you crying. Are you okay?"

"I will be," Naya replies. "Can we leave it at that?" She knows rehashing the day's events will send her into another fit of crying.

Harper nods in reply, tightening her embrace. "Boys are dumb," she mutters.

Naya chuckles at her little sister's intuition. She can read Naya like a book.

# CHAPTER 26

# ATLAS

Sunday crawled by at a snail's pace, each passing moment filled with the echo of Naya's abrupt departure from the rooftop. Despite his attempt to distract himself with mundane tasks, Atlas's mind kept wandering back to that night. He found himself replaying their conversation over and over, wondering what he could've done differently.

Monday morning arrived with a sense of apprehension as Atlas settled into Bargain Bytes for the day. It was only seven-thirty, but he needed a distraction. Plus, living upstairs made it easy to get an early start.

Putting a pair of old wired earbuds in, he immerses himself in repairing a laptop. Atlas is surprised when his hands move as if they have a mind of their own. His technical skills seem to reveal themselves when he's least expecting it.

As he disassembles the hardware, he identifies what needs to be replaced. Locating the parts from the containers near his desk, he begins carefully piecing everything back together. Lost in his work, Atlas barely notices the time ticking by. He methodically reassembles the device, each component clicking into place with precision.

Reaching for a screwdriver, a familiar voice breaks through his concentration, causing him to look up in surprise. Naya stands before him, observing his handiwork.

"You must've gotten an early start this morning. Looks like someone is remembering a few more tricks," she comments, looking more closely at his work.

Atlas feels a rush of warmth at her presence, his expression softening as he meets her gaze. He can still sense the underlying tension in her tone, though, a reminder of the way they left things. "Yeah, it caught me off guard" he admits hesitantly. "It's funny how these memories always seem to surface when I least expect it."

Naya nods, a sense of understanding in her eyes that sends a flicker of hope through him.

"Actually, there's something you might want to double check." She points out a small component Atlas had overlooked.

"I guess the past doesn't always have all the answers." Atlas leans in to examine the component Naya mentioned. As he does, a sudden rush of familiarity washes over him, transporting him back to a classroom from his past.

Atlas sits at a cluttered table, surrounded by computer parts and circuit boards. Beside him, stands the woman with warm brown eyes, her hair pulled back in a ponytail as she tinkers with a piece of technology.

"Hey, Cereal Thief, pass me the soldering iron, will you?" She extends her hand without a sideways glance.

"I'm surprised you trust me not to hand it over hot end first," Atlas remarks, prompting an eye roll in response.

"I trust that you wouldn't purposely injure your ticket to an A+ on this project," she replies, taking the soldering iron out of his outstretched hand.

Atlas clutches his chest dramatically. "Ouch, that stings. I've got skills too, you know!"

He watches as she expertly solders the metal connectors in front of her. When finished, she sets the soldering iron on its stand and gives him a pointed look. "Skills, yes. But more so with the software side of things. Hardware is my expertise."

"You have a point," he concedes with a smirk. "But can your expert tutelage help me land a job after graduation, too?"

She flashes him a playful grin, her ponytail swishing over one shoulder. "Oh, with my guidance, you'll be fighting off job offers left and right," she quips, her tone brimming with confidence. "Just make sure to mention who your mentor is on your resume."

The memory dissipates, leaving Atlas staring at the computer in front of him. He looks up at Naya, a resigned look now on her face.

"Her again?"

Atlas simply nods, unsure whether he should share more.

"Anything helpful?" she inquires further, sitting behind her own desk and spinning in her chair to face him.

"I apparently have more skills with software than hardware," he starts, thinking back on what the memory revealed. "And I get the impression that I went to a tech school for Computer Science."

Naya raises her eyebrows slightly. "Wow, a man with a degree? Maybe Mr. Jenkins will start paying you more."

Atlas chuckles, happy Naya is still joking with him even if her tone is a bit colder. She looks deep in thought, staring down at the floor. Abruptly she looks up, her eyes alight with a new revelation.

"It hasn't even been two full days since your last memory, Atlas! They're occurring more frequently now."

"You're right. I suppose that's a good thing, huh?" he replies.

Since his past seems to be pushing Naya further away, he's not as excited as he used to be about his returning memories.

"It is," she sighs. "Even if it can be hard to reconcile with the present."

Though she's smiling, it doesn't quite reach her eyes. She's keeping him at a distance, and he feels awful for being the cause of it. Her vulnerable moment with him had been overshadowed by his past, yet again. This weekend made him realize he needs to sort through his own past emotions before trying to move forward with Naya. It's not fair to her. If only he'd realized that sooner.

"Say, where is Mr. Jenkins?" Atlas questions, deciding to change the subject in hopes of breaking the tension.

Naya shrugs. "Not sure. He's usually here at the crack of dawn."

As if summoned by the mention of his name, Mr. Jenkins bustles through the shop door, sending the bell fervently ringing.

"Have you heard?" he exclaims, a wild look in his eyes. Atlas and Naya exchange a glance before they both shake their heads. They have no idea what he's referring to.

"Heard what?" Atlas replies.

"The government has released an official statement about the rumored VR technology."

# CHAPTER 27

# NAYA

The old shop TV crackles as it turns on, Naya quickly changing the channel to the news. Atlas and Mr. Jenkins pull up chairs, squishing together in the tight space to better hear the TV. A press conference is just beginning, the government PR woman starting with greetings to the nation.

"In response to recent speculation and concerns regarding virtual reality technology," she begins, her voice tinny through the TV speakers, "the government would like to clarify its position and provide reassurance to the public."

"First and foremost, the government is, in fact, in the preliminary stages of virtual reality technology development." A murmur goes through the reporters in the audience, quickly hushed as she continues speaking. "This has been undertaken with the primary goal of advancing various sectors for the betterment of society."

Naya exchanges a skeptical look with Atlas before returning her eyes to the screen.

"From enhancing educational experiences to revolutionizing training programs in critical fields like healthcare and defense, VR holds immense potential for positive impact."

A man's voice breaks through the crowd of reporters. "How does the government address speculation surrounding the potential permanent embedding of this technology via a microchip?"

The woman pauses briefly, making eye contact with the man in the crowd. "We want to assure the public that stringent measures have been implemented to ensure the safety and privacy of users. Rigorous testing protocols and adherence to established standards are vital parts of our approach to VR development."

The crowd of reporters grows loud, new questions arising after she didn't deny the microchip speculations.

"Why has the government been keeping this a secret until now?" a woman shouts.

"Is the government considering the ethics behind such an advanced technology as this? Are you testing on actual people?" another inquires, shoving his microphone closer to the stand.

The woman raises her hand, moving to silence the barrage of questions.

"Transparency is a cornerstone of our commitment to the public. We pledge to keep the public informed about the ongoing progress of VR technology, regularly providing updates to address concerns from now on. Ethical considerations are also of paramount importance. We are dedicated to prioritizing the well-being of individuals and society as a whole."

More questions are shouted, the roar of voices drowning each other out. The woman moves closer to the microphone to be heard.

"Thank you for your attention. We remain committed to the safe, ethical, and responsible advancement of Virtual Reality Technology and will be back with news in the coming weeks."

As she exits the stage, the questions continue, reporters trying to get every last detail. Naya mutes the TV, staring at the chaos while sorting through her own thoughts on the matter.

"Holy smokes," Mr. Jenkins murmurs, echoing Naya's internal feelings. "It's real."

Atlas remains silent, his face growing paler by the second. "I think I need a minute," he says, hauling his chair back to his makeshift desk.

Naya watches him go with concern. She notices Mr. Jenkins eyeing her closely as she does.

"Well, that was a bit… unsettling, huh Mr. J?"

He nods, an indecipherable look in his eyes. "Can you imagine total immersion like that? A seamless integration of the mind and technology. It's scary to think at some point we won't be able to tell what's real and what's not."

A shiver runs along Naya's spine at the thought. "Like being trapped in a digital prison housed in your own mind."

"Exactly. I may like technology, but I don't know that I'd want it to be a permanent part of me. We're surrounded by it enough, as it is."

"Well, we are in a computer shop," Naya jokes, hoping to lighten the mood.

Mr. Jenkins gives her a half-hearted chuckle. "I suppose it's time to get to work for the day. Turn that thing off."

Naya complies, turning the TV off and heading toward her desk. Atlas is sitting in his chair seemingly lost in thought.

"It's a lot to take in, isn't it," she says.

Atlas looks up as if shocked she's standing in front of him. He nods, not quite making eye contact with her. She notices he's rubbing his neck absentmindedly and thinks back to the scar he has there.

"What are you thinking?" she inquires, trying to pull him out of his thoughts. His reaction to the broadcast is starting to scare her.

He finally makes eye contact, a look of dread in his hazel eyes. "Naya, what if I'm one of them?"

"One of who?"

"One of the people they were testing the VR microchip on?"

Naya sits in her chair, letting the idea sink in. If Atlas were part of the government's trials, that would mean the facility they want to break into is government run. That would certainly complicate things.

"Although horrifying, it might explain the scar on your neck." Naya twirls in her chair, letting her mind work through the possibilities. "Actually, it might also explain your memory loss." She stops mid-twirl to face Atlas.

"How so?"

"Well, they said it was still in the early phases, right? Maybe they don't quite have the technology perfected and the chip causes issues with memory loss?" she proposes, using her computer hardware knowledge to make an educated guess.

"Or," Atlas challenges, "they did it on purpose. I highly doubt they only have good intentions for this device."

He has a grave look on his face that makes Naya feel suddenly chilled in the musty shop. The possibilities of an implanted device like this could lead to disastrous consequences, even some sort of mind control in the future. She wonders how many other people feel the same way they do or if more people are excited by the prospect. She supposes many people would jump at the opportunity to escape this crappy reality for something more utopian, even if it isn't real.

"Let's say your hypothesis is correct," Naya starts, making sure she has Atlas's attention before continuing. "That would mean the microchip is still implanted. Shall we attempt to find out?"

At that, Atlas furrows his brow, a mix of curiosity and apprehension on his face. "How would we do that?"

Naya grabs her laptop from her backpack and sets it on her desk. "By doing a little digital investigating," she answers, pulling up several programs on her device and getting to work.

She runs a network traffic capture, analyzing various packets of data currently being transferred on nearby networks. Among them, she spots something abnormal. Naya delves deeper into the anomalous packets, tracing their origin. After several minutes of analysis, she uncovers a peculiar pattern—a series of encrypted transmissions emanating from a nearby source.

"Found something," she exclaims, prompting Atlas to scoot closer to her computer. He watches as she continues investigating.

Naya focuses on unraveling the encryption protocols guarding the data, surprised to find them rather easy to crack. Though she has years of experience guiding her through the process, it's unusual for it to be this simple.

"Strange," she mutters quietly.

"What is? What did you find?" Atlas whispers, now only a few inches from her.

"I found encrypted data transmissions close by, traced it to its origin, and came across an encrypted software. The actual software's encryption has surprisingly weak protocols. If this is your chip, I don't know why it wouldn't have higher security," she explains, sharing a confused look with Atlas before returning to the data before her.

"Let me keep looking and see what I can find."

Naya scans through the inner workings of the software, expecting familiar structures and algorithms. But what she finds is unlike anything she's encountered before—a labyrinth of code, its structure both elegant and bafflingly complex. Curiosity piqued, she dives headfirst into the intricate network of algorithms and subroutines, her mind ablaze with revelation.

As she sifts through the lines of code, Naya deciphers a few of its functions and capabilities. Words like neural networks, spatial mapping, and sensory input jump out at her, the implications sending a chill down her spine. The code bears a striking resemblance to what one might expect to find in a VR microchip. She stops, closing the programs and leaning back in her chair.

"Why did you stop?" Atlas questions.

Naya turns to stare at Atlas, not sure how to break the news. "I think you were right, Atlas. I found lines of code that make the most sense in some sort of VR device."

Atlas stands suddenly, pacing in the small space between their desks. Naya notices his frenzied movements catch the attention of Mr. Jenkins, and she tugs Atlas's hand to get him to sit back down.

"Calm down, we don't want to freak Mr. Jenkins out too. Plus, I don't know for sure. It's just… Speculation?" She tries to inject as much positivity into her tone as possible—for both their sakes.

"Okay, so how come you stopped looking into it? Don't you want to be more certain?"

"Because the code is complicated. If it is your microchip, I don't want to accidentally mess something up and hurt you."

"Let me have a look," Atlas says, moving to grab her laptop.

Naya beats him to it, clutching it tightly to her chest. "Absolutely not. I know you had a revelation this morning that you're supposedly a software genius, but we shouldn't run the risk. We don't know what sort of chain reaction we could set off."

Atlas grumbles, crossing his arms obstinately. "Did you know you can be really bossy sometimes?"

The corner of Naya's mouth quirks up at his comment. He's cute when he pouts. She quickly shakes the thought away, reminding herself they're just friends. Since this weekend, she's been repeating it like a mantra in hopes to set aside her growing feelings for him. It's proving to be a more difficult task than she imagined.

"Let's get back to our actual jobs," Naya orders, leaning into her aforementioned bossy side. "Don't want to raise suspicion and have Mr. Jenkins ask questions. He doesn't need to be involved."

Atlas nods in agreement, settling in at his desk and resuming his work on the computer from this morning. Naya returns to her work as well, still mulling over her recent discovery.

Hours pass in a blur as Naya loses herself to conspiracy theories, her brain running rampant with possibilities. By closing time, she's barely accomplished anything. Looking over at Atlas, it appears he's having the same struggle.

She watches him organize his tools for the day, hunched over the containers on his desk. The faint pink shine of his scar catches the fluorescent light, and she subconsciously touches her own. As she does, Naya thinks about the hands behind their recovery, the various doctors that did their best to repair the delicate tissue. Suddenly, a frightening thought pops into her head.

"Atlas." She crouches next to him at his desk. "What if the lack of security on your microchip means something?"

He tilts his head, silently questioning her meaning.

"What if…" she pauses, almost scared to say it out loud. "What if they did the bare minimum because they didn't think they'd ever need to worry about it."

"I'm not sure what you're getting at," Atlas mumbles.

"The people that did this to you, they never planned on letting you leave the facility."

# CHAPTER 28

# ATLAS

Atlas lays in bed that night, unable to sleep. The sensation of an itch at the back of his neck persists, a constant reminder of the foreign device implanted in his head. He wants to crawl out of his own skin, to rid himself of the intrusive presence that disturbs his peace. The desire to be free from it grows overwhelming, thoughts of cutting it out of his skin sounding more and more tempting.

It's the memory of Naya's words that keep him from doing so, reminding him they don't know the risks. He'd rather not die in the process of trying to remove it.

As Atlas tosses and turns in bed, a storm of questions and doubts continues to brew. How did he end up at the facility in the first place? Did he agree to test the chip?

Frustration and confusion gnaw at him as he struggles to piece together the fragments of memories that now feel like shards of a shattered reality. The more he tries to make sense of it all, the more elusive the answers become. Eventually, exhaustion overtakes him, and he drifts into an restless slumber.

The next morning, Atlas wakes to the soft glow of dawn filtering through his window, signaling the start of another day. Despite the lingering unease from the previous day's events, he pushes himself out of bed.

Entering Bargain Bytes, Atlas is surprised to see Naya already there. Her presence is a reassuring anchor amidst the ocean of uncertainty in his mind.

"Now who's the early bird?" he calls out. She jumps in her chair, turning toward him with a scowl.

"You scared me!" she scolds, trying to slow her now rapid breathing.

"Sorry, didn't mean to." Atlas makes his way over to her desk, noticing the slight purple hue under her eyes.

She yawns and then stares timidly up at him. "Couldn't sleep," she explains.

"Glad I wasn't the only one."

Atlas scans her desk, trying to decipher what she's working on. She notices him staring, and picks up a small, half-finished device for him to see better.

"It's the comms device we talked about."

Atlas inspects the device, admiring Naya's ingenuity and resourcefulness. It's crafted from a hodgepodge of old components salvaged from Bargain Bytes, a marvel of makeshift engineering. At its core, the device houses a repurposed motherboard, its circuitry painstakingly rewired to serve a new purpose.

The casing of the device is a sturdy metal framework from an old desktop tower, its edges worn with age and use. Various knobs, switches, and dials from vintage radios and telecommunication equipment are attached to it.

"All I have left is the antenna," Naya says, interrupting Atlas's inspection. In her hands is a jumble of wires twisted together. She places a repurposed plastic casing over it, its unconventional design a testament to Naya's creativity.

Atlas hands the device back to her and watches as she carefully puts the finishing touches on her creation.

"Put it in your ear," she says, handing it back to him.

As he does, Naya leans into her laptop and says a few words, her voice coming through the speaker in his ear. Despite the device's somewhat crude appearance, it's surprisingly effective.

"Wow." Atlas's voice echoes back through Naya's laptop speakers.

He takes the device off, gingerly handing it back to her. "How far can it transmit?"

"Far enough," she replies.

The bell of the shop door interrupts them as Mr. Jenkins walks in.

"Didn't expect to see both of you here before me!" He walks back toward them, and Naya hastily scrambles to hide her device.

She's not fast enough, though, Mr. Jenkins motioning toward it. "Whatcha got there?"

Naya glances at Atlas, a worried expression on her face. "Just a little something I'm experimenting with," she starts. "I hope you don't mind. I've used some old shop parts."

"Not at all, glad to see them put to good use. What's it for?" he inquires further.

Naya stumbles over her words and Atlas tries to come up with a cover story.

"Teaching purposes," he blurts, silently imploring Naya to go along with it. "Most of my knowledge is with software so Naya has been teaching me hardware tips and tricks by making a new device. She's very talented."

Naya nods along with his story, her expression neutral as she listens to Atlas's explanation. Mr. Jenkins, on the other hand, looks doubtful but doesn't push the subject.

"I'm pleased you're trying to improve your skills, Atlas," he remarks, his tone laced with skepticism.

Mr. Jenkins pauses for a moment before continuing, his gaze flickering between Atlas and Naya. "It's always good to stay sharp, especially in… interesting times like these," he adds before parting ways.

Atlas lets out a sigh of relief, glad they dodged Mr. J's questions for now. They'll have to be more careful from now on if they don't want him to get involved.

Offering Naya a weary smile, Atlas settles into his routine for the day. It's not long until the bell chimes again, a well-dressed woman entering the shop with an air of apprehension.

"Excuse me," she says anxiously, "I need some help with this. It's urgent."

Naya steps forward, her professional demeanor kicking in. "Of course, we're here to help. What seems to be the problem?"

The woman sets a broken smartphone on the front counter, eyeing Atlas and Naya. "I've been to all the fancy repair places in town and they keep telling me to just upgrade to the newest phone. But with all this talk about," the woman leans in closer, lowering her voice to a whisper, "VR microchips, I'm worried."

Atlas exchanges a knowing glance with Naya, understanding the customer's concerns all too well. He watches as Naya admires the phone for a moment. They don't get to see many of them, these days. Phones are a luxury, something only the rich can afford to own.

"Do you think you can repair my current phone?" the woman asks.

"Don't worry," Naya reassures her. "We'll take a look and make sure everything's working in no time!"

Naya tells the lady to come back tomorrow to pick up the phone after repairs. It's not until the shop door closes behind her that Naya lets the smile on her face drop.

"So, it's not just us who are worrying about this new tech. Even the rich folk are apprehensive," she asserts, returning to her desk with the smartphone.

"That's good. People should be nervous."

"Should, yeah. But there are too many tech junkies who are probably thrilled by the idea. It's just one more way to escape their reality."

Atlas ponders her statement. A part of him can see the appeal of wanting to live in a better world, even if it's only a figment of your imagination.

"I suppose there isn't a whole lot to keep fighting for in this reality," he says softly. "Why toil away every day and still never be able to afford most of life's luxuries when you can have anything your heart desires in a virtual simulation?"

Naya gives him an incredulous look, stopping her examination of the smartphone to gape at him.

"Why? Because we were created for so much more than that. Because our time is limited. Because our weakest moments should drive us toward God instead of some virtual escape."

"Can't you find God inside the virtual escape?" Atlas counters, suddenly deciding to play devil's advocate.

"Maybe," Naya concedes, her tone softening. "But if you can also have anything you want, what's to stop you from making that new world your God? We aren't meant to cling to earthly things. We have an eternal life awaiting us with more peace, love, and joy than we could ever imagine."

Naya's passion is palpable, her conviction unwavering as she speaks of a faith that Atlas finds difficult to comprehend. He listens intently, though the concept of an eternal life filled with peace and joy feels like a distant dream to him.

"It's a bit hard to fathom," Atlas admits. "Especially with the way things are right now."

"Absolutely, if you're only focusing on the world. That's why it's so important to have a close relationship with the Lord. Walking daily with Him will open your eyes to see things in ways you never did before." As Naya speaks, there's a light in her eyes that Atlas envies.

"How did you get to that place?" he asks.

"By accepting Jesus Christ as my Lord and savior, repenting of my sins, and giving Him control over my life."

Atlas sits in silence, thinking about where he's at on that journey. Giving God control? He definitely still struggles with that. Unsure how to respond, Atlas thanks Naya for her insight and returns to his desk. His mind swims with thoughts, each one fighting for his attention. Tired of overthinking, Atlas focuses on crossing items off his to-do list for the day.

As he works, Atlas can't shake the feeling that something is off. Mr. Jenkins, usually preoccupied with his own tasks, seems unusually observant, his keen gaze lingering on him and Naya with a knowing intensity.

Atlas exchanges a cautious glance with Naya, silently communicating his unease. They've been trying to keep their plans under wraps, but it seems Mr. Jenkins may be catching on.

As closing time approaches, Mr. Jenkins pulls them aside, his expression serious. "Naya, Atlas," he begins, his tone low and measured. "I've noticed something's going on between you two."

Atlas's heart skips a beat, his mind racing to come up with a response. Mr. Jenkins's intuition has caught them off-guard, leaving them vulnerable. They didn't expect him to catch on so soon.

"I… I don't know what you're talking about, Mr. Jenkins," Naya stammers, her voice betraying her nervousness.

But Mr. Jenkins isn't fooled. His gaze flits between them, his expression unreadable. "I may not know the specifics," he says cryptically, "but I know enough to realize you're up to something. And whatever it is, I want in."

# CHAPTER 29
# NAYA

Naya's pulse quickens at Mr. Jenkin's sudden proposition. She shares a surprised glance with Atlas, uncertainty flashing across her face. They hadn't anticipated involving Mr. Jenkins, but it seems their plans may have just taken an unexpected turn.

"Mr. Jenkins, we appreciate your… interest," Naya begins cautiously, "but this is something we've been working on independently. It's not something we can just bring someone else into."

Mr. Jenkins's expression remains unreadable, but there's a steely resolve in his gaze that tells Naya he won't take no for an answer.

"I understand," he says firmly. "But whatever it is you're planning, it's clearly important. And if there's one thing I've learned in all my years, it's that sometimes, you need allies in unexpected places."

Naya hesitates, weighing the risks and benefits of involving him in their scheme. On one hand, his expertise and resources could prove invaluable. On the other hand, trusting him with their secrets could have dire consequences. Despite the risks, there's a part of her that believes they could use all the help they can get.

She looks over at Atlas, trying to gauge his reaction. He shrugs, apparently fine with whatever she decides. "Give us a second." Naya tugs Atlas toward the back of the shop. Mr. Jenkins nods, a curious gleam in his eyes.

"You're really fine with involving him?" Naya keeps her voice to a whisper.

"Originally, I wasn't so sure. But he's already suspicious, so what choice do we have? Plus, he's done so much for me. I trust him," Atlas replies earnestly.

"A few days ago, you were horrified to get *me* involved, and now it's no big deal? What changed?" Naya presses, confused by his change in attitude.

"Recent events—the government press release, the chip in my head. It's all a little overwhelming. We could probably use the help." Atlas looks back at Mr. Jenkins who is patiently waiting for them. Returning his gaze to Naya, he mutters, "Plus, he's not you."

Naya fights to keep the blush off her face. Though she's trying to keep him in the friendzone, he's doing a great job at fighting his way out. It feels good to hear him admit he cares, even in a roundabout way.

Clearing her throat, Naya heads back to Mr. Jenkins. She tries to ignore the flash of hurt she sees on Atlas's face as she brushes past him.

"Alright, Mr. Jenkins," Naya concedes, her voice steady. "But you need to understand this is dangerous. And if things go south, there's no turning back."

Mr. Jenkins nods, grinning ear to ear. "I could use a little excitement in my life. And if it means I can make a difference, I'm willing to take the risks."

"You might want to have a seat for this. It's kind of a long story." Atlas pulls up a few chairs for them all.

By the time Atlas and Naya have filled Mr. Jenkins in on all the details, the sun has set. He sat quietly the whole time, letting them speak without interruption.

"You're in quite the pickle there, Atlas." He scrubs a hand over his face. "And to think, we've had one of those newfangled VR microchips in our midst the whole time!"

Atlas laughs and Naya can't help but join in, the absurdity of their situation suddenly hysterical.

"It's actually really nice to be able to tell you," Naya admits. "It wasn't fun keeping secrets."

"And it wasn't fun being kept in the dark," Mr. J replies. "I may be old, but I still have my wits about me."

Mr. Jenkins wastes no time diving into the details of their plan, his years of experience and sharp intellect proving invaluable as they hash out the logistics. He offers insights and suggestions, his perspective bringing a fresh angle to their strategy.

"Let me see what I can dig up on this mysterious facility," Mr. Jenkins concludes. "But for now, let's call it a day. We all have a lot to think about."

Naya and Atlas agree, feeling weary with fatigue after a long night of planning.

"Naya, can we talk?" Atlas says, catching her before she leaves.

Naya hesitates, torn between her desire to hear what he has to say and the overwhelming fatigue that weighs heavy on her shoulders. Though she doesn't want to hurt him by saying no, she isn't sure she's ready to hear what he has to say.

"I'm sorry Atlas," she replies regretfully. "Another time? I'm really wiped after all that."

She watches as disappointment flickers across his features, a shadow of sadness clouding his expression. With a parting wave, he nods solemnly before letting her leave, locking the door behind her.

Naya tries to savor the refreshing evening breeze as she pedals her bike home, but her mind is still buzzing with today's events. She grapples with a wave of regret for letting her conflicting emotions create distance between herself and Atlas. Yet, a lingering apprehension holds her back from fully embracing the idea of reconnecting with him. She wants him to confront his past before she can entertain any hope for their present. However, Naya knows avoidance will only postpone the inevitable.

As she finally reaches her driveway, she walks her bike to the garage. Resting it against the wall, she steps inside her house, feeling a sense of relief wash over her at the familiar surroundings.

Naya kicks off her shoes with a sigh and pads into the living room. Fully prepared to sink into the couch, she's shocked to find Harper fast asleep in her spot. She's in her pajamas, her long dark hair spilling across her favorite pillow. *Of course she brought it to the couch with her*, Naya thinks to herself, a small smile playing on her lips.

She crouches down beside the couch, noticing the gold butterfly necklace tangled in her hair. Ever since Naya gave it to her for her birthday, Harper never takes it off.

Gently, she shakes Harper awake.

"Naya?" Harper asks groggily.

"Hey Little Butterfly," Naya greets. Harper smiles at the nickname Naya hasn't used in a while. "How come you're sleeping down here?"

"I was waiting for you to come home," she mutters, rubbing her eyes. "You worried me."

Harper's mussed hair and tired eyes make her look younger and more innocent. Naya tucks a strand of her little sister's hair behind her ear as she sits up. "You know I've been staying out later these days," Naya reminds. "I'm okay."

"I know," Harper says softly. "Just wanted to make sure you didn't disappear without saying goodbye."

Naya isn't sure what to make of Harper's comment, chalking it up to the remnants of whatever dream she was having.

"Never," Naya reassures her. "Now, let's get you to bed."

She helps Harper off the couch and walks her up to her room. Tucking her into bed, Naya kisses her forehead.

"I've been praying for you and Atlas," Harper whispers, eyes closed.

"Oh? What for?"

"That you'll figure things out," she replies, turning onto her side and burrowing further into the covers.

"Thanks, Harper." Naya closes the door softly and heads to her own room down the hall.

Harper's words fill her with hope. It's comforting to know she's looking out for her. Sprawling across her bed with a huff, Naya says a quick prayer of her own, giving her worries to the Lord. Only He knows what lies ahead, and she trusts Him to guide her in the right direction.

# CHAPTER 30
# ATLAS

A small stack of papers lands on Atlas's desk, interrupting his early morning work. He looks up in surprise, turning in his chair to see Mr. Jenkins staring at him over the rim of his glasses.

"That's all I could find on this mysterious facility of yours," he says, lowering himself into Naya's desk chair nearby.

Though it's not quite opening time, Atlas is keenly aware of her absence. Mr. Jenkins must be thinking the same thing because he gestures to her empty desk with a raised brow. Atlas shrugs in reply.

"They call themselves Genesis Laboratories," Mr. Jenkins says while Atlas sorts through the papers.

Among the stack are a few news articles, online forum posts, and vague social media posts. One image catches his attention, a logo branded in the corner. The concentric circles frame an abstract hexagram, an ominous yet familiar image.

He's seen this before.

"Flip to the last page," Mr. Jenkins suggests.

Doing as told, Atlas finds another forum post explaining the next stage in the VR development process. The user claims to be a family member of someone who works closely with this program.

"Human trials?" Atlas says aloud. "They're going to pay people to test it already?"

"Apparently. Look at the date! They're guessing it will be released to the public at the beginning of next week."

Atlas scans the rest of the post, seeing the date Mr. Jenkins mentioned. The government is moving this project along quickly. Rifling back through the stack of papers, Atlas hears the commotion of Naya wheeling her bike through the front door.

"Sorry I'm late!" she shouts. "Overslept. Did I miss anything important?"

"Only my most exciting discovery to date!" Mr. Jenkins jokes, a warm smile on his face.

Atlas hands the papers to Naya as she leans her bike against the back wall. "We were just talking about the last page."

Naya's eyes scan the post, growing wider the more she reads. She looks up when finished, an excited look on her face.

"This is perfect! Whenever they set the date for the human trials to start, that's the day we infiltrate. Take advantage of the extra flow of people." Naya flips through the other pages. "This is the same facility, right?"

Atlas nods, a lump forming in his throat at the thought of going back.

"Not a bad idea, little lady! Something to think on, at least." Mr. Jenkins lumbers back to his desk now that Naya is here.

Atlas takes that as his cue to get back to work and Naya does the same, plopping into her desk chair to repair the smartphone from yesterday.

The hours fly by in a blur of activity, helping customers, repairing devices, and organizing the shop. Atlas has put their impending journey out of his mind for now, but he can sense Naya is still mulling something over.

As he heads toward the stairs to his loft for a quick lunch break, Naya surprises him by asking to join. He tries to keep his tone casual as he accepts. She follows him up the stairs in silence, not speaking until the loft door is closed behind her.

"You know, I've been thinking," she begins, sitting on the couch while Atlas digs through his cupboards for food. "Maybe it would be better if I went into the facility instead of you."

Atlas is caught off guard by her sudden proposal, almost dropping the box of cereal in his hands. "I thought we already talked about this?"

"Hear me out," she pleads, setting her sandwich aside. "What if I sign up to be part of the human trials? They don't know who I am, and it would be a perfect way to get inside!"

"No," Atlas says sternly. "That's a horrible idea."

"No, it's not! You have to admit it makes more sense. How else are we going to get into that place?" Naya unwraps her food while she waits for Atlas's reply.

He racks his brain for ideas, knowing it's one of the few things they are still unsure of. "I don't know," he admits, "but we'll figure something out."

"Like?"

"Like anything to keep you out of there."

"You're so stubborn!" she huffs, taking an angry bite of her sandwich.

"Look who's talking." Atlas joins her on the couch with a bowl of cereal. "I don't know why you want to go in there so badly. You have no idea what you'll find."

Naya shrugs. "Maybe I just want to spare you the trauma of going back," she mumbles.

They sit in silence as they finish their lunch, neither one knowing what to say next. Atlas hates the awkwardness that's been festering between them since the night on the roof.

"I'm sorry," he announces suddenly, causing Naya to choke on the last bite of her sandwich.

She coughs, crossing to the kitchen to drink straight from the tap. Regaining her composure, she leans against the kitchen counter to stare at Atlas. The seconds tick by between them, Atlas unsure how she'll respond to his sudden apology.

"I'm sorry too," she says finally.

"What are you apologizing for?"

Naya shifts her gaze to the floor. "Leaving you on the roof like that. Pushing you away."

Atlas moves to stand in front of her, mindful of the distance between them.

"I never meant to hurt you," he says softly. "All these memories just make everything so confusing."

Naya looks up at him then, a resigned look on her face. She gives him a small smile. "I know. It's unknown territory. Neither of us are sure how to handle it. I guess I just wasn't expecting to be so hurt by something that's already happened."

She laughs, Atlas watching as a flurry of emotions cross her face. "It feels so lame to say it out loud," she admits, voice cracking.

"It's not lame. If roles were reversed, I'd feel the same way." He closes the distance between them. "I really like you, Naya."

She gazes up at him and he notices the flecks of gold in her eyes. They're full of intensity and Atlas can tell she feels the same way about him. She breaks eye contact, placing a hand gently on his chest.

"I like you too," she whispers, before pushing him away. "But I'm scared to be hurt like that again."

Atlas feels the pang of rejection pierce through his chest. Naya moves toward the door, stopping to look back at him.

"For now, I think it's best if we keep our feelings on the back burner." Her voice wavers slightly. "We should focus on getting your memories back."

Her words echo in the stillness of the room. He meets her gaze, seeing his own turmoil reflected in her eyes before she turns and closes the door behind her.

Alone in the quiet, Atlas can't shake the weight of her words. The ache of rejection lingers, a bitter reminder of the distance that now lies between them. Atlas drops his head into his hands, a familiar throbbing in his head preceding a memory that pulls him back into the past.

Atlas stands in a dimly lit office, tension in the air as the mystery woman stands facing him. Her face is still unclear in his mind, but he can see the anger in her brown eyes.

"I can't believe you're just going along with this." Her voice is laced with disappointment. "You're better than this, Atlas. You know it."

Atlas clenches his fists, struggling to meet her unwavering gaze. He knows she's right, knows deep down that he's compromising his morals for the sake of his job. But the thought of walking away, of abandoning everything he worked so hard for, fills him with a sense of dread.

"I don't have a choice," he argues. "This is my job, my livelihood. I can't just throw it all away."

She shakes her head, her expression filled with sadness and frustration. "You always said you wanted to make a difference in the world," she reminds him. "But what kind of difference are you making if you're willing to sacrifice your principles for a paycheck?"

Atlas winces at her words. He's always dreamed of using his talents to create something meaningful, but now, faced with the harsh reality of his choices, he feels like he's betraying himself.

As their voices continue to rise and the argument reaches its peak, the woman turns on her heels and storms out of the office, leaving Atlas alone with his thoughts. In the silence that follows, he can't shake the feeling that he's on the brink of losing something more precious than his job.

The last thing he sees before returning to the present is a logo emblazoned on the wall—an abstract hexagram surrounded by concentric circles.

# CHAPTER 31
# NAYA

Naya stands amongst the racks of clothing, searching for a retired pair of scrubs in the sea of thrift store items. Across the aisle, Atlas sifts through the clothes with Harper by his side, the trio diligently checking off the final item on their to-do list—finding Atlas a disguise.

A sense of relief washes over Naya as she notices the continued absence of awkwardness between her and Atlas since their candid conversation a few days ago. Though it was difficult, she's confident she made the right decision. Their current state of preparedness serves as tangible evidence, demonstrating they were able to prioritize finalizing their preparations over dwelling on their feelings for each other.

As they wander through the thrift store aisles, Naya steals glances at Atlas. Every time she catches his attention, his eyes seem to linger on her a little longer than necessary. He gives her a dazzling smile, holding up a hideously bright Hawaiian shirt. Warmth spreads through her chest at the sight of him, the ugly shirt only making him more endearing.

"Keep looking, mister," she says. "That shirt will get you caught in no time."

"Oh, I was considering this for personal reasons." Atlas's expression is serious.

"You're kidding, right?"

"What, is pink not my color?" Atlas holds the shirt right next to his face, looking from it to Naya and back again.

She laughs, charmed by his silliness. Moving to another aisle, Naya attempts to focus on rummaging through the clothing but her thoughts keep drifting back to Atlas. Despite deciding to prioritize their mission, she can't shake the lingering attraction between them.

Meanwhile, Harper, ever the social butterfly, strikes up a conversation with the thrift store employee. She elicits a laugh from both of them with one of her witty remarks. Her infectious energy fills the air, drawing smiles from both Naya and Atlas. Noticing she has their attention, Harper puts on a pair of sunglasses and strikes a pose.

Naya shakes her head at her, prompting Harper to pout. She comes running over, practically knocking Naya off her feet.

"Don't these look great on me? Can I get them?" she pleads.

"Harper, you don't need them. Put them back and then help us look for a surgical cap," Naya gently commands.

"Fine. What do you need all this stuff for again?" Harper inquires.

"You promised not to ask questions if I let you come along, remember?"

"Yeah, yeah, yeah," she replies with an eye roll, putting the sunglasses back and disappearing down another aisle of clothing. Focused on watching Harper's antics, Naya is taken aback when a ball cap suddenly lands on her head. She turns to find Atlas grinning down at her, sporting a straw hat of his own.

"To go along with the Hawaiian shirt," he says, pointing at his hat.

Naya quirks an eyebrow, a hint of amusement tugging at her lips. "And this one?" She gestures to the cap sitting backwards on her head.

"I just thought it would look good on you. I was right." Atlas winks, sauntering back the way he came.

His unexpected flirtation leaves Naya momentarily speechless, a flush creeping up her cheeks as she watches him go. *Keep it together, Naya,* she tells herself, returning to the search. Several minutes later, a light blue fabric catches her attention.

"Jackpot!" she declares, garnering a chuckle from Atlas.

He comes hurrying over, accompanied by an overly excited Harper.

"Me too!" she exclaims, holding up a small shirt in the same color. "Sort of."

Naya gives her a puzzled look, not quite understanding how a shirt could be a substitute for a surgical cap.

Harper looks eager to explain. "There weren't any scrub hats, or whatever you called it, so I found a shirt instead. I thought maybe Mom could turn it into a hat!"

Naya smiles, impressed by her sister's creative thinking. "Great idea, Harper."

"So, what did you find?" Atlas questions.

Pulling a worn set of nursing scrubs off the rack, she holds them up for his inspection. He takes them from her hands, splaying the clothes against his body to check for size.

"It's definitely a little small, but it'll have to work," he comments. "Nice job girls."

Harper beams at his compliment. "Told you I'd be helpful!" She sticks her tongue out at Naya.

"You were more helpful than me!" Atlas adds. "I didn't find a single useful thing."

"What happened to that wonderful Hawaiian shirt you loved so much?" Naya teases, pretending to scan the store for it.

Atlas mimics Harper, sticking his tongue out in reply and making both girls laugh. He looks ridiculously cute.

As they head to the checkout, Atlas plucks the pair of sunglasses Harper liked off the rack, sticking them on her head.

"My gift to you, Miss Harper. They suit you nicely." He turns to the clerk, telling them to add the glasses to his purchase.

"Atlas," Naya whispers, touching his arm gently. "That's not necessary."

"I want to," he says simply, giving her an affectionate grin.

"For only recently having a steady income, you're surprisingly generous with your money," Naya observes, earning another smirk from Atlas. He retrieves his wallet to pay, handing over some cash to the clerk.

"Just trying to take after another very generous person I know," Atlas replies, giving her a look of sincere admiration.

Naya is filled with joy at his words. It's rewarding to see the positive outcomes of her decisions, reaffirming she's on the right path. Each day, God reveals new blessings and Atlas is undoubtedly one of them.

The warm summer air greets them as they exit the thrift store, a gentle breeze cooling their skin. Around them, people walk along the sidewalks, enjoying the beautiful weather.

"Well, I guess I'll see you on Monday?" Atlas says slowly, clearly reluctant to say goodbye.

"See you Monday," Naya replies, parting ways with a small smile. Harper walks next to her, waving goodbye to Atlas over her shoulder.

Naya turns to see Atlas wave back before he heads in the opposite direction.

"I like Atlas," Harper says, putting the sunglasses over her eyes.

"Me too," Naya agrees. "He's a great guy."

Harper lowers her sunglasses slightly, peering over them at Naya. She raises a brow and purses her lips, forming a rather comical expression.

"What's that look for?" Naya questions, holding back her laughter.

"A great guy?" she repeats, making air quotes with both hands. "So why were you crying over him last week?"

Naya blushes and turns away, unsure how to respond. She was hoping Harper wouldn't mention that night again. And if she knows her little sister, the fact she's bringing it up means Naya can't give her another non-answer. She scrambles to come up with a reply that won't spill Atlas's secrets, not wanting to betray his trust or bring Harper into something dangerous.

"I thought you just said you liked him?" Naya stalls, hoping to distract her sister with another conversation.

"I can still like him and be disappointed by how he made you feel. Now spill." Harper points at Naya with a stern look while they walk.

Naya clears her throat, feeling suddenly awkward about confessing how she feels to her sister. "Well… I have feelings for Atlas, but he's still stuck in the past. I was hurt by…" Naya pauses, trying to find the right words. "By being compared to his prior relationship."

"And you're sure that's what he was doing?"

Naya sighs, knowing there was a lot more to it than what she's telling Harper. "I don't know. It's complicated, Harper."

"All your flirting at the thrift shop didn't seem complicated to me," she retorts.

Naya's jaw drops, embarrassed Harper noticed all that. She always forgets how observant she is.

"Why are you so curious, anyway?" Naya asks, changing the subject.

Harper shrugs in reply. "Like I said, I like him. I think you two are cute together but only as long as he doesn't make you cry again."

Naya hugs Harper to her side, appreciating her little sister's support. She's always looking out for what's best for her.

A couple walks hand-in-hand past them on the sidewalk, and Naya imagines her and Atlas like that. She shakes the thought away, annoyed with how hard it is to stop thinking about him. Boys have never been a big deal to her, so what's so different about Atlas?

As they round a corner, Naya is surprised to see a small canopy tent being put up by a group of people. She gasps when she notices the logo printed on the plastic matches the one Mr. Jenkins linked to the facility. *Genesis Laboratories,* she recalls.

Harper and Naya continue to approach the tent, intrigued by the spectacle.

"Wait here," Naya instructs Harper, leaving her standing on the sidewalk nearby.

Harper is about to protest but Naya jogs away, approaching the group securing the tent in place. She spares a glance back at her sister, noticing she now has her arms crossed in indignation.

Returning her gaze to the tent, she notices a woman in a suit observing its construction. Assuming she's the one in charge, Naya musters her confidence and walks toward her with a smile.

"Good afternoon!" she greets, prompting the woman to turn in surprise. "What's going on here?"

The woman looks Naya over head to toe, scrutinizing her.

"Government business," she says vaguely.

"This wouldn't have to do with that new VR technology, would it?" Naya inquires, injecting as much charm into her voice as possible.

The woman's eyes narrow and Naya decides to kick it up a notch. "I was so excited when they announced it! It's an incredible idea, one that has the potential to really revolutionize our society."

At that, the woman smiles, extending her hand. "Barbara, nice to meet you. And you are?"

"Nelly," she blurts, deciding at the last minute to use a fake name. "Nelly Blackwell."

"Well, Miss Blackwell, I'll let you in on a little secret."

She leans in conspiratorially close and explains the purpose of the tent is for voluntary sign ups in the next phase of the project. Excitement is evident in her tone as she details the human trials, reassuring Naya that participants will be well-compensated. Unease settles in Naya's stomach at the jovial way the woman discusses something so frightening.

"This first part will be for medical testing, ensuring only volunteers in peak health will move on to the actual trials," Barbara continues. "Would you be interested, Miss Blackwell?"

A sense of betrayal floods through Naya at what she's about to do, but she feels it's the best solution to their problem.

"Absolutely! Is there any way I can sign up now?" she replies.

"We aren't supposed to take applicants until Monday, I'm sorry."

"I'll be here bright and early Monday morning, then."

# CHAPTER 32

# ATLAS

Atlas is surprised when Naya rushes through the door of Bargain Bytes ten minutes late on Monday morning. She avoids eye contact as she settles into her desk, making Atlas worry.

"Everything alright?" he asks, noticing her strange demeanor.

"Yep." Naya keeps her eyes trained on the device in front of her.

Atlas is skeptical of her reassurance, unable to shake the feeling that something is off. He makes a mental note to check in with her later, hoping everything is truly okay.

As the day progresses, Naya's tension remains palpable, casting a shadow over their usual camaraderie. Atlas finds himself growing increasingly worried over her silence, but he knows better than to press her for answers. Instead, he focuses on their work, silently offering his support should she choose to confide in him.

The shop remains slow all morning, prompting the three of them to take an extended lunch break. Naya, Mr. Jenkins, and Atlas gather in the middle of the shop to finalize their plans. Naya proudly reveals the surgical cap her mom made from the thrift store shirt, eliciting impressed nods from Atlas and Mr. Jenkins.

"She was a little confused why I wanted this made," Naya explains. "But she didn't press for specifics. I told her I'd be going on a trip soon, too."

"And what did she say?" Atlas interrupts, worried her mom won't let her go.

"She was worried but felt relieved when I said I'd be going with you." Naya gives him a small smile. "She told us to stay safe."

Mr. Jenkins nods thoughtfully as he absorbs the information. "Your family has always been very supportive," he remarks, a hint of admiration in his voice.

"Yeah, they've always been there for me," she responds, the mention of her family visibly relaxing her tension from this morning.

"Oh!" Mr. Jenkins excitedly straightens in his chair. "Did you see the Genesis Laboratories tent in town? They started sign-ups today!"

Atlas leans forward, eager to hear more. "Did you find out the date for the medical testing?"

"A week from today. Their fast-paced timeline is disturbingly suspicious, and yet there was still a long line of people waiting to register this morning." Mr. Jenkins shakes his head in disappointment. "What has our society come to?"

Atlas glances over at Naya, noticing she's remained quiet at the mention of the sign-ups. He feels bad for squashing her idea the other day, but still doesn't like the idea of her being the one to enter the facility. He's grateful she relented and agreed to continue with their current plans.

"So, what's left?" Atlas asks, going through a mental to-do list of preparations.

"Packing our bags for the trip. That's pretty much it." Naya exchanges a glance with Atlas. Her eyes reflect the same anticipation he's feeling.

He's nervous to return to the sterile prison where his journey started but is ready to finally confront his past. Once his memories fully return, he can start living in the present. At that thought, a tendril of fear takes hold. What if the memories don't come back and Naya's hypothesis is wrong?

"Then we'll find other evidence to help us," Naya says, startling Atlas. He hadn't realized he'd said it out loud.

"And what if we don't like what we find?" Atlas asks, unable to shake the suddenly overwhelming fear of a past he doesn't like. The Genesis Laboratories logo flashes through his mind, a reminder of his most recent memory. He's not sure what he was doing there, but it didn't sound good.

Naya grabs his hand, jolting him out of his anxious thoughts. "Atlas," she starts, making sure he's looking at her before continuing. "Your past doesn't define you. No matter what you've done, God can forgive you, I can forgive you, and you can forgive yourself."

Atlas looks away, still doubtful. The past is what made him who he is today and he's not so sure it will be easy to forget.

As if reading his mind, Naya says, "Don't let your past shape your present. Focus on each day, moment by moment, as God reveals how he will shape your life for the future. Remember, you're created for eternity, not for a finite amount of time. You just have to put your trust in Him."

"Trust is not easily given these days," Atlas replies, letting his anxiety get the better of him.

Naya is undeterred, squeezing his hand in reassurance. "You learned to trust me. And I'm just some crazy stranger who almost crashed into you on a bike the first time we met."

Atlas gives her a weak chuckle as he remembers that day. He had no idea how much his life would change after that moment.

"Thanks, Naya."

Mr. Jenkins clears his throat awkwardly, disturbing the moment between Naya and Atlas. They look at the old man sheepishly, having all but forgotten he was there.

"Sorry to ruin the moment," Mr. J apologizes with a rueful grin. "Naya is right though, and you've got a good head on your shoulders, kid. Just focus on what's right in front of you and you'll figure it out."

"We'll figure it out together," Naya adds, her words provoking a sense of déjà vu.

Atlas stares at Naya, trying to make sense of the feeling. He gets the sense she's going to tilt her head and say his name, concerned with his sudden blank expression. A few seconds later when she does exactly that, Atlas is stunned. Just before he's about to mention the strange feeling to her, he feels the tug of a memory, giving into the pull.

"Atlas?" a female voice calls out, cutting through the hum of the coffee shop around them.

He looks up to find a familiar pair of brown eyes locked onto him. The rest of her face remains a blur, as if they're caught in a dream.

"How are things?" she prompts, her voice soft yet insistent.

Atlas's thoughts are scattered like leaves in the wind. He stares into the depths of his coffee cup, the dark liquid swirling as if mirroring the turmoil in his mind. As the foam clears, he notices the tired eyes in his reflection.

"Exhausting," he admits. "I miss you."

"You know that's all because of your own choices, right?"

Atlas nods in reply. He's been working himself to the bone, striving to get his new project up and running. It's been exciting, working on such advanced programming, but he's still wary of its potential uses.

"We have a name for it now." Atlas knows she's hesitant about the project. "Nowhere."

The woman's brow furrows in concern. "I worry about you, Atlas," she confesses. "You're diving into something that could change everything."

Atlas meets her gaze with uncertainty. "I know," he says quietly. "But it's important work. If we can harness this technology for good, imagine the possibilities."

She nods, understanding his perspective but still unable to shake her reservations. "Just promise me you'll be careful," she implores, reaching across the table to grasp his hand.

Atlas squeezes her hand reassuringly, offering a faint smile. "I promise," he assures her. "I'll do everything in my power to make sure this project stays on the right path."

"Just know that whatever happens, I'll be right here," she responds. "I care about you, Atlas. We'll figure it out together."

The memory recedes, bringing Atlas back to the present. Mr. Jenkins and Naya stare at him intently, a questioning look on their faces.

"A memory?" Mr. J asks, attempting to piece together what Atlas was doing.

Atlas and Naya both nod in reply.

"Wow, I've never seen you do that before. It's like your brain is taking a vacation from reality." Mr. Jenkins scratches his face in confusion. "Well, I suppose it sort of is, isn't it?" he decides with a chuckle.

"What did you remember?" Naya asks.

Atlas is reluctant to share, realizing he hasn't filled her in on his most recent memories that include Genesis Laboratories. He wants to be more certain before revealing it all, not wanting her to jump to conclusions like he's been doing. Hence, all the talk earlier about a past he won't like.

"I was working on some sort of coding project that was requiring a lot of my energy," Atlas describes, "and the mystery woman didn't like it."

Naya leans back in her chair, her face scrunched up in concentration. Mr. J gives Atlas a confused look and raises his eyebrows.

"Mystery woman?" he questions, a twinkle of intrigue in his eyes.

Atlas glances over at Naya, not really wanting to talk too much about this past woman in front of her. He knows it's not fun to hear.

"Someone I was close to in my past, apparently. Although I can never clearly see her face."

"The brain is a mysterious thing. It only lets you see what you're truly ready to see," the old man remarks.

Rising from his chair, he heads back to his desk, mumbling something about clearing his mind with busy work. Atlas decides to do the same, returning his chair to his workspace.

Naya joins him a bit later, moving as if in a fog. His memories almost seem to affect her more than him sometimes, spurring theories and questions as she tries to puzzle out his past. It's exactly why he's been keeping the logo in his memories a secret. No sense worrying her now when they're so close to unraveling the mysteries for good. At least, that's the hope.

# CHAPTER 33
# NAYA

Bargain Bytes was a flurry of activity the rest of the week, more customers coming out of the woodwork, spooked by the government's project. Naya still can't quite believe it's already Sunday, the day of their trip. Atlas arrived at her doorstep only moments ago, ready to lead Naya to the cabin that will house them for the night. Their goal is to be close enough to reach the facility bright and early tomorrow morning.

"Be safe," her mom says, crushing her into a warm embrace. She does the same to Atlas, though with a little less force. "Take care of my daughter."

"Of course," he replies with a smile. But Naya notices the twinge of betrayal in his eyes, knowing he's leading her into potential danger.

Harper hugs Naya next, wrapping her skinny arms around her with surprising force.

"I hope you get the answers you're looking for," she whispers. "I love you."

Naya is surprised by her sister's words, her intuition spot on once again. Maybe she's just referring to Naya's relationship with Atlas, but her words ring truer than she knows.

"I love you too, Little Butterfly. I'll be back before you know it," Naya says affectionately.

"Make responsible choices," her dad warns as they step out the front door.

"Love you too, Dad," Naya calls back.

He laughs gruffly, waving them off before closing the door. The weight of his words settles over her, adding to the nerves already fluttering in her stomach.

As they venture through her neighborhood, Naya's mind races with worst-case scenarios. Despite their preparations, the unknowns of their journey loom large, casting a shadow of doubt over her confidence.

"Are you sure you're okay to do this?" Atlas's voice breaks through her thoughts.

She gives him a tight-lipped nod, not wanting her voice to betray how she's truly feeling. Atlas gives her a skeptical look, concern evident in his gaze.

"It's okay to be nervous," he assures her, a small smile tugging at the corners of his lips. "I was starting to worry you were getting too excited about this dangerous adventure of ours."

Naya manages a weak smile in return, grateful for his attempt to lighten the mood. Despite her fears, she's comforted in knowing she isn't facing this journey alone.

As they reach the bustling city streets, Atlas takes the lead, weaving through the crowds with ease. Naya follows closely behind, her senses on high alert as they blend into the Sunday morning commuters.

"The forest isn't too far away. But once we're there, we have a bit of a hike ahead of us."

Naya nods. "Any last-minute thoughts before we venture into the unknown?" she asks, voice pitched low to avoid drawing attention.

"We stick together, no matter what."

Atlas leads them out of the city and through a neighborhood on the outskirts of town. They walk along the sidewalk until it ends, leaving them traipsing through dirt roads and fields. It's not long before the sounds of civilization begin to fade, replaced by the quiet rustle of leaves. As they leave the city behind and venture deeper into the forest, Naya takes a deep breath, allowing the fresh scents to wash over her.

"Feels like we're stepping into another world," she muses, her voice barely above a whisper.

Atlas nods in agreement, a sense of anticipation humming in the air between them. Birds chirp in the distance, a distant melody quieting Naya's unease. The forest is beautiful, a place she's never explored before. She watches Atlas move ahead of her, sure-footed and lithe as he maneuvers the underbrush.

The light breeze ruffles his brown hair and Naya is struck by the familiarity of the moment. A similar feeling of anticipation, following a boy heading through the woods. *The dream*, she thinks. *It was Atlas.*

Stunned by her sudden revelation, she trips over a tree root, stumbling forward into Atlas.

"Woah are you okay?" he asks, steadying her from toppling over.

"Yeah, sorry. I was zoning out I guess," Naya replies, debating whether she should reveal her thoughts to him.

His hazel eyes search hers as if he can see all the secrets she's harboring within. "Thank you," he murmurs. "For coming with me. I know it's overwhelming, but it means a lot to me."

His words strike a chord within her and she rushes forward, wrapping her arms around him. For a moment, he just stands there, surprised by her embrace. Then, he hugs her back, resting his chin on her head. They stand like that for a while, finding comfort in each other's arms.

"I didn't realize how much I needed this," Atlas mumbles into her hair.

"Me too," Naya replies, face pressed against his chest.

He smells of fresh pine and crisp outdoor air, a subtle hint of musk mingled within. She enjoys the feeling of his strong arms wrapped around her. He makes her feel safe.

Reluctantly, she pulls away. "I'm glad we're doing this together."

Atlas grins, tucking a stray strand of hair behind her ear. The simple gesture feels electric, the attraction palpable in the air between them. "After all this is over, can I take you on a date?" he asks.

"I'd like that." Naya giggles. "We better get on with it then. The sooner we get there, the sooner it's over."

Heading deeper into the forest, the dense canopy overhead shields them from the harsh summer rays. Atlas remains vigilant by her side, a reassuring presence amongst the wilderness. He offers a steadying hand whenever the uneven terrain threatens to trip her up, his touch a silent promise of protection.

Despite their peaceful surroundings, a sense of urgency hangs in the air, driving them forward with purpose. The weight of what lies ahead presses down on Naya, adding to the growing ache of carrying her heavy backpack.

As they continue their path, Atlas breaks the silence around them. "We're getting close," he explains, surveying the surrounding area.

Only a few minutes later, Naya spots the dark brown logs of a rustic cabin. Relief floods through her, excited for a chance to rest. The sound of a trickling stream greets them as they approach the front porch. It's a rather idyllic spot, the cabin built into a small clearing in the forest. She pictures a frightened Atlas stumbling upon this place, grateful for the shelter after fleeing for his life. It's hard to imagine what that would've been like.

Continuing toward the cabin, Atlas's arm shoots out without warning, preventing her from moving closer to the cabin. Looking ahead, she sees the door is halfway open, the peaceful sanctuary suddenly feeling very ominous.

"Wait here," he warns.

Atlas quietly ascends the steps, opening the creaky door and disappearing into the cabin. It's eerily similar to her dream when he stepped over the threshold and was swallowed by the darkness within. Naya's heart races at the thought, suddenly overwhelmed with worry. Her body is taut with apprehension, her senses on high alert.

She hears a scuffle inside and instinctively moves closer, wanting to aid Atlas in whatever he's discovered.

"Atlas?" she calls, hoping to hear his voice.

She takes a shaky step onto the porch just as something comes flying toward her out of the cabin. Naya screams in terror, tripping over herself to get away before landing in a heap on the ground. Nearby, a squirrel eyes her innocently as though it didn't just scare her half to death.

"Naya!" Atlas yells, rushing out of the cabin to check on her. "What happened?"

She tries to catch her breath, embarrassed by her extreme overreaction. "Sorry, the squirrel scared me."

Atlas takes in the sight of her sitting on the ground. He tries to hold back his laughter but fails miserably. Getting up, she smacks him playfully in the arm as she pushes past him into the cabin.

Worn wooden furniture adorns the interior. Though cozy, it's seen better days. A fine layer of dust coats everything and leaves and other debris are scattered across the wood flooring.

"It could be worse," Atlas comments, attempting to shut the broken door behind them. "I wasn't really thinking about leaving it how I found it when I broke the door, was I."

Naya sets her backpack on the small table in the kitchen before settling into the armchair by the fireplace. She kicks her boots off and sets her feet on the coffee table.

"Make yourself at home," Atlas jokes, finding a seat in the armchair opposite her. "So how should we spend the rest of our afternoon?"

Naya lists the options in her head, deciding what would kill the most time. She also considers the possibility that everything could change after this trip and realizes she wants to enjoy her time with Atlas as he is now. Hauling herself out of the armchair, she searches through the cabin in search of a game. Atlas watches her curiously as she does, a wide grin forming on his face when her search yields a deck of cards.

"What are we playing?" he asks, as they sit on the floor around the coffee table.

Naya skillfully shuffles the cards, dealing one to each of them. "I don't know the official name for it, but it's a game my family and I like to call Trump or Dump."

She explains the rules to him, detailing the process of adding cards each round and betting on how many hands you think you'll win.

"Remember, the lowest score wins in this game."

Atlas nods, still processing all the rules she just laid out. "Why do you call it Trump or Dump?"

"Because you either have a lead card, a trump, or you have a bunch of cards you need to get rid of, or dump. It's more fun with additional players, but for your first time, two people will be plenty." She gives him a playful grin as she reveals the trump card for the round. "Don't worry, I'll take it easy on you."

"Don't bother," Atlas remarks. "You know I like a good challenge."

An hour later, Atlas places the leading suit for the round, taking the last trick and earning Naya another point.

"How are you so good at this?" Naya grumbles, adding a tally to her rather embarrassingly long list of points.

"Beginner's luck?" Atlas suggests with a shrug.

"You're sure you haven't played this before?"

"Nope. Although I will say I'm a natural!" He gives her a cocky grin.

Naya scoffs playfully. "Reign it in, Mr. Confident. I still have time to dump on you yet."

Atlas chuckles at her determination and silly phrasing. He deals out the next round of cards and they stare at their hands, determining their moves.

By the time they've gone back down to one card, Naya has made quite the comeback.

"One." Naya figures she'll take this trick easily with her high card.

"One," Atlas responds, a competitive gleam in his eyes.

They stare at each other from across the table, trying to guess who's bluffing. With a growl, Naya smacks her card on the table and Atlas follows suit.

"What are the odds that you had a trump card?" Naya bellows, her outrage sending Atlas into a fit of laughter.

"I'm glad you find my anger amusing," she retorts, unable to keep a smile off her face.

"I didn't realize you were so competitive," he says, gathering the cards into a neat stack and putting them back in their box.

He stands, putting the cards back in the drawer and then moving toward the door. "Want to go for a walk?"

# CHAPTER 34

# ᗅTLᗅS

Stepping out into the afternoon sunlight, Naya and Atlas venture on a short walk around the cabin. The sounds of the forest envelop them, calming some of Atlas's nerves about the uncertainties that lie ahead. As they walk amongst the trees, Atlas notices the way Naya stares at the forest in awe.

"God really is the most magnificent artist," Naya notes, crouching down to touch the purple petals of a wildflower.

"An artist? I'd never pictured him that way." Atlas envisions an old man with a beard, a paintbrush in one hand and a palette in the other.

He notices Naya squinting at him as if she can see the mental image he's now pondering.

"He is the designer of the universe, after all. I can't imagine coming up with so many different creations!" She rises to a stand, leaning against the trunk of a nearby tree. "Just think of all the complexities in nature alone. It's astounding."

Atlas looks around at the forest, trying to see it through Naya's perspective. Despite his efforts, it just looks like a forest to him. Yet when he turns his gaze to Naya, a spark of appreciation flashes through him.

She catches him staring and a light blush colors her cheeks. His eyes flick to her lips and heat prickles along the back of his neck. He's always thought Naya is beautiful, but since getting to know her, she's become nothing short of stunning in his eyes.

Breaking through his reverie, Naya walks over to him and reaches out her hand. "Can I see your hand for a moment?" she asks softly.

Atlas nods, offering his hand to her with a raised brow, his curiosity piqued.

"If it's hard to see in nature, maybe you can see it in yourself. Take your hand for example," she begins, her voice filled with awe. "It's not just a tool used for holding and manipulating objects. It's a marvel of engineering, capable of performing intricate tasks with incredible precision."

Taking her other hand, she lightly traces his fingers. "Your fingers, for example," she continues, gently flexing them one by one, "are each equipped with muscles, tendons, and joints that work together to provide a wide range of mobility."

Naya directs her attention to the swirling lines etched into his skin. "And these lines," she says, "are not just random markings. They uniquely identify you. There are no others like them in the world."

Atlas listens intently, a newfound appreciation for his own hand blossoming within him. He never considered the complexity of something so seemingly ordinary.

"I've never stopped to think about my hand that way before," he admits.

Naya smiles softly, now marveling at her own hands. "Humans are remarkable creations. We're a testament to the intricacy of God's design."

She looks up at him then, staring intently into his eyes. He gazes back, tracing the swell of her cheek down to the delicate line of her jaw.

Atlas notices the way her lips curve into a soft smile, her eyes full of excitement and warmth. In that moment, he's struck by an overwhelming gratitude for Naya's radiant presence in his life.

"What?" she murmurs, her head dipping shyly in response to his appreciative gaze. "Is there something in my hair?"

Atlas shakes his head and smiles. "It's still a little hard to fathom God designing the world, but when I look at you, I see it clearly. You are a masterpiece, Naya, both inside and out."

"I could say the same for you," she whispers, meeting his gaze.

Atlas is filled with a mixture of nervousness and exhilaration as he leans in closer to Naya, his heart pounding in his chest. He reaches out to touch her face, gently brushing his lips against hers.

"Can I kiss you?" he murmurs, his voice barely audible above the rustling of the leaves.

In response, Naya stands on her tiptoes, closing the distance between them as she presses her lips against his.

Time seems to slow down, the worries about tomorrow fading into the background. Atlas is consumed by Naya's touch, the feeling of her soft lips against his.

When they finally pull away, Atlas's heart is still racing with the intensity of the moment.

"So much for putting our feelings on the backburner," Naya muses.

Atlas laughs softly, lacing his fingers through hers and leading them to the stream. "You have no idea how long I've wanted to do that," he exclaims.

"And here I was thinking you were too distracted by your past to be thinking about me," Naya replies playfully.

Atlas stops in his tracks, tugging Naya closer. He wraps an arm around her waist, his other hand tilting her chin to look up at him.

"Never," he says, searching her eyes for understanding. "I'm so sorry I ever made you feel that way."

Atlas sees a hint of hurt in her eyes and knows she's thinking about that night on the roof. "Naya, there's nowhere I'd rather be than with you."

"Nowhere?" she reiterates, shock evident in her tone.

"Nowhere," he vows.

The word hits him like a shockwave, sending a cascade of darkness over his thoughts as he descends into another memory.


"Nowhere?" the young man sitting next to him asks.

Atlas glances around, recognizing the familiar workspace as his own. Looking back to his left, he notices it's the man with the butterfly tattoo on his hand. *Michael*, Atlas thinks, the man's name suddenly coming back to him.

"Who came up with that?" Michael asks.

"I did, why? Do you not like it?" Atlas asks, slightly offended.

Michael shrugs and turns back to his screen, fingers clicking away on his keyboard. Atlas does the same, returning his attention to the lines of code on the monitor in front of him. He begins typing the next line, deep in concentration as he determines the right sequence.

"Oh, I get it!" Michael says suddenly, interrupting Atlas's thought process. "Because they really aren't going anywhere, it's all in their head."

"Sort of," Atlas replies. "I was thinking more about the mystery behind the program. It's a space that doesn't physically exist, a different type of no man's land, the true location unknown."

Michael stares at him in confusion and Atlas sighs in frustration.

"Like a realm that's disconnected from our world. It doesn't fit the usual constraints of time and space," he continues, trying to explain his thought process further.

"Sure, whatever you say, boss."

"I told you not to call me that," Atlas admonishes. "Just because I'm the lead on this project doesn't mean we aren't still best friends."

"Oh? I thought your new best friend was this project," Michael jokes. "You do spend most of your time with *it* these days."

Atlas punches Michael in the arm. He doesn't need another person in his life telling him to step away from this project. It's important work, wherever it may lead.

With a sharp inhale, the sounds and scents of the forest return. As the memory fades, Atlas blinks, taking in the gentle rustle of leaves and babble of the stream around him. He feels the warmth of Naya's hand in his and turns to see her worried face.

"Her again?" she asks nervously.

"No," he replies, noticing the immediate relief that floods into her brown eyes. "It was the man with the butterfly tattoo. Michael, apparently."

"What happened?"

Atlas rehashes the memory, trying to recall all the details, while Naya listens intently.

"Project Nowhere? That's new. Seems important, too," Naya says thoughtfully.

Atlas grimaces, suddenly feeling horrible for keeping things from her. "It's new to you," he replies quietly, watching as she registers his comment.

"You already had a memory about it? And you didn't tell me?" Her voice is full of disappointment, adding a weight to her words heavier than anger ever could.

"I'm sorry. I was scared," Atlas confesses. "And there's something else you should know."

Her expression is grim, preparing for whatever he might say next.

"I saw the Genesis Laboratories logo on the wall in one of my memories, too." Atlas watches as the weight of his words sinks in.

Naya bites her lip in thought, suddenly walking away from him toward the stream. He follows, watching as she finds a large moss-covered rock to sit on. She stares out at the water, avoiding eye contact.

"Do you know why you were there?" she questions.

"I was in an office," he replies vaguely.

"Your office," she states matter-of-factly.

"Yes, it seemed that way."

The silence stretches between them, both contemplating the implications of these memories. Atlas knows Naya will come to the same conclusion he has, that he used to work on the VR project. What he still can't figure out is how he ended up being a test subject for the project, too.

"So, you used to work for this company," Naya starts. "And it's likely you were helping to build the VR program."

Atlas moves closer, trying to read the expression on her face. She sighs again, picking up a nearby rock and throwing it in the stream. It makes a gentle splash, creating a momentary ripple amidst the flowing water.

"It sort of makes sense," she says quietly, as if thinking out loud.

"What does?"

Naya looks over at him. "I suppose it's my turn to share a revelation."

Atlas raises a brow, surprised by her confession.

"Before I met you, I had a dream. It was about a boy running through the woods. But, you know, it was a dream, so it had a weird twist as they always do."

Atlas listens carefully, not sure where she's going with this.

"He was running toward an exit door in the middle of the woods," she continues, her eyes searching his for understanding.

Atlas is stunned, taken aback by how similar her dream sounds to his experience before waking up at the facility.

"Atlas," Naya says, waiting to speak until she knows she has his full attention. "It wasn't until we were walking through the woods earlier today that I realized it was you."

Atlas braces himself on a nearby tree, attempting to wrap his mind around what she's saying. He has no idea how something like this would even be possible.

"I don't know how," Naya acknowledges, echoing his inner thoughts. "But I'm fairly certain it was you."

Atlas nods his head. "I remember that. It was right before I woke up in my hospital room."

Naya's eyes widen in surprise at his confirmation. She beckons him closer with an outstretched arm. Atlas takes her hand and sits beside her on the rock.

"What does this mean?" he asks, knowing Naya doesn't have the answer.

"We don't know now, but hopefully we will tomorrow."

# CHAPTER 35
# NAYA

The first light of dawn shines through the loft window, illuminating the specks of dust floating through the air. Naya can hear Atlas's deep breathing beside her on the bed, a makeshift pillow barrier between them. Naya suggested it as a solution for sharing the bed, though Atlas originally wanted to be a gentleman and sleep on the floor.

Propping herself up on one arm, she lets herself linger in the moment a little longer. Atlas looks so peaceful in his sleep, his slight brown curls falling over his forehead. Naya brushes one away, her heart pounding when his lashes flutter in response.

She hates to leave him like this, but she needs to stick to her plan. Yesterday made things more complicated than she would've liked and she's kicking herself for giving in to her feelings. It just makes what she has to do more difficult than it already was.

Carefully, Naya rolls out of bed, not wanting to wake him. Grabbing a small piece of paper and pen out of her backpack, she jots a quick note.

*Atlas,*
*I'm sorry for leaving without saying goodbye. Please don't come after me. I'll see you soon.*
*P.S. You better take me on that date when I get back.*

Gathering her things, she exits the cabin as quietly as possible. Last night, she talked through the plan with Atlas, getting him to tell her the directions to the facility from here. It's a decent jaunt, but she should make it in time to arrive with the other human trial volunteers.

The grass is damp with morning dew, making everything glisten in the sunlight. Naya can feel her hair start to frizz in the humidity. She tries to focus on her surroundings, not wanting to get lost along the way. Atlas's directions made it seem like it was a pretty straight shot to the facility.

The silence around her does little to keep her attention, her mind wandering back to Atlas. Their kiss replays in her head, the memory of his lips against hers sending a rush of warmth through her veins. A fiery blush spreads across her cheeks as she recalls the moment in vivid detail. The gentle touch of his hand against her cheek, the soft intensity of his gaze—it's a memory she won't soon forget.

Naya ponders what lies ahead for them. The revelation of Atlas's connection to Genesis Laboratories only adds to the complexity of their situation, leaving her with more questions than answers.

Thoughts of his confession to withholding memories still evoke a sense of betrayal. She mentally chides herself, knowing she has no right to feel that way considering how badly she's betraying him now. Picturing him waking up to find her gone makes her quicken her pace. She surges forward, her determination guiding her closer to the answers she seeks.

While she walks, Naya reviews the details of her strategy. Posing as a volunteer for human trial testing will get her into the facility, but it's after that where things get difficult. She'll need to use her limited knowledge of the space to navigate the halls undetected. It's a risky plan, but one she's willing to face for fear of Atlas being caught. After all, they know his face, not hers.

Up ahead, the trees begin to give way to a clearing. Naya squints to see further, spotting the imposing presence of a gray building beyond. The sight sends a shiver down her spine, but she refuses to let fear deter her.

Drawing closer, she takes in the building's architecture, noticing the lack of windows. A rusted metal staircase runs alongside the part of the building currently facing her. It stands in stark contrast to the natural surroundings, a reminder of the power and secrecy that lay within.

Taking a deep breath to steady her nerves, Naya stashes her backpack behind a fallen tree nearby. She runs along the tree line, finding the road that leads to the entrance. Crouching down amidst the cover of the underbrush, she waits for the others to arrive.

A short while later, she hears the hum of an engine followed by the bright yellow flash of a bus approaching the road. Naya dashes to the side of the building, heart racing as she presses herself against the brick. Peeking around the side, she watches as the bus slows to a halt near the front doors. Facility staff wait by the entrance, preparing to greet the volunteers. The bus doors swing open, and people begin exiting.

Now's her chance.

Naya smooths her hair and checks over her appearance, hoping she'll blend in with the other volunteers. Steeling her resolve, she waits until the staff are looking the other way and slips into the crowd of people now entering the facility. A few of the volunteers give her a strange look, noticing her sudden appearance. Thankfully, they don't say anything, focused on following the staff through the maze of halls.

"Welcome to Genesis Laboratories," says a woman with a friendly smile. "We're so glad you've decided to join us today."

Naya tunes out the woman's introductory spiel in favor of scanning her new surroundings. The interior is pristine and sterile, with bright fluorescent lights illuminating the space. She tries to keep her head down as she looks, avoiding eye contact with the other volunteers and staff members. An undercurrent of anticipation and nervous energy is palpable among the group.

As they reach a large room with rows of chairs and medical equipment, Naya's pulse quickens. The staff begin dividing the volunteers into smaller groups, each assigned to a different room. Naya keeps close to the back of the crowd, trying to locate the nearest exit. Panic rises up as she realizes there are none in sight.

"Nelly Blackwell," a male nurse calls.

A murmur goes through the remaining volunteers and Naya realizes this is the second time they've called that name.

"I'm here, sorry." She races to the front of the crowd, her heart pounding in her chest.

The young man looks around her age, his eyes widening slightly as she approaches. He almost looks more nervous than her, but she has no idea why.

"Follow me," he says, voice shaky.

Naya follows behind him through a set of double doors. As they enter the room beyond, Naya swallows nervously at the rows of futuristic-looking machines lining the walls. Each one emits a soft hum, adding to the eerie atmosphere.

She's guided to a hospital bed where she sits uncomfortably. Naya's hands fidget nervously in her lap as she waits for the next instructions, worried for what comes next. The room feels cold and clinical, sending goosebumps along her arms as she glances around anxiously.

She scolds herself for not slipping away sooner, regret gnawing at her as she realizes the gravity of her situation. But it's too late now—she's already confined to a separate room.

"I'll be right back," the man says, rushing out of the room.

Now alone, Naya wastes no time, her instincts kicking into high gear as she searches the room for anything useful. She rifles through drawers and cabinets, her hands moving swiftly as she searches for any useful tools or information.

Every second feels like an eternity as she scours the room for any signs of a clue. Naya frantically searches, her eyes landing on a computer nestled in the opposite corner of the room. Ignoring the panic rising in her chest, she hurries over to the terminal and powers it on, fingers flying across the keyboard as she attempts to bypass the login screen.

With each failed attempt, her frustration grows. She searches the nearby desk and drawers for anything that might indicate the password, refusing to give up. If she can gain access to the system, she might be able to uncover valuable information.

Footsteps grow louder in the hallway and Naya freezes. Her heart thunders in her ears as she runs back across the room, sitting hurriedly on the bed. Relief floods through her when the footsteps pass and the doors remain closed. *Enough of this*, Naya thinks. *Just focus on getting out of this room.*

She moves to the door, pressing her ear against it to listen for movement. After a few beats of silence, Naya grabs the door handle just as it begins turning from the other side.

Before she can turn back, the door swings open, revealing the male nurse from before. She barely registers the surprised look on his face, panic overtaking her. Caught red-handed, Naya backs away, bracing herself for whatever consequences lay ahead.

The man shuts the door behind him, locking it with a soft click. Fear courses through her veins, tears threatening to spill over. *Not again*, she thinks. *This can't happen to me again.*

As he moves closer, something on his hand catches her attention, jolting her out of her panic. It's a butterfly tattoo. Snapping her head up to meet his gaze, the man stops in his tracks.

"Naya, what are you doing here?" he questions, sending the world crumbling around her.

They know who she is.

# CHAPTER 36
# ATLAS

Stretching, Atlas yawns awake, content from a good night's sleep. He was worried he wouldn't be able to sleep from all his worries about today, but Naya's presence nearby worked wonders.

Atlas reaches his arm over the pillow barricade, sitting upright in a panic when he realizes the bed is empty.

"Naya?" he calls out, stumbling out of bed and down the stairs.

His bare feet sound loud against the wood floors, echoing in the empty cabin. Naya is gone.

Atlas searches the small space, his panic rising with each passing moment. Even though it's easy to tell she's not here, he checks every corner. His mind races with a dozen different scenarios, each more terrifying than the last. Has something happened to her? Is she in danger?

Fighting back the overwhelming sense of fear, Atlas forces himself to think logically. Maybe she went for a walk. He rushes out the front door, searching around the cabin.

"Naya!" he calls again. No response.

*Perhaps she left a note explaining where she went,* he thinks, returning to the cabin.

Running inside, Atlas spots a piece of paper scuttling across the floor. It must've fallen during his search around the cabin. He collapses onto the ground next to it, scooping it off the floor. A pit forms in his stomach, the words on the page making him feel sick. Atlas turns the paper over, hoping there's more on the back. Finding nothing, he sprints to his things and hurriedly begins packing. Why would she leave without him? And did she seriously think he wouldn't come after her?

He leans into his anger, knowing it will drown out the hurt of betrayal. Atlas focuses on the task at hand, not allowing his brain to run rampant with fear. Adrenaline fuels his movements, and he tries to avoid picturing all the worst-case scenarios. He hopes she hasn't been gone long. Maybe he can stop her before she gets there.

With a final glance around the cabin, Atlas pulls the door as shut as possible and takes off sprinting through the forest. Leaves crunch underfoot and he's reminded again of his VR experience. But rather than trying to escape the danger, he's running headlong toward it.

The trees fly past in a blur, several seeming to blink in and out of existence as he runs. Sweat breaks out across his brow and he swipes it away. Atlas tries to pace himself, but adrenaline still courses through him, urging him onwards faster and faster. Suddenly, Atlas remembers the comms device stashed in his backpack.

Skidding to a halt, he slings it off his back and rifles through it. When his hands touch the cool metal of the device, he grabs hold, turns the power dial, and shoves it in his ear.

"Naya! Are you there?" he calls into the device, straining to hear anything over the crackling static. His fear returns when there is no reply.

Not wanting to waste any time, Atlas zips his bag and throws it back on, taking off through the forest once again. He attempts using the device several more times on his journey, hoping she'll respond the closer he gets. But she never does. Knowing he must be getting close to the facility, his hope of running into her fades.

Finally, Atlas sees the building in the distance, the familiar staircase he escaped on visible from this side. Pausing at the edge of the tree line, he pulls out his nurse disguise. Hiding behind a thick tree trunk, Atlas changes into the scrubs and surgical cap. He puts the mask in his pocket for later.

Scanning his surroundings for a place to stash his stuff, he notices a fallen tree. As he makes his way over, his heart leaps at the sight of Naya's backpack.

She's here.

He snaps his head up, trying to spot her with no success. Setting his backpack next to hers, Atlas tries to think of a way inside the building. This was the part he and Naya knew they'd have to improvise, though now he knows she had a different plan altogether.

Atlas wants to throw caution to the wind knowing she's inside, not caring if he's spotted walking in. He stops himself, though, knowing he won't be able to help her if he gets caught.

The minutes pass painfully slow, every second increasing the likelihood that something could happen to Naya. Finally, Atlas watches as two nurses exit the building from the second story emergency exit. They stand on the staircase, leaning up against the railing as they chat. Their laughter echoes around them, making its way to Atlas and spurring another memory.

"Make sure it shuts behind you," Michael says, motioning to the emergency exit. "Wouldn't want our secret break spot to be discovered."

Atlas complies, pulling the door shut behind him. He joins Michael on the second-story landing of the rickety emergency staircase, the metal groaning softly under their weight. Leaning against the rusted railing, they gaze out into the dense forest that stretches before them.

Ever since they discovered the second floor's emergency exit was broken, Atlas and Michael have used it as their hangout. It's nice to escape from the sterile walls of the lab, even if only for a moment. Out here is the only place they can talk without prying eyes and ears.

The cool breeze rustles through the leaves, carrying with it the earthy scent of the woods. For a moment, they are just two friends taking a break from the chaos of their lives.

"I can't shake the feeling that something's off about Project Nowhere," Michael says, keeping his voice hushed. "The further we get with it, the more I worry they will go back on their word."

"I signed a contract, Michael. Genesis Laboratories is legally bound to my stipulations if they want me to continue with Project Nowhere," Atlas reassures him, though a seed of doubt is now planted in his mind.

"It's the government," Michael replies, his dark brown eyes filled with skepticism. "They're not always the most trustworthy."

Atlas nods in agreement, his gaze fixed on the distant horizon. "I can't say I haven't had that thought. I know I could be opening a Pandora's box with what I'm creating."

"But you want to change lives for the better, I know," Michael says, finishing his thought for him.

They've had this conversation many times, though this one feels more pertinent. Atlas clenches the metal railing, feeling worried and overwhelmed.

"I don't have all the answers, Michael. But I do know we shouldn't let fear dictate our actions." Atlas gives him an exasperated look. "We just need to stay vigilant, keep pushing forward, and trust that our intentions will guide us in the right direction."

The sound of the door closing brings Atlas back to the present. Rubbing his temples to reduce the oncoming headache, he makes sure the nurses have gone back inside. Certain no one else is around to watch him, Atlas sprints out of the forest to the staircase. He tries to keep his footsteps light, but the metal creaks under his weight.

As he reaches the second story exit, Atlas tugs gently on the handle. *Let's hope it's still broken,* he thinks. With a soft click, the door opens. Relief washes over him as he slips quietly inside and shuts the door behind him. He quickly pulls the surgical mask out of his pocket and straps it on, hoping his disguise will keep him undiscovered for as long as it takes to find Naya.

Atlas moves cautiously through the labyrinth of sterile white corridors. Memories of his escape dance at the edges of his mind, threatening to consume him. He tries to push them aside, focusing on his current mission to find Naya.

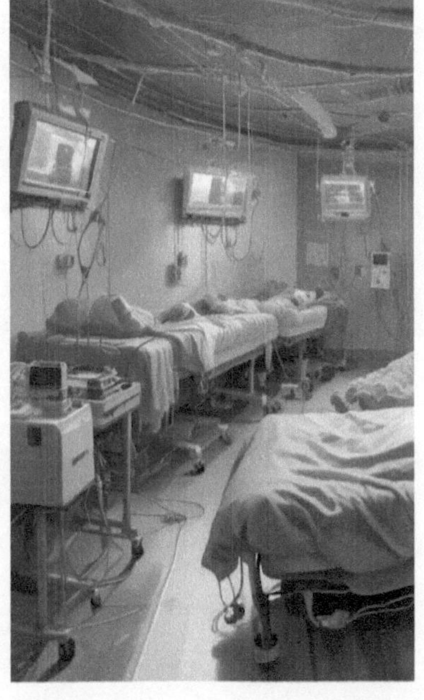

Peeking through the small windows of each door he passes, Atlas scans the rooms for any sign of Naya's presence. Some contain patients undergoing various tests, their faces uncertain. Others lie motionless on hospital beds, hooked up to an array of equipment like Atlas once was.

The sound of footsteps approaches around the next corner and Atlas panics. He frantically looks for an unoccupied room nearby, spotting one a few feet away. Atlas hesitates momentarily before pushing the door open and closing it as carefully as possible. He stands with his back against the wall, heart pounding as he hears the footsteps pass outside.

As the echoes of the footsteps fade, Atlas takes a moment to compose himself. He scans the room, his eyes adjusting to the light filtering in through the small window.

Rows of filing cabinets line the walls, their metal surfaces reflecting the muted glow. Atlas moves carefully, his steps silent as he navigates between the cabinets. Pulling open the nearest one, he sees files filled with documents containing patient information. Atlas's hands tremble with a mixture of anticipation and fear. This room could hold the answers he's been searching for.

Rapidly, Atlas searches through files for any clues that might lead him to Naya or mention his name. With each passing moment, his heart beats a little faster, the weight of his precarious situation pressing down on him. Time is of the essence and every second spent in this room could put Naya in jeopardy, but he can't afford to miss anything that might help them uncover the truth.

While Atlas sifts through the documents, the sound of footsteps approaching causes him to freeze. He quickly hides behind a row of cabinets as a nurse enters the room, flipping on the lights.

The nurse, engrossed in her task, moves to a nearby filing cabinet and begins rifling through the folders. Atlas holds his breath, praying she won't notice him crouched in the shadows.

Just as he starts to relax, the nurse pauses, her gaze sweeping the room. Atlas's heart pounds in his ears as their eyes meet for a fleeting moment. In that instant, he knows he's been discovered.

Before the nurse can react, Atlas bolts from his hiding spot and darts out of the room, his pulse racing with adrenaline. He needs to find Naya quickly and get them out of here before they're both caught.

# CHAPTER 37

# NAYA

Naya is silent, her gaze locked on the man with suspicion. She edges backward instinctively as he steps closer, her heart hammering in her chest.

"I don't want to hurt you," he assures her, holding his hands up in surrender. "I just wasn't expecting to see you here."

"Who are you?" Naya demands, her voice tight with apprehension. She watches him warily, her mind racing with questions.

"My name is Micah. I'm a friend," he offers cryptically, though his words do little to ease her tension. "You need to listen to what I'm about to say very carefully. It might come as a shock, but it's important."

Naya gives him a wary look, but stays quiet, waiting for him to continue. He opens his mouth but says nothing, as if he's having trouble finding the words. She furrows her brow at him, confused about what might be so hard to explain. Her patience wears thin as the seconds tick by.

"The butterfly," he finally begins, pointing to the tattoo on his hand. "Remember—"

Before he can finish his sentence, Micah's demeanor shifts abruptly, his expression going blank. Seconds later, a smile spreads across his face and he tilts his head in a friendly manner.

"Sorry about that, I just lost my train of thought." His voice has lost the urgency from before, his tone now light and casual. "Why don't you have a seat on the bed?"

Naya shakes her head adamantly, not wanting to move from her spot against the wall. Micah moves closer, this time in a more urgent manner. He reaches out to grab her but before he can, the door bursts open and a man rushes into the room.

Naya glances over Micah's shoulder, noticing the panicked look on the man's face. He looks right at her, and she immediately recognizes his hazel eyes.

Atlas.

"Naya!" he shouts, tearing off his mask and rushing toward her.

Before he can reach her, two men come barreling through the doors, seizing Atlas by the arms. Naya's heart lurches with dread as she watches them restrain him, her fists clenching in frustration. She surges forward but Micah grabs hold of her, keeping her at bay.

"Let go of him!" she cries out, struggling against Micah's grip as she tries to break free. But he holds her firmly, Naya unable to move as the men subdue Atlas.

"They've become an issue," one of the men holding Atlas says, his voice cold and authoritative.

"I'll grab the sedative," Micah announces, handing her off to one of the men.

Meanwhile, the other man grapples with Atlas, their struggle echoing through the sterile room. With practiced precision, he manages to pin Atlas against the wall, pressing one of his cheeks firmly against the cold brick surface. Atlas's hands are held firmly behind his back, rendering him temporarily powerless against his captors.

"It's going to be okay, Naya. We'll get through this," Atlas manages, prompting the man to press him harder against the wall.

"I told you not to follow," Naya replies.

"You really thought I could stay away?" He attempts to give her a grin.

"Shut up," the man restraining him warns.

Naya stumbles forward as she's pushed toward the hospital bed. She struggles against the man holding her, but to no avail. He shoves her onto the bed and straps her to it. Naya watches helplessly as Micah approaches Atlas, a needle in hand.

"I thought you said you were a friend!" Naya accuses.

Micah glares at her from across the room, unrelenting in his pursuit. Naya struggles against her restraints as she watches Micah tilt Atlas's head. He leans in as if inspecting Atlas's scar before plunging the needle into his neck.

"Atlas!" Naya's voice reverberates through the room, filled with horror at the sight of Atlas slumping to the floor. "What are you going to do with us?"

The men pay no mind to her cries, their faces impassive and unmoved by her desperation. Micah calmly disposes of the needle, his actions calculated and deliberate.

"I'll take it from here," Micah says softly, grabbing hold of Atlas and dragging him out of the room. There's a finality in his tone that sends a chill down Naya's spine.

Her scream echoes after them, a cry of anguish and despair. A tear slides down her cheek, her heart breaking as she watches Atlas's lifeless body disappear down the hallway. Despite Naya's best efforts, she couldn't keep him safe.

Nurses enter her room, obscuring her view. They grab various equipment and wheel them toward her bed. Their actions are blurred through Naya's tears as they approach, fear coursing through her veins. Continuing to struggle against her restraints, she's shocked by the cold grip of one of the nurses as she holds one of her arms still.

"What are you going to do?" Naya watches as the nurse sterilizes her skin with a wipe.

The other nurse preps an IV line, passing it off before setting up another machine.

"Please don't do this," Naya begs, wincing as the needle pierces her skin.

Suddenly, the room is filled with the buzz of machinery, the bed lowering beneath her. The ceiling comes into view as Naya is laid flat against the rough cotton sheets beneath her. She hears the click of dress shoes against the linoleum floors approach her bed and turns to find the source. A well-dressed man in a suit now stands beside her bed, staring down at her.

"Hello, Naya."

"Let us go," she pleads, knowing it's a longshot. "You don't have to do this."

"Oh, but we do." He leans in to brush a strand of hair away from her face.

Naya recoils, his touch triggering flashbacks from the night in the alley. Bile rises in her throat.

"Why?" she demands, voice hoarse from the screaming and crying.

"You know too much."

"Know what?" she questions. He doesn't answer. "What are you going to do with Atlas?"

"Don't worry about him, sweetheart. Before long, you won't remember a thing," he replies.

"What do you mean?" she frets, his statement sending a fresh wave of fear through her body.

The man smiles before backing away, murmuring something to the nurses. They quickly gather around her, busying themselves with the machines and equipment. A cold ache snakes its way up her arm and she knows they've started the IV.

"What's in that?" She tries to make eye contact with the nurses, but they refuse to look at her.

The world grows hazy, spots dancing at the edge of her vision. Her eyelids grow heavy, and she battles to keep them open.

"Don't wipe them all. We wouldn't want her forgetting her own name now, would we?" The man instructs, his deep voice echoing through the room.

It's the last thing she hears before she loses the fight against sleep.

# CHAPTER 38

# ATLAS

Atlas is shaken awake, confused by his surroundings. Blinking against the harsh fluorescent lights, he tries to push through the fog in his brain.

"Atlas, focus!" a man's voice says, his face temporarily shielding Atlas from the blinding lights.

"Where am I?" Atlas questions, memories of the moment before he lost consciousness flashing through his mind.

He remembers Naya's frightened face, and jolts upright, suddenly determined to get back to her. Atlas notices the hospital chair underneath him and tries to stand. He sways on his feet, still dizzy from whatever drug he was injected with.

"Take it easy, man."

"Who are you?"

The man's face comes into focus, and he recognizes him as the nurse who sedated him. Atlas jerks back in surprise, fearful of what he plans to do next.

"Micah," the man says, extending his hand for Atlas to shake.

He remains glued to his chair, unwilling to shake this stranger's hand. Atlas's eyes spot a butterfly tattoo, and he snaps his head up to inspect Micah. The man is blonde and blue-eyed, nothing like Michael from his memories. But it seems like a strange coincidence they both have a butterfly tattooed on their hand.

"Are you awake now? I need you fully alert for this," Micah says, waving his hand in front of Atlas's face.

Atlas scowls. "I'm fine, no thanks to you."

"Sorry, it had to be done to avoid drawing suspicion," Micah apologizes, glancing out the small window in the door. "I gave you the smallest dose so it wouldn't take you as long to wake up."

Atlas contemplates the man's explanation, unsure what his motives are. "What are they doing with Naya?"

"We can't worry about that right now. She'll be fine if I can convince you to wake up," Micah states, pacing across the room.

"I am awake," Atlas retorts.

"No, you're not." Micah's movements still as he turns to face Atlas with a serious expression. "None of this is real."

Atlas laughs at the absurdity of his statement. Micah narrows his eyes in reply, crossing his arms with a huff.

"Take this seriously!" he scolds, approaching Atlas in his chair.

Atlas leans back at his close proximity but can't avoid Micah as he flicks Atlas's forehead. "It's all in that thick head of yours."

"Ow! What was that for?" Atlas exclaims, perturbed by his actions.

This man is crazy.

"Atlas, you're in a virtual reality simulation right now." Micah's gaze is unwavering as he watches Atlas's reaction.

Atlas scoffs, his disbelief evident in his expression. "I don't know what you're trying to pull, but it's not working. You're crazy," he replies, his instinct urging him to retreat from the situation.

But Micah isn't deterred, stepping forward to block Atlas's path to the door. "Please, hear me out," he implores, his voice full of urgency.

Frustration mounting, Atlas shoves Micah's hand aside and takes a step toward the door. He needs to get away from this man as fast as possible. But Micah's next words stop him in his tracks.

"Do you want to save Naya or not?" Micah's question pierces through Atlas's defenses, stirring something within him.

Turning to look at Micah, Atlas hesitates, his mind racing with conflicting thoughts. He notices the pleading look on Micah's face and relents, albeit reluctantly.

"Two minutes. That's all I'm giving you," he concedes, leaning against the wall with a wary gaze fixed on Micah.

As he begins to speak, Atlas braces himself for whatever revelations may come. Two minutes won't be enough time to convince him he's in a fake reality, but he hopes this encounter will at least lead him closer to rescuing Naya.

"I know this sounds unbelievable, but you have to trust me. What you're experiencing right now isn't real. It's a simulation created by Genesis Laboratories."

Atlas narrows his eyes, skepticism painted across his features. "Why should I believe you? And even if what you're saying is true, how do you expect me to save Naya from inside this… simulation?"

Micah meets Atlas's gaze head-on, his expression earnest. "I understand your doubts, but think about it, Atlas. Does any of this feel right? The inconsistencies, the gaps in your memory… It's all designed to keep you trapped."

Atlas's brow furrows as he processes Micah's words. Despite his initial resistance, a seed of doubt begins to take root in his mind. "How do I know you're not just trying to manipulate me?"

"I don't expect you to trust me blindly," Micah replies calmly. "So, I'll give you evidence."

Micah stretches out his hand, pointing to the butterfly tattoo inked into his skin. "Does this look familiar?"

Atlas shrugs, not wanting to feed into his ludicrous ideas.

"It should. It may not have the word *Mom* alongside it, but it's the same butterfly Michael has," he states matter-of-factly.

A shiver runs down Atlas's spine at the mention of the best friend he only recently remembered. He attempts to school his expression into a mask of calm, trying not to show how Michael's name is affecting him.

"In the real world, I'm Michael. This person you see now, Micah, is an artificially generated person. Just lines of code I'm controlling."

"You seem pretty real to me," Atlas refutes. "And you have about a minute left."

Micah rakes a hand through his hair, his voice rising with panic. "I also have access to two other avatars in this world, both branded with a butterfly. Mr. Jenkins has a butterfly birthmark on his hand and Harper wears a butterfly necklace. I was trying to get you to realize it was me, but your memories are coming back slower than anticipated."

The names hit Atlas like a punch to the gut, knocking the air out of him. If what Micah is saying is true, both Mr. Jenkins and Harper aren't real people. He refuses to believe that.

"You're never going to convince me they're just lines of code."

"Haven't they said some weird things to you in the past? Cryptic comments about keeping your eyes open, noticing what's right in front of you? Mr. Jenkins even told you he felt like a computer!" Micah exclaims, throwing his hands up in the air.

"That's just an expression! How do you know all this, anyway?" Atlas argues, wanting more information.

"Because they are all me! I'm the one behind the screen," Micah protests, his eyes wide with worry.

"I don't believe you," Atlas declares. "And your time is up."

Atlas walks toward the door, reaching out to grasp the cool metal of the handle. It turns without resistance and he's thankful it wasn't locked.

"I thought you wanted to help Naya?" Micah calls after him.

"I do, and standing here listening to you isn't helping me." Atlas pushes the door open and scans the hall for people.

"Naya is the woman in your memories."

Atlas freezes, whipping his head back toward Micah. He's nodding now, realizing he's got Atlas's full attention.

"Your memories are snippets of the real world, everything that happened to you before you were put in the simulation," Micah continues, his voice unwavering.

Atlas slowly shuts the door, his mind reeling with Micah's claims. He wants to believe, to grasp onto any semblance of truth that could lead him to Naya. But the idea of this reality being nothing more than an elaborate simulation feels surreal, almost impossible to comprehend.

"It's also just as likely, if not more so," Atlas suggests, "that my memories are of this world. Naya could still be part of them like you claim. She is here right now, and she needs me. Maybe you're just trying to stall so they can do something to her."

"What's it going to take for you to believe me and just wake up?" Micah groans, his frustration simmering beneath the surface.

Atlas struggles to reconcile his doubts with the urgency of his situation. If what Micah says is true, then Naya's safety hangs in the balance, dependent on Atlas's willingness to accept the truth.

"I need more than just words," Atlas finally replies, his voice strained with uncertainty. "I need proof. Do something that wouldn't be possible in the real world. Float off the ground," Atlas insists.

Micah's expression softens, sympathy flickering in his eyes. "I understand but convincing you won't be easy. I can't do anything that would be an obvious anomaly in this reality. It's based on the real world and me floating off the ground would raise concerns."

"Raise who's concerns?"

"Genesis Laboratories. The people monitoring Project Nowhere. They're doing everything in their power to make this feel real."

"Why?"

"Because they have no intention of letting you leave," he admits, his words filling Atlas with dread.

Micah takes a deep breath, his gaze steady as he begins to list the ways he's attempted to break through the layers of deception woven into Atlas's reality.

"I've left breadcrumbs, subtle hints scattered throughout your experiences. And almost all of them involved either a physical butterfly or the image of one," Micah explains, his voice tinged with frustration and urgency. "Remember the butterfly leading you to the bathroom in the park? And the graffiti on the wall? 'They're always watching'? That was me, trying to warn you and get you thinking."

Atlas's brow furrows as he recalls the cryptic message, a sense of unease creeping over him at the realization of Micah's covert actions.

"And those coins you found in the fountain? Do you really think there'd still be money there in an economy like this?" Micah continues, his words coming in a rush now. "That was my doing as well. I wanted to guide you to Naya, to help you piece together the truth."

Atlas's mind swirls with the implications of Micah's revelations. Every seemingly harmless event, every chance encounter, now takes on a new significance as he realizes the extent of Micah's efforts to reach him.

"And Bargain Bytes." Micah's voice grows soft with remorse. "I had Mr. Jenkins hire you, hoping it would bring you closer to Naya, to trigger more memories from your past."

Micah's words weave an intricate web of deceit, one that Atlas had no idea surrounded him. Everything he's saying threatens to unravel the very fabric of Atlas's reality. Doubt gives way to clarity, and with a sudden jolt of realization, he understands.

"I'm in a simulation," he murmurs, the words tasting strange on his tongue, as if he's just now learning to speak them. His heart pounds in his chest, adrenaline coursing through his veins as the truth settles over him like a heavy shroud.

"Yes, Atlas. Now stay focused and find your backdoor," Micah encourages, hope evident in his eyes.

With a surge of determination, Atlas focuses his mind, summoning every ounce of willpower he possesses. The world around him shimmers and shifts, the door to the room dissolving into a new one. It's his favorite color, midnight blue and covered in stars. Atlas rushes toward it, turning the copper handle in excitement. As it swings open, he stops dead in his tracks. His enthusiasm is abruptly replaced by a chilling sensation creeping up his spine. Before him lies a void, a yawning chasm of darkness that seems to stretch into infinity. It's a tangible, suffocating blackness that seems to swallow everything in its path.

Atlas feels fear grip him as he stares into the abyss, unable to discern any depth or boundary. It's as if he's peering into the very essence of nothingness. Despite his instinct to retreat, Atlas finds himself rooted to the spot, unable to tear his gaze away from the terrifying emptiness before him.

In that moment, he realizes this is no ordinary void—it's a literal manifestation of nowhere. Stepping into the abyss means taking a leap into the unknown and being ready to confront whatever awaits on the other side.

As if she's standing right next to him, Atlas hears Naya's voice telling him it's just like faith. You have to trust what you can't see. So he does, stepping across the threshold into the void.

Gasping for breath, Atlas awakens from the reality that has held him captive for so long. He finds himself lying in a hospital bed as he blinks away the remnants of the simulation. He's awake now, truly awake, and nothing will ever be the same again.

# CHAPTER 39
# NAYA

A bicycle whizzes past Naya, narrowly missing her standing on the sidewalk.

"Get out of the way!" the rider yells as they continue pedaling toward their destination.

Naya glances after them in a fog, attempting to orient herself to her surroundings. She blinks, overwhelmed by the rush of activity around her. Across the street she recognizes the grocery store but can't recall what she was doing. With a shrug, Naya decides to walk back home.

As she sets off down the busy street, she feels like she's forgetting something important. She furrows her brow, trying to pinpoint what it is. Did she forget to buy something at the store? Where was she headed? The feeling gnaws at her, a persistent nagging in the back of her mind.

With each step, the feeling grows stronger, casting a shadow over her otherwise familiar surroundings. Naya glances around anxiously, her eyes scanning the crowded street for any clues that might jog her memory. But no matter how hard she tries to remember, the elusive thought remains just out of reach.

Her frustration mounts with each passing moment, mingling with the underlying sense of worry that clouds her mind. What is wrong with her? Attempting to bury the feeling, Naya focuses on the last few blocks toward home. But the feeling clings to her like a stubborn shadow.

Up ahead, her house comes into view, and she sees Harper standing by the window. Her eyes light up when she spots Naya down the road, and she disappears from the window. Seconds later, Harper runs out the front door, meeting Naya at the end of the driveway.

"You're back!" Harper hugs her tight. "Where's Atlas?"

Though the name is oddly familiar, Naya has no idea who Harper is talking about. "Who?"

Harper gives her a playfully confused look. "The tall, handsome man you went on the trip with?"

When Naya's expression remains blank, Harper drops the joking pretense. "You're joking, right?"

Naya shakes her head. "No, I don't know who that is. What trip are you talking about?"

"Well, you didn't give us many details, but you were gone for two days." Harper trails behind Naya as they walk inside.

"Two days?" Naya exclaims, shocked she doesn't remember going anywhere.

Her parents greet her warmly at the door, glad she's home safe. They also inquire about Atlas, assuming she dropped him off at the loft before heading here.

"Seriously, who is this Atlas guy you keep talking about?"

"Glad to see you making jokes again," her dad replies with a laugh.

"I'm not joking." Naya notices the worried glance her mom and dad share.

"What do you mean, honey?" her mom asks warily.

"I've never met anyone named Atlas. Is he a new friend of yours?" Naya continues, sitting on the living room couch.

She suddenly feels very tired, a headache beginning to form. As she massages her temples, her family joins her in the living room. Harper sits beside her, playing with the butterfly necklace around her neck.

"I'm sure Atlas will stop by soon and then it will all come flooding back," she says quietly, a knowing look in her eyes.

"You'll see him at work tomorrow, won't you?" Naya's dad asks from the armchair by the window.

"He works at Bargain Bytes?" Naya reiterates.

"Naya, he's been working with you for a while now. He lives in the loft above the shop, too," her mom explains. "You're really starting to worry us."

Naya gives a frustrated sigh, not sure why they all know who he is but she doesn't. It doesn't help that her headache just keeps getting worse. Getting off the couch, Naya returns to the front door and puts her shoes on.

"I don't know what this is all about, but I might as well go see for myself," she announces, opening the door. "I'm headed to the loft. I'll see you later."

"Naya—" her mom calls after her, the rest of her sentence cut off when Naya closes the front door behind her. She's tired of their worried looks and confusing statements. Maybe the walk to Bargain Bytes will clear her head.

Halfway down the driveway, she hears the front door open and close. The patter of footsteps sounds behind her, and Naya looks to see Harper rushing toward her.

"Wait for me!" she calls, haphazardly stepping into her shoes. "I'm coming with you."

"Harper, go back inside." Naya continues down the slope of the driveway and onto the sidewalk.

"No! You've been gone for two days and you come back with no memory of the guy you're crushing on. I have reason to be concerned."

"How is it possible that I don't remember someone you claim I have a crush on?" Naya argues, the headache making her tone sound harsher than she means.

Harper catches up with her, grabbing Naya's hand. "I'm not sure, but I want to help you figure it out."

With a sigh, Naya relents, continuing her walk to Bargain Bytes hand-in-hand with her little sister. Harper can be so persistent. They walk a while in silence, just enjoying each other's company. As the headache worsens, Naya decides she needs a distraction from her mess of thoughts.

"Tell me about Atlas," Naya suggests. "Maybe hearing about him will help jog my memory."

Harper's eyes sparkle with excitement at the mention of this mysterious man. "Well," she starts, a mischievous grin on her face, "he's very handsome, with dark brown hair and hazel eyes. He's tall, too."

Naya nods, trying to conjure an image of Atlas in her mind, but finding nothing. Her brain feels strangely blank. She listens intently as Harper paints a vivid picture of Atlas—his quick wit, charming smile, and the way he always seems shrouded in mystery.

"He's also funny," Harper continues, her voice tinged with fondness.

Naya smiles faintly, trying to imagine the playful banter they must have shared. As they navigate through the crowded streets, Harper's stories serve as a lifeline, offering glimpses of a foreign past. By the time they reach Bargain Bytes, Naya still hasn't recalled anything.

Opening the shop door with a jingle, Naya and Harper step inside. Mr. Jenkins greets them with a warm smile, maneuvering his way out from behind his desk.

"You made it! Where's Atlas?" he bellows.

"Not you too," Naya murmurs, frustrated she's the only one with a gap in her memory.

"She can't remember him," Harper explains, saving Naya the trouble. "Can we have a look in the loft to see if it jogs her memory?"

Mr. Jenkins gapes at them. "Uh, yeah, I suppose," he stammers, fumbling for his spare loft key. "Fill me in after you've had a look, will ya?"

Naya nods, wordlessly following him up the stairs and into the loft.

Hopefully this works.

# CHAPTER 40
# ATLAS

Atlas feels dazed, like he just woke from the deepest sleep of his life. Blinking groggily, he tries to get his bearings, but his body feels heavy, his thoughts sluggish. Atlas's head lolls to the side as he surveys his surroundings, his muscles abnormally weak.

He attempts to sit up, only to collapse back down at the sheer effort of the movement. Atlas lets out a frustrated sigh, feeling disoriented and disturbingly vulnerable. The machines around him begin beeping just as the door bursts open. A male nurse rushes in to silence them, clearly out of breath.

Atlas tenses, unprepared for what they will do to him. Micah said they never wanted him to escape. Is this where they finish him off?

The nurse pulls off his mask, revealing a familiar nose and crooked smile.

"Michael!" Atlas exclaims, the memories rushing back. "You're a nurse now?"

"I borrowed the outfit and came as soon as I saw you leave the simulation," he says, catching his breath. "It's good to see you back in the real world."

Atlas manages a smile, still overwhelmed with fatigue and the sensations around him. It's as if he forgot what the real world felt like, everything seeming more tangible and enhanced. "How long was I in there?"

"A month. You're already in rough shape so I knew I had to get you out of there."

"Only a month? But it felt like at least three," Atlas murmurs.

"Yeah, time works differently in your mind." Michael shrugs. "Now, we need to get you out of here before they've realized what's happened."

Michael checks his watch and then glances at the door. He starts unplugging machines, frantically working his way around the web of tubes and wires. "This isn't going to be easy. Your muscles are probably very atrophied," he states, motioning toward Atlas lying in bed.

"Michael, where is Naya? Please tell me she's okay."

Michael stops what he's doing, a grim look on his face. "She's still in the simulation."

Atlas's eyes go wide with shock, and it feels like the wind is knocked out of him. His mind races through the possibilities, trying to figure out why she would be here. Slowly, as if oiling a rusty machine, the wheels begin turning and the memories click into place. The last thing he remembers before being put into the simulation plays like a movie in his mind.

The rapid clicking of his keyboard fills the empty office as Atlas edits the program. Updates on Project Nowhere are becoming few and far between, once open areas of the facility now locked. The secrecy fills Atlas with worry, and he has a feeling Michael and Naya are right. Genesis Laboratories doesn't plan to stick to their agreement.

As the lines of code form on the screen, Atlas feels confident this is the right decision. A backdoor in the program needs to be made in case Project Nowhere is ever used for the wrong reasons.

Atlas puts himself in the shoes of the government, trying to determine how they might use the program. It could very easily hold people captive if it works like it should, the simulation seeming so real people won't know they're in one. If that's the case, there needs to be a way for them to escape.

*Why not make it an actual door,* he thinks, beginning the string of commands to make it happen. As long as a person is aware of being in the simulation, they should be able to manifest a door. Walking through it will trigger them to wake up in the real world.

Atlas develops a framework that will allow the door to generate based on a person's thoughts, each one unique to the individual. What they see when they open the door, he's not so sure of.

As he finishes the last line, the door to his office flies open. Atlas looks up, finding comfort in the brown eyes that stare back at him.

"Naya!" he exclaims, a rush of warmth flooding through him at the sight of her.

She gives him a glowing smile, racing over to hug him in his chair. "How is my handsome fiancé?" she says, kissing him on the cheek.

"Better now that you're here," he leans his head back, staring up at her. "I didn't expect you."

She grins down at him. "I figured you'd be working late again. Let's get out of here you workaholic."

Atlas chuckles, powering off his computer and getting out of his chair. He grabs Naya's hand, and they leave his office. Atlas is careful to lock it behind him.

"So how was work?" Naya asks, her cheeriness rubbing off on him.

He lifts her hand, admiring the modest diamond shimmering on her ring finger. With a smile, he kisses the back of her hand, enjoying the blush that spreads across her cheeks. "Fine," he replies, leaning in. "Let's not talk in here," he whispers.

They remain silent as they leave the facility, not continuing their conversation until they're a good distance away. Naya gives him a concerned look, not sure what his sudden secrecy is for.

"What's up?"

"I took your advice," Atlas starts. "I added a backdoor."

Her eyebrows raise in surprise, a soft smile gracing her lips. "I'm glad. What changed your mind?"

Atlas shrugs, staring off into the distance as they walk. "A lot of things. There's been a lot more secrecy in the recent weeks than there used to be. It wasn't sitting right with me."

Naya nods, listening intently. She's been telling him for a long time to be cautious, he just didn't want to hear it. Now, he feels like a fool for not listening to her sooner.

"Naya," he murmurs. "If they figure out I have my suspicions, I'm not sure what they'll do. If something happens to me, I want you to get out of here. Take your family and leave the city. I don't want you to be caught up in my mess."

Naya holds his hand tighter, her brown eyes growing serious. "What are you talking about? What would they do to you?"

"I'm not sure, I just want to be cautious," he explains. "Promise me."

Naya stops and drops Atlas's hand. He turns to look at her, noticing the way her long black hair sways gently in the breeze.

"You ask me to marry you, and now you're telling me to leave you if something happens," she states, her brow furrowed in irritation. "How can you possibly ask me that?"

Atlas walks back toward her, cupping her face in his hands. "I want to keep you safe. I wouldn't be able to live with myself if something happened to you."

"I appreciate the sentiment, Cereal Thief, but I'm not going anywhere without you. And neither would Harper," Naya announces, a small smirk on her face.

Atlas smiles back, knowing she'd argue. Naya's whole family has become like his, especially since losing his parents in an accident. It would be hard to leave them behind. "You're so stubborn," he grumbles.

"It's one of the many things you love about me," she retorts, sticking her tongue out at him.

"You're right," he admits, tugging her along as they continue their way home.

The memory blurs into another one, Genesis Laboratories flashing before his eyes.

"Good morning, boss," Michael greets as Atlas walks into the facility the next day.

Atlas gives him a scowl at the title, knowing Michael just uses it to annoy him.

"What's on the docket for today?" he inquires, following behind Atlas as they head to the lab.

"I was told there would be some preliminary tests today. I can't believe we've made it to this point," Atlas exclaims, excited by the prospect of seeing his program in action.

Stepping closer to Michael as they walk, Atlas lowers his voice. "What did you think of my last-minute addition?"

"Smart move," Michael whispers. "Let's hope it's never needed."

As they navigate the labyrinth of halls, Atlas hears the murmur of voices up ahead. He shares a curious look with Michael as they continue toward the noise. Up ahead, the doors to the lab are wide open, a flurry of people rushing to and fro.

"Atlas!" a man in a suit calls, his presence imposing and out of place. He extends a hand and Atlas shakes it. "I'm Mr. Ellis. We've been anxiously awaiting your arrival."

Surprised by his statement, Atlas feels wary of what's to come. Michael and Atlas follow Mr. Ellis into the lab, observing the people working around them. He's not sure what they're doing, the medical aspect of this project not his expertise.

"So, what sort of tests are we running today?" Atlas asks, looking around for clues.

"Our first human trial," Mr. Ellis declares.

"Already?" Michael interjects. "I didn't think we were prepared for that yet."

Mr. Ellis gives them a cryptic smile. "Our medical team has been hard at work behind the scenes."

"Who's the volunteer?" Atlas says nervously, unsure who would want to test something so new.

"You, of course!" Mr. Ellis responds, gesturing to the hospital bed now in front of them.

Instinctively, Atlas backs away. Michael does the same, but they don't get far before several well-armed men block their path.

"I didn't agree to this," Atlas says frantically, looking to Michael for help.

The men approach them, grabbing hold before they can think. Atlas is shoved toward the hospital bed while Michael is restrained in place.

"Who better to test Project Nowhere than the man who coded it himself!" Mr. Ellis claps his hands together in excitement.

The men holding Atlas stop in front of Mr. Ellis and he leans in close. "You've done your part, and we thank you immensely. Now, we have a better use for you."

Atlas cries out as he is wrestled onto the bed and strapped in place. Panic overtakes him, his worst nightmare coming true. Beside him, Michael's desperate pleas fall on deaf ears. Mr. Ellis warns him he'll be next if he doesn't cooperate. Michael's gaze falls to the ground, his silence a painful acknowledgment of their shared peril. The sense of betrayal cuts deep, though Atlas can't fault him for wanting to protect himself.

"I'm sorry, Atlas," Michael mutters, the words pulling him out of the memory.

In front of him, Michael is saying those same words, a look of genuine regret on his face. Atlas stares at him, the emotions from his past feeling fresh and unresolved.

"You left me in there for a month and now you tell me Naya's in there too? How did that happen? Wasn't I enough?" Atlas asks incredulously.

"I know, I feel horrible. But it's worse than that. Her family is here too." A look of sorrow crosses his face.

"All of them? Harper too?"

Michael swallows uncomfortably, an unreadable expression in his eyes. Atlas isn't sure what to make of it, growing more uneasy by the second.

"Spit it out. I need to know what's happened."

Michael hesitates, his gaze falling to the floor as he gathers his thoughts. "I… I'm so sorry, Atlas," he begins, his voice trembling. "Harper… she didn't make it."

Atlas's heart clenches at the words, a cold dread settling in the pit of his stomach. He struggles to comprehend the enormity of what Michael is saying.

"What do you mean?" Atlas manages, his voice strained with disbelief.

Michael meets his gaze, his eyes filled with sympathy and regret. "I mean… Harper died," he explains softly. "Two weeks ago. Her brain wasn't able to handle the strain of the simulation and her body couldn't keep up. She didn't survive."

The words hit Atlas like a physical blow, knocking the breath from his lungs. He feels as though the ground has been ripped out from beneath him, leaving him suspended in a void of despair.

"How…" Atlas trails off, unable to find the words to articulate the turmoil raging inside him.

Michael reaches out a hand, his expression pained. "I wish I had more answers, Atlas," he says quietly. "But they didn't know how to save her. I'm so sorry."

Guilt crashes over Atlas like a wave, consuming him in an ocean of shame. It's all his fault. If he hadn't made this program, none of this would've ever happened. Tears well up in his eyes, spilling onto his cheeks as he grieves the loss of Harper. How will he ever be able to face Naya again?

As he dwells on the consequences of his creation, his grief shifts into a seething anger that ignites every fiber of his being. Atlas clenches his fists, his knuckles white with rage, vowing to make those responsible pay for their crimes. No longer will he be a pawn in their twisted game, allowing them to manipulate and control innocent lives.

Atlas knows he must confront the demons of his own creation to seek justice for Harper. The weight of guilt still hangs heavy around his neck, but now it's accompanied by a burning desire for redemption. He needs to get Naya and her family out of the simulation before they suffer the same fate.

With a trembling hand, he wipes the tears from his cheeks, his jaw clenched in determination. He can't let Harper's sacrifice be in vain. Genesis Laboratories may have unleashed a monster, but they will soon learn that they've awoken a force far greater than they could ever imagine.

"Put me back in," Atlas demands.

# CHAPTER 41
# NAYA

The wood floor creaks softly beneath her weight as she enters the loft. Naya is surprised by the sparsely decorated space. Most of the furnishings are remnants of what she left behind when she moved out. If Atlas is living here, wouldn't there be more signs of him?

She wanders through the main room, taking in the books and pieces of tech scattered across surfaces. An assortment of papers clutters the coffee table and Naya sifts through them. Some look to be sketched-out maps, others are lists of items and to-dos. At the bottom of the pile, her heart skips a beat when she recognizes the handwriting as her own.

Sketched across the page is a schematic for some sort of device, various notes labeling the parts. What was she making? Naya scours over the sketch, disappointed when no memories are spurred. Setting the paper back on the coffee table, she moves to the bedroom.

The bed is made, though not as neat as she left it. There's a lighter on the nightstand, the scuffed silver casing reflecting the light from the small window. Across from the bed, Naya notices a few clothes hung in the small closet. She touches the worn fabric, noticing the faint scent of pine and musk. The smell sends a shiver down her spine, her brain on the verge of a memory. But it slips away, replaced by the familiar sensation of forgetting something.

The door groans behind her, alerting her to the presence of someone nearby. Naya flips around in surprise, relieved to see Harper standing in the doorway.

"Anything?" she asks hopefully.

Naya shakes her head in frustration and leaves the bedroom with Harper. Back in the main room, Mr. Jenkins stands in the doorway, his foot tapping nervously on the floor.

"Ready to explain what this is all about?" he inquires, lumbering to the couch.

Naya joins him and Harper squeezes in beside them, resting her head on Naya's shoulder. Although squished together on the small couch, Naya feels comforted by their presence.

"There's really not much to tell," Naya starts. "Earlier, I found myself in the middle of the city with no memory of what I was doing. When I got home, everyone kept asking about Atlas but I didn't know what to say. I don't know who that is."

Naya looks at Mr. Jenkins, unsurprised by his face now wrinkled with worry.

"So, you came here to try to remember, but it didn't work?" he clarifies.

Naya nods, resting her head in her hands. "It doesn't help that I have this killer headache that won't go away."

"Maybe you should go home and rest. I'm sure it'll come back to you at some point," Mr. Jenkins suggests.

The three of them sit in silence. Naya tries to ignore the relentless pounding in her head. Maybe Mr. Jenkins is right. Clearly being here isn't helping anything.

Naya feels bad for how she left the house, too. She knows her parents were just worried for her. Yet there is still a part of her that isn't ready to go home yet.

"I think I'll clear my head on the roof for a couple minutes," she states.

When Harper gets up to go with her, Naya motions for her to stop. "Can I go alone? Just for a bit."

Harper agrees reluctantly, dropping back onto the couch to wait. Naya makes her way down the hall and up the steps, squinting into the sunlight when she opens the door. As she steps onto the rooftop, she's greeted by the familiar sight of the city skyline sprawled out before her. The cool breeze carries with it a sense of calm, soothing her frazzled nerves. This was always her favorite place to relax when she lived here. The view of the city from above never fails to put her problems in perspective.

Closing her eyes, Naya lets the sounds of the city wash over her. The distant honking of a car horn, the murmur of voices, birds chirping in the distance—all of it blends together in a soothing symphony. As she sits there, lost in thought, she wonders if Atlas discovered this spot. It's weird how her mind keeps wandering back to him even though he's a stranger.

Suddenly, an image flashes through her mind. It's a fragment, just a fleeting glimpse of her sitting on this same rooftop. But she's not alone. There's someone beside her, their presence warm and comforting. Naya's heart races as she tries to grasp onto the memory, but it slips away like smoke. Who was that person? And why did being on the roof suddenly bring them to mind?

With a sigh, Naya pushes the thoughts aside, knowing she won't find answers here. Instead, she focuses on the present moment, allowing herself to simply be, for just a little while longer. She talks with the Lord, expressing her frustrations but not forgetting to be thankful all the same. *It could be worse,* she thinks. At least she still has her family by her side.

After a few more minutes, Naya heads back inside. Harper greets her in the hall, and they make their way to the front doors, waving goodbye to Mr. Jenkins before they go. Stepping outside, Naya feels Harper's arm loop through hers, a comforting gesture that speaks volumes without words.

They walk in sync, their footsteps falling into a reassuring rhythm.

"I'm sorry you didn't get the answers you were looking for," Harper says softly.

Naya looks down at her with a small smile. "Thanks for coming with me."

"Always. What would you do without me?"

Naya hugs her sister close. "I don't know. I can't imagine it."

They walk along the sidewalk, content in each other's quiet companionship. Naya watches the steady stream of people passing by, each headed to their own destination. Her mind drifts to the lives unfolding around them, astonished to truly consider it. Everyone has a unique story, a distinct journey that intertwines with countless others.

She wonders about the dreams and struggles hidden beneath the surface of each person. It's a humbling reminder of the vastness of human experience. Though realizing she's only one person in millions, Naya is comforted knowing God still knows and loves every detail about her. It's hard to fathom a love like that, especially when multiplied onto so many people.

Beside her, Harper senses her sister's introspection and offers a comforting smile, a silent reminder they're in this together. Just then, a butterfly lands delicately on Harper's shoulder.

"Naya, look!" Harper stares at it with wide-eyed wonder. "It's beautiful."

"Not as beautiful as my Little Butterfly." Naya admires her little sister now bathed in the warm glow of the setting sun.

Harper's amber eyes gleam like liquid gold, reflecting the fading light with a radiant warmth. Her long, black hair cascades in silky waves, framing her delicate features with a youthful elegance. Naya marvels at the beauty and resilience of her younger sibling, a source of strength and positivity in their shared journey through life. She looks forward to growing old with her sister by her side.

The butterfly flits away in a flash of color, and they turn to watch it disappear into the city. Its brief presence reminds Naya of life's fleeting moments, spurring her to reach for Harper's hand. Tomorrow isn't promised—she won't take for granted a single second spent with her sister. With a smile, she gives Harper's hand a reassuring squeeze and they continue walking.

When they get home, their parents fuss over them at the door before leaving them be. Naya kisses the top of Harper's head and goes upstairs, ready to curl up in her bed. The headache still lingers, and she hopes sleep will chase it away.

A knock at the door startles her awake. The clock shows Naya's been asleep for two hours. She lays in bed, listening to the faint murmur of voices downstairs. Rolling over to go back to sleep, Naya hears her mom call her down.

With a groan, Naya drags herself out of bed and attempts to smooth her wild hair. She pads down the stairs, rubbing the sleep from her eyes. Yawning, she doesn't notice the stranger in their house until he's suddenly crushing her to him in an unexpected embrace.

"Naya!" He says her name with genuine affection.

Pressed against his T-Shirt, Naya smells the familiar scent of pine and musk.

"Atlas?" she asks, pushing away from him.

He releases her, stepping back with an apologetic smile. "Sorry, I was just excited to see you. Are you okay?"

"I'm fine," she reassures. "So, you are Atlas, right?"

She watches as his handsome features furrow with confusion. His lean frame and hazel eyes certainly match the description Harper gave. This must be him.

Atlas laughs nervously, eyes darting from Harper to her parents before settling back on Naya.

"Yeah, that's me." He runs a hand through his tousled brown hair, and she notices the sweat dampening his brow.

"Did you run here?" she blurts.

"Mm-hm, I was in a bit of a rush. We need to talk," he explains, his tone now full of urgency.

Atlas strides into the living room and Naya reluctantly follows. Despite feeling tired and wary of this stranger, she's eager to hear what he has to say. Harper and her parents head to the kitchen to give them some privacy, but Atlas motions for them to join.

"I need to talk to all of you," he states, waiting until everyone is seated to continue.

He clears his throat nervously and Naya's heart pounds, uncertain what news he might share. Hopefully it's something that will jog her memory.

"Naya, I wasn't expecting you to have lost your memories. This is going to be even harder than I expected. I just ask that you all listen and give me a chance."

Naya's parents nod, their faces creasing with worry. It seems Atlas isn't always this cryptic.

"Naya and I visited a facility just outside the city called Genesis Laboratories."

"Oh, the company running the human testing for the government VR project, right?" her dad interjects.

Atlas nods. "There's a lot I haven't shared about myself, including my past with that company."

Naya listens, though not as attentively as her parents. The subject matter feels distant, like a dream just beyond reach. Atlas notices her disinterest but presses on.

"My job was to write code for the virtual reality program. I wanted to use the technology for good, but the government had other plans. Eventually, I became a test subject for the program, placed into the VR simulation against my will."

"How did you escape?" Naya's mom leans forward.

"I thought I had, but it was more complicated than that," Atlas admits, sensing their confusion. He must realize his story sounds unbelievable.

"This is going to sound crazy, but we're currently in that simulation. After Naya and I broke into the facility," Atlas continues, ignoring the shock on her parents' faces, "we were captured. A friend helped me realize none of this is real. That's when I was able to wake up in the real world."

Naya struggles to process Atlas's story, her mind swirling with questions. Harper remains strangely silent beside her. Her parents are the first to break through the stunned silence, quick to voice their concerns.

"You broke into the facility?" her mom asks, a touch of anger in her voice.

"You really believe none of this is real?" Her dad's forehead wrinkles in disappointment.

Atlas's hazel eyes darken with worry, and he lets out a frustrated sigh. "I knew this wouldn't be easy," he mutters.

"Let's humor your claim for a minute," Naya's dad begins, noticing Atlas's frustration. "If you really woke up in the real world, why are you here now?"

"Because I chose to re-enter the simulation."

"And why on Earth would you do that?" her mom presses.

"I couldn't abandon you all," Atlas says simply. "All of you are currently in the simulation. Your real bodies are wasting away in the real world while your minds are engaged by the chip in your brain."

Naya's parents sink back into the couch, overwhelmed by Atlas's claims. Harper still seems unphased by the news, her expression neutral.

"So tell me," Naya starts, "why can't I remember any of this?"

# CHAPTER 42
# ATLAS

Atlas's hope wanes with each passing moment, the weight of his task pressing down on him. He had expected challenges, but the unexpected loss of Naya's memories is throwing him off balance. He was counting on her support, her sharp mind and unwavering determination to see them through. But now he feels adrift, grappling with the enormity of their predicament.

His mind races through possibilities, searching for answers amidst the chaos. Why had Naya's memories been erased? What purpose did it serve? Frustration bubbles beneath the surface as he struggles to make sense of it all. He should've asked Michael more questions before coming back, but he knew they were short on time.

"It's likely Genesis Laboratories reset your memories in the simulation because we were getting too close to the truth," he answers, working through his thoughts out loud. "And they were probably going to do the same to me, if not worse."

"So why do Harper and my parents still remember you?" she demands, her tone laced with disbelief.

Atlas ponders the question, realizing he's been wondering the same thing. "Maybe they haven't had time?" he suggests, unsure what the reason could be. "I came back quickly because I knew we wouldn't have much time before they noticed something was up. A memory wipe could still be in the works for everyone else."

Naya's parents share a worried glance and Atlas knows how they all must be feeling.

"That's why it's so urgent you believe me," Atlas warns. "I don't know what they'll do if they realize I used a backdoor. We need to get out while we still can."

"So why don't we remember being put into the simulation?" Naya questions.

"You don't remember because they don't want you to know you're here," Atlas replies, pulling from his own experience.

"Why? What would be the point?" Naya argues.

"It's a way to keep us trapped here. If we believe the world around us is real, we'd have no reason to leave. But this isn't our home. Please believe me!" Atlas begs.

He gazes at the doubtful expressions on everyone's faces, knowing he has yet to successfully convince them. Racking his brain, Atlas tries to come up with more evidence to get them to believe. *His door,* he thinks.

"Hold on, I'll prove it to you," he promises, closing his eyes and concentrating on manifesting his backdoor.

When he opens his eyes, the front door of the house has shifted into his own, the night sky adorning the wood paneling. Atlas jumps out of his chair and runs to the door, excited to offer them tangible proof of the simulation. Why hadn't he thought of this before?

"Look!" He points to the door. "This is my backdoor. Each person has one to exit through once they can successfully manifest it. It was a fail-safe I added right before everything went horribly wrong."

Naya crosses her arms, her parents tilting their heads behind her on the couch. Harper shakes her head and shrugs.

"It just looks like our front door," Naya states.

Atlas looks back at the door, still seeing his own. Disappointment floods through him when he realizes the backdoor is only visible to the person it belongs to. With a frustrated sigh, he lets his concentration fade and the front door dissolves back into place. He paces anxiously in the entryway, trying to come up with a new plan.

"What finally convinced you it wasn't real?" Harper asks softly.

Atlas pauses, reflecting on what Michael revealed that made everything click into place. It was his memories, those fragmented glimpses into his real life, that had provided the key. If he can somehow trigger a memory for Naya and her family, maybe it will help them remember.

"My memories helped convince me," he answers. "What I thought was a past I had forgotten were actually glimpses into my real life."

Naya's parents listen intently, trying to understand where he's going with this.

"Naya was helping me remember my past," Atlas explains further. "Now, I need to help you remember yours."

Stepping back into the living room, Atlas decides to start with what he knows best—his own memories of joining their family.

"Naya and I first met at the grocery store," he begins, his voice tinged with fondness as he recalls their chance encounter. "I challenged her to a coin flip for the last box of Harvest Crunch, earning myself the infamous nickname of Cereal Thief."

He pauses, searching their eyes for a flicker of recollection, but there's nothing. Undeterred, he presses on, recounting another cherished memory. "We both graduated from college with Computer Science degrees," he continues, his gaze drifting to each member of Naya's family. "You threw a modest graduation party at your house and Harper smeared frosting on my face."

A bittersweet smile tugs at Atlas's lips as he reminisces, the memory vivid in his mind. "It was one of the first times I truly felt like part of your family," he admits softly, his heart heavy with the weight of their forgotten bond.

"I'm sorry, Atlas. I wish I could remember," Celeste, Naya's mom, says apologetically. Her words strike a chord within him, stirring a mix of understanding and hurt. Though he knows they can't help their lack of recollection, the pain of being so easily forgotten still cuts deep.

Atlas searches his memories for something that might be more impactful for them. Though the ones he shared were fond memories for him, they don't seem to have the same effect on her parents. As he thinks, an idea comes to him, and he rushes into the kitchen.

Frantically searching through the cupboards, he finally finds a box of Harvest Crunch. Grabbing it, he returns to the living room to stand in front of Celeste.

"My memories were triggered with familiar sights, sounds, or even emotions. If I can recreate those conditions, maybe yours will be too," he explains. "Can I borrow your wedding ring?"

Celeste hesitates momentarily before sliding the ring off her finger and placing it in his open palm. Atlas gives an appreciative nod and instructs them to move so they can see the door.

"Naya, you need to be the one to open the door," he directs, stepping outside and closing the door behind him.

The humid summer air clings to him, only adding to the nervous sweat wetting his palms. If this doesn't work, he's not sure what he'll do. Standing on the front step, he casts his mind into the past. For a moment, he just lets the memory wash over him, trying to capture every detail.

It's a gorgeous afternoon, the sunlight warming Atlas as he stands at Naya's front door, his heart pounding with anticipation. Should he knock? Ring the doorbell? His mind races with doubts, his nerves making him overthink everything. Pushing them aside, he decides to ring the doorbell.

Inside, he hears the soft shuffle of footsteps. Shortly after, Naya appears at the door, a playful smirk dancing on her lips at his surprise visit.

"Well, well, what do we have here?" Naya teases, quirking an eyebrow as she takes in the sight of Atlas holding a familiar box of Harvest Crunch.

"Hey there, Brown Eyes," Atlas greets, a nervous excitement fluttering within him. "I come bearing gifts."

Naya steps closer, her gaze flitting between Atlas and the box in his hands. "Gifts, huh? You know the way to a girl's heart, Cereal Thief," she remarks, pointing to the box when she notices it's open. "I see you've already had a taste?"

Atlas chuckles softly, unsurprised she noticed such a small detail. She's always been very observant.

"Quality control." He grins. "I had to make sure the bag inside wasn't tampered with. I promise I didn't eat any of the cereal. Have a look for yourself."

He hands the box to her and she takes it, eyeing him curiously. "We'll see about that."

Naya opens the box with a playful flourish. Peering inside, her brown eyes widen in surprise. She looks back up at him, mouth agape as she reaches in and takes out a small velvet box.

"What's this?" Naya asks, unable to contain the smile that spreads across her face.

Atlas takes the box from her with trembling hands, opening it to reveal a sparkling engagement ring. The diamond catches the light as he meets her gaze and sinks to one knee.

"Naya," he begins affectionately. "From the moment we met in the grocery store, I was captivated by you. For a while, I thanked our shared love of Harvest Crunch for bringing us together," he admits, gesturing to the cereal box in her hands, "but you helped me realize it was so much more than that. Thank you for being such a beacon of light in my life. I can't imagine it without you by my side. You are my best friend and the love of my life, and I want to spend forever with you. Will you marry me?"

Tears glisten in Naya's eyes. She nods enthusiastically, throwing her arms around him without hesitation. "Yes, Atlas, a thousand times yes."

Overwhelmed with joy, Atlas hugs her tightly, savoring the moment before pulling back to press his lips softly against hers. When they part, Atlas spots her parents and Harper watching from inside, and a flush of embarrassment colors his cheeks.

Naya turns to see their unexpected audience, laughing when she sees the tears in her parents' eyes and Harper's enthusiastic thumbs-up. Atlas slides the ring onto Naya's finger, and she admires it with a radiant smile.

"It's beautiful," she muses, her eyes full of love. "Though I would've said yes even with just the cereal," she whispers. "I do get to keep the box, right?"

Atlas returns to the present moment, the feelings from that day now fresh in his mind. He won't be able to reenact it perfectly, especially with Naya's missing memories, but he hopes it will be enough to help them remember. Taking a deep breath, he rings the doorbell.

# CHAPTER 43
# NAYA

When the doorbell rings, Naya answers the door like Atlas instructed. He looks ridiculous standing on the front step with a box of cereal in his hands.

"Hello?" she says, unsure what she's supposed to do.

Behind her, she can feel the gaze of her parents and Harper as they watch the strange encounter.

"Hey there, Brown Eyes," Atlas replies, a charming smile on his face. "I come bearing gifts."

The nickname feels strangely familiar, though she doesn't know anyone who calls her that.

"An open box of Harvest Crunch?" she questions.

He furrows his brow at her response but presses on. "I promise I didn't eat any of the cereal. Have a look."

Naya gingerly accepts the cereal out of his hands, looking at him with uncertainty. He motions for her to open the box and she does, surprised to see her mother's wedding ring amidst the cereal. An overwhelming sense of déjà vu settles over her, but she can't pinpoint why.

Atlas grabs the ring out of the box and drops to one knee in front of her. Naya can't hold back the shocked gasp that escapes from her lips.

"Though you don't remember me," he starts, voice trembling, "you are the love of my life. It pains me to imagine my world without you in it."

The sincerity in his words tugs at Naya's heartstrings. His hazel eyes are full of sorrow and something in her aches to take that pain away, to reach out and comfort him.

"I don't know how you'll ever forgive me for the mess I've created. I'm so sorry," Atlas confesses. "When all this is over, I'd be the happiest man in the world if you still want to marry me."

A sharp pain shoots through Naya's skull and she staggers backward, clutching her head. Atlas reaches out to steady her, but his touch feels strange and unfamiliar, making it even harder for her to process his claim that they were once engaged.

"Cereal Thief," her mom murmurs behind her. Naya turns to see a flicker of recognition in her eyes. "I remember that now. It's why I thought your proposal was so endearing."

Naya stares at her parents in shock as their eyes grow wide with recollection.

"Yes, I remember you telling me that," Atlas says, his excitement building as he rushes back inside. "Hold onto that feeling. That's what's real!"

Her mom frowns in concentration, mirroring her dad's expression. Naya looks over at Harper who seems untouched by the wave of memories. Why did Atlas's reenactment help her parents but not her or Harper? Naya tries to focus on the sense of déjà vu she felt, but nothing comes.

"What exactly are we supposed to be holding onto?" her dad questions. "I don't see anything happening."

"You won't at first," Atlas answers. "When you fully believe the world around you isn't real, you'll feel some sort of… shift inside you. It's hard to explain."

Naya's parents glance over at her and Harper. They look a little lost.

"Are you recalling anything, girls?" her mom asks.

They shake their heads no, and Naya offers a shrug.

"I've got quite the headache, though. If that means anything," Naya offers, glancing over at Atlas.

"Actually, yeah," he says, his excitement returning. "Every time I remembered something, I got a headache. I think it has to do with your brain fighting against the memory suppression."

Naya nods absentmindedly, the pounding in her head intensifying. She really hopes something good will come of it because it's rather uncomfortable.

"Atlas, I'm not getting any more memories," her mom admits softly, a forlorn expression on her face. "I'm really sorry."

Atlas shakes his head. "No, I refuse to believe that's it. Replay the memory in your mind. Try to remember what happened after that."

Her parents close their eyes, trying to think back. Naya does the same. When nothing comes to mind, she peeks at her parents with one eye open. They're still deep in concentration. Glancing at Atlas, she notices his contemplative look, his foot tapping lightly on the floor.

"It's almost ironic," he starts, drawing their attention. "You all taught me how to live by faith rather than sight, and now I'm trying to teach you the same thing. Though it's not quite in the same context."

"You weren't faithful before you met us?" Naya's mom asks.

"No, I favored luck instead. After my parents died in a car accident, I had a hard time believing there was a God who just let it happen." His eyes grow cold and distant as he recalls the painful memory.

"It's not God who causes bad things to happen. We just live in a fallen world. We have to deal with both the good and bad consequences of our free will—" Her Mom's response is cut short when she suddenly stops speaking. "I've said that before," she realizes, her forehead creased in concentration.

She looks at Atlas, her eyes widening in recognition as if seeing him for the first time. She rushes toward him, wrapping him in a tight embrace.

"I'm so sorry. I'm remembering more, but it's all still a bit foggy," she murmurs, releasing him from her arms. "I believe you. This isn't real."

As she pulls back, she points to the front door, a shocked expression on her face.

"The door!" she exclaims. "It changed."

Naya looks at the front door but sees nothing different. "Mom, what are you seeing?"

"Our front door. The real one."

"What does it look like?" her dad asks.

"It's teal," she says with a chuckle. "Though the paint is faded, and the wood is showing through. I think it's almost more beautiful this way." Naya's mom moves close to the door, touching it softly.

Naya yearns to see what she describes, but all that's there is the pristine dark wood of their current front door.

"I remember you painted it for me, Silas. After I told you how much I hated the sun-bleached wood. After that, I'd smile every time I came home. Not just because it was my favorite color, but because it reminded me of home. And you, darling."

Naya follows her gaze, noticing the shine in her dad's eyes. The corner of his mouth quirks up, forming a wry grin.

"I spilled the can of paint," he replies, laughing as a tear spills over. "And it created a permanent splotch on the front step."

"Yes!" her mom exclaims, walking over to him and cupping his face in her hands. "You remember that?"

"I do," he whispers, his voice trembling with emotion as he turns to face Naya. "Let's go back home."

Naya gives him a sad smile. "I don't see the door, Dad."

He glances between Naya and the door, a perplexed look on his face. "But it's right there!" He points to the door and stops, realization dawning on him. "You don't remember, do you?"

Naya shakes her head. "No. It all sounds so familiar, but nothing feels concrete."

"I promise I'll help her get to that point," Atlas interjects, moving closer to Naya's parents. "But you guys need to go before the backdoor is noticed. We're running out of time."

"But I can't leave my girls behind," her mom argues.

"I'll take care of them, Celeste," Atlas reassures, gently squeezing her hand. "We'll see you on the other side."

Her mom walks over to where Naya and Harper stand, wrapping them into a warm embrace. "I love you, my sweet girls." She pulls back, giving them each a peck on the cheek. "Trust Atlas, okay? He knows what he's doing."

She reluctantly lets them go, walking toward the door.

"You'll be right behind us?" her mom asks Atlas, still doubtful.

"Absolutely. There's no way I would leave them behind," he says, glancing over at Naya and Harper. There's a strange mixture of determination and regret in his eyes, but Naya's not sure why.

"I didn't expect you both to be seeing the same door," he continues, "but to be safe, go through one at a time. My friend Michael will be waiting for you on the other side. When you wake up, you're going to feel weak and disoriented. We've been in the simulation for a while."

Naya's mom nods, twisting the handle and staring outside. Her eyes widen in surprise, but Naya has no clue what she's seeing. It just looks like their front yard to her.

"Faith, not sight," Atlas reminds.

Celeste nods, giving them all one last parting smile before stepping through. The door closes softly behind her.

"I suppose it's my turn." Her dad gulps, gripping the handle and repeating her mom's actions. "Don't keep us waiting too long," he says with a wink.

After only a brief moment of hesitation, he steps over the threshold. The click of the door behind him echoes through the room with a firm finality. Naya's heart constricts now that they're gone, and her instincts urge her toward the door. She rips it open, her heart pounding in her chest.

"Wait!" she calls after them, rushing outside.

The warm summer air hits her like a shock, and she scans the surroundings desperately. Naya's breath comes in shallow gasps as she searches for any sign of her parents. But they're nowhere to be found, vanished as if they were never there at all.

A shiver runs down her spine, a cold, creeping realization that they are truly gone. The weight of the situation presses down on her, a mix of fear and determination battling within her.

"Atlas!" she yells.

He runs out of the house, skidding to a halt beside her. His hands skim her arms, his eyes frantic. "What? What happened?"

"What if we can't find them?" she whispers, her voice trembling. "What if this doesn't work?"

Atlas steps closer, placing a reassuring hand on her shoulder. "We will, Naya. Trust me. We're almost home."

Naya looks into his eyes, finding solace in his unwavering resolve. She nods, taking a deep breath to steady herself. The reality of their situation is daunting, but she can't turn back now. Her parents believed Atlas, so she can too.

"Okay," she says, her voice firmer. "I suppose my parents disappearing into thin air is pretty solid proof that none of this is real," she retorts, trying to joke away the panic.

Atlas surprises her with a radiant grin. "Glad to hear you joking around again. You can be really funny when you want to be."

His comment catches her off-guard, the affection in his tone making her blush. Naya looks away, hoping he hasn't noticed. When she turns her attention back to the house, she gasps at the sight before her.

The front door looks completely different, now a rich ebony wood with a large stained-glass window in the middle. The pattern is beautiful, the colored glass forming three butterflies. One at the top is a beautiful speckled black, reminding Naya of herself. At the bottom, is a butterfly with wings like the night sky. Something within her whispers it's Atlas. Then, nestled between them, is a butterfly with golden wings, just like the necklace Harper wears.

"I see it," she whispers.

Atlas follows her gaze, staring at the front door. "Your backdoor?" he questions, his voice dancing with excitement.

Naya nods, captivated by her door's beauty. She walks toward it as if hypnotized, reaching out to touch the cool metal handle. As she twists it, her eyes land on the delicate golden butterfly and she stops.

"Harper!" she exclaims, turning to face Atlas. Naya can't believe she was about to leave without her sister. "She's still inside the house. I can't leave her behind."

"She'll be okay, Naya. You can't lose this opportunity," Atlas urges, motioning toward the door.

"No! She needs to go before me," she argues, crossing her arms obstinately.

"Why are you always so stubborn?" Atlas growls.

"I can't go through this door without her. You go back inside and get her," Naya commands.

He sighs, running his hands through his already mussed hair. "I don't want to disrupt your backdoor," he replies.

"Seriously?" Naya comments incredulously. "Fine, how do I get rid of this thing, then?"

"Don't do that! Just go through! Please!" Atlas begs, his tone now desperate. "Your parents are waiting on the other side."

"I'm sorry that I won't trust my sister with a stranger while I venture into who knows where!" Naya's frustration mounts by the second, Atlas's insistence filling her with trepidation.

"I'm not a stranger!" Atlas bellows, his own pent-up frustration now evident.

Naya flinches at his tone and his eyes immediately fill with regret. He walks closer to her, stopping at the bottom of the front steps.

"I'm sorry," he whispers. "I'm just scared, and I don't know how much time we have left. Who knows if you'll be able to summon another backdoor. I don't want to take that risk."

"Well, I do." Naya closes her eyes in concentration.

"Naya," Atlas warns.

But she ignores him, focusing on bringing her front door back. She pictures the smooth, mahogany wood and her sister waiting inside.

When she opens her eyes again, the stained-glass door is gone. She turns the handle in a rush, stumbling inside. Harper is still standing patiently in the entryway, offering a lopsided grin when she sees Naya enter.

"Did you forget how to walk through a door?" she remarks.

Naya laughs, crushing her little sister into a hug. She hears the frustrated sigh of Atlas behind her as he steps back into the house. Without letting her sister go, Naya turns to glare at him.

"Harper goes first."

# CHAPTER 44

# ATLAS

The way Naya protectively holds her sister sends another wave of panic through Atlas. The determined look in her eyes is a sign she won't give in easily. Naya continues to glare at him, noticing his silence. Atlas doesn't know what to do. He was hoping to avoid a conversation about Harper until Naya was out of the simulation. Convincing her to leave her sister behind will be almost impossible.

A small voice in the back of his mind urges him to lie, to make Naya believe Harper went through a backdoor somehow. But he knows he'll never forgive himself for lying to her about something so important. He already feels guilty for being the one to get them all into this situation, let alone trying to hide the consequences of his actions to someone he loves. That will only push her away more than the truth already will.

Taking a deep breath, Atlas sees no other option than to tell Naya everything. "Harper can't come with us."

Naya balks at his statement, tightening her grip on her little sister. "What do you mean?"

"She isn't real. Harper is part of the simulation," Atlas continues, wary of saying more.

"Seriously?" Naya retorts, her accompanying laugh catching Atlas off guard. "I haven't lost all my memories. I know I have a sister."

"That's not what I'm saying," Atlas backpedals. "You do—did have a sister."

Naya catches the shift in his words, scrunching her brows in confusion. "Did? What are you saying, Atlas? Did something happen to Harper? I would remember that."

He swallows nervously, knowing what he says next could ruin everything. Harper's face looks confused as well, the AI not knowing what Atlas means either. He wishes Michael were controlling her now, helping him through this precarious situation. But he knows his friend has bigger things to deal with in the real world.

"Harper was put into the simulation like all of us," Atlas starts, letting his words sink in. "But the program put too much strain on her brain. She didn't survive the complications. I'm so sorry, Naya."

Naya's expression is blank, and Atlas can't tell what she's thinking. Harper looks up at her sister and then over at Atlas, a scared look on her face.

"So, I'm dead?" she asks, her voice trembling.

Atlas shivers at her words, realizing how strange it is to hear Harper talking knowing it's not really her. He wonders if he ever interacted with the real Harper in the simulation, or if it's been coding the whole time.

"The real Harper died two weeks ago, yes," Atlas replies.

His words cast a shadow over the room, and he's reminded of how he felt when Michael first told him. He can't imagine what Naya must be feeling.

"No," Naya mutters. "That's not possible. Harper is right here!" She grabs Harper's shoulder and turns her around. Kneeling, Naya stares into her little sister's brown eyes, searching for answers. "I would know if it wasn't really her."

Atlas grimaces, unsure how to handle Naya's denial. If he has any hope of getting her to wake up, she needs to be convinced of the truth.

"I had a hard time believing it, too. She feels really real," Atlas admits.

"I am real!" Harper argues. "I have memories and feelings. Why would you say this, Atlas?"

Harper's words send Atlas reeling, the betrayal on her face making his heart break again. He wasn't expecting her to argue with him, but then again, he had no idea how the artificial intelligence would respond. This makes it so much worse than it already was.

"Please don't make this worse," he begs. "You are just lines of code, programmed to behave like Harper. I'm not quite sure how they did it, or why, but Harper's memories and likeness were somehow saved into the simulation to create another version of you."

Naya is shaking her head now, still in disbelief. Harper wears a shocked expression, the AI struggling to comprehend the truth. Atlas looks away, searching for additional ways to help convince Naya.

"Naya," he says, drawing her attention. "Have you noticed anything about Harper lately that seems strange?"

She shakes her head again. "No. I don't know."

He sighs, knowing she's going through so many emotions right now it would be hard to focus on small details like that. Atlas looks over at Harper who is now fiddling with the gold butterfly necklace around her neck. *That's it,* he thinks.

"The butterfly necklace. It's not real. It's something my friend, Michael, added to Harper," Atlas exclaims. "It was his way of trying to tell us that she was an ally. He would sometimes use her to send messages to try and wake us up."

Naya rests her head in her hand, looking deep in thought. *Maybe this will be enough to convince her,* he silently hopes.

"Michael added the butterfly necklace," she reiterates, talking out loud. "But Harper wore a necklace in real life too."

Suddenly, she straightens, a recollection brightening her brown eyes. "It was never a butterfly. Harper," she says, turning to look at her sister. "What was the necklace I gave you on your birthday?"

Harper stares at Naya, a bewildered look on her face. After several moments of silence, she tugs on the butterfly necklace around her neck. "This was the necklace you gave me," she says adamantly.

Atlas watches as an unreadable mix of emotions cross Naya's face. Her mouth forms a thin line, and she looks down at the floor.

"No, Harper. It was a ladybug. I always called you my Little Ladybug. I can't believe I didn't remember that," Naya says, sliding to the floor in shock.

She sits with her knees to her chest, unable to look at either of them. Atlas watches her turmoil and imagines the conflicting emotions she must be dealing with. It's a pain he understands all too well, the agony of confronting a reality that defies everything you once believed.

He moves closer to her, wanting to anchor her amidst the storm that threatens to engulf them both. Reaching out his hand, he stops just short of brushing against her trembling fingers. *The last thing she would want is to be comforted by a stranger,* he thinks. It's a sobering reality, another reminder of how badly he wants to return to the real world. To be with the Naya that remembers him.

As if sensing his thoughts, Naya looks up at Atlas, her eyes filled with fear. He can see the depth of her pain, the rawness of her grief. It resonates with him, stirring memories he'd rather forget.

"I know this is hard to accept," he says softly. "But we can't stay here."

# CHAPTER 45
# NAYA

"My sister is dead," she murmurs, her voice barely above a whisper. The words pierce her heart like a knife.

Naya can feel Atlas's eyes on her as she considers the implications. A reality without her little sister is unfathomable. He's so insistent they need to leave, but she's not sure she can. She looks at Harper, her sister's familiar face now cloaked in uncertainty. Yet, as she stares, she sees the same warmth in her sister's eyes, the same grin that used to light up their childhood. It's a cruel paradox—the sister who stands tangibly before her isn't real, while the sister who was real is now gone forever.

"I can't go back," Naya whispers. "Not to a reality where Harper is gone. I won't."

Atlas reaches out to her, his expression filled with sorrow and understanding. He knows the pain of loss, the ache of longing for someone who's no longer there.

"I know how horrible this is, but if you stay, you'll die too. You can't do that to your parents." His hazel eyes fill with intensity. "Or me. I refuse to lose you, too."

Naya thinks of her parents waiting on the other side for them. A sob escapes her when she pictures telling them the news about Harper. They'll be devastated.

"This will break my parents," Naya says. "Losing their little girl."

"I know. But it will crush them if they lose both of you," Atlas implores. He moves to sit directly across from her on the floor, holding her hands in his.

Naya looks away, the weight of shame for wanting to give up mingling with her overwhelming desire to linger in her grief. Tears slip down her cheeks and another sob racks her body. Atlas tightens his grip on her hands, keeping her afloat amidst the sorrow threatening to drown her.

"Naya, you need to fight. Harper wouldn't want you to stay," he insists.

Naya envisions the unyielding spirit of her little sister, always striving for more, always bringing life and positivity to their family. Deep down, she knows Atlas is right. If Harper were truly here now, she'd be doing everything in her power to get Naya to wake up.

As if drawn by Naya's inner conflict, Harper walks over and sits beside her on the ground. She leans her head toward Naya's shoulder, pausing momentarily when Naya flinches. The once comforting gesture now feels hollow and foreign. Yet, in her grief, Naya can't push her sister away. She reaches out to hold Harper, even if it's just a shell of who her sister really was.

Naya sobs into her little sister's strawberry-scented hair. She tangles her hands in the silky strands, pulling Harper into a hug. Naya wants to burn the memory of her sister into her mind—the way her small body fits perfectly in her arms, the lull of her breathing. Everything feels so real, she lets herself imagine living here.

"Maybe I can stay, just for a while?" she asks hopefully, wanting to pretend for a little longer.

Atlas releases her hand for a moment to wipe a tear from his cheek. "No. The longer you stay, the more potential for your body to weaken and something to go wrong. We can't run that risk."

Harper pulls away, her amber eyes gazing into Naya's. "If staying with me means you'll get hurt, I don't want that."

Naya's heart aches at Harper's words, the logical part of her mind grappling with the emotional weight of the situation. Atlas and Harper are right, but letting go feels impossible.

"Harper," Naya rasps. "I don't want to leave you behind."

Harper's gaze softens, and she reaches out to gently hold Naya's face. "You're not leaving me behind. You're honoring my memory by living your life to the fullest. That's what I would want for you."

Tears stream down Naya's face as she looks at her sister. "I just… I can't believe you're really gone."

Harper wipes the tears off Naya's cheeks, giving her a bittersweet smile. "I'll always be with you, in your heart and memories. But you have to go home, Naya. You have to live."

Naya takes a deep, shuddering breath, feeling suffocated by the weight of her decision. She looks at Harper one last time, committing the image of her sister's face to memory.

"I love you, Harper," she whispers, her voice breaking.

"I love you too, Naya," Harper replies, her own voice filled with emotion. "Now go. Be strong for Mom and Dad."

With a final embrace, Atlas helps Naya stand.

"How do I do this, Atlas?" Naya falters, attempting to find some determination.

"Concentrate on waking up, on summoning your door again," he instructs, guiding her closer to the front door.

Naya stands to face it, envisioning the mahogany wood shifting into the ebony hues of her backdoor. It shimmers before her, on the precipice of changing. But it doesn't, the front door remaining stubbornly in place.

"I can't. It's not working," she says, fear creeping in. "I don't know if I'm strong enough."

Atlas grips her shoulders, bending down to stare into her eyes. "Yes, you are. You are one of the strongest, most determined people I know."

"But what about after? How do I face my parents? I couldn't keep my sister safe," she whimpers, the threat of tears making her throat constrict.

Regret flashes across Atlas's face. "None of this is your fault, Naya."

She sniffles and offers him a small nod. Closing her eyes, she pictures her door once more, willing it to appear. When she looks again, her door has appeared, but it doesn't look the same.

Naya's backdoor, once adorned with a beautiful stained-glass window, has transformed into a haunting reflection of her grief and sorrow. The wooden frame is dark and weathered, as if it has aged decades in mere moments. The rich, dark wood has now peeled away in long, jagged strips, revealing the raw, splintered wood beneath.

All traces of color have disappeared, the door itself now decorated with intricate carvings. They depict scenes of loss and longing—a hand reaching out to grasp empty air, a heart shattered into countless pieces, and eyes filled with tears. The doorknob is shaped like a wilted rose, its petals drooping as if burdened by an invisible weight. And there, molded into the rose, is a small, metal ladybug.

Naya steps closer, hearing the faint echoes of laughter and joyful moments now tinged with a melancholic undertone. As she places her hand on the doorknob, she feels a shiver run through her. The metal is icy to the touch, and for a moment, she hesitates. The door seems to pulse with her sorrow, a living entity that understands her pain. It's a gateway not just to another place, but to a deeper understanding of her own heartache.

With a deep breath, Naya turns the knob, and the door creaks open. An endless, pitch-black void stretches out before her. She gasps in fright, looking back at Atlas.

"There's nothing there," she exclaims.

"It's like taking a leap of faith," Atlas replies calmly. "You have to trust what you can't see."

Naya looks into the suffocating darkness, taking deep breaths to steady herself. She tries to focus on her faith and the strength of the Lord. But the blackness in front of her feels nothing like the bright, uplifting feelings her faith brings her. She turns away, facing Harper and Atlas in the house. Atlas's forehead creases in concern and Naya gives him a reassuring smile.

She allows herself a final, lingering look at her sister and Atlas before closing her eyes. With Naya's back now to the void, she pictures her parents waiting on the other side and lets herself fall backwards over the threshold.

Fluorescent lights blind her, and she squints against them. Machines beep incessantly around her, only adding to her sense of disorientation. Her body feels heavy, the scents of a hospital sending a wave of nausea through her.

She blinks drowsily, trying to take in her surroundings. Looking to her left, Naya spots long black waves spilling over her shoulder. She moves to touch it, noticing how stiff and sluggish her limbs feel. As her fingers graze the strands of hair, she's shocked by the enhanced sensations. She thought the simulation had felt real, but now it feels dull in comparison.

Her long hair seems unfamiliar after having short hair for so long. Instinctively, she reaches up to touch the side of her face to feel for her scar. To her surprise, her fingers brush the raised tissue, tracing it along the length of her hairline. *It was real,* she realizes, her last memory suddenly rushing back to her.

Naya can't sleep. She tosses and turns in bed, her mind racing with questions. Atlas hadn't talked to her at all today, which was strange. After his ominous warning yesterday about what Genesis Laboratories might do if they discover his backdoor, Naya can't help but think of worst-case scenarios.

With a huff, she climbs out of bed and heads to the kitchen for a late-night snack. Rifling through the cupboards, Naya finds a box of Harvest Crunch. Moving to pour it into a bowl, she's disappointed to find it's basically empty.

"Seriously? Why did I keep this?" she groans, talking to herself in the dark of her apartment.

Throwing on some clothes, Naya decides to make a quick trip to the store. Maybe the walk will clear her mind.

Naya knows what happened next, choosing to skip over the memories of her attack in the alley. She'd rather not relive that moment. As she does, the moments after the attack filter back to her.

The two people helping her in the alley exchange hushed words, assessing her injuries.

"Did he have to cut this deep?" one of them says, their voice deep and disapproving.

"He was just doing what he was told," a female voice says. "Let's get her in the van before the ambulance shows up."

Naya feels them lift her gently in their arms, hauling her through the alley. She still feels dazed from her attack, unsure what they're talking about.

"Where are you taking me?" she manages. "I need help."

She can still feel the trickle of blood down her face from her wound. Her long hair is plastered to her cheek.

"Don't worry, we'll help you, Naya," the woman says, smiling down at her as they lift her into a van.

"How do you know my name?" Naya asks, not remembering telling them.

"Prep the IV," the man interrupts, gathering items in the tight space.

Naya feels a makeshift cot beneath her and struggles to sit up. The woman gently pushes her back, smoothing her hair out of Naya's face.

"It's a pretty nasty cut, but we'll make good use out of it. It'll be stitched up and healed over in no time," she promises, cleaning the blood off Naya's face.

Naya's heart beats rapidly in her chest as these strangers busy themselves with strapping her onto the bed. She has no idea what they plan to do, but she no longer feels safe.

"Help!" she attempts to scream, her voice coming out weak and warbled. She's lost a lot of blood.

"Hurry up and put her under," the man says.

Naya feels the prick of a needle in her arm and turns her head to see the woman concentrating on inserting the IV. The vein in her arm feels cold and an immediate fog enters her brain.

She attempts to scream again, but it's hard to keep her eyes open. The sound of the engine roaring to life is the last thing she remembers.

# CHAPTER 46

# ATLAS

Waking up is easier this time, Atlas knowing what to expect. He takes his time coming to, allowing his brain to adjust to the sterile hospital room. He flexes his fingers and toes, relishing the feel of his physical body, though it's very weak. He knows he has a long road ahead to get back to the person he used to be.

The click of the door startles him out of his thoughts and his eyes fly open. Relief floods through him when he sees Michael entering his room, a lopsided grin on his face.

"You did it, man. You got them out," he exclaims, clapping Atlas on the shoulder.

Atlas laughs weakly. "You sound like you didn't doubt me for a second."

"I didn't have time to, boss," Michael replies, taunting Atlas with the title.

"You know I hate that. Especially after everything that's happened," Atlas says somberly.

"You're right, sorry," Michael apologizes.

"So where is everyone? Are we safe? What happened while we were in there?" Atlas questions.

Michael pulls up a chair next to the hospital bed and sits down with a sigh. "Naya and her parents are safe. The facility is vacated. I called the authorities and everyone fled. I suppose they didn't want to face the consequences of their crimes."

Atlas gives a frustrated groan. "Please tell me they caught some of them? They need to pay for what they've done."

Michael nods. "A few. None of the higher-ups, though."

Atlas feels the anger flare up within him and he fights to tamp it down. Now is not the time. They'll get what's coming to them eventually.

"Atlas, they have a lot of questions for you," Michael states.

"I figured. I'm the creator of the program, after all. Did you destroy it?" Atlas asks, remembering his last request of Michael before reentering the simulation.

"It was the first thing I did. The servers are wiped," Michael reports.

The words fill Atlas with satisfaction. His creation can't hurt anyone anymore. Though he knows it was evidence, Atlas wanted to ensure Genesis Laboratories couldn't take the program with them. He'd rather face the consequences of getting rid of it than let it fall into the wrong hands again. Project Nowhere needed to die.

"Thank you, Michael. For everything," Atlas expresses, gratitude evident in his tone. "I'll answer whatever questions they have for me, but can I see her first?"

Michael grins, knowing Atlas would ask. "Of course, let's get you situated."

After several minutes, Michael is wheeling Atlas down the hall in a wheelchair. Though Atlas protested at first, a few steps was all it took to know his legs were too weak to carry him.

The halls are a flurry of activity, men and women in uniform hurrying about. Atlas ignores them, eager to see Naya. As they round the next corner, his heart speeds up at the sight of her dark hair through a window up ahead.

Michael flips Atlas around, wheeling him backwards into the room as he holds the door open. As he's turned back around, the sight of Naya fills him with joy. Her long, dark hair looks different from the shorter cut she had in the simulation, but she's no less beautiful.

"Atlas," she breathes, giving him a small smile as Michael parks the wheelchair next to her bed.

"I'll give you two a minute," Michael says, heading into the hall and shutting the door behind him.

Atlas reaches out to tuck a strand of hair behind her ear, his fingers brushing against a raised bit of skin. Looking closer, he's shocked to see a familiar scar running along her hairline. Naya notices the look on his face, her eyes darkening.

"It was real," she murmurs, twisting a strand of hair anxiously around a finger.

Atlas's stomach twists at her words, a fresh spark of rage igniting within him. He had hoped it wasn't real, though he knew the trauma would still affect her either way.

"How?" he asks, wondering when it happened.

Naya swallows, her eyes glossed over as she recalls that night. "It was them," she whispers. "Genesis Laboratories. I remember snippets of conversation while they carried me into a van. It was like it was all planned out. I think it's how they got me here."

Guilt makes Atlas feel sick, the consequences of his actions worse than he could have ever imagined. He can't believe the extent Genesis Laboratories went to get her here.

"Your parents?" he adds, suddenly worried how they ended up here. "Have you spoken with them?"

"Not yet. I haven't been awake for long. You must've been right behind me," Naya notes. She reaches out to hold Atlas's hand in hers, squeezing it lightly. "Thank you, for getting us out."

"Don't thank me, Naya. I'm the one who got you into this mess in the first place." Atlas looks down at their hands, his shame making it hard to look her in the eyes.

He notices the ring on her finger, a reminder of the promise he made to her before everything went wrong. Atlas lightly touches the diamond, wondering if she still feels the same. As if reading his mind, Naya lifts his chin with her hand, leaning down to kiss him softly.

"I remember, Atlas. It's me," she whispers against his lips.

Atlas's heart races, a mix of relief and disbelief flooding through him. "Naya, I was so scared. I thought I'd lost you."

Naya's eyes well up with tears. "You almost did, but I'm here now. We're together. That's what matters."

He pulls her into a tight embrace, burying his face in her shoulder. Naya takes a deep breath, her body relaxing into his touch. "What happens now?" she asks.

"We recover," Atlas replies. "And we make sure Genesis Laboratories pays for what they've done."

Naya nods. "Can we go see my parents?"

# CHAPTER 47
## NAYA

Michael pushes Naya into her parents' room, the door creaking closed behind him as he goes to get Atlas. Her parents look haggard and worn, but their faces light up when they see their daughter.

"Naya!" her mother exclaims.

Her father's expression softens beside her, a mixture of relief and concern.

"Mom, Dad," Naya says, her voice cracking. "You're here."

"We're here, sweetie," Celeste replies. "We've just been waiting for you to wake up."

Silas nods, beckoning Naya closer. "How are you feeling?"

"Tired," Naya admits. "But… relieved."

Her parents exchange a glance before Celeste speaks again. "We were so worried when we realized what had happened. It was like waking up from a nightmare. Where's your sister?"

Dread pools in Naya's stomach. She'd almost forgotten she would have to break the news. Before she can decide what to say, the door opens behind her.

"That must be her now!" her father interjects.

Naya turns to see Michael wheel Atlas into the room, parking him beside her.

"The gang's all back together again," Michael exclaims, a content smile on his face.

"Except for Harper," Celeste says. "Where is she?"

Michael looks nervously at Naya and Atlas, swallowing uncomfortably. The room is silent. No one is sure what to say.

"Atlas," Celeste continues, her voice rising with panic. "You promised me you wouldn't leave her behind. So where is she?"

Naya grabs Atlas's hand for support and takes a deep breath. "Mom, Harper didn't come with us. We had to leave her behind because she was part of the simulation."

Silas narrows his eyes, trying to discern the meaning of her words. "I don't understand," he states.

Atlas squeezes Naya's hand, giving her a knowing glance. With a nod, she knows he'll take it from here. She appreciates Atlas sharing the weight of this burden with her.

Atlas's voice is gentle and filled with sorrow as he meets the eyes of Naya's parents. "The Harper you left behind in the simulation was no longer your daughter," he begins, his words heavy with grief. "Two weeks ago, Harper passed away due to complications from the simulation."

Celeste gasps, her hand flying to her mouth as tears well up in her eyes. Silas's face contorts in pain, his grip tightening on the edge of his hospital bed.

"I'm so sorry," Atlas continues, his voice breaking.

Celeste's sobs fill the room and Silas pulls her into his arms, his own tears streaming down his face. Naya feels a pang of deep sorrow, the weight of the loss settling heavily in her chest. She wheels herself closer to her parents, reaching out to hold their hands.

Naya's parents cling to each other, their grief palpable. She rests her head in her mom's lap, her own tears flowing freely now. They comfort each other amidst the overwhelming sadness, letting themselves mourn the loss of Harper.

"C-Can we see her?" Celeste stammers, wiping away a tear.

Naya watches as Atlas looks toward Michael for an answer. He sighs, his own eyes wet with emotion.

"I'm not sure. I can check to see if they kept her body in the lab," Michael replies somberly, leaving the room.

Atlas moves closer to comfort Naya, the four of them lost in their grief. Naya isn't sure how long Michael is gone, their sobs and ragged breathing the only sounds in the room. By the time he returns, everyone's eyes are rimmed with red, their tears dried up.

"She's here," Michael says. "I'll take you to her."

Harper lies unnaturally still on the table, her once golden skin now deathly pale. Her dark hair fans out around her, framing her youthful features. Naya's vision blurs as she gazes at Harper's lifeless form, fresh tears pricking her eyes. They spill over, wetting the hospital gown covering her sister's body.

Naya touches her little sister's cheek, her skin cold to the touch. The vibrant girl who once brought so much joy and energy into their lives now lays cold and still, a stark reminder of the cruel reality they've woken up to.

Beside Naya, her mom clutches Harper's hand tightly, tears falling freely onto the sterile metal table. "My sweet baby girl. What did they do to you?" she sobs, her voice trembling with anguish.

Naya's dad is on the other side of the table, his face a mask of grief and helplessness. "She didn't deserve this," he whispers. "None of us did."

Atlas, sitting in a wheelchair next to Naya, reaches out and takes her hand, his touch warm and reassuring despite the tears in his own eyes.

"I just can't believe she's gone," Naya mutters. "It felt like she was just here with us, full of life and laughter."

Celeste looks up, her eyes red and swollen. "We need to make sure this never happens to anyone else," she says, a determined edge creeping into her voice. "We can't let Genesis Laboratories get away with this."

Silas nods, his expression hardening with resolve. "We'll fight for her," he agrees. "We'll make sure the truth comes out and those responsible are held accountable."

Beside her, Naya senses Atlas shifting uncomfortably in his wheelchair. He drops her hand, staring into his lap.

"It's all my fault," Atlas confesses. "I'm the one who designed Project Nowhere. I'm so, so sorry. I never meant for any of this to happen."

Naya reaches over, wrapping her arms around him in a comforting embrace. "No, you didn't do this to us. You tried to make something that would help the world."

Atlas's shoulders shake with sobs as Naya holds him tighter, her own tears mixing with his.

"Atlas," Silas begins, his voice steady and firm. "We don't blame you. If anyone is to blame, it's those who misused your creation. They twisted your work for their own ends."

"It's not your fault," Celeste adds, placing a hand on Atlas's shoulder. "Harper would never blame you."

Atlas looks up, his handsome features contorted with regret. "How can you forgive me so easily? If I hadn't written the code, Harper wouldn't have died. I should have known. I should have stopped them" he cries, raw emotion making his voice waver.

"You couldn't have known how they would use it," Celeste reassures. "You are a victim of their deceit just like the rest of us. Blaming yourself won't bring Harper back."

Naya knows how Atlas feels, having blamed herself for not being able to protect her little sister. "Atlas, you built the backdoor. You're the one who saved us," she argues.

"We've all made mistakes," Silas interjects. "What matters is what we do moving forward. We have a chance to fight for justice and make sure no one else has to suffer like she did.”

“And we’ll see Harper again,” Naya insists, an encouraging reminder for all of them. “She’s in a better place now and she’d want us to keep going.”

Naya pulls back slightly, looking into Atlas’s eyes with fierce determination. “We need you, Atlas. You’re the only one who truly understands the system. You can help bring down Genesis Laboratories.”

Atlas nods slowly, the spark of resolve rekindling in his eyes. Naya smiles through her tears, a glimmer of hope shining through her grief.

“Together?” Naya prompts.

Atlas gives her a weak smile. “Together.”

The room falls into a moment of quiet resolve, the weight of their shared mission settling over them. Despite the pain, there’s a newfound sense of purpose. They’ve been through hell, but they had each other, and together they will face whatever comes next.

Atlas takes a deep breath, and Naya can tell his burden of guilt has lifted just slightly. “Thank you,” he whispers. “I don’t deserve your forgiveness, but I’ll do everything I can to make things right.”

Naya leans in, pressing her forehead against his. “You already are, Atlas. You already are.”

CHAPTER 48
# ATLAS

It's been two weeks since leaving the simulation. After undergoing questioning, everyone was eager to get back to their real lives. Harper's funeral was small and intimate, a final goodbye for the family. With a month having passed after they all just vanished, Naya and her parents didn't want to involve friends and neighbors.

Genesis Laboratories concocted a story saying the Callaway family had moved out of the country to live as missionaries. The lie covered their tracks well but made returning to society even more difficult. Naya lost her apartment and is now living with her parents. Thankfully, Genesis Laboratories hadn't gotten around to listing their family home. It just sat empty all this time.

In an attempt to placate the family, the government is footing the bill for biweekly physical therapy. They also paid for the surgeries to have each person's microchip removed. Everyone is working hard to recover from the operation and rebuild their atrophied muscles. Naya and Atlas have made significant progress, but it's slower for her parents whose age makes it more difficult.

The government also offered other financial compensation, but they turned it down. It feels like hush money, a way to keep them quiet while the controversy around Project Nowhere dies down.

Amidst everything, Atlas is consumed by getting justice, but it's proving more difficult than he imagined. Due to the government's involvement with Project Nowhere, there is a lot of red tape slowing down the investigation. To make more progress, Atlas and the Callaways are doing their own research.

He shuffles through the papers laid out on the table before him, frustrated with the lack of information they've gathered so far.

"Why don't you take a break, Atlas? Go home, get some rest," Celeste instructs, stretching in her wheelchair.

"Agreed, it's time we call it for the night," Silas grumbles, rubbing his tired eyes.

Atlas sighs, leaning back in his chair. They're getting nowhere with their search for the Genesis Laboratories employees who disappeared. It's like they vanished into thin air. Every day, Atlas searches for any leads, often coming over to visit Naya and her parents who are just as invested in the search.

Naya is already in bed, having called it quits much earlier in the night. She's been a bit distant lately, finding it harder to adjust to her old life.

"Mind if I use the restroom before I head out?" Atlas asks, pushing back his chair.

"Not at all," Celeste says with a weary smile.

Atlas grabs his walker and makes his way toward the bathroom. Though his rehabilitation feels painfully slow, Atlas is told he's made remarkable strides these past two weeks. As he shuffles down the hall, Atlas glances at the family photos hung on the walls. Harper smiles back at him in several, his heart constricting at the sight of her.

Atlas admires the resilience of Naya and her family, not allowing their sorrow to taint the past. Although they were able to leave the pictures up, Harper's bedroom still sits untouched down the hall. He glances at her closed door before disappearing into the bathroom.

Atlas splashes water on his face, attempting to clear his mind. In the mirror, he notices the weariness etched on his face. The bathroom light enhances the dark circles under Atlas's eyes, making him look haggard and older.

By the time Atlas is back in the dining room, Celeste informs him they called Michael and he's almost here.

"I appreciate it," Atlas says, grateful they have a landline.

Michael is the only one with a cell phone, having had a steady income longer than the rest of them. Although recently, he's been thinking he might have to get rid of it. Being a former employee of Genesis Laboratories is making it hard to find another job. Even so, Michael graciously let Atlas move in with him, Atlas having also lost his apartment.

Heading into the living room to wait, Atlas collapses onto the couch. He rests his head against the cushions, tired from his jaunt to the bathroom. Atlas hates feeling weak and easily exhausted, though it makes him appreciate a healthy, functioning body that much more.

A knock on the door interrupts the silence, Celeste wheeling over to open it. Michael steps inside, his expression warm. His straight brown hair flops over his forehead and he brushes it aside.

"Any progress?" Michael asks hopefully, looking from Celeste to Atlas.

Celeste shakes her head solemnly. "No, but it hasn't been long. I know we'll find something eventually."

"I always appreciate your positivity, Mrs. Callaway," Michael answers.

"Thanks for coming to get me," Atlas interjects, standing and walking over. He feels the pull of exhaustion with every step.

Bending down to hug Celeste, he thanks her for her hospitality. With a wave goodbye to Silas who still sits at the table, Michael helps Atlas outside.

The cool night air hits Atlas like a balm, momentarily refreshing him. They walk to Michael's car, a battered but reliable sedan that has seen better days.

The drive to Michael's apartment is quiet, punctuated only by the hum of the engine and hushed radio. Atlas stares out the window, noticing the dilapidated state of the city. It's not as clean as it used to be, with trash littering the sidewalks and alleys. He watches as a homeless man pushes an old grocery cart down the sidewalk, likely trying to find shelter for the night.

Michael finally breaks the silence as they pull into the parking lot of his apartment complex. "How are you holding up?" he asks, glancing over at him.

Atlas sighs, running a hand through his hair. He really needs a haircut. "I'm… managing. It's just a lot to process."

Michael nods, his eyes reflecting a deep understanding. "I get it. There's a lot to sort through now that you're back. Just take it one day at a time."

Michael helps Atlas up to his apartment, a modest but comfortable space that feels like a sanctuary compared to the sterile confines of the facility. The living room is decorated with mismatched furniture, and a small kitchen table is cluttered with books and papers.

"I'll get us some water," Michael says, gesturing to the couch before heading into the kitchen.

Atlas sits, the cushions enveloping him in a comforting embrace. He watches Michael move around the kitchen, the familiarity of the scene grounding him in reality.

Michael returns with two cups of ice-cold water, handing one to Atlas before sitting across from him. They sip in silence for a moment, the cool liquid refreshing Atlas's tired mind. Michael turns on the TV, the nightly news illuminating the room.

Footage of a mass protest flashes across the small screen, people holding signs and banners demanding justice. Some scenes show clashes between protestors and police, with tear gas and smoke filling the air. The TV cuts to people looting nearby stores, others holding signs demanding economic relief.

"Protests are erupting in cities around the country, people in an uproar over the government's VR experiment," the news anchor says. "The government claims Genesis Laboratories acted alone, that the VR technology was never intended to be used in such a manner. But people are skeptical of their official story, with many believing it's just a cover up."

Michael and Atlas eye each other, shocked with what's going on. The world is a far cry from what Atlas left behind when he was put in the simulation, the recent protests only serving to make it worse. He returns his attention to the TV, watching as the screen splits into scenes that illustrate the turmoil.

"The economy has worsened, social unrest is at an all-time high, and the government's grip on information is tighter than ever," the news anchor relays, solemnly delivering the grim updates.

Footage shows long lines of people outside of job centers, waiting in hope for employment opportunities. Faces of despair and frustration dominate the screen.

"Unemployment has sky-rocketed, people are struggling to make ends meet."

Images of overcrowded homeless shelters and food banks flit across the screen. Families huddle together on the streets, looking anxious and weary. The footage cuts away, a short interview with a middle-aged woman named Janet taking its place.

She stands in front of a small, run-down grocery store, her expression a mix of anger and fear. "I've seen my grocery bill double in the last year. Rent keeps going up, but my paycheck stays the same. It's like they want to squeeze every last penny out of us. And now this? Using virtual reality to mess with our minds? It's a whole new level of control."

The camera zooms in on her face, capturing the raw emotion in her eyes. "Project Nowhere is a nightmare. Just the thought of being trapped in some fake reality makes my skin crawl. And the Callaway family? They were just regular people, like you and me. To think they were used like guinea pigs, without a say in it, it's horrifying."

Atlas gulps, feeling guilty knowing he's much more than an ordinary citizen. He's thankful the authorities agreed to keep his part in designing the program under wraps.

Janet takes a deep breath, trying to calm herself. "We need transparency, we need accountability. If they can do this to one family, what's stopping them from doing it to everyone? We deserve better than this constant state of fear and manipulation and we're not going to stop until we get the truth. This is our lives they're playing with, and we won't be silenced."

The camera pans out, showing Janet standing defiantly among other concerned citizens, determination evident on their faces. The interviewer nods, clearly moved by her impassioned plea.

"Thank you for sharing, Janet. Your concerns are echoed by many."

The camera cuts back to the news anchor in the studio. "The fallout from Project Nowhere is far from over, and the public's demand for justice and transparency continues to grow."

Another story takes over and Michael turns the TV off. "Have you thought about what's next?" he asks.

Atlas shakes his head. "Not really. It's hard to think beyond the immediate. We've only just started the recovery process. Naya and her parents are trying to find jobs since turning down the government's payout."

"And you?" Michael inquires seriously, leaning forward. "Bringing Genesis Laboratories down won't pay the bills."

Atlas takes a deep breath, feeling overwhelmed by his situation. "I know. It's just… Harper. I can't get her out of my mind."

Michael's brown eyes soften. "We all have our ghosts, Atlas. But right now, we need to focus on the living. I have my suspicions that Genesis Laboratories won't just let us walk away. Especially with the country up in arms. We need to figure out what they might be planning next."

Atlas takes a deep breath, steeling himself for the challenges ahead. "You're right. With so many of them out there, who knows what they might try to do."

Michael places a reassuring hand on Atlas's shoulder.

"We'll find a way to expose them, to make sure no one else suffers like we have."

# CHAPTER 49
# NAYA

Naya's childhood bedroom feels eerily similar to the simulation, making it hard to fall asleep. She rolls onto her back, staring at the ceiling to avoid looking at the familiar surroundings. Plastic stars glow above her, forming peculiar shapes and patterns. Naya smiles, letting a memory wash over her.

"What's that supposed to be?" Harper asks, pointing at the shape Naya just finished making.

"Lay down on the bed," Naya instructs, flopping onto her back next to her little sister. "Can you see it now?"

Harper tilts her head, her eyes lighting up when she sees what Naya made with the little plastic stars. "A ladybug!"

"Mm-hm. For my Little Ladybug," Naya says, tickling Harper beside her.

She giggles, a joyful sound that's impossible not to smile at.

"Well now I have to make one for you, too! Our galaxy isn't complete without the both of us up there!" Harper jumps up and grabs another handful of stick-on stars.

Naya remains on the bed, watching her sister work. Harper starts by making a circle before adding lines radiating out from it.

"A sun?" Naya asks. "How come?"

"Because you're my sunshine," Harper declares. "I admire your positivity. You always help me see the light, even in dark situations."

Naya is stunned by her sister's words, warmth spreading through her chest. Harper snuggles in beside her on the bed and Naya hugs her tight.

"Thanks, Harper. You don't know how much that means to me."

A tear slides down Naya's cheek, the bittersweet memory almost unbearable. Naya swipes it away, struggling to sit upright in bed. She doesn't feel anything like the Naya in her memory, the positivity Harper described fading with each day. She's not sure why, but lately she's felt a tug to do things she normally wouldn't.

Wanting to clear her head, Naya decides to get out of bed. Slowly, she swings her legs over the side, gripping the walker parked nearby. Naya hauls herself to her feet, shuffling to the door. She feels like an old lady.

Walking into the kitchen, she's thankful her parents' house isn't exactly like it was in the simulation. It's strange how some things changed, and others stayed the same. Her bedroom is almost exactly as she remembers it, but other details feel distorted, like in a dream. Rather than having an upstairs, the house has a basement. With everything vital on the main floor, the basement remains unused until they can more easily use the stairs.

Grabbing a glass of water, Naya braces herself against the kitchen counter. Even standing is a lot of work, but she doesn't feel like moving a few more feet to sit in a dining chair. She stares out the backdoor, sipping on the cool liquid. The backyard is wild, most of their efforts spent dusting and cleaning the interior since their return. Her dad is in no state to mow the yard, anyway. Naya makes a mental note to ask Michael to do it next time she sees him.

A tapping on the glass breaks the silence, sending Naya's heart racing. She glances around, uncertain what made the noise. A flash of white at the backdoor catches her attention and she squints to see the source. There, on the back porch, sits Gizmo.

Naya's heart skips a beat at the sight of their cat. They thought he was gone, Genesis Laboratories having been humane enough to let him out of the house when they left it empty.

Gizmo paws at the glass, wanting to be let inside. His white and brown fur is matted and he looks skinnier than when they left him. Naya walks to the door as fast as her legs will allow, sliding it open enough for Gizmo to slip inside. Immediately, he rubs against her legs, purring loudly.

She bends down to pick him up, snuggling him in her arms. "How's my little gremlin? Where were you, huh?" she whispers into his fur.

Naya is comforted by his presence, a piece of home she thought she'd lost. He meows and she puts him down, getting him some food and water. When he's all set, Naya moves into the living room, curling up onto the couch. Gizmo is close behind, jumping onto the couch to lay beside her. Though he's dirty, she pulls him close, letting his rhythmic purring lull her to sleep.

The next morning, Naya sits on the padded table in the physical therapy room, her legs dangling off the edge. The familiar scent of antiseptic and rubber mats fills the air. It's a high-end therapy center on the rich North side of the city, one her family could've never afforded on their own. Although Naya still feels out of place amongst the modern interior, she's grateful her family is receiving the best therapy possible.

Naya's been working hard to regain her strength, making good progress since waking up from the simulation. Today, her usual therapist, Rachel, told her there would be a new specialist to help her with the next phase of her recovery.

As she waits, she glances around the room, wondering which machine they'll have her try next. In the corner, Naya sees her parents going through their routines. Though their progress is slower than hers, they haven't given up on themselves. The determination on their faces is inspiring, and it reminds her of her own resolve to get back on her feet.

The sound of footsteps draws her attention, and she turns to see a blonde, well-built man with a friendly smile. He looks to be around her age, maybe a few years older. He extends his hand to her with a smile.

"Hey there, Naya. I'm Lucas Thorne, your new physical therapist," he says.

Naya takes his hand and shakes it. "Nice to meet you Mr. Thorne."

"Lucas is fine," he replies, his blue eyes sparkling with a warmth that puts her at ease. "I've heard great things about your progress from Rachel. Ready to take it up a notch?"

Naya nods, feeling a surge of confidence. "Absolutely. Let's do this."

Lucas guides her through a series of exercises, pushing her just enough to challenge her without causing discomfort. His encouragement and enthusiasm are contagious, making the session fly by. By the end, Naya feels exhausted but accomplished.

"You did great today, Naya," Lucas says, handing her a towel. "Keep this up, and you'll be back to full strength in no time."

"Thanks, Lucas. I appreciate it," Naya says, wiping the sweat from her forehead. "It's nice to have someone pushing me."

"Anytime," he says with a smile. "With all you went through, don't forget about your mental health, too. Recovery isn't just physical, you know."

His words strike a chord with Naya. She gives him an absentminded nod before getting to her feet, appreciative he's treating her like a normal human being so far.

Sometimes she forgets that her time in the simulation is public knowledge. The constant stares and whispers whenever she goes out make her feel like a stranger in her own city. Naya has become a reluctant celebrity to some, and a victimized outcast to others. It's a peculiar limbo, being simultaneously avoided and scrutinized, and she's still not used to it.

Noticing her parents are still chatting with their therapists, Naya decides to get some fresh air. As she steps onto the sidewalk, she basks in the sun's warmth. It's another reminder this world is real, the heat much more palpable than it was in the simulation. She takes a seat on the bench outside, watching people go about their day.

The affluent north side of the city, dubbed Uptown, stands in stark contrast to the old, dilapidated downtown where Naya grew up. Wide, tree-lined boulevards are meticulously maintained, their greenery a testament to the wealth that flows through this part of the community. Luxurious high-rises with modern architectural designs pierce the sky, their glass facades reflecting the sunlight in dazzling patterns.

People in Uptown move with a purposeful grace, their designer clothing and polished accessories signaling their social status. Naya notices the latest tech gadgets clutched in their hands or peeking out of pockets and purses. She'd love to get her hands on one of those, but she can only dream of ever affording it.

Cars glide smoothly down the pristine streets, Uptown's residents not needing to walk or ride a bike to their destination. A jogger runs past, clad in the latest athletic wear. Naya follows their path, eyeing the manicured park to her right. Couples stroll along the scenic paths and children play on the shiny, well-equipped playground.

A flash of long black hair catches her attention and her heart lodges in her throat. *Harper,* she thinks, shielding her eyes to see better. Blinking, disappointment floods through her when she realizes it's just her mind playing tricks on her.

Naya sets her head in her hands, letting out a frustrated sigh. Nearby, she hears a car door open. Looking toward the parking lot, Naya sees Michael's beat-up sedan. It sticks out like a sore thumb amidst the other cars in the lot.

Atlas climbs out from behind the wheel. Grabbing his walker from the backseat, he makes his way to the building.

"Naya!" he calls, beaming as he spots her. "I was hoping I'd catch you before you left. How was your session?"

She smiles back, giving him a small wave. "Good. I'm doing so well they moved me to a more advanced trainer!"

Atlas sits beside her on the bench. "That's amazing. You're blowing me out of the water."

Naya chuckles, reaching out to push a stray curl off Atlas's forehead. "Thanks, but you're doing great too."

"I feel like I don't get to see you as often anymore," he says softly, his hazel eyes filled with a mixture of longing and regret.

"I know, I'm sorry," she replies, feeling a bit guilty. "I feel like there's not much we can do, being somewhat crippled," Naya jokes, motioning toward their walkers.

"So you're saying when we get old, you won't want to hang out anymore?" Atlas wrinkles his nose in mock offense.

"Exactly!" she retorts with a smirk. "You'll be too boring, sitting around talking about your aches and pains."

Atlas feigns shock, clutching his chest. "Boring? Me? Never! I'll have you know, I plan to be the most exciting old man around. You'll be begging to hang out with me."

Naya laughs, rolling her eyes. "Oh, really? And what thrilling activities do you have in mind for our golden years? Bingo nights and early bird specials?"

"Absolutely," Atlas says, nodding sagely. "And don't forget the heated debates over which brand of prune juice is superior."

Naya giggles, playfully nudging him. "Well, when you put it that way, how can I resist? Although, we've got to up our game now if we want to be the cool old couple."

Atlas leans in closer, lowering his voice conspiratorially. "Agreed. We should start training now. I'm thinking after physical therapy we start salsa dancing and skydiving."

"Salsa dancing, huh?" Naya says, raising an eyebrow. "You can't even manage a slow dance without stepping on my toes."

"Practice makes perfect," Atlas replies with a wink. "And as for skydiving, I'll make sure we get a tandem jump so you can't escape."

Naya bursts out laughing, shaking her head. "Alright, Mr. Adrenaline Junkie, you're on. But just remember, when we're eighty and jumping out of planes, you better not chicken out."

Atlas grins, his eyes twinkling. "Deal. But if we're doing this, you're going to have to promise not to call me boring ever again"

"Deal," Naya agrees, sticking her pinky out. "Pinky swear?"

Atlas hooks his pinky with hers, a playful seriousness in his gaze. "Pinky swear."

She looks down at their pinkies intertwined, and a sudden twinge of sorrow pierces her heart. It reminds her of all the times she and Harper used to pinky swear, sealing their sisterly promises with a giggle and a secret smile. Every time Naya feels a flicker of happiness, a wave of guilt crashes over her, knowing Harper will never experience life's little joys again.

She averts her gaze, looking back at the children playing in the park, her thoughts clouded with uncertainty. Atlas can sense her introspection and gently reaches out to hold her hand.

"Seriously, though, how are you?" he asks softly, his concern evident.

Naya takes a deep breath, looking back at him. "I don't know, Atlas. Everything feels different. We've been through so much, and now that we're out, I'm struggling to find my place again. The world doesn't feel like how we left it."

Atlas squeezes her hand reassuringly. "We'll find our way, Naya. It's going to take time, but we'll figure it out together."

She looks into his eyes, finding solace in his words. "I hope so. It's just hard, you know? I miss Harper so much, and it feels like part of me is missing without her."

Atlas's expression softens with understanding. "I miss her too, Naya. Every day. But we have to keep going, for her sake."

Naya nods, tears welling up in her eyes. She angrily wipes them away, annoyed with how little it takes to get her emotional these days. "I know you're right. It just feels like I'm constantly fighting against this grief."

"One day at a time. Never forget I'm here for you, always," Atlas reminds, gazing into her eyes. "And you have your faith. Remember you told me once, our weakest moments should drive us toward God?"

Naya nods, recalling their conversation in Bargain Bytes a while back. "It's easier said than done, I guess."

Atlas pulls her into a hug. Naya leans into him, resting her head on his shoulder. "Thank you, Atlas. I don't know what I'd do without you."

They sit in silence for a moment, drawing strength from each other's presence. After a while, Naya pulls back, wiping her tears. "I guess I should get going. My parents are probably waiting. Lucas wants to see me tomorrow morning for another session."

Atlas raises an eyebrow. "Lucas? Your new trainer?"

"Yeah, he was great today. Challenged me just the right amount."

Atlas nods, though there's a hint of something in his eyes that Naya can't quite place. "Just be careful, okay? I want to make sure you're safe."

Naya smiles, touched by his concern. "I will, I promise. You've become such a worry wart lately," she teases.

"Yeah, yeah, yeah. Can you blame me?" he says, giving her a wry grin as she rises from the bench.

"Go kick some butt in your session, Cereal Thief. I'll see you later," Naya says, parting ways.

As she leaves, Naya catches a glimpse of Lucas watching her from inside, but when she glances back, he's gone. She must be seeing things again. Her parents climb into the therapy center's complimentary shuttle car and Naya follows behind. The whole way home, she can't shake the feeling that things are changing, both within herself and around her.

# CHAPTER 50

# ATLAS

The rest of the week is a monotonous blur. Physical therapy. Dig up dirt on Genesis Laboratories. Watch depressing news updates. Attempt to find a job. Repeat. Tonight, Atlas is excited for something different, hoping to surprise Naya with an impromptu date.

Atlas pulls into Naya's driveway, grateful Michael let him borrow his car for the night. With a bit of effort, he makes his way to the front door, excited to have graduated to a cane instead of the walker. It makes him feel a bit more dignified.

Celeste answers the front door, greeting Atlas warmly before calling for Naya. It isn't long before she appears at the door, her outfit catching Atlas off guard. She wears a fitted black tank top with a scoop neck and tight ripped jeans—quite different from her usual style.

"How did you know?" Atlas asks, motioning toward her outfit with a playful grin, as if she'd somehow anticipated his date night plans.

Naya glances down at her clothes, arching an eyebrow in confusion. "What do you mean?"

"Just that you're dressed differently. Thought you might've heard about the date I was planning," Atlas comments.

She shakes her head in reply, offering him a casual shrug. "After my apartment was rented out and my stuff was thrown away, I needed new clothes. Thought I'd try a new style for a change."

Although Atlas can certainly appreciate the way her new clothes accentuate her figure, it feels strange and unfamiliar. He's more accustomed to her modest, comfortable style. Shoving his uncertainty aside, Atlas focuses on appreciating his gorgeous fiancé.

"Well, you look amazing," he says, offering his arm. "Are you up for a date night?"

Naya smiles, looping her arm through his. "Absolutely. Lead the way."

By the time they reach the park, the setting sun has bathed everything in a warm, golden glow. Atlas moves toward a spot beneath a willow tree, realizing halfway there that someone is sleeping beneath it. Heading in the opposite direction, he finds an idyllic patch of grass beneath a large oak tree. Spreading out a soft blanket, Atlas carefully unpacks his picnic. Amidst the charcuterie, sandwiches, and sparkling cider, he sets a brand-new box of Harvest Crunch.

Naya sits down gingerly, smiling at the spread before her. "You found a box," she says, her eyes sparkling with delight.

"Of course." Atlas sits down beside her. "I've checked the grocery store every day since we got back and finally managed to snag one. It wouldn't be a proper picnic without it."

"No challenging strangers to a coin toss to get the last box?" Naya teases.

"Not this time," he says, the memory filling him with affection.

Despite the park's desolate appearance, there is a certain peacefulness about it. The absence of daytime crowds brings a rare, almost serene silence, broken only by the occasional distant siren or the chirping of crickets. It's a welcome respite from the chaos of their daily lives, and they enjoy their meal in the comfortable ambience.

Atlas observes the park, noticing the new graffiti on the playground, the colorful tags distorted by the waning light.

The swings creak softly in the breeze, and the slide now casts a long, unsettling shadow. Atlas looks over at Naya who also eyes the playground in contemplation. He wonders if she's thinking about Harper.

Hoping to lighten the mood, Atlas breaks open the box of cereal and points to the flower garden in the middle of the park. The tiered circles of tulips and lilies are a bit wild and unkempt, but still beautiful.

"In the simulation," Atlas starts, swallowing his handful of cereal. "That was a fountain, not a flower garden."

"Huh," Naya says, tilting her head to imagine a fountain. "I can see how it sort of looks like a fountain."

Atlas gives her a mischievous grin. "You know when I first met you at the pastry vendor?"

Naya nods, her brown eyes full of curiosity.

"Right before that, I waded through the fountain to get the coins that were scattered at the bottom. I thought it was my lucky day, but I later found out it was Michael trying to orchestrate us meeting each other," he explains, gazing at the middle of the park as if the fountain is still there.

"Really?" Naya asks in surprise. "I had no idea. What else did Michael do?"

"Hired me at Bargain Bytes."

Naya's jaw drops. "And here I was thinking it was my sweet talking that got you the job." She smiles ruefully, her expression turning thoughtful. "I keep forgetting that Mr. Jenkins wasn't real. It's weird to think about Michael controlling him behind the scenes."

Atlas stares at Naya, noting the faraway look in her eyes. Though he understands what she's experiencing, he knows it's different for her, having been much closer to Mr. Jenkins than he was.

"Yeah, looking back on it, there are a lot of things that feel weird," Atlas says softly, offering the cereal to Naya.

She takes a handful and then closes the box, setting it aside. Finished eating, Atlas packs up the picnic with Naya's help.

"I have a little surprise for you," he says when they're done, offering his hand to help her up.

They walk slowly along a weathered trail lined with cherry blossom trees, the path illuminated by the fading light. Up ahead, Atlas finds a cozy spot on a hill, directing Naya that way. When they reach the top, he sets his bag down and pulls out two paper lanterns.

"I thought we could write messages to Harper on these and say goodbye," he says softly.

Naya's eyes fill with tears, but she nods, touched by the gesture. They write their messages and light the lanterns, waiting for them to puff up before letting go. Atlas pulls Naya to his side as they watch the lanterns float upward until they look like distant stars in the approaching night sky.

"Thank you," she murmurs, wiping her tears away.

Atlas kisses Naya's forehead and pulls her to him in a tight embrace. They stand like that for several long moments, finding strength in each other's arms. Atlas looks down at Naya, brushing her long hair away from her face.

"How about some stargazing, like the good old days?"

She nods, giving him a small smile. He places the blanket on the hillside, and they lay side by side, the stars growing brighter as the sun dips below the horizon.

"Have I ever told you the story behind my favorite color?" Atlas questions, turning his head to face Naya.

"No, tell me," she whispers.

"It's the color of the sky on the night when I first realized I loved you."

Naya turns to face him, reaching her hand up to touch his face. "That night you said you didn't need to wish for anything?"

Atlas nods. "And when you brought me onto the roof in the simulation. I was falling for you all over again, although that night didn't end how I wanted it."

"Who knew I'd be jealous of myself," she jokes, inching closer to press her lips to his.

Atlas kisses her back, tangling his hands in her hair. For a moment, the world around them fades away, leaving only the two of them. Naya pulls away, leaving him breathless as he gazes into her beautiful brown eyes.

"I love you, Brown Eyes."

Naya stares back at him, uncertainty flashing across her face. Her demeanor shifts suddenly, as if a switch has flipped, and she averts his gaze. "What if I'm not the same girl you fell in love with back then?"

"Of course you're still her, Naya. The simulation affected you and I both, but it could never change who we are at our core," Atlas reassures.

She looks away, her voice tinged with frustration. "I appreciate your positivity, Atlas, I do, but it almost feels like we're trying to live in the past. The world is different now. I'm different. Ever since we woke up, it's like parts of me are missing. I don't know how to explain it."

Atlas reaches out, taking her hand in his. "We've been through a lot, Naya. It's going to take time to heal and to adjust to real life again. But you don't have to do it alone. I'm here with you, every step of the way."

Naya pulls her hand away, sitting up and hugging her knees to her chest. "You don't get it, Atlas. You're still you. You're still fighting to make the world a better place. To bring Genesis Laboratories down. I'm the one who feels lost."

Atlas sits up too, his expression pained. "I do get it, Naya. How could I not? You don't think I feel lost after everything I worked so hard for ended in such a nightmare?"

Naya is silent for a while, staring out at the horizon. When she finally looks back at him, her brown eyes have grown hollow.

"I guess we've both changed, then," she whispers. "We're not the same people who fell in love and I'm scared we never will be."

Atlas reaches out to touch her shoulder, but she pulls away, standing up. "Naya, please. We can work through this. I love you."

Naya looks down at him, her voice trembling. "Maybe that's the problem, Atlas. Maybe I need to figure out who I am on my own, without you always trying to fix everything."

Atlas feels a pang in his chest, her words cutting deep. "So, what are you saying?"

A tear rolls down her cheek and she wipes it away. "I don't know, Atlas. I just need some space to figure things out."

Atlas stands, his heart heavy. "I understand. If space is what you need, I'll give it to you. But please, don't shut me out completely. We've been through too much together to just give up now."

Naya nods, her eyes filled with sorrow. "I'm not giving up, Atlas. I just need time."

They stand in silence for a moment, the weight of their shared past and uncertain future hanging between them. The cool night air wraps around them, a stark contrast to the warmth they once shared. Atlas steps closer, hesitating before speaking.

"I'm sorry for trying to ignore the changes. I know we're different people now, living in a different world. But change doesn't mean the end. It can be a new beginning, too. We just need to find our way back to each other."

Naya's shoulders slump as she absorbs his words. "I wish it were that simple. But every time I look in the mirror, I see someone I don't recognize."

Atlas takes a deep breath, his voice steady but filled with emotion. "We've both faced our fears before, and we've always come out stronger. This time is no different. Take as much time as you need, Naya. Just know that I'll be here waiting for you."

Naya's eyes shimmer with unshed tears. She steps forward, her fingers brushing against his cheek. "Thank you. I just need some space to learn how to love myself again."

Atlas closes his eyes at her touch, savoring the brief moment of closeness. When she steps back, he looks at her, the mixture of hope and heartbreak in her eyes mirroring his own.

The ride to Naya's house is filled with an uncomfortable silence, the joy of the evening having evaporated. When Atlas walks Naya to her door, there's a palpable distance between them.

"Goodnight, Naya," he murmurs, trying to bridge the gap.

"Goodnight, Atlas," she replies, her voice void of warmth. She steps inside, closing the door gently behind her.

Atlas stands there, staring at the closed door, feeling a deep sense of unease. Though the night started with such promise, it ended in uncertainty, leaving him questioning everything.

# CHAPTER 51
# NAYA

Monday morning, Naya pushes herself to her limit during physical therapy. She enjoys drowning out her thoughts with the exercises, focusing only on the burn in her muscles.

"You're even more determined than usual," Lucas observes. "Something on your mind?"

"I just want to get better fast, that's all," she replies, starting another set.

"Well, you don't want to overdo it, either. That can set you back," Lucas cautions, glancing at the clock. "Your session is about over, anyway. After this set, call it quits for today."

Naya grunts in affirmation, putting her all into the last exercise. Sweat drips down her forehead and stray hairs from her ponytail stick to her neck. Lucas hands her a towel and she dries off, catching her breath.

"Think I can get rid of my cane soon?"

"Maybe not completely, but you can try some intervals of walking without it," he says, his words filling her with hope.

She's satisfied with her progress, feeling well on her way to functioning normally again.

"Thanks again, Lucas. I'll see you Wednesday?" Naya confirms, heading toward the door.

"Yeah. And Naya? I'm serious, don't overdo it."

Naya gives Lucas a nod before leaving. As she stands on the sidewalk, she feels a bit guilty for planning to walk home. *So much for not overdoing it,* she thinks.

The humid summer air does little to cool her down as she walks. Naya eagerly anticipates the day she can start riding her bike again. Considering Lucas's assessment of her progress, she hopes it will be soon.

Naya tries walking a few feet without the support of her cane, noticing the renewed strength in her legs. She still feels tired faster than she used to, but rehabilitation has been freeing.

As she navigates the pristine sidewalks of Uptown, Naya admires the elegant window displays of the boutiques that line the streets. Well-dressed pedestrians stroll by, their conversations a murmur of business deals and weekend plans. Several of them glance her way, whispers of her name making her feel self-conscious.

A couple walks by her on the sidewalk. Her heart drops at the sight of them, a reminder of how she hasn't talked to Atlas since their date. Naya doesn't feel great about how she left things, but knows it was the right call. She's been feeling more distant lately, not sure who she's becoming. It will be nice to spend some time by herself trying to figure it out. Atlas deserves to be with someone who knows who they are.

Naya notices the buildings change as she walks, the polished opulence of Uptown giving way to the grittier, more eclectic ambiance of Downtown. The high-rises become fewer, replaced by older, brick buildings decorated with colorful murals and graffiti.

There is a distinct presence of military police as she moves further south, their stern faces and imposing uniforms creating an atmosphere of tension. They stand in pairs at street corners and patrol the sidewalks, their presence a stark reminder of the ongoing unrest in the city.

The sight of them makes her quicken her pace slightly, the cane tapping rhythmically against the pavement. Despite the discomfort, Naya feels a strange sense of determination. This is her city, and she will find her place in it once more, no matter how much it has changed.

Down the block, a dilapidated shop catches Naya's attention. The faded words written above the door make her blink again, sure she's imagining things. The shop's name is Bargain Bytes.

Walking fast, Naya moves closer to the building. As she nears the windows, she sees someone working inside. Squinting, she tries to get a better look. The man's back is to her, but his balding head, glasses, and round belly are startlingly familiar.

Pushing the door open with the jingle of a bell, Naya calls out to the man. "Mr. Jenkins! I can't believe it's you!"

The man turns in his chair, a surprised look on his unfamiliar face. It's not Mr. Jenkins.

"I'm sorry, may I help you?" he questions.

Naya glances around the shop, realizing it looks nothing like Bargain Bytes. Newer devices are lined neatly on shelves, everything tidier and better kept.

"Sorry, I thought you were someone else," Naya mutters, embarrassed by her outburst.

She turns to leave but stops just short of the door. Pivoting on her heel, she gives the man a smile. "Actually, are you hiring? I'm looking for a job."

Several minutes later, Naya exits the computer shop with an interview scheduled for Thursday afternoon. She feels rejuvenated, excited by the prospect of working with computers again. Walking back toward home, Naya glances back at the shop, the words clearly spelling Budget Bits. She sighs, a bit worried how often she struggles to discern reality from her imagination.

When Naya arrives home, her mom greets her warmly at the door, standing out of her wheelchair. "How was physical therapy?"

"Great. Lucas says I can start walking intervals without my cane," Naya relays, a little out of breath from her walk home. "Oh, I also have a job interview on Thursday at a local computer shop!"

"That's amazing, sweetie. What inspired that?"

"Saw it on my way home and stopped in to ask." Naya decides to leave out the part about her seeing things.

Her mom pulls her into a hug, still a little wobbly on her feet. Gingerly, she steps back. "I think you need a shower," she politely declares.

Naya gives her mom a wry grin before kicking her shoes off and heading into the bathroom. She takes her time in the shower, enjoying the feel of the hot water. Massaging shampoo into her hair, a part of her misses her short hair. It was so much easier to take care of.

By the time she's done, the bathroom is full of steam and the mirrors are fogged over. Naya smears a hand over the glass to see her reflection, her scar more visible with her damp hair slicked out of her face.

She stares at herself for a while, as if her reflection holds all the answers to her unending questions. But the more she looks, the more troubled she feels. Her eyes trace the contours of her face—the lines of worry etched into her brow, the dark circles under her eyes. Her appearance is a stark reminder of the sleepless nights and endless tears.

Naya's gaze shifts to her long hair, cascading down her shoulders. It used to be a source of pride, something she and Harper would laugh about, comparing lengths and styles. It was undeniable they were sisters, some people even mistaking them for twins despite their age difference. The memory of Harper's dainty fingers braiding Naya's hair brings a lump to her throat.

Naya touches a strand, feeling its texture between her fingers. It feels heavy, a tangible connection to her sister that suddenly feels like a burden. Looking back into the mirror, it's Harper's face that stares back at her.

Stumbling backward, Naya braces herself against the wall. An intense urge rises within her, a desperate need to reclaim herself, to find some semblance of control amidst the chaos of her grief. The impulse to chop her hair off hits her like a wave.

She did it in the simulation in response to her traumatic attack, so why not now? Though Harper had initially cried when she saw the drastic change, she eventually came around, saying it made Naya look fierce and strong. She could really use those feelings right now.

Without thinking, Naya grabs a pair of scissors from the vanity drawer. Her hands tremble as she lifts the blades to her hair, her breath quickening. Tears blur her vision, but she steadies herself, focusing on the strands between her fingers. She hesitates, the weight of the decision hanging heavily in the air. Cutting her hair will be real this time, a length like her current one taking years to regrow.

Harper's face still stares back at her, a hollowness in her eyes. Naya looks away. Her sister is gone, and she needs to accept that.

"Goodbye, Harper," she whispers, the words catching in her throat.

With a sharp, decisive snip, the first lock falls to the floor. The sound of the scissors slicing through her hair is oddly satisfying, a cathartic release of pent-up emotion. The hair piles up around her feet, the beginning of a new chapter.

When she's done, she drops the scissors and looks at herself in the mirror once more. Her hair is jagged and uneven, nothing like the perfect cut she'd magically given herself in the simulation, though she thought nothing of it at the time. Still, Naya feels a strange sense of liberation.

The reflection that stares back at her is different, not just in appearance but in spirit. It's still her, but it's also someone who has faced unimaginable pain and is slowly finding a way to move forward. Another tear spills onto Naya's face as a small, determined smile forms on her lips. Her new hair feels fresh and weightless, both a symbol of a new start and a reminder of her past.

It's perfect.

# CHAPTER 52

# ATLAS

"Yesterday, police followed a lead regarding the whereabouts of Mr. David Ellis, the CEO of Genesis Laboratories."

Atlas scrambles for the remote, turning the TV volume up. Michael joins him in the living room, listening intently to what the news anchor has to say next.

"After staking out the location, the authorities determined the suspect had fled. There are no further leads at this time."

Atlas slumps into the couch with a groan, frustrated with the lack of progress. Genesis Laboratories is managing to stay very well hidden.

"It's been just over three weeks since the government's VR experiment at Genesis Laboratories was uncovered. The victims are still in recovery, though they seek justice for the loss of their daughter, Harper," the woman on the screen continues, a picture of Harper popping up on the side.

Atlas shuts the TV off, not wanting to hear any more. Michael sits beside him in silence, both feeling disappointed with the news. After a while, Michael gets up to finish preparing his lunch.

"You want one?" he asks, holding up a cup of noodles before popping it in the microwave.

Atlas's stomach twists at the sight as he remembers making those for him and Naya in the simulation. He's felt on edge since their date, worried Naya's need for space will lead to their breakup.

"No thanks, I'm good," Atlas replies with a half-hearted smile.

"Suit yourself." Michael shrugs, leaning against the counter as he waits for the microwave to finish.

Turning away, Atlas stares at the blank TV, his eyes glazing over. It's been too easy to get lost in his thoughts lately, letting his melancholy attitude waste the day away. There's plenty he could be doing, but it's hard to focus with Naya constantly on his mind. As much as he hates his current situation, it's made him realize he needs to get his life together outside of his relationship with Naya.

The beeping of the microwave jolts Atlas out of his mental fog. He drags himself off the couch, stretching his muscles as he meanders into the kitchen. Around the apartment, Atlas moves as much as possible without the use of his cane. His legs can carry him much further than they used to, but he still finds the need to occasionally brace himself against the furniture.

Michael eats his noodles at the small dining room table, watching Atlas maneuver through the kitchen.

"Have you talked to Naya lately?" he asks.

Atlas shakes his head. "Not since Friday."

"What about her parents? Aren't you still working with them on Genesis Labs stuff?" he inquires further, slurping another bite of noodles.

Atlas sighs, temporarily pausing his search for food. "Yeah, but Naya said she wanted space, so I'm trying to give that to her. Figured I could work from home for a while, though we've pretty much exhausted all of our resources."

Michael chews thoughtfully, narrowing his eyes in concentration. Without warning, he sets his food down and disappears into the bedroom. Atlas ignores his friend's strange behavior, peering into the fridge.

Torn between several options, Atlas doesn't notice Michael's return to the kitchen.

"Dude!" Michael shouts excitedly.

Atlas's head jolts up in surprise, whacking the top of the refrigerator. He scowls in pain, rubbing the back of his head as he stands to look at Michael.

"What?" He eyes the manilla folders in Michael's hands.

"I totally forgot about these! I snagged them before the police arrived. Thought you'd get better use out of them than they would." Michael hands the folders to Atlas.

He takes them, opening the top one to reveal his picture staring back at him. Thumbing through the stack, Atlas realizes it's his file from Genesis Laboratories. A quick glance at the other folders shows they belong to Naya and her family.

"Michael! This is amazing!" he gasps, bear-hugging Michael. "And probably illegal."

Michael laughs, and Atlas moves past him to set the folders on the dining table. He pulls his file from the pile, unceremoniously spreading its contents out before him. The information here will take him hours to look through. Grabbing the first page, Atlas sees it's a patient intake form listing his medical history.

Michael stands behind him, looking over his shoulder. "I hate to disrupt your riveting search for information, but don't you have physical therapy soon?"

Atlas looks up at the clock on the wall, realizing he's going to be late. "I didn't notice what time it was! I'll look at these later. Thanks again, Michael!" Atlas grabs Michael's keys off the counter and hurries out the door.

Halfway to the stairs, he realizes he forgot his cane. Groaning, he turns back around, only to see Michael exiting his apartment with his cane in hand.

"You forgot this!" he says, handing it off to Atlas.

Atlas grins. "You're the best."

An hour later, Atlas leaves the therapy center feeling satisfyingly tired. His therapist has kicked things up a notch, testing Atlas's endurance. He thought maybe he'd get a new physical therapist like Naya did, but it seems he gets to keep his for the duration of his therapy.

Heading to the parking lot, Atlas sees Naya walking on the sidewalk. His heart skips a beat and he jogs over to say hi. She looks at him, her hair making him do a double take.

"You cut your hair," he comments, taken aback by how similar she looks to their time in the simulation.

"Yeah, it was an impulse decision. My mom had to help even it out. It was a bit of a mess when I was finished with it." She laughs, grazing her hands along the freshly cut ends.

Atlas smiles, though his heart aches at the memories it stirs. "It suits you."

Naya shrugs, her fingers still playing with her hair. "I needed a change. I thought maybe this would help me feel more like myself again."

Atlas nods, understanding the sentiment. As he admires her new haircut, it dawns on him that she was walking when he saw her. "Did you walk all the way here?" he asks, noting the cane she carries in her arms.

"Yep! I did it on Monday, too. Lucas keeps telling me not to overdo it, but I feel so accomplished when I walk here."

"That's incredible, Naya. I haven't even tried walking for that long," Atlas acknowledges, looking back at Michael's car. "Hey, would you want a ride back home after you're done with your session? I don't mind hanging around. It's a long walk to your house."

Naya smiles. "Ever the gentleman. Thanks for the offer, Atlas, but I'll be okay. See you around?"

He's disappointed but pastes on a smile. "Of course."

# CHAPTER 53
# NAYA

"Wow, Naya, I really like your haircut," Lucas declares when she walks through the doors. "It looks great on you."

"Thanks!" She sets her stuff down on a floor mat.

She's grown very comfortable with Lucas, his easygoing nature making the grueling process of rebuilding her strength more bearable.

"How were your intervals without the cane? I hope you didn't overdo it." He gives her a knowing smile, the resulting dimple sending a flutter through Naya's stomach.

It catches her off guard and she quickly dismisses the feeling. "It's been good. I feel strong."

"You are strong, Naya," Lucas says, bringing over some weights and resistance bands to place on the mat beside her. "Your progress is remarkable."

His compliment makes her blush. She appreciates that he's noticed her hard work. Turning away, Naya begins stretching. Lucas oversees her routine, ensuring she maintains proper form. His touch is light, correcting her only when necessary, and yet she notices it more than usual. *What is wrong with me today*, she thinks.

Lucas guides her through a new stretch to add to her routine, watching as she repeats the motions. "Besides your incredible steps toward recovery, what else do you have going on?"

"I actually have a job interview tomorrow," Naya replies with a hint of excitement. "It's for a local computer shop."

Lucas raises an eyebrow, genuinely interested. "A computer shop, huh? That sounds cool. Do you think it's something you'll enjoy?"

Naya shrugs, leaning forward to touch her toes. "I'm excited, but part of me wonders if I'm just going through the motions. Everything has changed since the simulation and now I'm not sure what life after it should look like."

Lucas nods, his expression thoughtful. "Maybe this job isn't the right move for you."

Naya looks at him, surprised by his directness. "What do you mean?"

He sits back, his blue eyes meeting hers with an intensity that makes her heart skip a beat. "Maybe taking another job in the same field isn't the change you're looking for."

His words surprise her, as if he's able to read her mind. "How did you know I'm looking for a change?"

Lucas motions toward her new hair, giving her a shy smile. "I just assumed, considering your short hair and all."

Naya is impressed by his keen observation. Though it's a change for him, it almost feels more familiar to her than her long hair did.

"Have you thought about exploring something entirely new? Something that excites you?" Lucas asks, interrupting her thoughts.

Naya bites her lip, considering his words. "I guess I haven't really thought about it. I just assumed I needed to get back to something familiar to find stability."

"Stability is important," Lucas agrees, handing her a weight, "but so is finding something that makes you happy. You deserve to be excited about your future, not just settling for what seems safe."

Naya notices his eyes drift to the engagement ring on her finger and she looks down at it. Lucas is making her ponder things she's not sure she's ready for. "I wouldn't even know where to start," she murmurs.

Lucas reaches out, placing a reassuring hand on her shoulder. "Start with what you love, what you're passionate about. The rest will follow. You don't have to have it all figured out right away."

Naya looks back at him, a small smile tugging at her lips. "You're right. I'll think about it."

Lucas grins, reaching out a hand to help Naya off the mat. "Glad to hear it. Now, let's get to work. We've got some progress to make."

As they move through the exercises, Naya notices his strong jawline and the way his eyes crinkle when he smiles. Her growing attraction to him is sudden and unexpected.

The light catches on her ring, reminding her of the promise she made to Atlas, and shame floods through her. Naya tries to focus on her recovery and the repetitive motions of her exercises, but Lucas's words replay in her mind. They've sparked something inside her, a curiosity about what her future could hold if she dared to take a different path.

Finishing the session, Naya's workout endorphins fill her with a renewed sense of determination. "Thanks for the pep talk and another challenging session, Lucas," she says, giving him a genuine smile. "I needed that."

He smiles back, his eyes warm and encouraging. "Anytime, Naya. You've got this."

As she leaves the therapy center, Naya's mind buzzes with possibilities. She still has doubts, but for the first time in a long while, she feels a glimmer of hope. Maybe change can be a good thing.

"Well, you're in a good mood!" her mom says, watching as Naya plays with Gizmo on the living room floor.

She tosses the plastic spring across the room, delighted when Gizmo picks it up in his mouth and brings it back to her.

"You're such a good boy!" Naya praises, scratching him under the chin. He purrs loudly.

"Did you have a good physical therapy session today?" her mom asks, sitting on the couch. It's nice to see her mom out of the wheelchair, having moved to a walker earlier this week.

"Yeah, Lucas says I'm making really good progress. I think I might be able to get rid of my cane soon." Naya throws the spring across the room again.

"I'm proud of you, Naya." Her mom reaches down to pet Gizmo, distracting him from their game of fetch. He collapses onto the floor at her mom's feet, purring contentedly.

"Traitor," Naya mutters, a fond smile on her lips.

Gizmo meows, his bright blue eyes a stark contrast to the brown patches over his eyes. He's adorable and impossible to stay mad at. Scooting close to him, Naya rubs his face.

"I'm glad he's back," she comments, looking up at her mom.

She nods in reply, gazing down at Gizmo lovingly. "Me too. You know Harper loved him to death. It's like having a little piece of her back."

The sound of her sister's name puts her on edge. "I don't want to talk about her."

Naya's mom widens her eyes, their amber hue sparkling with concern. "Since when? I know it's been difficult, but you have never been one to shy away from the past. Especially when it comes to your sister."

Naya stands, a sudden anger urging her to leave. "Since now. I don't know, Mom. Maybe I'm just sick of being stuck in the past like you still are." Her words come out with an edge, sending a flash of hurt across her mom's face.

Naya wants to immediately take it back and apologize, her heart constricting at the pain she caused her mom. But something in her brain is tugging her to walk away. So, she does, storming off to her bedroom. She slams the door behind her, falling face first into her bed.

Laying there, the burst of anger fades like it was never there, leaving Naya feeling sad and confused. She's never been quick to anger before, this new side of her not one she likes. Naya groans into her pillow, frustrated with herself.

It isn't long before she hears a knock at the door, her mom's voice on the other side. "Can I come in?"

When Naya doesn't reply, her mom opens the door and peers inside. Closing it softly behind her, she sits on the bed next to Naya.

"What's going on, honey? This isn't like you," she whispers, gently placing her hand on Naya's arm.

Naya turns to look at her, filled with regret. "I'm sorry, I know I'm acting like a moody teenager. I don't know what's up with me lately."

Her mom laughs softly, carefully maneuvering her legs up onto the bed in front of her. Naya rolls over, sitting up to rest her head on her mom's shoulder.

"With everything you've been through, you deserve a moment of moodiness. Though next time, I'd appreciate it if you don't take it out on me."

"Sorry." Naya hugs her mom apologetically. "Where's dad?"

"Your father has found a new hobby to occupy his time. He's woodworking in the shed, although I think it's just an excuse to hit things with a hammer," she says with a skeptical smile.

Naya giggles, imagining her dad aimlessly nailing things together. She closes her eyes, comforted by the reminder that her parents are still adjusting to their new life too.

"Do you still have some of those?" her mom asks, pointing at the plastic stars on her ceiling.

"Yeah, why?"

"I want to add to your galaxy."

Naya gets up to grab the bag of remaining stars from her desk drawer. Handing them over, she watches as her mom stands on shaky legs to stick them on the ceiling.

"Careful, Mom."

"I'll be fine," she assures, focusing on forming her new shape.

Naya's eyes remain glued to where her mom stands on the bed. She reaches her arms out to steady her right as she finishes her new creation. With a grin, her mom gives the bag back and sits down on the bed.

Glancing up, Naya searches for the new variety of stars placed up above. She spots it, nestled between the ladybug and sun. It's a cross.

"You will shine among them like stars in the sky as you hold firmly to the word of life," her mom recites, Naya recognizing the line of scripture. "I thought you could use a reminder that you're never alone. Even on your darkest days, know that you can shine bright with the help of the Lord."

# CHAPTER 54

# ATLAS

Thursday morning, Atlas is only half awake when someone knocks on Michael's apartment door. Though he doesn't want to get up, Michael is already gone for the day, having started a new IT job last week. He throws on a pair of sweatpants and stumbles out of the bedroom toward the door. Peering through the peephole, Atlas sees a woman in a pantsuit standing in the dingy apartment hallway. She looks uncomfortable, her eyes anxiously darting around.

"Atlas Williams?" she calls, knocking again. "It's Ms. Harrington!"

Recognizing her as his government case manager, he opens the door with a sigh. She takes in his appearance, his sweatpants and bare chest earning him a disapproving look.

"Come on in," he says, ushering her into the apartment and shutting the door behind her. "What do you need, Ms. Harrington?"

She stands hesitantly inside while Atlas grabs a shirt from the bedroom. When he gets back, she hasn't moved, looking like she'd rather be anywhere else than here.

"I've come to make you another proposal on behalf of the government," she states, digging a piece of paper out of her bag.

He takes it, looking it over. "An apartment lease?"

Ms. Harrington nods, giving him a broad smile. "Yes! We want to offer you a brand-new apartment in Uptown to compensate you for everything you endured with Project Nowhere."

Atlas shoves the paper toward her, disgusted. "I already said I didn't want the government's hush money. An apartment is no different. Thanks, but no thanks."

She doesn't take the paper from his hands, unphased by his rejection. "You have a week to decide. If I don't hear from you by then, I'll assume your answer is still a no. You should really consider it, Atlas. It would be a wonderful new start."

Ms. Harrington leaves, the door creaking to a close. Atlas stares at the lease in his hands, unsure how to feel. For a second, he entertains the idea of a new start on the rich side of town. Living in a new apartment sounds rather appealing. The prospect of leaving behind the cramped space and constant reminders of the past is tempting. He imagines the modern amenities, the quiet, the comfort. A fresh start, free from the ghosts of Genesis Laboratories.

But as quickly as the thought comes, guilt floods in. How could he even think of accepting such an offer? It feels like a bribe, a way to silence his pursuit for justice, to make him forget about Harper and everything they've been through. The anger and shame well up inside him, making his hands tremble. If he accepts their offer, his decision will haunt him forever.

Atlas tosses the lease onto the coffee table and grabs his Genesis Laboratories file. He tries to distract himself with his continued search for information, scrutinizing each page. Several documents in, Atlas finds a section detailing the psychological effects of prolonged exposure to the simulation. It's filled with clinical language, but the implications are clear—Genesis Laboratories knew the potential for harm.

They predicted and documented the kind of trauma he, Naya, and others would endure. He reads about memory fragmentation, identity confusion, and the potential for dissociation. The text describes how he was observed closely, with detailed notes on his behavior and responses to stimuli.

"The patient exhibits a high level of engagement within the simulated environment," one note reads. "He responds to stimuli as if the experience is entirely real, showing no signs of awareness regarding the artificial nature of his surroundings."

Another entry goes into disturbing detail about the specific psychological impact. "Subject displays consistent emotional responses aligned with real-world interactions. Notable instances include expressions of fear, joy, anger, and even love. Patient appears fully invested in simulated relationships."

The words make his skin crawl. It's as if they were observing a lab rat, not a human being with thoughts, feelings, and a life outside their cruel experiment. Each word cuts deeper, fueling his resolve to bring them down.

He flips the page and sees the word "reset" in bold, red letters. Underneath is a detailed account of the process for resetting Atlas's simulation experience in order to continue suppressing his memories.

"Subject exhibits signs of memory resurgence, an anomaly not anticipated in initial projections. Reset procedures were employed to maintain control over the subject's memory. Close observation and further investigation will be required moving forward."

Atlas knows Michael was behind his returning memories, trying to manipulate situations to get him to wake him up. He's grateful for his friend's efforts, especially in shielding him from the reset procedure through his nurse avatar, Micah. If it weren't for him, he would've had his memories wiped just like Naya.

Scanning another section, Atlas notes the label "Physical Deterioration." Here, the language shifts to the state of his real body, lying dormant in the facility.

"Subject's physical condition has shown marked decline over the extended period of immersion. Muscle atrophy is significant, with notable loss of mass and strength. Nutrient absorption is suboptimal due to prolonged intravenous feeding. High levels of stress on the brain are also evident, likely due to the extended simulation exposure."

Atlas swallows hard, remembering how it felt when he first woke up. Each day, he fights to rebuild his strength, to regain what was stolen from him. It makes him sick to see the doctors' focus on their experiment's success rather than the well-being of their patient.

A knock on the door snaps him back to reality. Expecting Ms. Harrington has returned with more false promises, he opens the door with a scowl. "I told you, I'm not interested in your stupid—"

His words die in his throat, shocked to see Naya standing in the doorway, her expression unreadable. For a moment, they just stare at each other. Then she steps inside, holding something small and shiny in her hand. Atlas's heart sinks when he realizes what it is.

"I… I can't keep this," she says, her voice barely above a whisper. She holds out the engagement ring, the diamond catching the light.

Atlas feels like the wind has been knocked out of him. "Naya, please—"

She shakes her head, cutting him off. "It's not fair to you, Atlas. You deserve someone who knows what they want."

He takes the ring from her, his fingers brushing hers. The contact is electric, a painful reminder of what he's losing. "This doesn't change how I feel about you," he says, his voice breaking.

Naya looks down. "I know."

With that, she turns and walks out the door, the sound of her footsteps fading away. Atlas wants to yell after her, to convince her to stay, but he can tell she's made up her mind.

Closing the door, he leans against it, the weight of the world pressing down on him.

He looks at the ring in his hand, a symbol of a future now uncertain. Its perfection seems to mock him, gleaming untouched while his heart lies in pieces. In a moment of rage, he flings it across the room, yelling into the empty apartment. Tears blur his vision as he storms into the living room and swipes the files off the coffee table, papers scattering across the floor.

"Why?" he sobs, sinking to the floor. "After everything I've been through, why do you take her away from me too?"

Doubt and anger course through him, threatening to extinguish the fragile flame of his faith. It's a familiar, suffocating feeling, like when his parents died. A black void that threatens to swallow him whole, closing him off to the very source of strength and peace he fought so hard to find.

His anger dissolves into sobs that echo through the apartment. The raw sound of his heartache fills the room. And yet, amidst the despair, Atlas feels a flicker of resilience. He doesn't want to follow the same dark path again, letting his circumstances lead him astray. *Come back to me*, a small voice whispers. *When you are weak, I am strong.* It's a familiar reminder, a lifeline that keeps resurfacing in his darkest moments.

"I'm sorry," Atlas murmurs, taking a deep breath. "Help me through this heartache, Lord. It feels like I just fell into a pit with no hope of ever getting out. But I will trust that you have a plan. That you will work this pain into something good."

He begins gathering the scattered papers around the room, as if picking up the pieces of his shattered heart. Each piece of paper, each step, is a small act of defiance against the despair threatening to consume him. As he meticulously collects the documents, he silently prays for strength, for guidance, and for the resilience to face whatever lies ahead.

A glint of light from across the room catches his attention and Atlas's eyes fall on the ring lying on the kitchen floor. He walks toward it, reaching out with trembling hands. The ring, still pristine and whole, feels heavy with unfulfilled promises. As tears blur his vision once more, he clutches the ring tightly, now a reminder of the hope and strength he needs to rebuild.

# CHAPTER 55

# NAYA

"What did I just do?" Naya mumbles, standing on the sidewalk outside Michael's apartment building.

She turns to look at it, wondering what Atlas is doing inside. The thought of the pain she's putting him through makes her stomach twist. She suddenly wants to take it back, to apologize to Atlas and forget this ever happened. But her mind is telling her no, to let the past go and find a new way forward. It feels like her heart and her head are going in opposite directions, each vying for her attention.

Hoping to distract herself from her conflicting feelings, Naya starts walking. With no destination in mind, she lets her feet lead the way. After a while, the rugged ambience of Downtown begins to ebb away and Naya realizes she's headed to the north side of the city.

As the manicured lawns and sleek high-rises begin to dominate her surroundings, Naya's eyes catch sight of a sleek technology shop. It's minimalist design and gleaming windows showcase the latest gadgets, beckoning her closer. The neon sign reads "Tech Haven." On a whim, she decides to go in, hoping the shiny gadgets will offer a temporary escape from her racing thoughts.

Inside, the air is cool and filled with the faint hum of electronics. Rows of the latest devices—tablets, smartwatches, VR headsets—are displayed on polished counters. Naya wanders aimlessly through the aisles, her fingers brushing against the smooth surfaces. The technology feels both familiar and alien, the updated designs unlike anything she's had her hands on before.

Suddenly, a strange urge grips her. She's never stolen anything before, but the thought of taking something, anything, feels thrilling—a way to exert control in a life that's been spiraling. Her eyes fall on an elegant, compact smartwatch. Heart pounding, she glances around to make sure no one is watching. With a swift, practiced motion she didn't know she was capable of, she slips the watch into her pocket.

As she turns to leave, she hears murmurs behind her. A group of shoppers nearby is staring at her, whispering. "Isn't that Naya Callaway?" one of them says.

Panic seizes her. Without thinking, she bolts out of the store, her heart racing. The stolen watch presses against her thigh with every step. She runs until her lungs burn, not daring to look back. It's almost exhilarating, the adrenaline giving her a burst of strength.

Slowing to a stop around the corner, she catches her breath. Not wanting to go home and face her parents, she keeps walking, ending up at the therapy clinic. The familiar sign outside the door feels like a lifeline. She pushes the door open, the air-conditioned interior a stark contrast to the heat of her flushed cheeks.

Lucas is working with a patient, but he looks over when he hears the door open. His blue eyes widen in surprise, and he says something to his patient before walking over.

"Naya? What are you doing here? You don't have a session today."

Suddenly embarrassed for barging in unannounced, she forces a smile. "I just… I was in the neighborhood and wanted to say hi?"

Lucas narrows his eyes, noticing she's out of breath. He glances back at his patient, running a hand through his short blonde hair. "My session is almost over. If you hang around for a few more minutes, we can talk after."

"Okay," she says, going back outside to sit on the bench out front.

Not sure what else to do, she stares through the window, watching Lucas work. Naya admires the way his muscles flex as he demonstrates an exercise. Turning to watch his patient repeat the motions, he looks up and catches Naya staring through the window. He smirks and she looks away, her face hot.

Suddenly self-conscious, she glances down at her outfit. Naya adjusts her crop top and tight jean shorts. As she does, she notices the bulge in her pocket and remembers the watch. She shimmies it out, admiring it before strapping it to her wrist.

"That's a nice watch you got there," Lucas says from behind her.

Naya jumps in surprise, making Lucas laugh.

"Sorry, didn't mean to scare you," he says apologetically, taking a seat next to her on the bench.

Naya smiles, trying to calm her rapidly beating heart. She's not sure if it's from being scared or Lucas sitting so close to her. The thought makes her question herself, still surprised by her sudden and rapidly developing feelings for Lucas.

"Cat got your tongue?" he asks, his lips curving into a dimpled smile.

Regaining her composure, Naya smiles. "Sorry, I didn't expect you to be done so soon."

"I told you it was almost over. And maybe I was a bit more motivated knowing I had you waiting outside," he admits, looking down at his hands.

Naya's not sure what to say, uncertain if he's flirting with her or not. The silence stretches between them, growing more awkward by the second.

"I broke up with Atlas," Naya blurts, attempting to start a conversation while also validating her desire to flirt with Lucas.

Lucas looks over at her, not as surprised by the information as she expected. "I'm sorry to hear that."

"It's okay, it was for the best," Naya reassures, somewhat shocked by her own words. Something about Lucas's presence makes her forget everything else, her doubts about breaking up with Atlas fading away.

Lucas's eyes shimmer with hope. "Really? You didn't seem so certain the other day."

Naya shrugs. "Today is a new day. Feelings change."

The words sound callous, but suddenly Naya doesn't care. Lucas's brows are raised in surprise, equally shocked by her nonchalance.

"Well then, would you want to grab a drink with me later?" he asks.

His proposition shocks her and she's not sure what to say. She wasn't expecting him to ask something like that. Misinterpreting her stunned reaction, a blush creeps onto Lucas's face and he looks away.

"I'm so sorry, that was way too soon," he exclaims, his words coming out in a rush. "I shouldn't have asked. Can we just pretend that never—"

"I'd like that," Naya interrupts.

The Uptown bar looks busy when she gets there later that evening. It's far fancier than any of the ones Naya's seen in Downtown. The modern interior is tasteful and pristine, high-top tables scattered throughout. Rows of glass shelves illuminated by blue light line the wall behind the bar, colorful bottles of alcohol arranged neatly on them.

The space is packed, people laughing and having drinks as if they actually come here to hangout. It's nothing like the dilapidated bar in her neighborhood where people only go to drown their sorrows in alcohol. Naya scans the bar for Lucas, spotting him at a table in the back. She makes her way over to him, noticing the way his face lights up when he sees her.

"You made it!" he says. "I half thought you changed your mind."

"Sorry, I left the house a little late and it's a long walk," she explains, taking a seat across from him.

"You should have told me, I would've picked you up," Lucas answers.

Though the offer is nice, the thought of him picking her up at her parents' house is rather mortifying. She pictures how out of place he'd feel driving through the dirty streets of Downtown.

"That's alright, I like the walk. It's much more doable now that I don't need my cane."

Lucas beams. "Your determination never ceases to amaze me."

She blushes, thankful for the dim lighting in the bar. The atmosphere is lively, with laughter and clinking glasses filling the air, but Naya feels a little uncomfortable, a combination of the crowds and her lack of experience in a bar. It's never really been her scene.

"Can I get you a drink?" Lucas asks, noticing her tension.

Naya nods. "Surprise me," she says, not sure what to order.

He slides out of his chair, giving her a charming smile before leaving to get their drinks. She watches him weave through the crowd, grabbing the attention of the bartender and ordering with ease. He gives off an air of confidence, clearly at home in the space. It makes her wonder how often he comes here and how many other girls have joined him.

As she waits, she looks around, trying to acclimate to the energetic setting. People are chatting and dancing, seemingly without a care in the world. It feels like a completely different universe, the civil unrest and economic instability not a worry for these people. Naya feels like an outsider looking in, unsure of her place here.

She glances down at the stolen watch on her wrist, keenly aware of its small, cold weight that seems to grow heavier with every passing minute. Naya nervously looks around, half expecting someone to come up to her and demand it back. The thrill of the theft has faded, replaced by a gnawing guilt.

Lucas returns with two drinks, handing her a cocktail with a smile. "Here you go, one signature Uptown Sunset. It's got a mix of fruit juices and a little bit of a kick. Sweet and fiery just like you," he says with a wink.

"Thanks." Naya takes a sip. The flavors burst on her tongue, sweet and tangy with a subtle warmth. She smiles, genuinely pleased. "This is really good."

"I'm glad you like it," Lucas says, his eyes sparkling. He scoots his chair next to hers, their knees almost touching. "So, how are you feeling?"

Naya takes another sip, trying to gather her thoughts. "A bit overwhelmed, to be honest. Everything's been so chaotic lately. I just needed a break from it all."

Lucas nods, his expression understanding. "I get it. Sometimes you just need to step away from everything and clear your head."

She looks at him, feeling a wave of gratitude. "Thanks for inviting me out, Lucas. I didn't realize how much I needed this tonight."

"Anytime, Naya." Lucas raises his glass. "To new beginnings."

"To new beginnings," she echoes, clinking her glass against his.

As they drink, Naya feels a flicker of excitement for the future, a feeling she thought she'd lost. They sit in comfortable silence for a while, sipping their drinks and listening to the lively music. Naya feels a sense of calm begin to settle over her, the stress of the day beginning to fade.

Lucas leans in closer, his voice dropping to a playful whisper. "You know, if you ever need a distraction, I've got plenty of ideas."

Naya laughs, the tension easing from her shoulders. "Oh really? Like what?"

"Well," Lucas says, a mischievous glint in his eyes, "we could start with another round of drinks and see where the night takes us. And maybe I could show you some of my secret spots around town. I've got a feeling you'd love them."

She raises an eyebrow, intrigued. "Secret spots, huh? Are you trying to impress me, Lucas?"

"Is it working?" he asks, flashing her a confident smile.

Naya feels a flutter in her chest, enjoying the playful banter. "Maybe," she replies, leaning in slightly. "Guess you'll have to keep trying."

Lucas chuckles, his eyes never leaving hers. "Challenge accepted."

Finishing their drinks, Lucas orders another round and leads Naya toward the back corner of the bar. The clatter of balls colliding and the low hum of conversation greets them as a pool table comes into view. It sits beneath a trendy neon light, the one beside it already being used.

Naya raises a brow, feeling a mix of excitement and nervousness. Turning, she gives Lucas a tentative smile. He steps behind her, one hand placed gently on her hip as he dips his head down to hear her better.

"I've never played pool before," she says into his ear, the thought of making a fool of herself in front of Lucas a bit daunting.

Lucas gives her a surprised look before a devilish grin takes its place. "No better time to learn, then."

Setting their drinks on a nearby table, Lucas grabs a cue stick and hands it to her. "Alright, first things first. Let's get you set up."

Naya wears a concerned expression, gripping the cue stick awkwardly. He laughs, placing his hand on hers to adjust her grip. "Don't worry, I'll go easy on you. It's all about technique and a little bit of strategy," he whispers into her ear.

His touch is warm and steady, and Naya feels a rush of confidence as he guides her through the basics. He explains how to hold the cue, how to position her body, and the importance of aiming. Naya listens intently, trying to absorb everything he's saying, though his close proximity is a little distracting. This kind of closeness is nothing like their physical therapy sessions.

"Let's start with a simple shot," Lucas says, placing a ball near a pocket. "Line up the cue ball with this ball and try to sink it in the pocket."

Naya takes a deep breath, bending over the table and lining up her shot. She feels Lucas's presence close behind her, his hands gently adjusting her stance. His breath tickles her ear, sending a shiver down her spine.

"Take your time," he murmurs. "Aim carefully and follow through with your shot."

Naya concentrates, focusing on the ball and the pocket. With a steady hand, she pulls back the cue stick and strikes the cue ball. It rolls smoothly, hitting the target and sending it straight into the pocket.

Her eyes widen in surprise and delight. "I did it!"

Lucas grins, clapping his hands together. "Nice shot! You're a natural."

She beams, feeling a burst of pride. "Thanks to your expert coaching."

He winks, leaning against the table. "I knew you had it in you. Let's try a few more shots and then we can play a game."

After a bit more practice, Lucas sets up a game, racking the balls and explaining the rules. "Alright, we'll play eight-ball. The goal is to sink all your assigned balls—stripes or solids—and then the eight ball. Got it?"

Naya nods, finishing the last of her drink. "Got it. Let's do this."

They take turns, the game becoming a fun challenge. Lucas's skill is evident, but he's careful not to be too competitive, ensuring Naya has fun. She surprises herself with a few impressive shots, earning genuine praise from Lucas.

At one point, Lucas lines up a tricky shot, leaning over the table with a focused expression. Naya watches, admiring his concentration and skill. He makes the shot effortlessly, sinking the ball into the pocket.

"Show off," she teases, sticking her tongue out at him.

He laughs, his dimpled smile returning. "Just giving you something to aspire to. Your turn."

As Naya lines up her next shot, she feels his eyes on her. The game has become more than just a distraction—it's a chance to connect with Lucas in a new way. She feels a flutter of excitement, taking her shot and sinking the ball perfectly. Lucas cheers, both of them grinning from ear to ear.

"You're getting really good at this," he says, his voice full of admiration.

"Thanks," Naya replies, feeling a blush creep up her cheeks. "I'm having a lot of fun."

"Me too." Lucas's gaze lingers on her. "Do you want to get out of here?"

"But we haven't finished the game," Naya protests.

"That's alright, I'd win anyway," he declares, earning a playful smack from Naya.

"Aren't you supposed to let the lady win on the first date?" she asks.

"Oh, so this is a date?" he says, pulling her close.

She shoves him away with a blush. "Answer the question, mister."

"Normally, I'd say yes, especially if I thought it would win you over. But I can tell you're competitive and hate when someone lets you win," Lucas says, his astute observation catching her off guard. He grabs her hand, paying their tab before tugging her out of the bar.

"Where are we going?" Naya asks.

"To one of my secret spots," he replies, continuing his pursuit toward their mysterious destination.

They walk closer to the edge of Uptown, the buildings becoming less maintained. Lucas directs her into an alley beside an older looking high-rise. Her heart skips a beat, and she pauses, causing Lucas to stop and turn around.

"Just a little further," he says, looking up at the old, creaky fire escape. "The climb is a bit of an adventure, but trust me, the reward is worth it."

Naya nods and follows him up the stairs, glad they're not staying in the alley. As they ascend, the air feels fresher, the sounds of the city below growing more muted. When they reach the top, Naya gasps. The roof offers a stunning panoramic view of the city.

"This is where I like to go to think and escape the chaos of the city. I figured you might appreciate it, too," Lucas says, admiring the view beside her.

It's strange how similar this feels to Naya's rooftop escape in the simulation. She would've never guessed Lucas likes to clear his mind the same way she does.

"It's beautiful," she murmurs. "How did you find this place?"

Lucas shrugs. "I like to explore. Not everything in Uptown is as polished as it seems. There are still plenty of places left in disrepair, forgotten relics of the past not yet demolished."

He steps closer, his expression softening. Gently taking her hand, he pulls Naya toward him. "There's something about being up here that makes everything else seem so far away."

Naya looks up at him, her heart pounding in her chest. Lucas's eyes search hers, his gaze intense and unwavering. The air between them feels charged, every heartbeat magnified. He moves even closer, their bodies nearly touching. Naya's breath catches in her throat as she feels the warmth radiating from him.

Lucas's hand comes up to cup her cheek, his thumb gently tracing her jawline. "Naya," he whispers, his voice low and intimate. "I've been wanting to do this for a while."

Before she can respond, Lucas leans in, his lips hovering just inches from hers. The anticipation is electric, and Naya feels like time has slowed. Finally, his lips meet hers, soft and tentative at first, as if testing the waters. But then, Naya slides her hands up to his shoulders for support and Lucas deepens the kiss. His arms wrap around her, pulling her closer until there's no space left between them.

When they finally pull apart, Naya's cheeks are flushed, her breath coming in short gasps. Lucas's eyes are dark with desire, but there's a tenderness there as well. He brushes a strand of hair away from her face, his fingers lingering on her skin. "How about we head back to my place for a drink?" he suggests, his tone casual but his eyes still searching hers.

Naya startles at his offer, her mind racing. Lucas quickly reassures her, sensing her hesitation. "We don't have to do anything you're not comfortable with," he says gently. "We can just talk. I want to get to know you better, Naya. That's all."

She studies his face, finding sincerity in his gaze. Slowly, she nods, a small smile forming on her lips. "Okay," she agrees. "Just talk."

# CHAPTER 56

# ATLAS

"Atlas!" Michael yells, peeking his head into the spare bedroom. "Celeste is on the phone wanting to talk to you."

Atlas groggily rubs the sleep from his eyes, grabbing Michael's cell phone from his outstretched hand.

"Hello? Mrs. Callaway?"

"Hi, Atlas, sorry to wake you." She sounds a bit strained.

"No, that's alright. What's wrong?"

"Hopefully nothing, but have you seen Naya lately? She didn't come home last night."

His stomach drops and he bolts upright in bed. "What?"

"She went out last night but hasn't come home yet. I was hoping she was with you?" Celeste reiterates.

"Naya didn't tell you, then," Atlas says, a bit surprised. "She gave back the engagement ring yesterday morning. I haven't seen her since."

On the other end of the line is stunned silence. After several moments, she speaks. "Atlas, I'm so sorry. Naya's been going through a lot lately, but you've always been her support system. I don't know why she'd break things off."

"You and me both," Atlas replies. "Do you know where Naya was headed last night?"

"No, she was rather distant when she came home. I suppose it makes sense now knowing what she'd been doing."

Celeste stops speaking and Atlas hears a commotion on her end of the line. He thinks he can hear Silas's voice in the background. "Hang on, Atlas," she says, followed by a moment of static as she sets the phone down.

Several long minutes pass, Atlas straining to hear what's going on. There are multiple voices, one in particular he doesn't recognize. His heart rate quickens as he imagines the voice belonging to a police officer, sharing awful news about Naya.

"Come on, Celeste," he mutters.

Finally, he hears her labored footsteps approach the phone. "She's home, Atlas."

The words send relief flooding through him. "Thank goodness. Did she say where she'd been?"

"No, but her breath reeks of alcohol and her physical therapist, Lucas, is the one who dropped her off," Celeste answers, disapproval evident in her tone.

"I'm coming over," Atlas announces, worried about Naya's out-of-character behavior.

"Thank you, Atlas," Celeste replies. "See you soon."

Flying out of bed, Atlas puts on clothes and barges into the kitchen. "Michael, can I borrow your car?"

"Sorry, Atlas, I have to go to work."

"Oh yeah, sort of forgot about your new job," Atlas says, pulling on his shoes.

"Where are you off to in such a rush?" Michael asks.

"Naya's parents' house. Apparently, her physical therapist, Lucas, just dropped her off hungover."

Michael's eyebrows shoot up in surprise. "Dang, that's not like her."

Atlas grimaces, nodding in agreement.

"How about I drop you off on my way?" Michael offers.

Silas greets him warmly at the door when he arrives, informing him Celeste is talking with Naya in her bedroom. Atlas heads that direction, pausing just outside her bedroom door when he hears raised voices.

"Don't you have an interview this afternoon?" Celeste reminds.

"I'm not going," Naya snaps.

"Why not? I thought you were excited about this job!"

"Not anymore."

Celeste sighs in frustration. "So what's your plan, then? Are you going to look for another job?"

"I don't know, mom! But I'm an adult. I'll figure it out. Now leave me alone," Naya retorts, clearly agitated.

"Remember young lady, you are living under our roof. If you keep acting like this, we'll be forced to reconsider," Celeste warns, exiting her room.

She jumps slightly at Atlas's presence in the hall, her eyes softening when she realizes it's him. "Maybe you'll have better success than I did," she says sympathetically, patting him on the shoulder before walking down the hall.

Atlas takes a deep breath, steeling himself in preparation for Naya's rage. He doubts his conversation will go any better.

"Naya?" he calls, pushing open the door.

"What are you doing here?" She scowls, lifting her head from the bed.

"Your mom called me this morning when you hadn't come home yet. I was worried."

She lays her head back down, staring at the ceiling. "Well I'm here now, no need to worry."

"Naya, this isn't like you." Atlas steps further into her bedroom.

He takes in the state of her room, noticing the clothes piling up on the floor and surfaces gathering dust and clutter. It's unusually dirty, especially for Naya's taste.

"How many times have I told you? I've changed. Get over it," she grumbles. "And what's it to you, anyway? We're broken up, over, done!"

Her words sting, but Atlas tries not to take them to heart. "You're hungover, Naya. You'll feel better when you drink some water and eat some breakfast or something."

Sitting up, she glares at him. "Leave!" she shouts. "I don't want to see you."

"You don't mean that," Atlas whispers, holding onto hope that she wouldn't discard him so easily.

"I do, I've moved on," she replies, her expression cold.

"Just let me help you and then I'll leave," Atlas begs, not wanting to leave her this way.

"I. Said. Get. OUT!" she yells, suddenly sitting to grab the framed photo of her and Harper from her nightstand. She holds it over her head, preparing to throw it at him.

"Naya, put that—"

The frame comes flying toward him before he can finish. He ducks just in time, the glass shattering against the wall behind him.

Atlas is shocked by Naya's violent rage. He's never seen her like this before.

"What is wrong with you?" he growls. "You loved that photo!"

"Loved. Past tense. Get it through your head, Atlas. I'm not the same girl you fell in love with," she says, breathing hard.

"You're right." It hurts to admit, but Atlas can't deny it any longer. "You're not the Naya I used to know. It's disappointing to see you act this way."

"Good thing I found someone else who can appreciate the new me, then," she replies. "I quite enjoyed kissing him last night."

Atlas feels as though the ground has been ripped out from under him. Her words cut deeper than any physical wound ever could. His mind races, trying to process the reality of what she just said. He struggles to keep his voice steady, the shock and pain evident in his eyes.

"So soon?" he asks, his voice barely above a whisper.

She smirks, a coldness in her eyes that he's never seen before. "Yes, Lucas understands me in ways you never have."

Atlas's heart pounds in his chest, a mix of anger and heartbreak coursing through him. "How could you? After everything we've been through together?"

She shrugs nonchalantly, her demeanor unnervingly detached. "At least I gave the ring back before I did it."

Atlas takes a step back, his hands shaking. He can hardly believe what he's hearing. This isn't the Naya he fell in love with, the Naya who fought alongside him to regain his memories. This is someone else, someone cold and unrecognizable.

"The Naya I know would never hurt me like this. She wouldn't throw everything we had away so easily," he says, his voice cracking.

Her expression softens for a moment, a flicker of the old Naya shining through, but it's gone as quickly as it appeared. "She's gone, Atlas. And she's not coming back."

The finality of her words hits him like a punch to the gut. Atlas turns away, unable to bear the sight of her any longer. When he speaks again, his voice is firm.

"Fine, if that's how you feel. But I won't stop fighting for the Naya I know is still in there somewhere."

He walks out of her room, each step feeling heavier than the last. Atlas heads down the hallway, his mind a whirlwind of emotions. Naya's actions are so unlike her that he feels there has to be something else going on. He's not sure what, but he's hopeful that the woman he loves is still in there somewhere, waiting to be found.

"Atlas, are you okay?" Celeste asks, worry etched into her features. "I heard something shatter."

Atlas's expression is grim as he looks at Naya's parents. "She threw the framed photo of her and Harper at me."

Celeste covers her mouth in shock, Silas comforting her with a hand on her shoulder.

"Are you hurt?" Silas asks.

Atlas shakes his head. "Not physically. But the things she said to me—that's not the Naya I used to know."

"We see it too," Celeste agrees. "But I don't know what to do."

Atlas shrugs, feeling the same way. Though she's been through a lot, so have they, and they aren't acting nearly as different as she is.

"It reminds me of when she lost her memories in the simulation," Silas notes. "Except this time, she's forgotten who she is completely."

His words stir something in Atlas, reminding him of the Genesis Laboratories files laying in Michael's apartment.

"Actually, that reminds me of something. Thank you, Mr. Callaway. I need to go," he replies, rushing to the front door.

"Atlas!" Celeste calls after him. "What are you thinking?"

"I'm not sure yet. But if I find something, you'll be the first to know," he reassures, leaving the house and closing the door behind him.

With a burst of adrenaline, he sprints to Michael's apartment, ignoring his protesting muscles. When he arrives, he's panting and out of breath, but he pushes himself up the stairs, jamming his key into the lock and stepping inside.

The files sit in a neat pile on the coffee table where he left them the night before. Atlas picks them up, shuffling through them to find Naya's file. Rifling through its contents, he scans the documents as fast as he can, looking for anything that catches his attention.

On Naya's intake form, he notes the description of her attack, the cut along her hairline clearly detailed. He reads on, the words at the bottom of the section sending a shiver along his spine.

"Though a bit excessive, the cut along the patient's hairline proved viable for successful insertion of Project Eclipse."

The project name is unfamiliar to him, something that was never discussed when they were building Project Nowhere. Atlas flips through the pages, searching for any other mention of Project Eclipse. He finds it at the end of Naya's file, one last mention of this secretive experiment.

"Patient is responding well to Project Nowhere, indicating a high likelihood of success with Project Eclipse. Enough data has been collected to begin trials soon. Patient will need to be taken out of the simulation for proper implementation to take place."

Atlas is filled with dread as the meaning of the words sinks in. Naya has had another chip this whole time. He wonders what it's been doing to her, the implications of such a secretive project making him very concerned for her safety. He paces around the apartment, his mind racing. Glancing out the window, Atlas spots the old payphone on the corner of the street. It's a relic, but it still works.

Running into his bedroom, Atlas searches for change. He rifles through drawers and pockets, finally gathering enough to make a call. Heading outside, he reaches the payphone in several hurried strides. He fishes the coins from his pocket and inserts them, dialing a familiar number. The phone clicks, and a voice on the other end breaks through the silence.

"Hello?"

"Michael, it's Atlas. You work IT at the hospital, right?"

"Yeah, why?"

"Please tell me you've made some new friends."

# CHAPTER 57

# NAYA

Naya lays on her bed, reeling from her conversation with Atlas. Part of her is ashamed of how she acted, agreeing with Atlas's assessment that it's nothing like her. But another part is proud, feeling as if she accomplished some unknown goal.

The sound of the doorbell draws her out of her thoughts. She hears her mom answer it, another woman's voice ringing out in reply. Naya moves close to her bedroom door, listening to the exchange.

"Thank you, Ms. Harrington, but we don't want the government's money."

"Can I speak with Naya? We'd like to offer her something as well."

"No, sorry. She's a bit… unwell at the moment," her mom replies. "I'll relay the offer to her."

"Sorry to hear that, but I need to speak directly with Naya since she's well over the age of 18," Ms. Harrington argues.

Curious about the government's offer, Naya walks down the hall and into the entryway.

"Naya!" Ms. Harrington says with a smile. "Glad to see you're well enough to talk with me."

"Yes, I'm feeling a bit better," Naya replies. "What is it you are here for?"

Ms. Harrington grabs a piece of paper from her bag and hands it to Naya. "The government would like to pay for a brand-new Uptown apartment for you to have a fresh start."

Naya looks at the lease in her hands, shocked by the generous offer. By the looks of it, this apartment is very expensive, including all the modern amenities Naya could ever imagine.

"Wow, this is incredible," she breathes, looking over the document.

"Indeed. What do you say, Ms. Callaway?"

Her mom moves closer, placing a tentative hand on Naya's shoulder. "Naya, I'm sorry for what I said earlier. But this isn't something you want to accept. Think of your sister."

Ignoring her mother's pleas, Naya walks into the kitchen. Her dad sits at the dining room table, worry lines creasing his forehead.

"Naya don't do this," he warns.

She searches for a pen, finally finding one in a drawer. Without hesitation, she signs the lease in a fluid motion. Her dad looks disappointed, but she walks by, unphased. When she hands it back to Ms. Harrington, the woman smiles radiantly.

"Excellent decision. How about you grab some of your things and I can take you to your new apartment?"

Naya nods, going back to her bedroom and shoving clothes into a bag. Her mom follows close behind, shouting for her dad. They stand in her bedroom doorway, watching her pack.

"Don't leave, Naya," her mom begs.

"We're worried about you, sweetie. Moving away right now isn't going to help," her dad adds.

"I appreciate the concern but look at this as a good thing. At least now you won't have to reconsider me living under your roof," Naya spits, shoving the last of her clothes in the bag and stalking out of her room.

"Naya!" her mom calls after her, grabbing her shoulder. "If you have to go, take this with you." She holds out a framed family photo, waiting for her to take it.

Naya looks down at the picture, feeling a sharp pain in her chest at the sight of the happy family they used to be. She doesn't take it, turning away from her mom and walking to the front door.

"Lead the way, Ms. Harrington."

Naya's new apartment in Uptown is a sophisticated, modern space that feels worlds away from her old life. The entrance opens into a spacious living room with floor-to-ceiling windows, flooding the room with natural light and offering a stunning view of the city skyline. The walls are painted in soft, neutral tones, and the floors are a polished hardwood that gleams under the light.

The living area is furnished with a minimalist style, featuring a plush, cream-colored sectional couch, a glass coffee table, and a large, flat-screen TV mounted on the wall. Naya brushes her fingers along the couch as she walks further into the space.

Next to the living room is an impressive kitchen with stainless steel appliances, quartz countertops, and a stylish island with bar stools. Everything is spotless and appears unused. Naya almost doesn't want to touch anything for fear of ruining it. She's never been surrounded by such expensive furnishings before.

Looking back at Ms. Harrington, she gives Naya an encouraging smile. "It's magnificent, isn't it?"

Naya nods, at a loss for words.

"Well then, I'll leave you to explore so you can make yourself at home! Your keys are on the kitchen counter," Ms. Harrington declares, departing with a wave.

Now alone in the new space, Naya continues her tour. At the back is her bedroom, which is just as spacious as the other rooms. A king-sized bed dressed in luxurious linens dominates the middle of the room. To the left, is a walk-in closet with ample space for Naya's new wardrobe. She sets her bag on the plush carpet, planning to unpack it later.

Attached to the bedroom, Naya finds the bathroom, complete with a deep soaking tub, a glass-enclosed shower, and marble accents. She catches her reflection in the mirror above the sink, stopping to stare at herself briefly. As she does, three buttons illuminate on the bottom right of the mirror's glass. She reaches out to touch each of them, watching as the light around the mirror changes to simulate different times of day.

"Wow," she breathes. "Fancy."

Her words echo in the bathroom, another reminder that she's alone in this giant apartment. The space feels ridiculous for just one person, and Naya can't believe people live like this. *Now I live like this,* she thinks, reminding herself this is her apartment now.

Venturing back into the living room, Naya sees a sliding glass door that leads to a small, private balcony. It looks like a perfect place to relax and enjoy the cityscape. Standing just on the other side of the glass, she looks at the city beyond. Another apartment building is nearby, close enough that she can see people going about their day through the windows. It makes her keenly aware of her own gigantic windows, and she glances nervously around as if someone might be watching her.

"Are there no shades for privacy?" she asks aloud, searching for some.

"Privacy shades engaged," a voice says suddenly, the windows growing a shade darker as if tinted on the outside.

Naya jumps, surprised by the response. "Hello?"

"Hello. I am your smart home assistant."

Naya takes a cautious step back, her heart pounding. The voice is calm and soothing, but the unexpected interaction unsettles her.

"Oh right, I forgot about the smart home system," she mutters to herself, recalling the description on the paperwork Ms. Harrington gave her. "Thank you… um, assistant."

"You're welcome, Naya. Is there anything else I can assist you with?" the voice responds smoothly.

Naya hesitates, still getting used to the idea of having an automated system managing her home. "No, that's all for now. Thanks."

The assistant falls silent, leaving Naya alone with her thoughts once more. She takes a deep breath and steps out onto the balcony, letting the cool breeze wash over her. The sounds of the city below soothe her nerves a bit, a temporary escape from the silence of her new apartment. Despite the luxurious surroundings, Naya feels a pang of loneliness. The apartment, with all its modern conveniences, feels impersonal.

Reluctantly returning inside, she sits on the plush sectional couch and lets out a heavy sigh. The day has been overwhelming, and it's not even lunchtime. Not sure what to do, Naya searches for a TV remote. Not finding one, she tentatively breaks the silence.

"Smart home assistant?" she calls out.

"Yes, Naya?" the voice responds promptly.

"Can you… turn on the TV?" she requests.

"Of course," the assistant replies, the TV in front of her blinking to life.

The screen is crisp, the colors more vivid than the small, old TV at her parents' house. The news is playing, an anchor seated at a sleek desk in the studio. The headline scrolling across the bottom reads, "Genesis Laboratories Employee Comes Forward."

Naya leans forward, her interest piqued.

The anchor's voice is clear and authoritative. "New details have emerged about the unethical practices involved in Project Nowhere, and the public outcry continues to grow."

Footage of a recent press conference fills the screen, a government spokesperson standing behind a podium flanked by officials. "The government is committed to uncovering the truth and ensuring justice is served," the spokesperson says. "We are providing support to the victims and their families, and we will hold those responsible accountable."

The screen changes again, this time to an interview with a former Genesis Laboratories employee. The person's face is obscured for anonymity, their voice altered. "We knew what we were doing was wrong," they say. "But we were pressured to continue, to push the boundaries. Some people enjoyed it, excited by the prospect of such powerful technology. But I found it unsettling. Now, I just want to make things right."

As the interview ends, the news anchor reappears. "In related news, the government has announced new regulations for the development and use of advanced technologies, aiming to prevent future abuses."

"Change the channel," Naya says, the smart home assistant quickly complying.

A sensationalized talk show pops up, also discussing the recent scandal with Genesis Laboratories.

"Again," Naya commands, frustrated when yet another program discussing Project Nowhere pops up. "TV off."

Naya feels overwhelmed, unable to escape her past. She knows the scandal is far from over, and the consequences will likely be felt for a long time. The reality of her situation hits her hard—she's not just a survivor, but a key player in a story that's capturing the nation's attention.

# CHAPTER 58

# ATLAS

"You're lucky I'm such a charmer," Michael says with a lopsided grin.

"Or just annoyingly persistent," Atlas retorts, remembering when he and Michael first became friends.

He walks through the doors of the hospital, Naya's file clutched tightly to his side. Michael said they could meet with his new friend over their lunch break, so Atlas rushed over here. They still have some time to kill, though, which is perfect for Atlas to break the news.

"So what's so secretive you couldn't tell me over the phone?" Michael asks, guiding him into his small office.

Atlas shuts the door behind them before speaking, wanting to ensure their privacy. With the door closed, the office feels more like a closet, with barely enough room for the two of them next to Michael's desk and computer.

"Naya has been acting like a completely different person lately," Atlas starts.

"Thanks, Captain Obvious. She broke up with you. I never thought I'd see that happen," Michael interrupts.

Atlas gives him a pointed glare before continuing. "Anyway, it's strange enough that I thought there might be something else going on." He grabs the documents mentioning Project Eclipse out of Naya's file and hands them to Michael. "Read what I found in her file."

Michael scans the documents, his eyebrows raising. "Project Eclipse?"

"You haven't heard of it either?" Atlas asks. "I was hoping maybe you knew more than me."

Michael shakes his head. "No, never heard of it. From what I'm reading, Project Nowhere wasn't the end of Genesis Laboratories' experiments?"

"Yeah. I think Naya has another microchip."

The silence stretches between them as they process their predicament. There's no telling what this other chip does, so it's difficult to know how to move forward.

"Where's Naya now?" Michael asks.

"According to her parents, she just moved into a new apartment in Uptown, courtesy of the government," Atlas replies, still disgusted by the news.

"Naya? Living in Uptown? Now pigs really are flying."

Atlas chuckles, grateful for Michael's sense of humor. "You do actually have a friend who can help, right?"

"Knowing the extent of the situation, her help will be a little less extensive, but yes," Michael reassures.

"Her? You didn't say it was a lady friend," Atlas teases with a smirk.

Michael rolls his eyes. "Friend, future girlfriend—didn't think the specifics were important."

"And you've known her for how long?"

"Almost two weeks? But that's beside the point. I told you, I'm a charmer. Add in the fact that she'll be helping basically a celebrity, and I'm sure she'll be all in," Michael replies with confidence.

Atlas gives him a skeptical look but doesn't push the issue. "Alright. When's her lunch break?"

"Any minute now. I told her to meet me in my office after she grabbed food."

"Oh, she's familiar with your office, is she?" Atlas asks, satisfied by the blush that's now creeping onto his best friend's face.

"Don't you have enough to worry about without adding my love life to the list?" Michael retorts, standing up to open the door. "Please don't embarrass me when she gets here."

Atlas holds his hands up in surrender. "I promise. You're right. After we talk with your… friend, we need to figure out how to get Naya here."

"Naya? As in Naya Callaway?" a female voice exclaims behind him.

Atlas turns to see a woman standing in the doorway of Michael's office. Her black hair is tied into a long ponytail at the base of her neck, a pair of glasses framing her deep brown eyes. She's dressed in well-fitted scrubs, a simple wristwatch her only accessory.

"Bec, you made it!" Michael greets, breaking out into a grin.

She smiles over at him before extending her hand toward Atlas. "Rebecca Langley. Nice to meet you, Atlas Williams. I wasn't told I'd be helping one of our nation's newest celebrities."

Atlas shakes her hand, a bit unnerved she already knows who he is. It's easy to forget his face is plastered constantly on the nightly news.

"Nice to meet you Ms. Langley. I appreciate the assistance. It does, actually, involve Naya Callaway," Atlas replies warmly.

Rebecca eyes the space momentarily before speaking again. "I think your office is a bit crowded, Michael. Let's go somewhere else to talk."

Michael and Atlas follow her to a secluded exterior courtyard. Rebecca sets her tray of food on one of the tables and starts eating. Atlas scans the area anxiously, ensuring no one else is around.

"I'm one of the few people who eats out here," she reassures. "Now fill me in on what I'm supposed to help you with."

Atlas is surprised how willingly she's getting involved. *Maybe Michael really is a charmer,* he thinks. Michael takes the lead with filling Rebecca in, catching her up with their recent discovery. Her jaw drops before she hastily closes it, forgetting she has food in her mouth.

"And you know this, how?" she asks.

Atlas opens Naya's file, showing Rebecca its contents and pointing out the paragraphs about Project Eclipse. She reads it, digesting the medical terminology faster than Atlas did.

"So, what do you want me to do?"

"Rebecca is a radiology tech," Michael adds, looking over at Atlas who's piecing together a plan.

"I know this might be asking a lot, but could you arrange for a scan of some sort to identify the chip's location? It might help convince Naya, too," Atlas proposes.

Rebecca sets her fork down with a sigh. "Naya doesn't know about this?"

Atlas shakes his head. "No. She's been acting differently lately, which is what prompted me to look for a cause. I think the chip is doing something to her. Please, can you help?"

Rebecca looks away, contemplating his words. She fiddles with the food on her plate, her inner turmoil etched onto her face. Atlas knows the severity of messing with someone's medical care without their consent, but he's hoping his desperation will convince her.

"I'm not sure, Atlas, I could lose my job if we get caught," she finally says, her voice tinged with uncertainty. "But if what you're saying is true, Naya could be in real danger. Why haven't you just gone to the police with this?"

Atlas looks down at his hands. "For a lot of reasons. With the government's involvement in everything, I'm not sure if I can trust them. And even though they're supposedly helping us, it's at a very slow pace." Atlas looks at the file on the table next to him, reluctantly adding, "And legally, I probably shouldn't have this file."

Rebecca sighs again, rubbing her temples. Michael leans forward, his expression earnest. "Rebecca, you're the only one who can help us right now. This would mean the world to us if you could."

She stares at Michael, her lips pressed into a thin line. "Okay, I'll do it," she relents. "But we need to be careful. I can schedule a scan under the guise of a routine checkup."

"No," Atlas interjects. "It needs to be off the books. If Genesis Laboratories is still behind the scenes, they can't know we're onto them."

Rebecca glares at him, probably silently wishing she hadn't gotten involved. Atlas feels bad for asking more of her, but this is the only way. He needs to ensure Naya's safety.

"Fine, I can be discreet. We'll do the scan between appointments when the room isn't being used. Right around now might be the best time, actually. Bring Naya in under some pretense, and I'll handle the rest," she says, her resolve hardening.

Atlas lets out a breath he didn't realize he was holding. "Thank you, Rebecca. You're a lifesaver, literally."

She looks between the two men with a mix of anxiety and determination. "Don't thank me yet. You've got an hour to get her here," she replies, grabbing her tray off the table and walking back into the building.

Atlas watches as she disappears down the hospital hallway. His mind starts racing, trying to figure out how to get Naya to the hospital without arousing suspicion.

"Michael," he says, an idea forming. "Naya likes you still, right?"

He shrugs, eyeing Atlas curiously. "I think so? Why, what are you planning?"

# CHAPTER 59
# NAYA

"Naya, someone is at your door," her smart home assistant says, waking her from her nap on the couch.

"Huh?" she mutters, rubbing her eyes.

"A man is at your door," the voice reiterates.

Naya sits up, rising from the couch with a stretch. She makes her way to the front door, momentarily fascinated by the small screen on the wall showing who stands outside. It's Michael.

"Michael? What are you doing here?" she asks upon opening the door.

"Hey, Naya. I have a favor to ask," he says.

She notices the desperation on his face and steps aside to let him in. "Okay, come in. How did you know I lived here, by the way? I literally just moved," Naya questions, shutting the door as he steps inside.

"I called your parents," he admits. "Desperate times call for desperate measures."

"What are you so desperately in need of?" Naya asks, unsure what he would need her help for.

Michael takes a deep breath, looking a bit sheepish. "I got a new job working in the IT department at the hospital, and I've gotten myself into a tough situation. It's urgent and I could really use your expertise."

Naya raises an eyebrow, motioning for him to sit on the couch. "What kind of situation?"

"There's this machine—an advanced imaging system—and the software needs fixing. I'm not 100% certain how to do it, and I really don't want to mess up such a big task," Michael explains, rubbing the back of his neck. "I can't lose this job."

Naya gives him a reassuring smile. "I doubt they'd fire you over something like that, Michael. Everyone needs a bit of help now and then. What exactly does the machine need?"

"It's one of the latest MRI machines. The software is supposed to integrate with the hospital's new patient management system, but it's been glitching," he says, sounding a bit panicked. "I need to get it running smoothly as soon as possible."

Naya nods, already formulating a plan in her mind. She's almost grateful for the distraction from the loneliness of her new apartment. "Alright, I can help you with that. No problem. You won't lose your job over a software issue, trust me."

Michael lets out a sigh of relief. "Thanks, Naya. I really appreciate it."

She chuckles, shaking her head. "Why didn't you ask one of your colleagues for help?"

Michael shifts uncomfortably. "Well, um… There's this girl, Rebecca. She's a radiology tech. I might have mentioned to her that I was good with this sort of stuff and now she's expecting me to fix it. I guess I wanted to impress her."

Naya bursts out laughing. "So, you need my help to impress a girl?"

Michael grins shyly. "Pretty much, yeah. I thought I could handle it, but it's more complicated than I anticipated."

Naya shakes her head, still smiling. "Alright. But you owe me big time. How about you stop by my parents' house and mow the yard for them?" Michael nods eagerly. "And next time, Michael, don't bite off more than you can chew just to impress a girl."

Michael laughs. "Deal. Thanks, Naya. You're the best."

Naya follows Michael out of the apartment and gets into his sedan. It's a short drive, the hospital looming up ahead. Michael parks and they enter through the staff entrance. He leads her through a maze of hallways until they reach the MRI room. Naya takes in the sleek, advanced machinery nestled between the sterile white walls.

"Alright, what computer should I use?" she asks, looking around.

But before she can begin, the door swings open and Atlas steps into the room. Naya's eyes widen in shock.

"What are you doing here?" she demands, her voice cold and sharp.

Atlas looks at her with a mix of determination and regret, blocking the door. "Naya, please, just hear me out."

"Was this all a setup?" Naya turns to Michael, betrayal evident in her eyes.

Michael looks down, guilt written all over his face. "I'm sorry, Naya. It was the only way to get you here."

A woman steps into the room behind Atlas, shutting the door.

"It wasn't all a lie," Michael says. "That's Rebecca."

Naya scoffs and crosses her arms. Atlas steps forward, a file in his hands.

"Please, read this. It's important," he says, opening the file and pointing to a few paragraphs.

Reluctantly, Naya takes it. Her eyes scan the documents, her expression shifting from confusion to horror as she reads about Project Eclipse. Her hand moves up to touch the scar on her face. She gently pushes along the raised tissue, searching for a lump or anything to indicate a microchip.

"This can't be real," she whispers, her voice trembling. "You're saying they orchestrated my attack not only to get me to the facility, but to implant another microchip?"

Atlas nods solemnly. "Yes. I think the chip is affecting your behavior."

Naya's hands shake as she clutches the file. The weight of the revelation presses down on her, a mix of anger, fear, and betrayal swirling inside her. "And you think a scan will prove this? Is that why I'm here?"

"Yes," Atlas says softly. "We just need to see where it is."

Naya looks at Michael, her eyes filled with hurt. "Why didn't you just tell me?"

Michael sighs, throwing his hands in the air. "We didn't think you'd believe us. We had to get you here first."

Naya takes a deep breath, trying to steady herself. "Fine."

Atlas and Michael guide her to the MRI machine. Rebecca moves closer, her expression professional yet sympathetic.

"We'll start with a basic brain scan," Rebecca explains. "It will show us any foreign objects in your head."

Naya lies down on the machine's table, her heart pounding in her chest. As the machine whirs to life, she closes her eyes, trying to calm her racing thoughts. The scan takes a few minutes, each second feeling like an eternity. It reminds her of being hooked up to the simulation and she starts to feel panicked.

"Almost done," Rebecca says, noticing Naya's tension.

When it's finally over, Rebecca pulls up the results on a nearby screen. There, clear as day, is a small, metallic object embedded in the side of Naya's head.

Naya stares at the screen, her worst fears confirmed. The room is silent, everyone processing the horrific news. Naya turns to look at Atlas, a combination of regret and anger on his face.

"What do we do now?" she asks, her voice barely above a whisper.

Atlas looks at her and then over at Rebecca. "Can it be removed easily?"

Rebecca examines the image and shrugs. "It's hard to tell, I'm sorry. I just run the machines. I'm not trained to interpret the results."

"But from what you can tell?" Naya questions, eager for any answer at all.

"Well, we don't know the purpose of the microchip, but from its location, it's likely attached to very sensitive nerves and tissue. A surgery to remove it would probably be very complicated and risky," Rebecca replies.

Naya nods, still processing the reality of having another microchip embedded in her body. Atlas thanks Rebecca and helps Naya off the table.

"You guys really need to go now. I'm sorry I can't help more," Rebecca apologizes, ushering them toward the door.

"You've done more than enough, thank you," Atlas says, leaving the room.

Naya follows, leaving Michael to talk with Rebecca alone for a few seconds. When he exits the room, Rebecca gives him a small smile that sends a light blush across his cheeks. She shuts the door, and they start walking down the hallway.

"I'd invite you back to my office, but it would be a little crowded," Michael says, breaking the silence. "Plus, my lunch break ended fifteen minutes ago, so I really need to go back to work."

"Thanks, Michael. I really appreciate your help. I'll keep you updated," Atlas says, watching as Michael hurries off down the hall.

Naya continues walking absentmindedly, unsure where to go. Atlas falls into step beside her, the silence stretching between them. Nurses walk by, several giving them suspicious stares. Naya ducks her head and Atlas guides her outside.

"What's next?" she asks, stepping onto the pavement.

Atlas sighs, running a hand through his hair. Naya notices it's getting long, the slight curls touching the tops of his ears.

"We find someone to remove the chip, I guess," he replies.

"Yeah, like I can afford a surgery like that," she retorts, suddenly angry again.

Something about being around Atlas brings out unwanted emotions Naya can't control. Instinctively, she reaches up to touch her scar, wondering if her chip is the culprit.

"I don't know, Naya! But we can't leave it in your head. It's changing you," Atlas argues, his voice tinged with desperation.

"And then what? We just go back to normal as if nothing happened?" Naya fumes, her anger flaring up again.

"Yes! Right now, normal sounds amazing. I'd give anything to have the old Naya back," Atlas admits, his voice softening as he steps closer to her.

"And what if the surgery goes wrong? It could blind me or paralyze me or even kill me, Atlas!" Naya's voice cracks.

"Are you saying you don't want the chip removed?" Atlas questions, his tone accusatory.

"Of course not," Naya declares, though a part of her hesitates. She pushes the doubt down, worried it's the chip talking again. "I want it out, but I'm scared of what might happen."

Atlas sighs. "I know it's risky, but we have to try. We can't let them continue to have a hold over your life. Who knows what they plan to do with that thing? Or how much control they have? You deserve to be free."

Naya looks away, frustration gnawing at her. "Why do they keep toying with my life?" she mutters, channeling her anger toward Genesis Laboratories. It's easier said than done, a part of her fighting against the feeling. It makes her even angrier, more aware of the chip's influence over her feelings. "I want to bring them down, Atlas."

"I understand, Naya. But you are more important. The longer the chip stays embedded, the more potential for you to keep changing."

With a huff, she starts walking down the sidewalk. "I need time to think," she calls behind her.

Atlas's footsteps grow louder, and Naya shakes her head, turning to face Atlas. "Alone."

A flash of hurt crosses his face, quickly replaced with a scowl. "Absolutely not. I'm not leaving you alone right now!"

Ignoring him, Naya continues walking, keeping a quick pace.

"Where are you going?" Atlas asks.

"Home!"

"Your parents' house?"

"No, to my new apartment," she explains, annoyed with his questions.

Atlas catches up to walk beside her. "Don't you think your parents should know what's going on?"

The thought of telling her parents more disturbing news makes her feel sick. Naya knows they deserve to know, but she doesn't want to worry them anymore. She needs to figure out what she's going to do about this new discovery, first.

"Naya?" Atlas prompts, noticing she's ignoring his question.

"If you think they must know right this second, how about you tell them and leave me alone. By now, you have a better relationship with them than I do," she remarks.

"And there it is again! That anger and bitterness toward me. It's not you, Naya!" Atlas implores. "This is exactly why we should go back to the hospital and schedule a surgery to have the chip removed!"

Naya walks faster, trying to get ahead of Atlas. He just keeps pushing her buttons, her anger threatening to explode out of her. Suddenly, Atlas grabs her hand and tugs her to a stop. She whips around, pulling her hand out of his grasp.

"The surgery is going to take too long!" she yells, her breathing more rapid.

Atlas flinches at her tone, avoiding eye contact. His expression sends a wave of regret through her, and she softens her voice. "And the recovery… it might ruin my chances of stopping them. I don't have that kind of time."

"What are you suggesting?" Atlas asks, his brows furrowing in concern.

"I'm not sure yet," Naya says, a spark of determination lighting her eyes. She turns to keep walking, ignoring the stares of people passing by on the sidewalk.

Atlas continues following her, this time staying behind her. "Maybe I can disable parts of it," Naya exclaims, thinking out loud. "If I can weaken its control or make it less operational, I might temporarily solve my problem."

Naya can feel Atlas's eyes on her, boring a hole into the back of her head. She turns to look over her shoulder at him.

"That's risky," he replies. Naya scowls, turning back around as he continues speaking. "But if anyone can do it, it's you."

She stops unexpectedly and Atlas almost runs into her. Looking up at him, she searches his hazel eyes for support.

"I know how you feel. I've been trying to bring them down for weeks. If this is how you think we can do it, I'm with you." He reaches out his hand, his fingers brushing hers. As she looks down at their hands, a raindrop lands on her cheek.

Naya looks up at the sky right as it opens up, pouring down onto them. "Great," she says with a laugh, "just what we needed."

Looking back at Atlas, there's an unexpected intensity in his eyes. She feels his fingers intertwine with hers and she lets it happen, his touch sending a shiver up her arm. The rain drips down her face, but she's no longer worried about getting soaked.

"What?" she asks, his gaze catching her off-guard.

Atlas leans closer, his damp curls dripping water onto her face. "Will you come back to me?"

Naya feels the weight of his words. She bites her lip, trying to sort through her conflicting emotions. Her head is telling her no, she's with Lucas now and she needs to let the past go. But her heart says something different. Its voice is muffled, as if trying to speak through a wall. Naya focuses, wanting to hear what it's saying. And for once, it breaks through the chaos in her mind, bringing her a clarity she hasn't felt in a long time.

"I never really left, Atlas," she whispers, her voice barely audible over the rain.

His hazel eyes fill with hope. Naya reaches up to touch his face, watching as he realizes she's back, if only for a moment. His lips curve into a relieved smile and he laughs softly. It's a broken sound, as if he thought he'd never get her back. A tear rolls down his cheek, getting lost on his rain-soaked skin.

Naya brushes her thumb across Atlas's lips, her heart pounding in her chest. Atlas's breath catches in his throat and he pulls her closer. The closeness, the rain, it all feels like a dream. She stands on her tiptoes, leaning in to kiss him.

He pulls back slightly, stunned by her actions, but then he crushes his lips to hers again. The kiss deepens, becoming more passionate. Naya feels herself melting into him, her hands cupping the back of his neck. Atlas pulls her into him, the world around them fading into the background. She can feel his heart beating wildly against hers.

"Together," he murmurs against her lips.

"Together," she echoes.

As she pulls back, Naya feels another surge of clarity. It's as if knowing about the chip is giving her the power to push its influence aside. She can distinguish her true feelings from the fabricated ones, and the realization makes her feel powerful.

"I can feel it now," she says, her voice trembling. "The chip. It's like a dark cloud trying to smother my thoughts, but I can fight it."

Atlas's eyes widen, his lips curving into a radiant smile. "I knew you were still fighting in there somewhere."

Their lips meet again, the kiss full of longing and resolve. The rain cascades around them, washing away their doubts. Naya looks into Atlas's eyes, seeing his unwavering love. It gives her strength and a renewed sense of purpose. She has faith that together, they are unstoppable.

# CHAPTER 60
# ATLAS

Atlas follows Naya into her apartment, dripping water onto the polished wood floors. He can't help but gawk at the space, staring at the expensive furniture.

"Dang, so this is what I'm missing out on," he says, kicking off his shoes and exploring the main room.

"You were offered an apartment, too?" Naya asks, disappearing into the back room.

"Yeah, right before you came over to give back the ring," he replies, disliking the feelings still attached to that memory.

Naya reappears with two towels, her expression remorseful. She gives one to Atlas before attempting to dry her hair with a hand towel.

"I'm sorry, Atlas. I was horrible to you. And I can still feel the urge to keep acting that way," she admits softly.

He nods, trying to focus on drying himself off before he gets the whole apartment wet. He's not sure what to say to Naya. It's still hard to distinguish the real her from the fake one, and he's worried he'll set her off. Their moment in the rain only confused him more. Getting a glimpse of the Naya he fell in love with filled him with a fragile hope, one he's tentative to hang on to. He's not sure he can take another rejection.

Atlas folds the towel and lays it on the couch. He sits down, hoping Naya won't mind. She walks into the living room, her bare feet tapping softly against the floors. To his surprise, she sits directly on the couch, tossing the towel onto the floor.

"I appreciate your attempts at keeping my apartment dry, but I think it's a lost cause at this point," she declares with a rueful grin. "I'm just glad they staged this place at all, or we wouldn't even have these towels."

Atlas laughs softly, savoring the moment with Naya. He tries not to let his eyes linger on the wet clothes clinging to her figure, but it's nearly impossible. The urge to touch her is overwhelming—to run his fingers through her wet hair and kiss her again.

He looks away, blushing at the thought, feeling like he's been starved for her attention. Now that he has a piece of her back, the craving for her touch is even more intense. He mentally scolds himself, trying to keep his priorities straight. There will be plenty of time to spend with Naya once the chip is dealt with.

Looking back over at her, he can see she's deep in thought. Her brown eyes are glossed over, her full lips pressed into a contemplative line. It's the expression she gets whenever she's trying to solve a complex problem.

"Talk to me, Brown Eyes. What master plan are you hatching in that magnificent brain of yours?"

She smirks, leaning her head on the back of the couch. "You've always had such a way with words, Cereal Thief," she replies, the nickname making his heart skip a beat.

Turning toward the ceiling, Naya speaks as if there is someone else in the room. "Is there a computer in this place, by chance?"

"Good afternoon, Naya," a voice says, making Atlas jump slightly. He raises a brow at Naya, and she mouths, *"Smart home assistant."*

"Yes, there is a laptop in the top drawer of the desk in your bedroom," the voice continues.

Naya's eyes light up. "I guess I didn't do a very thorough job of exploring!" she exclaims, running into the bedroom.

She's gone for a while and Atlas wonders if he's supposed to follow. Getting up from the couch, he wanders toward the bedroom. The door is open, a massive bed in the center of the room. He sees a shiny new laptop sitting on the desk in the corner, but no Naya.

Venturing further inside, he spots a walk-in closet. The edge of Naya's bag is visible, clothes haphazardly shoved inside. Peering around the corner, he catches a glimpse of Naya's bare stomach as she changes clothes.

He whips around, staring at the wall in front of him. His face is hot, his heart beating wildly. Clearing his throat to announce his presence, he wonders if Naya saw him.

"Well, someone's impatient," she calls out. "I figured I'd change into dry clothes since I'm back here. I'll be done in a second."

"Okay, I'll just wait in the living room."

Atlas forces himself not to look back as he leaves the room, trying to get his mind out of the gutter. Naya doesn't keep him waiting long, returning in a pair of sweatpants and a loose-fitting T-shirt. Distracted, Atlas doesn't react in time to catch the shirt now flying at him from across the room. It hits him in the face, falling into his lap.

"Here. It's the biggest size I have. It might fit?" Naya says, collapsing onto the couch next to him.

"Thanks," Atlas says, pulling off his damp T-shirt and putting the other one on. He can feel Naya's eyes on him but doesn't look over at her.

The shirt fits, but barely. It hugs his lean frame, tight around his broad shoulders. He hears a muffled giggle beside him and turns to see Naya stifling her laughter.

"What? It's not that bad, is it?"

"No, it's not. I guess I'm just more used to wearing your shirts than you wearing mine," she responds, sitting cross-legged on the couch.

She sets the laptop across her legs, powering it on. "Wow, the government really is trying to butter me up. This thing is amazing."

"You still haven't filled me in on what you're planning," Atlas reminds, scooting closer to her.

"I'm going to attempt to hack into the chip," she states, as if it's the simplest task in the world.

"You can't be serious."

Naya looks up at him, her eyes narrowed. "I thought you had full confidence in me?"

He sighs. "I do. But you hardly know anything about this chip. Is it even safe to hack into while it's active?

Naya shrugs, her eyes glued to the laptop screen. "Probably not. But if I don't try, who will?"

Atlas watches anxiously as Naya's fingers fly over the keyboard. Her determination is palpable, and he feels a swell of pride and awe as she works.

"Found the signal," she mutters, her eyes scanning the data that fills her screen. "It's piggybacking off common Wi-Fi frequencies. Clever, but not clever enough."

Atlas leans closer, watching the packets of information as they stream past. Though he's able to decipher bits and pieces, it's nothing like the code he uses to build programs. "What does it all mean?"

Naya pauses, her brow furrowing. "From what I can tell, the chip is receiving regular updates and commands from a central server. I need to get past these layers of encryption to figure out what they say."

She works for several minutes in silence, her focus unwavering. Atlas feels useless in this situation, watching from the sidelines as she attempts to crack the chip's encryption.

"There," Naya exclaims, letting out a sigh of relief. "They actually put some effort into security this time."

She pulls up several pages of decrypted data and Atlas looks over it with her. Various command patterns are evident, each signal serving a different purpose.

"It looks like there are protocols for behavior modification, emotional regulation... even hormone secretion," Naya comments, her voice trailing off as a hint of anger seeps in.

"And those protocols, they're the commands changing you," Atlas says, realization dawning on him.

"Exactly." Naya starts typing again, faster this time. "First, I need to block their access without alerting them. A firewall should do the trick, but I don't have the software I need. I suppose we can take a momentary pause while I download the required tools."

She gets the software to start installing before setting the laptop on the glass coffee table. "Have you eaten anything today?"

Atlas ponders the question, realizing he's been so caught up with everything he never stopped for food. His stomach growls in response to the thought.

"I'll take that as a no," Naya says, going into the kitchen.

"What's on Chef Naya's menu? Has your taste in food upgraded along with your house?" Atlas teases.

She opens the fridge staring inside before giving Atlas an embarrassed look. "Unless you count an empty fridge as an upgrade, no. Guess we have to find food elsewhere."

Atlas chuckles, getting up and following Naya to the front door. "If only the apartment had come freshly stocked with groceries. Now that would be a bribe."

"I suppose they thought the computer was enough," Naya replies with a sly grin. "I certainly don't mind."

Atlas follows Naya outside. Thankfully, the rain has subsided, the sidewalk and streets now covered with puddles of water. Naya heads to the right and Atlas follows.

"So where is the best place to eat around here?" he asks.

"No idea," she admits with a smile. "Figured we could wander around until we find a spot."

Atlas nods, appreciating her sudden positivity. They navigate the manicured sidewalk, keeping their eyes peeled for food. Uptown is the complete opposite of the parts of the city Atlas is used to. Here, the streets are lined with elegant trees and well-maintained flower beds, their vibrant colors standing out against the grayness of the wet pavement. Modern skyscrapers tower above, their glass facades reflecting the shimmering puddles below. People hurry by, dressed in fashionable attire, giving the area a lively feel.

They pass by various boutiques and cafes, the smell of fresh coffee and baked goods wafting through the air. Naya points to something up ahead, and Atlas spots a cozy bistro nestled between two larger buildings. The sign above the door reads "The Urban Garden." Its exterior is adorned with hanging plants and fairy lights, giving it a warm and inviting atmosphere.

"How about this place?" Naya suggests as they approach the building.

Atlas glances through the windows and nods. "Looks perfect."

They step inside, greeted by the gentle hum of conversation and the clinking of cutlery. The interior is charming, with exposed brick walls, wooden tables, and a small indoor garden in the center. It's like a small taste of what Downtown could look like with a bit of effort.

A hostess greets them, unable to hide her shocked expression after scrutinizing their attire. Atlas glances down at himself, having forgotten he was wearing Naya's tight-fitting shirt. He rubs the back of his neck, embarrassed.

Naya grabs his hand unexpectedly, giving him a reassuring squeeze. She looks unphased by the hostess, giving her a smile as she leads them to a small table by the window. They sit down, the menu filled with a variety of dishes. Naya's eyes light up as she scans the options, the tension of their situation momentarily forgotten.

Atlas looks over the menu, gulping at the prices. Though it's probably not the most expensive place in Uptown, it's still much more than what he's used to.

"What are you thinking of getting?" he asks, glancing over the top of his menu.

"Everything looks so good," she says, biting her lip in indecision. "Maybe the rosemary chicken with roasted vegetables. What about you?"

"I'm leaning toward the truffle pasta," Atlas replies. "I haven't had anything like that in ages. My wallet will suffer but my stomach will not."

Naya laughs. "I'll pay, Atlas."

"No, it's fine. I got it."

She sets her menu down, giving him a determined stare. "Seriously, I'll pay." She leans closer, dropping her voice to a whisper. "The government may have also given me a small deposit in addition to the apartment."

Atlas raises his eyebrows in surprise. "Alright Ms. Money Bags."

They place their orders, and as they wait for their food, they talk about everything and nothing, the conversation flowing easily between them. Atlas is amazed by the shift in Naya's behavior. If only he'd realized what was happening sooner.

When their food arrives, it's as delicious as it looks. Atlas savors each bite, feeling a warmth spread through him that's not just from the meal, but from getting to share it with Naya. Atlas watches her, a soft smile playing on his lips, happy to see her relaxed and enjoying herself.

"This place is amazing," Naya says between bites. "I'm glad we stumbled upon it."

"Me too," Atlas agrees, raising his glass in a silent toast to their unexpected but much-needed moment of peace.

As they finish their meal, Atlas feels satisfyingly full.

"Are you ready to head back and get to——"

He stops abruptly when he sees the look of horror on Naya's face. "Naya?"

"Lucas is outside."

# CHAPTER 61
## NAYA

The sight of Lucas sends a flurry of emotions through her. She sees the worried look on Atlas's face and fights the urge to make a rude remark. An overwhelming feeling threatens to overtake her, telling her to leave the restaurant to be with Lucas. Naya clings to the table for support.

"Naya, what's happening?" Atlas notices her tension.

"Seeing Lucas is making me feel a complicated mix of emotions," she grinds out, trying not to lose her grip on herself.

Lucas heads closer to the restaurant and Naya instinctively ducks.

"What is he doing here?" Atlas asks.

"Well, he does live in Uptown. Maybe we just happened to stumble into one of his favorite restaurants."

"Doubtful," he replies, his jaw clenched in irritation. "I'm not really in the mood to have a conversation with him right now."

Naya nods, knowing the situation she's created is painfully awkward. She hands her card to Atlas, instructing him to pay for the meal and leave when the coast is clear. "I'll go distract him."

She leaves before Atlas can argue, appeasing her inner desire to head in Lucas's direction. Stepping onto the sidewalk, it doesn't take long for Lucas to notice her.

"Naya!" he calls, walking the last few steps toward her. "What are you doing here?"

"I was wondering the same thing!" she answers. "I actually just moved to a new apartment in Uptown and was grabbing a bite to eat."

Lucas beams. "Really? That's amazing. Where is your new place?"

Naya is tentative to answer, and Lucas notices her hesitation. "Just down that way," she says evasively.

He nods, a strange expression flashing across his face. It's gone in a second, replaced with his signature dimpled smile. "You'll have to show me sometime. I really enjoyed our date last night. Hopefully your parents weren't too angry with me."

"I'm an adult, they'll get over it. Sorry you had to drive through Downtown," Naya replies, the words coming involuntarily. She feels the chip's hold over her, pushing her to say and do things she normally wouldn't.

"Don't be," Lucas responds, looking away nervously. "Any chance I could take you out again?"

Naya nods, a rush of excitement making her stomach flutter. *What is happening to me,* she thinks, unable to control her own emotions. "Can we talk more about it on Monday during physical therapy?"

"Alright," he says, looking a little surprised by her response. "See you Monday, Naya."

He leaves with a wave, continuing down the sidewalk and past the restaurant. Naya feels silly for assuming he was headed to the bistro, motioning to Atlas inside that it's clear to come out. He leaves the restaurant slowly, looking in the direction Lucas went.

"What did he say?" Atlas asks as he approaches.

Naya hesitates, knowing Atlas won't like the answer. She clears her throat nervously. "He asked if he could take me on another date sometime."

Atlas's expression turns grim, and he looks away. "And you said?"

"I pushed off talking about it until Monday."

Atlas nods and starts walking back to her apartment. Naya follows, jogging to catch up with his long strides. They walk the rest of the way in silence, the tension festering between them. It's an awful feeling.

They reach her apartment door and Naya steps in front to unlock it. As she puts the key in the handle, she stops and turns to face Atlas. He looks down at her curiously.

"I'm really sorry, Atlas," she begins, "for everything that I've put you through since we've been back. I know I've been awful, pushing you away and behaving like a brat. You don't deserve to be treated that way. I'm so sorry for dragging you into my mess."

Atlas smiles sadly, nodding his head as he processes her apology. Slowly, he reaches out his hand to intertwine his fingers with hers.

"I forgive you, Naya," he says softly. "I won't lie and say it's easy. You really put me through a lot. And this whole thing with Lucas, it's weird and feels wrong. But I know a lot of it isn't your choice. Let's just focus on getting this chip disabled and we can sort the rest out later."

"Okay," she replies, squeezing his hand before unlocking the door and walking inside.

The tension has dissipated slightly, and Naya feels better as they move to sit on the couch. She grabs the laptop off the coffee table, checking to see if the software is done installing. Everything looks in order.

Naya looks over at Atlas who sits silently beside her. He looks lost in thought. "What are you thinking about in that magnificent brain of yours?"

He smirks. "Hey, that's my line."

She smiles back, waiting for him to answer.

Atlas sighs, sensing her determination. He suddenly looks embarrassed, avoiding her gaze as he speaks. "I'm thinking about Lucas."

Naya's eyebrows shoot up in surprise. "Lucas? Why?"

"I don't know, I just get this weird feeling about him showing up by the restaurant. And then seeing him caused your chip to act up? It can't just be a coincidence."

She ponders his words, thinking through the possibilities. It does seem a little strange how it all played out.

"If it wasn't a coincidence, then what was it?" Naya asks.

Atlas doesn't answer right away. He looks up at the ceiling as if the answer is written up there. She watches him think, her own brain trying to piece together the puzzle. A spark of realization flashes across his face, quickly turning into fear.

"What? What is it?" Naya questions, setting her laptop aside and scooting closer to Atlas.

"Is it possible," he starts, his voice full of dread, "that Lucas is working with Genesis Laboratories?"

The idea sends a shiver down Naya's spine. Is he? Has she been blind to it this whole time?

"But why?" Naya's not sure what the motive would be.

"To monitor you? I don't know. This technology is so new, they probably want to keep a close eye on you and see if it's working. At least, that's what I would do," Atlas explains, shifting nervously on the couch.

Naya replays every interaction she's had with Lucas, searching for any sign of his involvement. As she does, the pieces begin to fall into place.

"Did you get a new therapist when your sessions got more advanced?" she asks Atlas.

He shakes his head. "No. I did think it was a little weird that you did but I didn't." As he speaks, his eyes fill with a new sense of understanding. "Wait, do you think Lucas became your therapist so he could be closer to you? To report back to Genesis Laboratories?"

"Maybe," she breathes, still working through her thoughts.

Everything Lucas has ever said to her now takes on a new meaning. His comments about change, urging her to take a new job and reconsider her current situation feel suspicious. His romantic interest now seems like a twisted way for him to get close to her. Even taking her to his secret rooftop spot feels oddly perfect, as if he had inside knowledge into Naya's preferences or her time in the simulation.

"Atlas, I think you might be right," she admits.

He appears almost surprised she agrees with him, turning to face her. Atlas takes her hands in his, offering silent support as she processes the revelation. The more she thinks through it, the more she's convinced Lucas is involved somehow.

"If he really is working for them, then his appearance at the restaurant wasn't a coincidence. He was looking for me."

"How did he find you? You didn't tell him you moved to Uptown, did you?"

Naya shakes her head. "No, he didn't know."

She grabs her computer off the couch, an idea suddenly spurring her to search through the chip's decrypted data again. As she does, she notices a protocol she'd missed the first time—one that's designed to track her location.

"It's a tracker," she mutters, turning her computer screen to show Atlas.

He reads through the data, his mouth parting slightly when he discerns what she means. "Can you turn it off?"

Naya moves to begin reanalyzing the chip but stops before she gets very far. "Even if I could, it would immediately alert Genesis Laboratories that we're onto them. If we have any hope of catching them, I have to leave it active."

"I don't like that," Atlas states.

"I don't either, but I don't see another option."

Naya moves to sit cross-legged on the floor. She sets her laptop on the coffee table and resumes her attempts to hack into the chip. Her fingers fly over the keyboard as she navigates through layers of encryption and security protocols trying to access the firmware. If she wants her firewall to work, she needs to be able to find the best places to insert the code.

"How can I help?" Atlas interjects.

"Can you start writing the code for the firewall? It needs to be able to intercept, filter, and block the commands controlling me," Naya replies, her eyes never leaving the screen.

She hears Atlas rooting around her apartment to find a writing utensil and piece of paper. When he comes back, he has a pen, but no paper. Instead, he sets her file from Genesis Laboratories on the table and pulls out a piece of paper that has a blank back. He starts writing, giving her a reassuring smile.

His support renews her determination, and she redoubles her efforts. Naya tries multiple approaches, using every hacking trick she knows. The minutes tick by, turning into hours. Each failed attempt only fuels her resolve.

Atlas stops writing, watching her with an expression that grows more concerned with each passing moment. "Maybe we should take a break," he suggests gently. "You've been at this for hours."

"I can't stop now," Naya replies, her eyes glued to the screen. "I'm so close."

She types in another command, watching as the code begins to unravel. Her heart races as she feels she's making progress, but then the process stops. An error message takes its place, indicating another barrier.

"No!" she mutters, slamming her fist on the table in frustration.

Atlas places a hand on her shoulder. "Naya, it's okay. We'll figure this out. You're doing everything you can."

She sighs, feeling the weight of the situation pressing down on her. "I just... I need to get into this chip."

Naya tries another approach, this time attempting to exploit a potential vulnerability in the chip's firmware. She runs a diagnostic tool, watching as it maps out parts of the chip's architecture. The screen fills with lines of code, each representing a different aspect of the chip's functions.

She hones in on the communication protocols which is the most comprehensive part of the scan. If she can't inject a firewall code, maybe she can find a way to intercept and analyze the signals being sent. The process is slow and tedious, requiring her to sift through mountains of data.

Atlas sits beside her on the floor, his shoulder touching hers. He knows how much this means to her and how much is riding on their success.

After several more attempts, Naya finally leans back into the couch, exhausted. "I can't do it. Nothing is working."

Atlas squeezes her shoulder. "You did your best, Naya. We'll find another way."

She nods, her frustration alleviated by his reassurance. "Yeah, maybe."

Naya closes her laptop, the atmosphere heavy with unspoken concerns. She tries not to think about what might happen if she can't deactivate the chip. Atlas wraps an arm around her shoulder, sensing her tension. He pulls her into him, and she rests her head on his shoulder.

"We should get some rest and then we can try again in the morning," he suggests.

Naya wants to argue, but she can feel her brain's exhaustion. It doesn't help that she's still trying to fight the chip's control. The constant focus it requires is causing a headache that's becoming too intense to ignore.

"You're right," she whispers, kissing Atlas on the cheek before getting up off the floor.

She heads to her bedroom, glancing back at Atlas who's making himself comfortable on the couch.

"Goodnight, Atlas," she says softly.

"Goodnight, Naya. I'll see you in the morning."

She offers him a small, tired smile before disappearing into her room. Naya lies in bed, staring at the dark ceiling. It looks unusually blank, and she misses the soft glow of the makeshift galaxy in her childhood bedroom. She remembers her mom's latest addition, a reminder to hold tight to her faith.

"Long time no talk," she murmurs, realizing it's been a while since she's prayed. "I'm sorry. I've been pulling away from everyone in my life, and that includes you. I'm ashamed to admit I started blaming you for all the horrible things that were happening to me. But I know that isn't true. I'm sorry I keep trying to take control over my own life when I should be trusting you to guide me through this crazy minefield. You're the only one who can give me true peace in such a fallen world."

A sense of comfort washes over her, and she feels a burst of gratitude. "Thank you for helping me gain a piece of myself back. Thank you for bringing me back to Atlas. And thank you for the relentless support of my family. It's so easy to lose sight of the many blessings I still have in my life with all the chaos going on. Say hi to Harper for me," Naya says, her voice cracking. "It's been really hard letting her go but I know she's with you now, her positivity a welcome addition to your heavenly kingdom. And I know I'll see her again. Please, Lord, give me the strength to keep fighting until that day comes."

# CHAPTER 62

# ATLAS

Atlas wakes bright and early the next morning, the floor-to-ceiling windows letting in enough sun to light the whole room. He sits up, not feeling quite as refreshed as he hoped. He had a fitful night of sleep, his dreams filled with shadows of the challenges they still face.

Getting off the couch, Atlas heads to the wall of windows, admiring the view. "It's certainly quite the sight to wake up to," he murmurs.

Quietly, he walks to Naya's bedroom and peeks inside. She's laying in the middle of the bed, the covers a tangled mess around her. At first, she looks asleep, but Atlas notices her feet shift slightly.

"Naya?" he whispers.

She lifts her head off the pillow, looking half-awake. "Morning," she mumbles.

Atlas chuckles, walking over to stand next to the bed. "I'm going out to find us some donuts for breakfast."

"Donuts?" Naya smiles, sitting up.

"Yeah, you know, sugar and carbs. Brain food," Atlas says with a wink. "I'll be back in a bit."

"I'll try to look more alive when you get back."

Atlas heads out of the apartment, stepping into the brisk morning air. He meanders down the streets, realizing he has no idea where to find donuts in Uptown. As he navigates, Atlas notices how out of place he feels on this side of the city.

The buildings are taller, the streets cleaner, and the people dressed sharper than he's used to.

He wanders aimlessly for a while, the frustration building as he passes coffee shops and bakeries, none of which seem to have the simple donuts he's searching for. *What, are Uptown people too snobby to eat donuts,* he silently grumbles.

After what feels like an eternity of wandering, he finally spots a small, old-fashioned donut shop between two sleek, modern buildings. The neon sign flickers, casting a warm glow on the sidewalk. Atlas sighs in relief and pushes the door open, the smell of fresh pastries immediately lifting his spirits.

Inside, the shop is cozy, with vintage decor and a friendly clerk behind the counter. Atlas orders a dozen assorted donuts, the clerk packing them into a pink box with practiced ease. He figures they can snack on them throughout the day. As he pays, he feels a sense of accomplishment, small as it is.

With the box of donuts in hand, he makes his way back to Naya's apartment. The walk back seems quicker, the sight of familiar buildings guiding him. As he reaches the apartment complex, he feels a strange mix of anticipation and anxiety. He knows donuts won't solve their problems, but maybe they'll offer a small respite from the stress.

Atlas takes the stairs two at a time, eager to get back. When he opens the door, he's surprised to see Naya isn't in the living room.

"Donuts! Come and get 'em," he calls out, setting the donuts on the kitchen counter.

When he hears no reply, he heads back to the bedroom, assuming Naya fell back asleep.

"Wake up, sleepy head," he says, entering her room.

But the bed is empty.

His heart drops at the sight. Atlas rushes into the closet, but she's not there either. Her bag is on the floor like it was the night before, clothes spilling out of it.

"Naya? This isn't funny!" he yells, turning the lights on in the bathroom. It's empty. His heart is racing, the scenario eerily similar to when she left him in the cabin.

The memory makes him think to check for a note, like the one she left last time. He races into the kitchen, scouring the surfaces. Not finding anything, he looks in the living room by her laptop. Sure enough, a small piece of paper sits on top of the glass coffee table next to her file. Atlas picks it up with trembling hands.

*Last night was fun, but it didn't change anything. I expect you to be gone by the time I get back.*

The words hit him like a punch to the gut. It's exactly what he feared—another rejection to dash his rekindled hope. Atlas shoves down the heartbreak, trying not to let his emotions cloud his judgement. He rereads the short note, wondering why Naya would write this.

The more he looks at it, the more he realizes how strange it is. Naya was fine last night and this morning, acting more like herself than she has in weeks. The only thing that would change that is the chip. Did it regain control?

Atlas latches onto the thought, determined to believe this isn't what Naya wants. He stands, placing the note in his pocket. Not sure where to start, Atlas decides to call her parents. He heads outside in search of a payphone. There are none in sight, all the old relics destroyed in favor of the new Uptown aesthetic. *And everyone here owns a cell phone,* Atlas remembers, his annoyance morphing into a spark of hope.

Scanning the street for someone who might help, Atlas sees a man in a suit only a few feet away. He tries to smooth his hair, taking a deep breath to calm his nerves.

"Good morning, sir" he greets, walking up to the man. "I really need to get a hold of someone and was wondering if I could borrow your cell phone?"

The man gives him an inscrutable look, checking his watch. "Sorry, man. I really have to get to work."

"But it will only–" Atlas tries again, trailing off when the man keeps walking without looking back.

"It's fine," Atlas mutters to himself. "I'll just try again."

Several ritzy women walk by, but Atlas can't work up the courage to ask them. He's not sure he has enough confidence or charm to win them over. Atlas continues down the sidewalk, looking for someone with a friendly face.

Finally, another middle-aged man walks by, looking less stuck-up than some of the others.

"Excuse me!" Atlas calls, walking up to the man.

"Yes?" he says, his tone more inviting than expected.

"I really need to get a hold of someone and was wondering if I could borrow your cell phone really fast?" Atlas asks, trying his best to sound casual despite the panic rising within him.

The man glances around nervously. "For just a moment?" he asks.

Atlas nods eagerly. "Yes, I won't take long."

Reluctantly, the man pulls his cell phone out of jacket pocket and hands it over. "Alright," he replies.

"Thank you so much!"

Atlas dials Naya's parents' landline, listening as it rings. *Pick up, pick up, pick up.* After several painfully long seconds, Celeste answers the phone.

"Hello?"

"Celeste, it's Atlas."

"Oh, hi Atlas. It's good to hear from you. I didn't recognize the number."

"Yeah, I borrowed someone's phone. Listen, this is urgent. Have you seen Naya this morning?" Atlas asks hurriedly, walking a few steps away from the man. He notices his anxious stare, so Atlas attempts to give him a reassuring smile.

"No, we haven't seen her since she moved out," Celeste answers.

Another wave of panic washes over Atlas. He doesn't speak, trying to keep his emotions in check.

"Atlas, what's wrong?" Celeste responds, sensing his unease through the phone.

"It's a long story. But I was with Naya last night and…" Atlas pauses, wondering if now is the right time to tell her. He decides to keep it brief, knowing he needs all the help he can get. "And we discovered another chip in Naya's head."

Celeste gasps, but Atlas keeps talking. He fills her in on the basics, describing their speculations about the chip's purpose and their attempts to disable it.

"She was able to fight it, Celeste. The real her was back. But this morning, I went out to get donuts and when I came back, she was gone. She left a note saying nothing changed and she wanted me out of her apartment before she got back."

Celeste is silent for a long while, processing everything Atlas just told her. He glances over at the man whose foot now taps softly on the sidewalk. Atlas waves at him, signaling it will only be another minute. The man nods his head and Atlas breathes a sigh of relief.

"Celeste? I can't talk much longer, but what do we do?"

"Do you have any idea where she went?" she asks, her voice warbling.

"No. That's why I called you."

Celeste sighs, silent as she thinks. "Have you asked the neighbors if they saw anything?"

"No, I haven't. That's brilliant, Celeste. I have to go. I'll keep you updated."

"Atlas—" she starts, but he ends the call. He hands the phone back, not wanting to waste any time.

"Thank you so much, sir. You have a wonderful day."

The man gives Atlas a surprised smile. "Yeah. You too."

Racing back into the apartment, Atlas flies up the stairs to Naya's floor. He strides into the hallway, catching his breath as he knocks on the neighbor's door. An older woman answers, eyeing Atlas with suspicion.

"Hi," Atlas starts, feeling a bit awkward. "Um, I was just wondering if you happened to see the girl next door leaving?"

The woman shrugs. "No. I didn't realize anyone moved into that apartment. Sorry," she replies, shutting the door before he can reply.

Atlas stares at the closed door for a moment before turning around. He goes to the door across the hall, hoping maybe someone else saw something. Knocking, he hears muffled footsteps on the other side. When no one comes to the door, he knocks again. It flies open, revealing a middle-aged man in a robe.

"What?" he bellows, scowling at Atlas. "I'm not buying whatever you're selling."

"Sorry to disturb you this morning. I'm not selling anything. I was just wondering if you saw the young woman who lives across from you leave her apartment?" Atlas says quickly, trying to get it all out before the man closes the door on him.

The man scrutinizes Atlas's appearance with a sigh. He glances at Naya's apartment door. "What does she look like?"

"She has short, wavy black hair. Brown eyes. Average height or a little shorter?"

The man narrows his eyes in thought. "Actually, yeah, now that you mention it. I wondered who that was."

"Was she alone?"

The man shakes his head. "No, some guy was knocking on the door quite loudly this morning. When I looked outside, a young lady was walking away with him."

"Willingly?"

The man raises a brow, wary of Atlas's question. "Yeah, it didn't seem like there was a problem to me."

"Do you remember what the guy looked like?" Atlas inquires, hoping for more details.

The man leans against the doorframe, looking a bit annoyed with the questions. "Blonde, I think? Muscular guy. That's all I remember."

*Lucas.*

Atlas thanks the man for his time and heads toward the stairs. He tries not to jump to worst-case scenarios, thinking through logical reasons why Naya would leave with Lucas. Maybe he came to take her to physical therapy?

He starts down the stairs, intending to stop by the therapy center. Halfway down, he stops, remembering she wasn't scheduled to be there until Monday. At least, that's what Naya told him.

A pang of jealousy twists in his gut—had Lucas come by to ask Naya on another date? The thought is ridiculous, and he shoves it away. If Lucas really is working for Genesis Laboratories, he wouldn't be here for something so trivial. So why would he come?

*They know.*

The realization hits hard. Fear slithers through him, coiling around his chest. Atlas grips the railing for support, his heart pounding, breaths coming in ragged gasps. If they have her, he has no idea what they plan to do. Horrifying thoughts overtake him, images of Naya being hurt or killed flashing through his mind. His knuckles turn white as he clenches the railing harder.

*This is all my fault,* he thinks. *I'm losing her all over again and it's all my fault.* A cry of anguish tears from his throat, echoing through the empty stairway. He feels hopeless, at a loss for what to do.

*Think, Atlas, think.*

But nothing comes.

Atlas slams his fist into the railing, angry with himself for being so useless. His mind is a chaotic mess, an onslaught of thoughts and emotions threatening to bury him in despair. He can't bear the thought of something happening to Naya. Surrendering to the fear, he collapses onto a step, burying his head in his hands.

Minutes pass in silence, the sound of his own heartbeat thundering in his ears. Then, through the haze of anxiety, a faint, inaudible voice breaks through.

*I did not give you a spirit of fear.*

A sudden clarity washes over him. All this time, he's been acting as if he's alone—the only one in control. But he's not. The realization fills him with shame. Is his faith that weak?

*Yes,* a small, insidious voice whispers, beckoning him back to fear and doubt. It would be so easy to listen to it, to renounce his faith and blame everything that's happened on the Lord. But the thought of Naya makes him hesitate.

He knows what she'd say in this moment, gently reminding him not to rely on his own strength and understanding. He's always admired the peace and positivity that Naya radiates, longing to experience it himself.

Atlas takes a shuddering breath, feeling a tremor of determination take hold. He closes his eyes and begins to pray, pouring out his heart to the Lord. He surrenders control, laying his life down and repenting for trying to do it all on his own. Atlas prays for Naya's safety, for strength and guidance, and for the courage to face whatever lies ahead.

As he prays, a calmness envelops him, soothing his frayed nerves. The storm in his mind begins to quiet, replaced by a sense of peace he hasn't felt in a long time. It isn't a promise that everything will be okay, but a reassurance that he's not alone. Whatever happens, he will face it with faith, knowing the Lord is with him.

Atlas rises from the step, his resolve strengthened. He will find Naya, no matter what it takes. Even if he can't see the path ahead clearly, he'll trust in the Lord's plan. With renewed determination, he turns and heads back up the stairs.

# CHAPTER 63

# ATLAS

The computer screen blinks to life, his only hope of finding Naya. He says a silent prayer, checking to see if the computer still has access to the chip's signal.

It does.

Atlas breathes a sigh of relief, thankful Naya didn't close any of the programs. He tries to recall her process for gathering the data, repeating it as best he can. It's not as thorough as hers was, but it will do the trick.

Using the same decryption algorithm Naya determined last night, Atlas turns the data to plaintext. He scans the protocols, searching for an output that looks like coordinates. If there really is a tracker in her chip, it might lead him to where she is now.

Several lines down, he finds it, his heart skipping a beat. Fumbling for the pen he left on the coffee table, he writes the coordinates down on a piece of paper. Grabbing the laptop, the file, and the scribbled coordinates, Atlas sprints out of the apartment.

Part of him wants to head directly to her location, but he has no idea what he'd be up against. He can't run that risk. Not caring how crazed he must look, Atlas gets the attention of the nearest person—a woman walking her dog.

"Can you direct me toward the police station, please?"

After a moment's hesitation, she points. "Down that way and to the left."

Atlas takes off running in that direction, not bothering for more directions. He weaves through the crowds of people, ignoring the stares and shouts of dismay. Every second counts.

Rounding a corner, he sees the police station up ahead. With a final burst of speed, he crosses the street, earning a few honks from passing drivers. Pushing open the doors, he sets the computer and coordinates on the small counter ledge.

"My name is Atlas Williams. I'm one of the victims in the Genesis Laboratories investigation. I need to speak with someone about Naya Callaway. I think she's in danger. It's urgent!" Atlas pleads, getting the attention of several police officers in the back.

Thankfully, the front desk attendant must recognize the name, quickly signaling for a nearby officer. He strides over with a look of concern. Atlas, breathing heavily from his sprint, tries to steady himself as the officer approaches.

"Officer, my name is Atlas Williams. I need your help. Naya Callaway is in serious danger. I think she's been kidnapped by people from Genesis Laboratories—the same ones you've been searching for," Atlas explains urgently, his eyes wide with worry.

The officer's expression shifts from concern to alarm. "Genesis Laboratories? We've been trying to track them down for months. What makes you think they have her?"

Atlas gestures to the computer and coordinates he's placed on the counter. "I found this tracking signal. It's from an encrypted chip implanted in Naya's brain. One that we didn't know about. I managed to decrypt the signal, and it led me to these coordinates. I'm certain it's where they're keeping her now."

He opens the laptop, and the officer quickly scans the screen. "You're sure about this? These coordinates could be a major break in our case."

"Absolutely. We need to act now before they move her again or something happens," Atlas insists, desperation lacing his words.

The officer nods sharply, then turns to the front desk attendant. "Get Captain Monroe up here immediately. Tell him it's urgent."

Within moments, Captain Monroe, a tall, stern-looking man with a commanding presence, joins them at the front. The officer quickly briefs him on the situation.

Captain Monroe turns to Atlas, motioning for the evidence Atlas brought. Tentatively, he hands it over.

"Alright, son. We'll take a look at those coordinates. If what you're saying checks out, we'll mobilize a team immediately," the captain explains. "Can you come with us and explain everything in detail?"

"Of course," Atlas replies, relief washing over him as he follows Captain Monroe and the officer into a back room. "How long is this going to take?"

"Hard to say, but let's get your statement first."

As they walk, Captain Monroe speaks into his radio, instructing officers to prepare for a potential raid. Atlas can hear the buzz of activity already starting.

In the back room, Atlas explains everything he knows about the chip, Genesis Laboratories, and how he and Naya managed to decrypt the signal. He speaks in a rush, trying to relay it as quickly as possible. The officers listen intently, asking questions to clarify details and understand the situation fully.

"We've had our eye on Genesis Laboratories for a while," Captain Monroe says, leaning back in his chair. "But they've always been one step ahead, slipping through our fingers. If these coordinates are correct, this could be our chance to shut them down for good and find Naya."

Atlas clenches his fists, his frustration boiling over at the captain's lack of urgency. "I'm telling you, they are correct. Now can we go, please?"

Captain Monroe gives him a measured look. "Atlas, we're moving as quickly as we can. But these things take time. We need to make sure we do this right."

Atlas shakes his head vehemently. "We don't have time for careful planning. She could be in immediate danger!"

The captain's expression hardens. "I understand your urgency, but we can't go in unprepared. It's too dangerous. And you won't be joining us."

"I need to be there," Atlas insists. "I know the details, I can help."

"Sorry, son," Captain Monroe says firmly. "You're not trained for this. We can't take you with us. It's too risky."

Atlas opens his mouth to argue, but the captain cuts him off. "No, Atlas. You're staying here. We'll handle it."

"Will you?" he yells, his anger getting the better of him. "Because you've been searching for Genesis Laboratories for weeks and haven't made any progress!"

The captain doesn't respond, clenching his jaw as Atlas speaks his mind.

"You can't afford to lose this lead. Please." Atlas's voice breaks as his anger turns into desperation.

"We'll do our best," Captain Monroe says, shutting the door and leaving Atlas alone in the room.

Feeling a mix of anger and helplessness, Atlas reluctantly stays put. He reminds himself of the promise he made to put his trust in the Lord, although it's proving rather difficult right now.

"Lord give me strength," he murmurs. "Please keep Naya safe. Be with the officers as they plan, and please help her be unharmed when they get there."

Atlas paces the floor, his mind racing. As he thinks, he realizes he needs to call Naya's parents. They need to know what's happening. Leaving the back room, he heads to the front desk and asks to use the phone.

Naya's parents arrive in a flurry of worry and concern. Atlas quickly fills them in on everything he knows.

"Are they leaving soon?" Silas asks, glancing around the lobby.

Atlas shakes his head. "Not that I know of. No matter how many times I told them it was urgent, they just kept saying they needed to do it the right way. The captain didn't know how long it would take to be ready."

Silas's expression hardens, his weathered hand clenched at his side. "I'm going to have a word with the captain." He walks off to speak with the front desk attendant.

Celeste watches him leave before wrapping Atlas into a hug. "Thank you," she whispers.

"For what? I'm the one who got you all into this mess," Atlas mutters.

Celeste pulls back, her hands gripping Atlas's shoulders. He averts his gaze, not sure how to face her after everything he's put them through.

"Atlas," she says, moving to look him in the eyes. "We've been through this before. This isn't your fault. Stop blaming yourself. You're the one who figured out she has another chip. And you're the one who brought the information here, advocating for our daughter's safety."

Atlas stares into her eyes, finding only love and understanding. He hugs her again, thankful for her unwavering support. "I'm sorry," he whispers.

Celeste hugs him tighter. "I'm sorry, too. You've been through so much."

She releases him and they move to sit in the station's lobby. Silas is gone from the front desk, presumably taken back to speak with the captain. Atlas taps his foot impatiently, trying his best to have faith. He looks over at Celeste who's praying silently beside him. After a while, she opens her eyes and gives Atlas a small smile.

"What do you pray for?" he asks.

"Naya's safety. Peace and patience to get through this moment. And faith to accept whatever the outcome is."

"And if the outcome is bad? If Naya isn't—" Atlas can't bring himself to say it.

Celeste pats his hand gently. "Then we'll rely on the Lord to get through it. Losing Harper was really hard, so I can't imagine losing Naya, too," she replies, her eyes glistening with tears. "But let's not worry about that right now."

"Aren't you angry this keeps happening?"

She laughs sadly, a tear slipping down her cheek. "It's human to be angry. We have such finite perspectives, it's easy to focus on the immediate and not realize how it will impact our future. But the Lord knows. And I believe he works it all out for the good."

She is silent for a moment, gathering her thoughts. "I don't believe God causes bad things to happen. It's just part of our fallen world."

Her words remind Atlas of something Naya once said to him. The thought of her makes his heart ache.

"But I know he weeps along with us," Celeste continues. "Caring so deeply for his children that he takes no satisfaction in our pain. And I know that Harper is in a better place. One that's perfect and beautiful and has no pain." Celeste turns to look at him. "And I also know that I'll see her again someday when it's my turn to join her in heaven. The same goes for Naya, if something were to happen to her."

Atlas stares at the wall in front of him, letting the weight of Celeste's words sink in. He says another prayer, voicing his concerns and laying his worries in God's hands.

"I strive to have a faith like yours one day, Celeste."

She looks at him, wiping her tears. "I'm so proud of how far you've come, Atlas, but my hope is that you find a faith of your own. We all have unique relationships with the Lord, you just need to work on building yours.”

Her words strike a chord with him, reminding him that everyone’s journey to faith is different. There’s no use comparing himself to others. Atlas thanks Celeste for her wisdom just as Silas walks over to join them.

“They’re on their way,” he informs them, easing himself onto a chair.

Atlas breathes easier, glad they finally left. They wait together in the station’s lobby, the minutes ticking by. He tries not to worry, but it’s hard, the tension creeping back in with each passing moment.

As they sit anxiously, the television mounted on the wall flickers to a breaking news segment. The headline reads, “Police Raid Suspected Genesis Laboratories Hideout.”

“Can you turn the TV up?” Atlas calls out, watching intently as a reporter on the scene describes the raid in real time.

“We’re here live at what appears to be a major police operation on the edge of Uptown. Officers entered the building moments ago. Sources indicate this raid is connected to the elusive hunt for Genesis Laboratories, a group implicated in the Project Nowhere scandal.”

The camera pans to the building, showing the police vehicles parked outside. Naya’s parents hold each other, their faces etched with worry. Atlas stands, his fists clenched.

The reporter continues to narrate, “We’re hearing unconfirmed reports that a young woman may be held inside.”

Finally, there’s a flurry of activity, and the camera captures officers in tactical gear leading people out in handcuffs. The reporter’s voice rises with excitement. “It appears the police have taken numerous suspects into custody. We’re still waiting for confirmation on whether the missing woman has been found.”

Atlas leans forward, his eyes fixed on the screen, silently praying for good news. The wait is excruciating, each second stretching longer than the last.

Suddenly, the reporter presses a finger to her earpiece, listening intently. "We have just received confirmation—not one, but two victims have been rescued. They are alive, though their conditions are unknown at this time."

A collective sigh of relief sweeps through the station. Naya's parents embrace each other, tears of joy streaming down their faces. Atlas feels his legs give way as he collapses into his chair, overwhelmed by the news.

The screen shows stretchers being wheeled into the building and Atlas hopes she isn't seriously injured. Minutes later, the camera zooms in as they are wheeled back out. Naya sits partially upright in the first one, wrapped in a blanket with a bandage around her head.

Following closely behind is someone lying unconscious on the other stretcher. Atlas squints to see who it is, managing to make out a bit of blonde hair sticking out from the bandage around his head.

It's Lucas.

Atlas is stunned, wondering what happened to put him in such a state. His attention is diverted when Captain Monroe appears on the screen, giving a brief statement.

"We have successfully rescued Naya Callaway and Lucas Thorne, apprehending at least a dozen suspects connected to Genesis Laboratories. This is a significant breakthrough in our investigation."

Atlas watches as the screen cuts back to Naya, who looks around with a confused expression, searching the crowds now gathering around the scene. Atlas wishes he could be there with her but says a silent prayer of thanks that she's okay.

He turns to Naya's parents, the weight of the past hours lifting slightly. "She's safe. She's really safe."

# CHAPTER 64

# NAYA

When Atlas and her parents walk into her hospital room, Naya cries tears of relief. Her mom embraces her first, followed immediately by her dad, who wraps them both in his arms.

"I'm so glad you're safe," her mom says, checking her over. "What happened?"

"They removed my chip," Naya explains. "They kept saying they needed to destroy the evidence."

Atlas walks to the other side of the bed. He grabs Naya's hand, and she pulls him into an embrace.

"You're the one who found me, aren't you?" she whispers.

He nods, burying his head in her shoulder. "Yeah. But only because you paved the way for me."

They pull apart, and Naya is touched by the raw emotion on Atlas's face. He looks on the verge of tears, his eyes locked on hers as if she'll disappear if he looks away.

"We make a good team," Naya says with a soft smile. "I love you, Atlas."

His eyes search hers, checking to see that she truly means what she says. "I love you, Naya," he breathes, pulling her to him again.

With their reunion complete, everyone pulls up chairs beside Naya's hospital bed. She fills them in on everything she remembers, starting from when Atlas left that morning.

"The chip started feeling more invasive, and I was still tired from fighting it the night before. Then, Lucas showed up at the door and urged me to leave with him. With the chip's influence and Lucas right there, it was hard to resist. I followed blindly as he led me through Uptown."

"What about the note?" Atlas interrupts.

"Oh, yeah. I told Lucas I would leave a note for you so you wouldn't be worried about my sudden disappearance and come after me. He was watching over my shoulder while I wrote it, but I hoped you'd see through the harsh words and know something was up."

Atlas nods thoughtfully, considering her words. "I'll admit it surprised me at first, but I figured it out."

Naya smiles, grateful her idea worked. Atlas motions for her to continue her story.

"The building Lucas brought me to was one he'd taken me to before," Naya says, remembering the night on the roof. "Genesis Laboratories had been in the city this whole time."

She explains how terrifying it felt to step inside, not knowing what would happen next. It was fast—a group of unfamiliar people seized her and guided her to a makeshift surgical area. Everyone was in a rush, packing up while a few people prepped Naya for surgery.

"So, they were preparing to leave?" her dad interjects.

Naya nods. "It seemed that way. I think they realized their hideout would be discovered soon."

"Where was Lucas in all this?" Atlas asks.

"That's what was weird. Lucas was being prepped for surgery too. The medical team said they'd get to him after me," Naya recalls. "I don't remember much after that. They put me under. When I woke up, I was being lifted onto a stretcher by the police. Before they took me outside, I saw the medical team with their hands in the air. It looked like the police interrupted them mid-surgery."

The room is quiet as they all process Naya's story. Reliving it sends goosebumps along her arms, the fear of not knowing if she'd wake up still fresh in her mind.

"So, your chip is really gone?" her mom inquires, squeezing Naya's hand for reassurance.

"Yeah."

"And they didn't hurt you?" her dad confirms.

"The doctors said I have a bit of nerve damage, but nothing severe."

Naya turns to look at Atlas. He gives her a relieved smile.

"I'm glad you're okay," he says.

She leans her head against the pillow, feeling comforted by their presence. It's almost hard to believe it's finally over. They did it—they brought Genesis Laboratories down. As she thinks it, a thought hits her.

"Mr. Ellis!" she exclaims. "They got him, right?"

"He was there?" Atlas asks.

"Yes. I saw him."

"I don't remember seeing him on the TV, but then again, I was so focused on looking for you that I wasn't paying much attention," Atlas admits.

Naya's dad stands, moving toward the door. "I'll go see if I can find out," he says, stepping quietly into the hall.

Her mom heads that way as well, giving them a knowing smile. "I'll just give you two a moment alone," she says, closing the door behind her.

Atlas leans in, pressing his lips softly to Naya's temple. Seconds later, the door bursts open again and Michael flies into the room.

"I came as soon as I heard!" he says, out of breath.

Naya laughs at Michael's dramatic entrance. She waves him closer, giving him a hug. "Thanks for coming, Michael. And for all your help."

"How did you get in here?" Atlas remarks, looking slightly irritated by his friend's interruption. "Aren't they only letting in the family right now?"

"What can I say? I'm friends with the guy who manages the ER's front desk, too. He's always needing tech help," Michael replies with a grin.

Atlas chuckles, and Naya appreciates the normalcy of their friendly banter.

"Glad you still know how to make friends," Atlas retorts. "Now can you get out of here so I can have a moment alone with Naya, please?"

Michael crosses his arms. "But I just got here! Maybe I want a moment alone with Naya, too?"

Atlas gets up, walking over to Michael. He grabs him by the shoulders, turning him around and pushing him to the door. Naya laughs as she watches the encounter.

"Alright, alright, I'll go," Michael relents. "But I'm only giving you five minutes! And then I'm coming back and I expect to hear all the juicy details."

Atlas nods, shutting the door after Michael with a sigh of relief. He stares at Naya from across the room, his back to the wall. His gaze is intense, his eyes lingering on every feature like he's committing her face to memory.

"A part of me thought I'd never see you again," he breathes.

Naya beckons Atlas closer, and he sits beside her on the bed. She gently cups his face with her hands, looking deeply into his eyes.

"I'm here, Atlas. I'm not going anywhere," she vows, pulling him toward her so his head rests on her chest.

She runs her fingers through his hair as they hold each other, their hearts beating in sync. They enjoy the stillness of the moment, the room falling into a comfortable silence. After a while, Atlas lifts his head to meet her gaze.

"I don't know what I would have done if I had lost you," he admits, his voice thick with emotion.

"But you didn't lose me, so you don't need to worry about that," Naya reassures him. "Let's think about the future."

Atlas smiles, moving to lay beside her on the bed. Naya leans into him.

"So, when do I get my ring back?" she asks softly.

Atlas turns to look at her with an endearing expression. "As soon as you'd like," he replies. "Although maybe I should make you work for it after all you've put me through."

Naya smacks him playfully on the arm. "It wasn't by choice!" she refutes.

Recognizing the truth to his words, she drops the joking pretense. "I really am sorry for everything, Atlas. Thank you for fighting for me and never giving up."

"Of course. I knew you were still in there."

He pulls her into him, resting his head on hers. Just then, the door opens, and Michael peeks his head inside.

"Time's up, lovebirds."

Naya's parents follow Michael in and they all get settled.

"Good news," her dad begins. "They have Mr. Ellis in custody."

Naya breathes a sigh of relief, feeling a weight lift off her shoulders. "I'm glad."

"Indeed," her mom says, smiling through her tears. "This nightmare is finally over."

Atlas squeezes Naya's hand. "We'll make sure it stays that way."

Michael clears his throat nervously, drawing everyone's attention. "I've actually been meaning to apologize to you all for my part in this." He turns to face Naya's parents. "I'm so sorry for not doing more—for not helping sooner. If I had, maybe I could've saved Harper."

Naya's mom sets her hand on Michael's shoulder. "Thank you, Michael, but don't blame yourself. You found your way in the end, and you helped get us out."

Michael smiles sadly, touching her hand briefly before directing his attention to Atlas. "And I'm really sorry for not fighting harder when they put you into the simulation, Atlas. I stood by just watching while it happened."

Atlas stands, walking over to Michael and pulling him into a hug. "I forgive you, man. I get it, you did what you had to. If you had fought harder, they would've put you in the simulation too, and we'd all be stuck."

Michael's hand tightens around Atlas, his butterfly tattoo catching the light.

"Speaking of getting us out," Naya says, prompting their bro hug to end. "Why the butterfly? And don't just say the tattoo."

Michael grins, staring down at the tattoo on his hand. "Two reasons. One, my mom would always remind me the butterfly doesn't count months, but moments. When she passed, I got this tattoo as a reminder to live in the present and appreciate each moment as it comes."

"And the other?" Atlas interrupts, settling back on the bed beside Naya.

"The butterfly effect," Michael muses. "The idea that even one small action can have a huge impact kept me going when I thought about getting you guys out."

"That's beautiful, Michael," Naya replies, moved by his story.

The moment is interrupted by a knock on the door, and a nurse walks in. "I'm sorry to interrupt, but I need to check on Naya."

Atlas reluctantly moves aside, still holding her hand as the nurse checks her vitals. The nurse smiles kindly at the group. "She's doing well. Just make sure she gets plenty of rest."

As the nurse leaves, Naya's dad steps forward. "We should let you get some sleep, Naya. We'll be right outside if you need us."

Her mom gives her one last hug. "We love you, sweetheart."

"I love you too," Naya replies, feeling grateful for her family's unwavering support.

Atlas moves to get comfortable in a chair, but Naya urges him to leave. "You need to get some rest, too."

"I can sleep here," he argues.

"No, I mean real rest."

He sighs. "Have I told you how stubborn you are?"

"Many times," she says with a smile.

Atlas leans in for one more kiss on her forehead. "I'll be back first thing in the morning," he promises.

"Me too," Michael says with a wink, roughhousing with Atlas as they leave the room.

With everyone gone, Naya settles back into her bed, exhaustion finally catching up with her. Though she's tired and her head hurts from the surgery, she feels a profound sense of peace. Closing her eyes, Naya says a silent prayer of gratitude before she drifts off to sleep.

# CHAPTER 65
# ATLAS

The next morning, Atlas heads to the hospital with a cup of coffee and a bouquet of flowers. Sunlight filters through the hospital room window, bathing Naya in a golden glow. She looks angelic.

"Good morning," Atlas says, his eyes lighting up when he sees she's awake.

"Good morning," she replies, sitting up with a bright smile. "You're here early."

"I couldn't stay away," he admits, handing her the flowers. "How are you feeling?"

"Better," she says, taking a deep breath of the floral scent. "Much better."

They spend the morning talking, her parents joining them a little while later. Their visit is interrupted by a steady stream of visitors, with Michael being the first.

"Told you I'd be back!" he says excitedly, making himself at home in a chair by the window.

He stays long enough to hear about everything that happened after Atlas and Naya left the hospital. Michael listens intently, asking a variety of questions. Their chat ends when there's another knock on the door and Captain Monroe steps inside.

Everyone pauses, shifting their attention to Captain Monroe. He moves closer, his kind eyes betraying his commanding presence.

"Good to see you recovering, Naya," Captain Monroe says, giving her a warm smile.

"Thank you, Captain," Naya replies. "And thank you for everything you and your team did."

Captain Monroe nods. "We're just glad you're safe. I wanted to give you an update on the situation with Genesis Laboratories."

Everyone in the room listens as he continues. "We've arrested twelve key members, including Mr. Ellis. They're being held for questioning, and we're gathering more evidence to ensure they face justice for their actions."

Naya grabs Atlas's hand, giving it an excited squeeze. "That's good to hear."

Atlas nods in agreement. "It's a huge step forward. It's about time they're held accountable."

Captain Monroe turns to Atlas. "And I have to commend you, Mr. Williams. Your quick thinking and determination played a crucial role in this. We couldn't have done it without you."

Atlas shifts uncomfortably but gives a brief nod. "I just did what I had to do. We all did."

The captain smiles. "Well, you did an excellent job. Now, unless you have more questions, I won't take up any more of your time. I just wanted to ensure you had the latest information."

"Captain?" Naya says. "Do you have any information you can share about Lucas? How is he?"

"Ah, yes. Lucas Thorne. He's awake and recovering. Would you like to speak with him?"

"If I could, I'd really appreciate it."

Michael excuses himself, hugging Naya goodbye. Celeste helps Naya navigate to Lucas's room, Silas and Atlas close behind. It's only a few doors down, and Atlas lingers outside while Naya gets situated. He stops the captain briefly, catching him before he leaves.

"I have some additional files that should help you build your case against Genesis Laboratories. Is it okay if I drop them off at the station later today?"

The captain raises a brow but doesn't ask questions. He nods his assent. "See you later, Atlas."

Celeste and Silas join him in the hall, letting Naya have a moment to speak with Lucas alone. Atlas watches nervously through the window, trying his best not to eavesdrop. Only a few minutes later, Naya waves him inside.

"We were wrong," Naya says when he closes the door. "Lucas wasn't working for them. He was a victim like me."

Atlas stares at Lucas, the bandage around his head now making sense. "You had a chip, too?"

Lucas nods.

Atlas has a seat next to Naya, a bit uncomfortable with the situation. He's not sure what to say to Lucas or how to handle everything that's happened between the three of them. It's rather unconventional.

"I'm sorry. To both of you," Lucas starts, his tone remorseful. "I know this whole thing is a little weird."

"Maybe a little bit," Naya agrees with a light-hearted laugh. "But you were being controlled by a chip. We understand."

Atlas nods his agreement. "So, uh, do you remember how it happened? The chip, I mean."

"Yeah. Before the chip was removed, I had a gap in my memory. But now, I remember what happened," Lucas replies, taking a deep breath. "I was attacked in the alley beside the building we were found in. I only remember bits and pieces, but they took me inside and sedated me. I'm sure that's when they embedded the chip."

Naya shifts nervously in her chair and Atlas recalls how similar this sounds to Naya's experience.

"I woke up in the hospital the next day and was told I'd been mugged. I had a small scar along my hairline to show for it."

"So how did you become my therapist?" Naya asks.

"When I heard you were starting therapy at our clinic, I had a sudden urge to work with you. I realize now that it was partially the chip's doing. But we had a similar experience, and I used it to convince my boss I could relate to you better than your other therapist."

His story makes sense, explaining why Atlas never transitioned to a new therapist. Beside him, Naya twirls a strand of hair around her finger.

"And the, uh," she swallows nervously. "The romantic advances?"

Lucas blushes, looking down at his hands. "That was all me, actually. I really did fall for you, Naya. I found your determination very attractive. I think the chip just enhanced those feelings."

Atlas clenches his jaw and Lucas senses his unease.

"I'm sorry, Atlas. I thought Naya broke up with you."

Atlas takes a deep breath, letting his frustrations go. "I know. I forgive you, Lucas. It's all in the past."

Lucas breathes a sigh of relief, visibly relaxing in front of him. "I appreciate it. And I'm sorry for putting you in that situation, Naya."

She smiles over at him. "You're a great guy, Lucas. But the Naya you fell for isn't the real me. I know you understand."

He nods, a resigned smile on his face. "I do. I can tell you really love Atlas. If it's not weird, can we still be friends?"

Naya beams, nodding earnestly. "Of course! I think you'll get along really well with Michael and Atlas, too. Once they get to know you, of course."

Lucas chuckles, resting his head against the pillow behind him. He looks drained, far less recovered than Naya.

"Not the exact same!" Naya replies. "Spelled K-n-o-w-a-r-e. Like Knowledge Ware? Get it? Because technology is made of soft*ware* and hard*ware* and gives us knowledge?"

Atlas laughs, finally understanding. "I like it."

"So, you'll do it?"

"Absolutely. I'm in. Wherever you go, I'll follow."

"Together?"

"Forever," he says, stealing a kiss.

Naya's laughter dances in the air, a melodic sound that fills Atlas with joy. In that moment, he feels the weight of their past lift, replaced with an excitement for the future—a future filled with endless possibilities.

# EPILOGUE

Atlas hurries down the sidewalk, coffees in one hand, a box of donuts in the other. It's a gorgeous morning, the rising sun warming him as he walks. As he shifts his grip on the coffee tray, the light glints off his silver wedding band. Even after two years of marriage, he still gets a thrill at the sight of it. Being married to Naya is a blessing he'll appreciate for the rest of his life.

Up ahead, the building approaches, its new facade a testament to all the work they've poured into it. It really is a labor of love, and he hopes they've created a space that can become a beloved community hub. He opens the front doors, precariously balancing the coffee on the donut box. Naya stands just inside, the sight of her making his heart flutter.

"How is Mrs. Williams?" Atlas kisses Naya's cheek.

"Excellent."

"And baby Williams?" Atlas continues, moving to kiss Naya's belly.

She laughs softly, gazing down at Atlas. "Same as usual. Feisty and constantly kicking."

"And that's why it's a boy," Atlas replies, setting the coffee and donuts on a nearby table.

"I still think it's a girl."

"You just want a girl so we can name her Harper."

"Maybe," Naya says, drawing out the word.

Atlas moves to stand next to her, pulling her to his side. "Well, I'd be happy either way. Anyway, I brought breakfast. Today is a big day!"

She sighs, staring at the space before them. It's a harmonious blend of old and new, the ground floor dedicated to the technology thrift shop. Shelves and displays are filled with a curated selection of refurbished gadgets and electronics. It reminds Atlas of an upgraded version of Bargain Bytes.

On the left side of the space is an open and airy layout, with comfortable seating areas scattered throughout. More shelves adorn the walls, lined with vintage electronics and components. Each item is meticulously labeled with its history and potential uses, encouraging visitors to explore and learn. The space is thoughtfully designed to invite people to tinker with gadgets while fostering collaboration between the communities.

In the center of the shop, a large, interactive touchscreen table serves as both a display and communal workspace. Here, visitors can engage in DIY projects, attend workshops, or collaborate on tech innovations.

One of Atlas's favorite parts is the wall decor. Naya made each one, repurposing electronic components to create art that adds a whimsical touch to the space.

"We've come so far," Naya muses, admiring everything.

"And it's all because of your brilliant idea." Atlas grabs a donut and coffee for each of them, before leading Naya up the staircase to the second floor.

Up here is the Internet Café—rows of desks and computers decorate the space, each one available for the public to use. The centerpiece of the cafe is a state-of-the-art digital archive, where visitors can access a vast array of online resources, including e-books, research papers, historical documents, and tutorials. Bookshelves surround it, seamlessly integrated with the digital archive, encouraging a blend of traditional and modern learning.

"What are we up here for?" Naya asks.

"I figured it would be a better view."

Naya braces herself against the railing that overlooks the space below. Atlas hands her a coffee and donut before settling in beside her. They stare at the front facade of the building which is full of large glass windows. Natural light floods the interior, a major improvement from the original industrial design. It also offers a close-up view of the crew now hanging the finishing touch.

Although it's backwards, Atlas and Naya watch with glee as the sign bearing the shop's name is fastened to the building. It takes a bit for the crew to finish it, but they don't mind. They sit in comfortable silence, enjoying the view while they finish their breakfast.

"I want to see it from the front!" Naya exclaims when they're done, making her way down the stairs and out the front door.

Atlas follows closely behind, standing beside her on the sidewalk.

"Kno-Ware," Atlas reads, still enamored with the name. "You're so brilliant, Naya."

"Only after I explained it to you," she teases, poking him in the ribs.

"Hey! It was just a bit hard to comprehend when I couldn't see it spelled."

"Mm-hm," she replies, giving him a skeptical grin. "Did you ever come up with a slogan? That one is still stumping me."

Atlas gazes at the building they've created, a symbol of innovation and community in the heart of the city. He considers their purpose—making technology accessible for everyone—and an idea hits him.

"Empowering minds, one device at a time."

"Oh, that's good!" Naya compliments. "I think that means we're ready for business. What do you say, Cereal Thief?"

"Let's do it, Brown Eyes."

CAMRYN VAN LINGEN is an artist and avid reader who lives in the Midwest with her husband and two cats. She first had the idea for Nowhere in elementary school. Since then, it's changed drastically, and she thanks the Lord for the opportunity to turn her childhood idea into a finished novel. She could not have accomplished it without His presence and guidance throughout the process.

Camryn has a degree in Art Education and currently teaches high school Media Production and Cybersecurity. Her newfound knowledge of Cybersecurity proved invaluable while writing this book.